SONS &
DAUGHTERS

SONS & DAUGHTERS

ANN HANIGAN KOTZ

BookPress®
publishing

Published in Des Moines, Iowa, by:
Bookpress Publishing
P.O. Box 71532
Des Moines, IA 50325
www.BookpressPublishing.com

Publisher's Cataloging-in-Publication Data

Names: Kotz, Ann Hanigan, author.
Title: Sons and Daughters / Ann Hanigan Kotz.
Description: Des Moines, IA: Bookpress Publishing, 2023.
Identifiers: LCCN: 2023913228 | ISBN: 978-1-947305-67-0 (hardcover) | 978-1-947305-87-8 (paperback)
Subjects: LCSH Norwegian Americans--Fiction. | Pioneers--Fiction. | Frontier and pioneer life--Fiction. |
Women--Fiction. | Middle West--History--19th century--Fiction. | Historical fiction.| BISAC FICTION /
Historical / General
Classification: LCC PS3611.O74938 S66 2023 | DDC 813.6--dc23

First Edition
Printed in the United States of America
10 9 8 7 6 5 4 3 2 1

For John

For my siblings

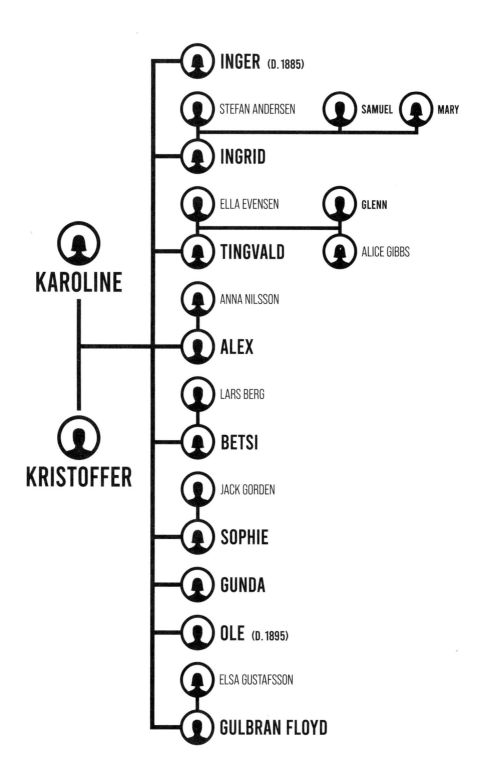

1905

Karoline

Time had passed without him. No support. No help with the farm. No help with the children. Yet, Karoline did not miss her husband. No anger. No disappointment. No obedience.

Each step she had taken in the direction away from his grave freed her further from him. The first few steps were mixed with bitterness and sadness; a few more brought relief; the final steps, peace.

Karoline wished she could turn back time, needing only fifteen minutes. If she could, she would return to the moment before she opened that horrible letter and, instead, fling it into his grave, leaving his last hurtful words undelivered. But she couldn't. And she could never unknow them, never forget them. Any chance of forgiving her husband for his bruising words and cutting chastisements while they were married, leaving Karoline to remember any remaining words of love and respect, was now lost, carried away like seeds in the wind.

Her anger and resentment toward him sealed themselves into her heart, her soul, her every drop of blood pumping through her body.

Karoline turned from her thoughts and reminded herself she was free. Free to raise their children as she saw fit, free to name the child she was carrying anything she wanted, free to do and say as she pleased.

Her life would begin anew. Instead of *wife*, she was now *widow*. To her, widow did not mean a woman who'd lost her husband; she was instead a woman without a husband. The possibilities floated through her head. The decisions about the children, the farm, even herself were hers to make. She could do as she pleased without asking for permission or apologizing for her choices.

Karoline thought about her position as a single woman. Iowa was a conservative state, filled with farms run by men with wives to support them. Iowans were good neighbors, offering a hand whenever it was needed; however, they could also be judgmental, each community bonded by their own origins and setting standards of comportment based on their religious beliefs. If she chose not to marry, she may be ostracized for being too modern, too independent in a state filled with women who partnered as soon as it was appropriate.

Karoline chose to walk back to the house, waving away offers of buggy rides. She wanted the time and space to think about her future instead of her past. From a favorite vantage point, she could look around the Loess Hills, the town of Soldier nestled in their midst. The hills—usually green—were brown with drought but still beautiful with their curved tops and sloping valleys. The trees—oak, maple, ash, and walnut—still held their green foliage against their black trunks, standing individually in this once desolate prairie. Looking beyond the hills, Karoline could see what remained of the Soldier River digging its way through the landscape, its muddy bottom turning the water a chocolate brown. Black and rust cattle dotted the hills, finding the little green among the brown vegetation; most of the land was better suited for animals than crops. The steep slopes could easily roll a wagon loaded with corn.

Karoline had not chosen this land for her home. She had only followed Kristoffer when they emigrated in 1883. They had first established themselves in Minnesota; but the cheap, fertile Iowa land had beckoned her husband, offering a way to own his own farm, a dream long imagined.

Iowa had been settled from east to west, the early settlers clearing forests along the powerful Mississippi. Pioneers who chose the middle of the state waded through flatlands of tallgrass prairie, their curved plow blades slicing through the tough roots. Rising two hundred feet above the Missouri River valley, the Loess Hills with their steep, rugged terrain comprised the western side of Iowa, inviting only the toughest newcomers.

Covered by thick prairie grass, the land of the Loess Hills was a brawling brute, fighting the hot summer sun and drying winds. Its thick prairie exterior withstood torrential rains, punishing snow, and severe droughts. The grass roots grew deep into the soil, their diameter as thick as a tree branch.

The men who brought their families to this area carried with them an ache to replace the wild grass with their own corn, beans, and wheat. The land would not be easily tamed, resisting muscle and plow. But the men were stronger and more determined. Their feet walked every mile, and their bodies watered every inch with the sweat from their labors. Until eventually man won over nature.

Kristoffer, along with the Svensen brothers, had chosen this area to settle. They found a community of other Norwegian immigrants and began breaking the tough sod, carving out thirty acres for their farm, which sat a little over six miles away from the town of Soldier.

Karoline, arriving after the men had built her a home, found the land beautiful and determined, much like the people of the Loess Hills.

The town of Soldier had been established only twenty-five years before she and Kristoffer started their farm. The town's name always intrigued her. Unlike Denison or Dow City, the small settlement was not named after a founder. It was named for the Soldier River, which ran close to the original Soldier Township. While the citizens of Soldier did not know with certainty from where the name of the river derived, local legend told of a man found on the riverbank, wrapped in an army coat with metal buttons, indicating he was a soldier.

Even if that were not true, Karoline liked the name of the town. It reflected the type of pioneer who had settled this wild land, battling against the elements to grow a new life.

Soldier Township had started with only a few houses, a general store, a post office, and a blacksmith shop. A mercantile had been built, burned down, and built again. The store had changed hands several times and was currently run by Anton Anderson. Little by little, house by house, and business by business, the town fought the harsh elements and grew. With the coming of the railroad, Soldier Township became the current town of Soldier.

Karoline had imagined the reaction of the Soldier community if they knew how she really felt about her husband's death. Instead, she plastered a look of mourning on her face. For the first week or so, neighbors and Lutheran church members continued to bring her food. Her kitchen filled with pies and canned fruits and vegetables. With each food gift, she had invited the giver inside and patiently listened to all the good they said about Kristoffer. She herself was forced to dig up small stories about his goodness as a husband. Telling her true feelings would have alienated her from others and confused them. As necessary, she played the role of the grieving widow.

Within a week of the funeral, she was picking apples when a

new, ornate buggy pulled up to the house. The Olsens' own buggy, purchased a year before Kristoffer died, was open air with a wooden seat in the back and one in the front, carrying four people. This carriage, however, had an upholstered seat and a fine black cab, protecting the rider from the elements. A middle-aged man in a fine black suit with a black bowler hat looked down and around the property, seeming to assess the farm and its merits. He jumped down and let his horse find its way to her flowers.

"*Hallo*, can I help you?" Karoline yelled out in Norwegian from her position in the tree.

"Are you Mrs. Olsen?" the man responded, matching Karoline's language. As he was asking, Karoline noticed his continued surveying, taking note of the implements and animals in particular.

"I am. What can I do for you?" As he started to speak, Karoline left her basket of ripened apples and climbed down her ladder.

"My name is Horace Twigg, and I am the bank manager. I don't usually make calls to our customers' homes but, considering your situation, I thought I could make an exception," he said with condescension, irritating Karoline.

"I appreciate that, but you didn't say *why* you are here." Karoline could feel her impatience rising.

Twigg cleared his throat and looked around some more. "Is there an older son I can speak with?"

"My son Tingvald is in the field. There is no one but me. How can I help you?"

"Well, ma'am," he said as he started to flush red, "I'm here about a loan made to your husband. You see, he borrowed from the bank for some land and cattle. The loan hasn't been paid in two months, and I've come to make arrangements for the back payments as well as the current payment. Perhaps I can return when your son is available to discuss this with me?"

"You can talk to me about this. How much is the total loan and how much are the monthly payments?"

"Do you mind if we go inside and sit down? I can try to explain all of this to you."

Karoline invited the banker into her kitchen, the place where she felt the most confident. It felt odd to sit across from a man she didn't know without a male relative present. Women stayed with their own and let the men handle anything relating to the farm, business, or politics. Women had been relegated to children, birthing, and household matters. She had never talked of money before, and now she must begin this life as a widow with bank loans. She felt like she was on shifting ground, and she didn't have sure footing with this topic. Manners dictated an offer of coffee and some type of sweet treat for all visitors, but Karoline felt unfriendly toward him and sat without offering him anything.

Taking out his papers, Horace Twigg started to explain the history of the farm loans.

"Well, Mr. Olsen first borrowed for ten acres and then leveraged that to borrow for another ten. Overall, he owes on the total twenty acres. He bought the land for $24.00 per acre. That brings the loan to $480.00 without interest. With interest we're looking at near to $500.00 plus a few more dollars."

"We owe $500.00?" Karoline's body froze with the shock of this news.

"Not exactly," he said. "There's the matter of the cattle. He bought thirty head of cattle, which was when cattle were at their lowest, and now they are much higher."

"And how much for the cattle?"

"Well, let me see here. He paid $23.57 per head at thirty head, which adds up to…$407.01…plus the interest."

"We owe the bank $900.00?" She had never seen that much

money. Nothing she owned was worth that amount of money.

"Closer to $1,000 with the interest," he replied.

She could see these were merely math sums to him. They didn't add up to a homeless family. They didn't add up to a lost farm. And, they certainly didn't add up to a penniless widow.

"How are we supposed to pay it back? We don't have that kind of money. How much is the payment each month?"

"Again, Mrs. Olsen, I would really rather talk to your son about this. I can see that I'm upsetting you."

"Please continue, Mr. Twigg. How much is the monthly payment?" she repeated, mustering as much calm as she could. She didn't want to prove him correct by giving in to any of her female feelings.

"Seventy-five dollars. Might I suggest you sell some of the cattle to get yourself caught up? Right now, cattle are going for $27.44 a head. You are behind $150.00 and with this month's payment that adds up to…"

"Two hundred and twenty-five dollars." Karoline might not know about bank loans, but she did know her sums. "Mr. Twigg, I appreciate your taking the time to come here. I need to discuss this with my son, and we'll come up with something. I give you my assurance you will have your money within the next two days. Have a pleasant day." She stood up and started walking toward the door.

The banker's face turned red. He replaced his hat, turned on his heels, and walked briskly to his buggy. Karoline wasn't sure whether it was her impertinence at interrupting him with her math skills or whether it was because she hadn't asked him for his help, but Mr. Twigg was clearly annoyed by something she had done.

Karoline didn't know if they had the money, but debts needed to be paid. The farm was not only their sole income; but it was the center of their life, the home to which her family could return.

Tingvald had no more than shown his head through the door before Karoline accosted him. "Did you know your *fadir* had debt on this farm?"

"I did. Why?"

"Do you know how much? The banker came today. We're overdue on our payments by two months and now we have another month to pay."

Karoline started to pace the kitchen, thinking about how they were going to pay back the money Kristoffer owed the bank.

"I was never sure how much was on the loan, but I knew it was pretty large. And I knew we were behind two months. *Fadir* thought he could pay what we owed and get ahead when he went up north. What money we did have went toward his funeral."

They had spent far more than needed to honor Kristoffer in a proper way. His grave marker, a large obelisk, towered over the other tombstones. That marker told the community he was a loved man. What would they think about him if his wife and children were homeless? Would he still be a hero?

"Why didn't I know about all of this?"

"*Fadir* said business and money couldn't be understood by women, so it wasn't their place to know. I've been trying to figure out a way to get us even again."

Tingvald sat down at the kitchen table and looked into the cup of cold coffee sitting in front of him. His dejected face told Karoline how much her son had been burdened by this secret.

"The banker said we should sell some cattle."

"I don't want to do that. The price of cattle has been going up, and I think if we hold on to them, we can pay off more of the loan. I was planning to sell them in another year."

Karoline sat down at the table with him and put her head into her hands. She was angry Kristoffer had put them in this position and worried about how they would come up with the money.

"Tingvald, we don't have a choice. We have to sell some cattle."

"I have some money saved. I've been putting away money I earned from raising hogs. *Fadir* never paid me an income, so that's why I've had hogs the last two years. I wanted to put it toward the lumber for the house I want to build for Ella and me. We can put off marriage for two years. We're both young, and her father doesn't want her to marry until she is eighteen."

Her heart sank with his generosity. How had such a hard man raised such a thoughtful and gentle soul?

"Do you have enough for the payments?"

"I have almost half. If we sell two cows, we'll be able to make it."

"Tingvald, if you do not have the money to build a house when you are ready to marry, you and Ella can live here with us. It's only appropriate the man of the farm lives in the big house. I'll give up the large bedroom and share with the twins. Once we get past this crisis, we need to come up with a plan on how to make the payments every month."

"I think we should raise hogs along with the cows. Meat is always needed, and even in drought the animals can be sold."

Karoline had watched her son grow and change. He had recently taken to smoking a pipe and went by his initials T.A. instead of his given name. She had meant to scold him for his smoking, but she would remain quiet and let him make his own decision. His name, though, was another matter. While she did not mind others calling him T.A., she would not be doing so herself. His name meant something important to her, a reminder of her strength.

Not only was he using his initials, but he also had changed the spelling of their last name. She noticed this trend with the next generation. They were all using *son* instead of *sen*. When she asked her neighbor about this, Kristina explained they wanted to use the American spelling of the word *son*, not the Norwegian spelling. Also, it separated them from the Danish, who spelled with the *sen*. She supposed the young people had no personal ties to their homeland, which allowed them to shuck off their surname system.

Beyond these physical changes, this day Tingvald showed how much he had taken on the role of being a man. He had sacrificed himself and his desires to save the family and his father's dream. He had also taken his first step in making farm decisions. She needed to respect him as the man he had become instead of always thinking of him as her child.

Karoline was relieved they had gotten through this crisis and saved her husband's farm, the family's legacy. To her, though, it was more than a legacy or a way to make a living. The land held their past and gave her children a permanent place in which to return. Having given up her own childhood home when she moved to America, she knew the feeling of being untethered, of not having a place of unconditional acceptance and love and safety. As their only parent, she made it her purpose not only to maintain their Norwegian heritage but also their home, no matter where they may someday live.

1906

Karoline

Karoline's last child with Kristoffer was born in March 1906, seven months after Kristoffer's funeral. She named him after her father Gulbran and chose a modern American middle name, Floyd, a name popular among silent movie characters. Gulbran did not appreciate his unusual Norwegian name and changed it as soon as he was old enough to correct people, going by his middle name. His mother was disappointed but allowed it. Karoline and the rest of the family overindulged him. He did as he pleased and said what he pleased. Karoline, too soft-hearted for this last child of hers, never said 'no.'

If he wanted his dessert before he finished his meal, so be it. If he stole into his mother's garden and filled up on strawberries; instead of punishing him, Karoline laughed with delight at his red-stained mouth and hands. His older twin sisters, Sophie and Gunda, gave him what he wanted before he could ask. He was their play doll.

Being able to name her child anything she pleased and raise him as she saw fit gave Karoline an immense feeling of freedom. That freedom grew stronger with every decision that was hers and began permeating every aspect of her new life.

As Elfred Svensen predicted, bachelors and widowers flocked to her front door, small gifts in one hand and hat in the other.

Her first offer of marriage, which came only a month after the burial, was from her brother-in-law, Valter Olsen. Valter had immigrated to Iowa in 1883, five years after Kristoffer and Karoline's arrival in America. The Olsen farm in Norway was so heavily mortgaged the family eventually lost it to the bank. Valter, with no land of his own to farm, hoped Kristoffer, his younger brother, would offer some of their land—"just to get him started," he said—but Kristoffer was already farming with the Svensen brothers and hadn't wanted to include his less-than-productive brother. Valter stayed with them for six months until his presence was like a rug in Karoline's kitchen—worn and in need of throwing away. With no land to farm and no money to purchase it, Valter started his own business cleaning chicken houses. He hauled out the chicken manure and sprayed the coop to get rid of pests. It was an unpleasant job, but one that needed to be done regularly.

Kristoffer noticed his brother never received a second job from anyone. When he investigated, his neighbors reluctantly admitted that when Valter finished the job, he often took off with one or two of their chickens. Because they thought so highly of Kristoffer, they never said anything but never asked the other Olsen brother back, either. When Valter asked Kristoffer if he could be hired to clean their chicken coop, Kristoffer told Karoline they might as well get work out of him because he would steal their chickens whether he cleaned their coop or not.

When Valter showed up on Karoline's doorstep, his black hair, now threaded with grey, was long and uncombed. His overgrown beard and mustache held remnants of chewing tobacco juice. His shirt and pants were dirty and frayed. His most notable feature was his freshly made black eye. When Karoline opened her door, he stood without a gift or a smile. He looked her up and down like a heifer he was considering buying.

"Valter, what happened to your eye?"

"I hit a tree limb when I was out riding my horse," Valter said, spitting tobacco into her flower bed.

Karoline knew the answer to her question before she had asked him. She just wanted to hear him lie. The tale of Valter had spread through the valley like smoke. In the dark of night, Valter had snuck across his neighbor's pasture and stolen a pig. When his neighbor went to the pen, he noticed one fewer pig and followed the tracks across his pasture right to Valter's house. When Valter opened his door, the neighbor punched him in the eye and then went to retrieve his pig.

"What can I do for you, Valter?" Karoline asked with impatience.

"I come to marry you, Karoline. You need a man to run this farm. And I think it's my duty to my dead brother to take care of his widow."

Karoline knew his supposed concern was also a lie. They had never gotten along, and she found him revolting. He wanted nothing more than to get his hands on his brother's land.

"Valter, I appreciate your concern, but I already have a man to run the farm."

"Who?"

"Tingvald. And, Ingrid's husband Stefan is also part owner and farms with him."

Valter's face turned into a sneer. "That little britches? He don't know how to run a farm. You need an experienced man for the job."

"Well, you may be right, but so far we've been doing pretty well. If I need any help, I'll certainly let you know. For now, I'm not interested in marrying. And I would appreciate it if you would keep your hands off our chickens. Kristoffer never said anything to you, but I'm different. If you steal my property, you're going to suffer the consequences."

"You always was a hard woman, Karoline. I don't know how my brother ever put up with you." With that, he turned around and left.

Every time Karoline saw Valter, she thought of her friend Runa. Valter and Runa danced several times the evening she met Kristoffer. Karoline had briefly envisioned Runa and her becoming sisters-in-law. That did not come to pass; Valter never courted Runa beyond that night. Once again, Karoline thought to herself how Runa had slipped the noose by not marrying Valter. While Karoline was sure Runa came out better for it, she sometimes wondered if Valter would have been a better man if he had married Runa, a fine woman who might have brought out the best in him. As it was, it did not matter since they never married. Runa eventually married the man on whose farm she was working the last time the two women had seen each other. The man's wife died, and he married Runa shortly after.

Karoline had other suitors, but they waited the appropriate year before they came knocking on her door. Most were Norwegian, but some were German or Irish. They were all ages and sizes. Some were younger than Karoline, and others were far older. They wanted to take her for a buggy ride or escort her to a community dance. Karoline politely declined each one of them.

Fourteen months after her husband's funeral, Karoline was hanging clothes on the line, hoping the menacing clouds coming from the west would not produce a tornado. A buggy pulled up to the house. A rather elderly man—he looked like he might have been in his seventies—stepped down. He was wearing a white shirt and black pants with a black bowler hat. His hair was white, which matched his short-cropped beard. As he walked toward her, she could see he was somewhat bent over, from hard labor she supposed.

"Hello, madam. My name is Henry Wagner, and I am from Schleswig. I've come to court you, if you please."

Karoline tried to keep her face placid, but in her mind, she was wondering how an old man, who didn't even know her, would think she would want to be courted by him.

"It's nice to meet you, sir. How is it that you have heard I am looking for a husband?"

"I was at the Dunlap auction, and some of the men were talking about a widow with a farm who was in need of a husband. I'm not in my prime, obviously, but I can still manage a farm."

Karoline needed to politely but firmly rebuff him. "I'm honored that you would consider my need and make such a long trip to my farm. I have three sons who will inherit this farm. I would hate to see you work hard for something that will never be yours. My oldest son and son-in-law are now working the farm and have been able to meet its needs, so you needn't worry about me. Please have a safe trip back and enjoy the lovely day."

Looking annoyed, the suitor said, "Perhaps I could come in for some coffee and cake, and we could talk about this a little more?"

Karoline could see he wanted to get something out of his visit, and if it were only a home-baked good, he would be satisfied. She, however, did not want to let him into her house for fear it would be hours before he would leave.

"I hope you can forgive my poor manners, but if I don't get my laundry hung up we won't have clothes for tomorrow. I'm sorry, but I need to decline."

Like the rest of the men, Henry Wagner had never considered Karoline as a human being—one who would be a partner to them, one who needed love. They thought of themselves first, wanting a farm or a woman to take care of them. It wouldn't be long before Henry would need a nursemaid, which is why he came to marry her. He thought of his own needs, not the woman who would be saddled with an old man.

The last of them to arrive was Elfred Svensen, just as he had promised. The previous suitors were easy to decline, but Elfred was a different matter. They already had a history together, and he loved her as a woman instead of a woman with a farm or a woman who would take care of his needs. He did not put on his best outfit or carry a bunch of wildflowers in his hand. He came as himself, honest and true, to her front door.

Combing his hair down with his hand, Elfred cleared his throat and asked, "Karoline, are you ready to marry me?"

"Elfred, it's good to see you. Please come in, and I'll pour you a cup of coffee."

Karoline shooed the children out of the kitchen, grabbed two cups, and poured from the pot on the stove. She took her time, looking in her pantry for something to serve, putting off the inevitable. Then, she sat across from Elfred.

"Well, Karoline? Will you marry me?"

She had thought about this day since he made his feelings known to her while standing at Kristoffer's gravesite. She had gone back and forth on her decision like a weed in the wind. His presence in her life had always been a comfort and made daily living easier. If she married him, she would be using him the same way all of those other men wanted to use her. She would be asking him to take care of the farm and help raise her children. She was also afraid. She and Kristoffer had started off loving one another and through circumstances and their own changes, they had become strangers, and at times, even adversaries. She respected Elfred too much to treat him that way.

Looking across the table at him, Karoline laced her fingers together and set her hands on the table. She looked directly into Elfred's eyes and took a deep breath.

"Elfred, you are my oldest friend. I have relied on you since the day we met. I think highly of you and know you would make a good husband. But… I told myself I would not marry again. I do not make a good wife. I have my own opinions and will not obey. I enjoy our time together, but if we married we would spoil that. We have never had a cross word or a disagreement. Marriage would bring about both of these. I'm sorry, but my answer is no."

His face fell, and he dropped his eyes down to the floor. Clearly, he had expected a different response.

"I'm sorry, too. I mean it; I love you. I had myself set to marry you when a year of mourning was up. I can't tell you I'm not disappointed. This will take me some time to mend. You may not see much of me."

"I hope we can get past this, Elfred. I value our relationship as it is. I would hate to lose you as a friend, and I'm going to need your advice from time to time. I'll understand if you don't stop by anymore. You're a fine man."

Elfred, embarrassed from being rejected, left quickly.

Karoline felt bad about having to tell Elfred no, and she sincerely hoped he would continue to be a part of her and her children's lives, but as someone on the outside rather than on the inside.

Karoline, like a mother blue jay keeping her young in her nest, desired a life in which she and her children lived their expanding lives as one with no one telling her how to raise them. The farm, their nest, would always pull them back together and give her children a permanent home.

1906

Gunda

The Olson twins, Gunda and Sophie, were sixteen when their father died. The young women were just beginning to date young men as well as thinking about what would come next after high school. Perhaps they would marry, as was common for most women once they received their high school certificate, or perhaps they would continue with their schooling. Their father would have approved or disapproved of their choices, and they would have had to follow his decisions. Gunda had always obeyed her father's commands, but she was strong-willed and had a mind of her own.

Gunda didn't mind being a twin, but she never knew what it was to have a life of her own. She was always paired with Sophie. Her mother had dressed them alike when they were children. People assumed they thought alike and liked the same things, which wasn't true. The only difference seemed to be their names. Sophie's name was easy to spell and never mispronounced. Gunda's name was never pronounced correctly, the first syllable always being pronounced like *gun*. And, if people pronounced her name correctly, they always spelled it *Goonda*, as it sounded. Her name was the only thing about her Gunda would trade with her sister.

The twins were fraternal rather than identical, so they were never mistaken for one another. Gunda somewhat mirrored Sophie in appearance. She also had long dark hair, but hers was straight rather than curly. Sophie's face was heart-shaped, and Gunda's was more squared like her father's. They both had bright blue eyes. Their real physical difference was their size. Sophie was willow-tall like their father, and Gunda was petite-plump like their mother.

Their personalities were as opposite as sand was to sky. While Sophie focused on fashion, Gunda focused on her education. Sophie thought only of her own desires; Gunda generally thought of others before herself. Sophie hated the farm; Gunda loved being outside on the land and spending time with the animals.

When Gunda was old enough, she begged her parents to allow her to take care of their horses. She fed, watered, and brushed their coats. Gunda enjoyed taking a horse out for sunset rides. She had a special place on the top of a hill where she could look out across the Loess Hills. She treasured the steep hills, ditches with bright sumac, and patches of farmed acres.

Even when the animals hurt her, like when a cow stepped on her foot and broke it, she never blamed them or became afraid of them. When Gunda was eight years old, her mother's rooster had climbed up her back and pecked her, leaving a scar on the side of her right eye. Gunda begged her mother to forgive the rooster, but Karoline caught that rooster and killed it, serving him for supper. That didn't deter Gunda; she still loved going to the chicken coop to gather the eggs, talking to the hens as she reached under them to claim her prize.

Gunda was gentle and soft spoken. At gatherings, she rarely spoke, preferring to sit and listen instead. If she did speak and all eyes turned to her, she could feel her face turning bright red. She would prefer any attention go to her twin. Instead of sitting with the adults, she gravitated toward the children, placing herself in the midst of them, playing games and taking care of their hurts. When her mother had Floyd, she took care of him whenever she was home from school. She liked to pretend he was her baby and even changed his dirty clouts without complaint. Whenever Floyd was scolded, he rushed to Gunda for sympathy.

Gunda wanted to be both a teacher and a mother. She planned to earn her high school diploma and then attend a normal school when she turned seventeen. Her dream was to attend the Iowa State Normal School in Cedar Falls to receive her four-year degree. If she could go to Cedar Falls, she would earn her state certificate, which would earn her higher pay. Unfortunately, the family's lack of finances would require her to scale back her plans and attend summer training instead. A summer program was better than the two-week county program, which was slowly being eliminated in the county schools. A summer program would not earn her the highest certificate, but it would give her more credibility than the current country teachers.

Her own teacher, Miss Anderson, had generously spent time with her after school to discuss her best options in becoming a teacher. They laid out all the nearby programs and their costs. If she could go to the summer program, the town of Moorhead just southwest of Soldier would need a teacher the following term.

Morningside College in Sioux City had the closest summer program, which also included room and board. The learning would be intense, covering many curricula in a short amount of time, but Gunda loved to learn and wanted to fulfill her dream. Her only hurdle would be getting money and the family's permission.

1906

Gunda

Finishing her last year in school, Gunda left for teacher training in May and would be gone from home for eight weeks. After much family discussion and debate, her mother had finally convinced Gunda's brothers to send her to Morningside College for the summer. The family agreed Gunda would teach for as long as it took to pay back the money her brother Alex had loaned her for her schooling.

Many young women taught for one or two terms until they married. Those teachers hadn't gotten the better training. They had trained for two weeks and earned the lowest teaching certificate available, and their education was scarcely better than the students they taught. They had no real investment in their career.

Gunda was different. She wanted to spend years in her profession. Her own time and Alex's money would be sacrificed to achieve this endeavor. This would not be something to keep her amused until she found a man to marry. Gunda did plan to marry someday, but she would wait until she was in her mid-twenties to do so.

Gunda was the first family member to leave the farm, and she was the only one to receive additional education. She felt fortunate her mother, a more modern thinker, supported Gunda's desire to work outside the home. She, unlike most of the women in the community, did not believe a woman's sole purpose was to marry and raise children. Karoline wanted her children to follow their dreams, just as she and Kristoffer had followed theirs.

Gunda had not known her father well when he died. But her impression of the marriage was of her father's anger. She could remember times in the house when she sensed she should be quiet; she should cause no commotion because they were all trying to be good for the sake of an angry Kristoffer. As she had grown older, her sister Ingrid spoke of a mother who defied, a mother with her own opinions. Even now, Gunda could see why the marriage had not worked; her mother had her own way and would take no direction from another.

With her valise packed, Gunda kissed her family good-bye, and she and her mother left for the train station. Once she arrived in Sioux City, she would need to find a hansom cab to take her from the train station to the college. This responsibility worried her the most. She had never been away from home by herself. She had never ridden in a cab much less hailed one. Every time she spoke to strangers, her face flushed red, and she had difficulty speaking loudly enough for them to hear her. She worried she would get lost. For weeks, she had dreamt of all kinds of bad things happening to her as she traveled. She felt once she was safely deposited at the college gates, she would be less frightened.

Nervous and with feelings of regret, Gunda hugged her mother at the station with her mother's voice issuing confidence in her ear.

If her father Kristoffer had lived another year, he would have been at her mother's side. Gunda wondered if he would have approved of her decision to attend teacher training.

Leaving with many hugs and kisses, Gunda was finally on her own. She told herself often that, after today, she would be at the college, safely ensconced in her room, and her dream would begin.

After a long train ride with many stops in small towns, Gunda stood on campus and looked across the Missouri River valley. She marveled at wide expanses of farmland with the Missouri River snaking through, dividing the land. Compared to the Soldier River, the Missouri looked like an ocean to Gunda.

The college buildings, made from red brick, loomed in front of her. She threw her head back and observed the many windows looking down on her. Gunda had never seen such opulence. The buildings that impressed her the most in Soldier looked puny next to these elegant giants.

Once in her room, Gunda took note of two single beds on either side of the space. The window was devoid of curtains, and the room's sparseness contrasted greatly with the room she shared with Sophie. Eventually, another young woman entered the room and introduced herself. "Hi, I'm Hazel. I guess we'll be rooming together." Gunda welcomed her, and the girls sat for a while and exchanged information.

Hazel lived in Kingsley, a small town north and east of Sioux City. She was the same age as Gunda but looked like her complete opposite. Hazel, tall and slender, had long blonde hair and green eyes. She, too, came from a farm family and wanted a career of her own. More so, Hazel wanted to leave the farm without having to marry in order to do so. Her own teacher was marrying, so she encouraged Hazel to get her training and take her place for the fall term.

The young women had much in common, coming from a farm and a small community. They became fast friends and promised to help each other through the rigorous curriculum.

The student teachers would study two subjects for two weeks, one subject in the morning and one in the afternoon. Their classes were held in Charles City Hall, another imposing building; but their classroom looked little better than the one she attended for her own schooling. The room held small tables for two and matching chairs. The walls were devoid of any decorations. Unlike her own classroom, this one was hot and stuffy. The students were expected to dress professionally, which meant the women wore their petticoats, an additional layer, trapping in the sweltering condition.

The young women would start with basic content: writing, reading, arithmetic. It was assumed the students were proficient in these areas, but the school wanted to be sure all of them had the same standard of excellence. They would all be educated to the high school level for arithmetic, which was algebra, in the event they had a particularly bright student. Gunda flew through the algebra lessons, enjoying the new learning, but Hazel struggled in not only the algebra but some of the basic arithmetic concepts.

Their next session focused on government. They studied school government in the morning: its organization, duties of the county superintendent, and school board obligations. Teachers needed to understand how schools were run, so they could participate in school board elections, the only time a woman could vote. Learning state and federal government in the afternoon would prepare them to teach citizenship class. Public school teachers were responsible for turning out strong Iowa citizens who understood how their state and federal governments operated.

Their third session taught agriculture science for their male students and home economics for their female students. Hazel and Gunda felt fortunate they had grown up on farms. There was much they already knew. However, many of the female students' faces looked scalded when they studied animal husbandry.

"I can't imagine teaching this!" Hazel whispered to Gunda during a lesson.

Shaking her head, Gunda replied, "It's just farm animals. If you live the farm life, these are things you must know. I've seen this a hundred times. But I also can't imagine teaching this lesson to a classroom of boys."

Gunda was also very proficient at home economics, her mother making sure she knew how to sew, knit, cook, and garden. Hazel had not had the same training. Her mother had died when she was young, and her father had not remarried. Hazel could cook and run a household; however, her sewing was weak and her knitting, non-existent. Both girls were surprised by the study of chemistry in this session. They applied the science to soil composition and bread making.

Their last session focused on the art of teaching. The students were taught some techniques for teaching reading, writing, and arithmetic. Their instructor spent a whole day on the importance of discipline, keeping it and applying it. Gunda's own schoolhouse teacher ran a tight ship, and students did as they were asked. Gunda thought it was unnecessary to spend so much time on one topic. She envisioned herself with quiet children who hung on her every word and loved her ardently.

Their teacher education was quite difficult and required a great deal of memorization. Gunda had always learned easily, but Hazel was not as strong a student. The women spent every evening studying with Gunda pulling Hazel through the chemistry session. Gunda also guided Hazel's sewing and knitting.

At the end of the summer training, the students had to pass an exam for each subject with no individual score lower than seventy percent. Any part not passed meant no teacher certificate. The student could repeat the entire session if she so wished and try the exams once again the following summer. Since Gunda and Hazel had teaching jobs waiting for them in September, it was critical they both pass the exams on the first try.

In mid-July, all teacher candidates sat for their exams. They would take one exam each morning and afternoon for a full week of testing. Their scores for each day would be posted the next morning for everyone to see. Their first test was arithmetic. Gunda worried for Hazel and did her best to prepare her friend both intellectually and spiritually.

After the test began, Gunda flew through the basics: addition, subtraction, division, multiplication, and fractions. She felt confident in her answers and went into the second section, algebra, with little worry. Working the problems carefully, Gunda slowed her progress, making sure she made no silly errors. At one point, she looked over at Hazel, who was chewing on her pencil and bouncing her right knee. *A sign of struggle,* she thought. Gunda tried to think good thoughts and send them to her friend, but it didn't look like Hazel would finish on time. Gunda finished with twenty minutes remaining and left the testing room. She waited outside for her friend.

"How did you do?" Gunda asked Hazel as her friend came through the outside doors.

"Not very well, I'm afraid. I've never been good with fractions. My own teacher hurried through them, and now I'm suspecting she wasn't very good at them either."

"How was the algebra section?"

"Terrible. Everything I knew just flew out of my brain. I got so nervous; it was difficult to think logically. I kept worrying about losing my teaching position."

"I'm sure you'll be fine. Let's get lunch and prepare for the next test."

The women returned after lunch to sit for their next exam,

agriculture. Both of them worried about how much chemistry there would be on the test since they both still felt rather inadequate in that subject. Fortunately for Gunda, there were only two questions, and she knew the answers to both of them. Hazel was unsure of her answers, but she felt confident in her remaining responses.

With two tests completed and a number yet to take, the women ate supper with the other students, reviewed the information for the following day's tests, and went to bed early.

When they reached their classroom the next morning, they saw scores for both tests posted outside of the classroom. Gunda found her name quickly: 90% on arithmetic and 95% on agriculture. She beamed with pride and exhaled in relief. After her own scores were securely tucked away, Gunda remembered her friend and turned to look for her. Hazel was nowhere. Gunda looked at Hazel's scores: 67% on arithmetic and 85% on agriculture. She did not have the requisite score to continue with her certificate.

Gunda's stomach sank to her knees. It was as if she herself had received inadequate scores. She ached for her friend, who would now have to relinquish her future teaching contract.

Once Gunda finished her morning test, she went back to her room to find Hazel. There were no signs of her. Her clothes were gone, and the bed was made. Gunda found a note on her bed:

Good luck on the rest of your tests. I'll always remember you. Hazel.

Gunda would remember Hazel, too. As sad as she was, Gunda still had other tests and needed to focus on those instead of worrying about her new friend.

On the last day, the students took only one test in the morning. Their scores would be posted in the afternoon; those who passed would receive their teaching certificate. Gunda felt proud of her work, passing all of her exams with nothing less than 85%. Her final test, home economics, earned her the highest score, 100%.

With her certificate in hand, Gunda boarded the afternoon train to return home to her mother; Sofie; her baby brother; and her older siblings, Alex, Tingvald, and Ingrid. She was especially excited to share her adventure with her twin.

While she missed them terribly, she had enjoyed being on her own and meeting new people. She loved the challenge the learning had brought and was excited to get her own classroom where she could endow her students with that knowledge.

1906

Gunda

Gunda, a fresh teaching certificate in her hands, was hired in the fall by the town of Moorhead, nine miles southwest of Soldier, to teach in their country school. Gunda sat in the empty classroom, facing the county superintendent, Mr. Higgs. She was both anxious and nervous to meet her superior and to find out her duties as the new teacher for Moorhead.

The schoolhouse was newly built, sitting on donated land east of the town. Some of the children from Soldier lived closer to the Moorhead school than they did the Soldier school, so they attended the one closest to them. The small, white building sat on a sand lot, so it did not have a basement like those nearer the larger towns. The importance the community placed on education showed by the entrance hall for children's coats and boots, which had cost extra money to build. The interior of the classroom was already decorated

by past teachers with posters of presidents lining the top of the wall.
A blackboard ran along the front of the room with cursive alphabet
letters donning the top of it. A large map of Iowa and the United
States covered the west wall opposite a bank of windows. In the back
of the classroom sat a coal stove, black and squat. The room was
cheerful and clean—*a perfect place to teach,* Gunda thought.

"Miss Gunda Olson, it's a pleasure to meet you. I have to admit,
I'm a little concerned about your size. I thought you would be taller."

Gunda didn't like the way he pronounced her first name, holding
onto the vowel like her name had double *o*'s.

"Why is this a concern?" Gunda didn't think there was a size
requirement.

"Some of our boys are bigger than you. Are you sure you can
control them?"

"I can," she lied. She had never thought about teaching the older
students when she pictured herself in a classroom. She had only pictured young children gathered around her.

"Well, then, let's get down to the job. You are hired on a term-by-
term basis. Your pay is $33.00 per term. You will be given free board
with the Christensen family, who will also provide your food. They
have three daughters and a son who attend this school. School starts at
eight, so you should be here no later than six, so you can prepare the
classroom. In the winter, you are expected to start the stove and have
the room warm by the time the children arrive. Is this suitable for you?"

"Yes, of course."

"You are responsible for keeping the schoolroom clean: scrub
the floors at least once a week, sweep every evening before you
leave, clean the blackboards once a day. In the winter, you will need
to shovel the front entrance. Someone will come and shovel the rest.
Does this meet with your approval?"

"Yes. I can do that."

"We have a few rules you will need to abide by. If you violate them, you may lose your position. Of course, you may not marry. If you do, you'll need to resign. You are not to keep the company of any man, especially riding in a carriage, unless it is one of your male family members. You may not travel out of county limits; your home is acceptable, but you must get permission from the chairman of the board. Your behavior must be impeccable: no smoking or drinking. No loitering in the ice cream shop. You must attend church each Sunday. I believe you are Norwegian, are you not?"

"Yes, I am. Is that going to be a problem? I know this is a Danish town."

"Not as long as you attend our church and keep your Norwegian to yourself."

"Yes, sir." Gunda didn't appreciate the discrimination, but she wanted the job so badly she was willing to make those concessions.

"Your attire is also important. Under no circumstances are you to dye your hair, do not wear bright colors—not even outside of school—and always wear two petticoats. Your dresses must not be any shorter than two inches above your ankles. Now, let me see, did I forget anything? Oh, yes, and you must be home no later than eight in the evening unless, of course, you are attending a school meeting. And, you are required to attend all school meetings and vote in all matters pertaining to school. Do you understand?"

"Yes, I understand." Gunda wanted him to leave, so she could be alone in her classroom, but he did not stand up.

"Now, let's talk about the curriculum. You will use the approved textbooks: The *McGuffy Reader* and the *Hoosier Schoolmaster* for grammar. If you bring in your own books for the children, you will be fired."

"Are the Jack London books not acceptable? I thought *White Fang* would be a wonderful tale for the boys."

"Absolutely not. A man tramping about instead of settling down with a family is immoral. And we don't want the children getting ideas in their head about leaving their communities in search of adventure. You can use the *McGuffy* and the Bible, but nothing else."

"I'm sorry. I understand." Gunda was particularly upset by his disapproval of *White Fang*. He failed to understand the bigger meaning of the novel and instead applied his own narrow-minded prejudices. Gunda knew the world was bigger than Iowa, and she felt preparing children for its constant change was an important responsibility of a teacher.

"Miss Olson, your job is to instill morals and values. You also have the important job of creating proper citizens. There is no job more important than that of a teacher. Am I understood?"

"Yes, sir. I completely understand."

"Good, then. I'll leave you to your job. Let me know if there are any questions or there is anything you need. There shouldn't be, but just in case."

He smiled at her, but she didn't feel like it was a welcoming smile. She felt like a naughty school girl who had just been chastised. Their rules didn't surprise her, except the one about attending their church. Both communities were Lutheran; however, she felt at home in her own church and had planned to attend there, but she would follow his dictate.

As she looked around her classroom, she envisioned herself teaching. She was excited and frightened at the same time. She had always wanted to teach, but thinking about the learning of the children solely in her hands was an important responsibility. The ones who wanted to continue to high school would rely on her to pass their exams. All of them would need those basic foundational skills in order to succeed in life. Gunda had never been given such trust, but she would do whatever was necessary to ensure she prepared them for whatever road lay ahead of them.

1906

Sophie

Sophie Olson lived on a farm—but she was no farm girl. She knew she was born in the wrong place, the wrong town, and the wrong state.

When Sophie was sixteen years old, her father died. Her relationship with her father was one way: he lectured her on morals and behavior, and she obeyed. When she was young, he broke his leg in a farming accident and was laid up in bed for a month. She avoided him during that time, afraid of his yelling and ranting. She, of course, was sad when he died; but she did not miss the tense atmosphere every time he was in the house. Her mother seemed much more at ease. But her oldest brother thought it was his job to teach her morals and watch after her. She thought it unfair Tingvald obsessed over the young men who came to court her and tried to tell her who she could date and who she couldn't.

Sophie, like her niece Edna—Tingvald's only daughter—was considered one of the beauties of the county, and at seventeen years old, she drew the young men to her. She had dark brown hair, which hung in ringlets down her back. Her long black lashes framed her bright blue eyes. Young men stuttered around her, and her sweet giggle while she covered her mouth was one of the reasons they had difficulty talking to her. Sofie was tall like her father, and her shapely form made her look years beyond seventeen. Her mother Karoline harped at her to wear loose clothing, but the fashion of the day was a cinched-in waist, making her hips and bosom bloom from bottom and top.

Sophie knew she affected the male species, and she delighted in it. She had perfected a downward look, which showed off her long lashes, and just at the right moment, she would look up and left while keeping her lids half closed to appear coquettish. She had perfected her ability to flirt with young men, a quality that brought them to her front door only to be questioned like a thief by her brother.

Sophie hated living on the farm. When she was asked to help with the harvest, she complained loudly and constantly about being in the field. Her primary task, pulling ears from the corn stalks and throwing them into the wagon, made her hands rough and her shoulders sore. In the summer, she sometimes had to help with cutting volunteer corn from their fields. She was hot and dirty and hated bugs.

Sophie wasn't any better with the animals. They smelled and were unpredictable, which often frightened her. Gathering eggs from the henhouse made her cringe. The hens pecked her while she thrust her hands under them to retrieve their eggs. It didn't take her long to outfox them, though. She kept a big stick hidden in their coop, and before she put her hand beneath them, she took the stick, clamped it across their necks, and held their heads down. It kept them from pecking her.

Often when she was reading books in the hayloft, she could hear family members calling her name. Knowing the pigs or cows needed chasing, she slid deeper into the hay to hide from her family obligations. Her brother Alex had lost his foot because cows had stampeded him, and Gunda had the incident with the rooster. Sophie was terrified of animals.

She also despised the solitude of the farm. She could not visit her school friends, nor could they make the trip to the farm. There was no entertainment, except to read and reread the same books. Sophie felt trapped in a world not for her.

Iowa, still young in its statehood, was naïve to the practices of the states bordering the Atlantic. It had yet to allow much of the modern world in. While the East Coast established new industries and built mansions in the styles of Europe, Iowa preferred to wear its work clothes. Its residents favored the simple life of farm, family, and church.

Soldier, secluded by the hills, felt like the middle of nowhere. This provincial town had few entertainment offerings. Nothing seemed to happen if it wasn't connected to one of the churches or farm life. It didn't have a movie theater. If she wanted to see a silent film, she needed to go to Denison. With the family's one truck, a trip necessitated getting a ride with another family or a group of friends, which didn't happen more than once a year.

A barn dance with her brother Tingvald playing his violin was a "real treat" for the community. When Soldier residents congregated, their conversations revolved around farming and the local gossip. To Sophie, nothing could have been more boring or provincial. She wanted to discuss the latest fashions or the doings of the silent stars. Who cared if someone's pig went missing?

Other than the men who would eventually go overseas during the war, most people didn't travel any farther than Denison or Sioux

City. Sophie wished to see more of the world than her family and neighbors did.

Once, Karoline had promised her she could travel to Chicago to visit her namesake, her Aunt Sophie, Karoline's sister. Sophie nagged her mother for weeks the summer she was thirteen to contact her aunt and purchase the train ticket. Karoline put her off until eventually there was no more talk of the trip.

The little she saw of Iowa made her wish for distant destinations. Fields of corn, wheat, and beans along with cows, hogs, and sheep made up most of western Iowa. Every town, to her, was the same. She had never visited the large cities, like Sioux City, Omaha, or Des Moines. She was sure there had to be more to those places than fields and farm animals. Even if she couldn't get out of Iowa, she would still have preferred to live in a larger city.

Therefore, Sophie did what she could to manage through her childhood, a girl born in the wrong place. Instead of completing her chores, she hid in the hayloft, looking at fashion magazines that had been handed down by a friend of hers. She could imagine herself as those models in the magazine, wearing the latest fashions and traveling all over the world. She paid special attention to the ads in the back, promising modeling careers through agents.

When she was alone in her room, she wore her hair in different modes, replicating the hairstyles she saw in those magazines. She looked at herself in the mirror, pinching her cheeks and biting her lips to redden them. She sat and stood in different poses, copying the magazine models.

Eventually, her pretending ended and, instead of wearing Paris designs, she was stuck on a dirty farm, wearing her mother's and sisters' hand-me-down clothing, which was hopelessly out of style.

Even if she were allowed to go shopping, Soldier's stores carried the necessities of a farming community, not the fashionable dresses and hats of the big city.

Sophie knew she was destined for more, for better things. She wanted to travel, to experience culture. She had no intention of living on the farm, living in Soldier, or even staying in Iowa. She had no intention of marrying some farm boy who would be approved by her family.

She wanted off the farm. She wanted a glamorous life.

1907

Sophie

For her eighteenth birthday, Sophie requested something very unusual. She wanted to have her picture made. No one in the family had ever paid for this privilege. She would have liked Gunda to travel the nine miles to accompany her and possibly have her picture made as well, but Gunda's superintendent was rather strict on her sister's movements.

Even though Karoline found the birthday request unusual, Sophie was an unusual daughter. She was not satisfied with thinking about marriage and a family. This daughter had plans Karoline thought far-fetched and silly. However, she allowed Sophie her dreams, knowing one day she would see the real world and understand her place in it. Karoline didn't feel her daughters needed to marry, but they did need to have an appropriate career if they chose a single life. They could be a nurse or a teacher, perhaps even work in a store, but Karoline thought Sophie's dreams of modeling in the big city were sheer fantasy.

Karoline believed the idea of a picture was unnecessary—and very vain—but since this was her daughter's only request, she consented. She would ask Sophie's older sister Betsi to drive her and Sophie to Denison on the day of Sophie's birthday. They could even make a day out of it, window shopping along Denison's streets.

When Karoline told Sophie of the birthday plans, she squealed with delight. She needed to find the perfect hairstyle and outfit for the picture. None of her own clothing was suitable. Much of it was ill-fitting or out of style. Only one person liked fashion as much as she.

Sophie admired Helen Fost, one of the two young shop girls at the mercantile. Helen was far more sophisticated than any member of Sophie's family. This young woman embodied modern fashion. When Karoline asked Sophie if she wanted help to prepare for the picture session, Sophie told her mother she preferred to have Helen's help instead.

Her first decision was what to do with her hair. Wear it up or wear it down? Stylish women piled their hair on top of their heads with a loose bun. There were other variations of that, but mostly women piled their long hair on the tops of their heads. The other option was to wear it free around her shoulders. Since she wasn't married, it was still appropriate to wear her hair down.

The clothing concerned Sophie the most. She borrowed a blue and white pinstriped dress from Helen. As was the fashion, the dress was layered, one shorter layer on top of a longer layer, creating a fountain effect, hitting just above her ankles. The dress was cinched in with a white belt. Her long sleeves had white sheer cuffs at the end, which matched her V-neck collar. Her friend loaned her an expensive faux pearl necklace. She would have loaned her the matching pearl earrings, but Sophie did not have pierced ears. Helen paired the dress with a white, large-brimmed hat. Even though her mother thought it very risqué, Sophie wore lace-up boots, which were tan with black patent leather spats. When Sophie looked at herself in the mirror, she beamed. She looked modern and older than her seventeen years.

The day of her birthday, Sophie exuded excitement and nervousness. She was thankful her brother's car had a top, so her coiffed hair and perfect ensemble remained pristine.

When she and her mother walked into the studio, the town outside disappeared. The photographer had hung a large sky-blue backdrop against the back wall, a color that would enhance Sophie's outfit. The room was quiet and seemed a world of its own.

Henry Norton came from the back room of his studio. He was a short, pudgy man with thinning hair and small-set eyes. When he saw Sophie, he raved about her beauty. He immediately went to his back room and brought out a white parasol.

"This is perfect for your picture," he said, handing her the parasol. "You look like a model."

Sophie blushed with the praise. She immediately stood taller and gave him one of her coquettish looks, which she thought mimicked a model.

"Were you thinking we take a head and shoulders shot or a full-length shot? Or, since she is such a vision, I would suggest both," the photographer said with an oily voice.

Sophie looked quizzically at her mother. They did not know which would be better. Karoline asked, "How much for one?"

"One picture is two dollars and fifty cents," the photographer answered.

The cost of the picture was exorbitant. Her mother spent that kind of money once a fall. Even one photo was more expensive than they had planned. They certainly couldn't afford two photos.

When the photographer saw the skeptical look on Karoline's

face, he knew finances were a concern. He was worried they would leave without even having one photo taken. "Since she is so beautiful, she deserves to have both pictures. I will take two pictures for the price of one."

Sophie's eyes widened, looking at Karoline with such desire that Karoline couldn't refuse, even though the cost would need to be made up somewhere else in her monthly household budget.

Henry Norton placed Sophie in front of the backdrop for the full-length picture. He placed the parasol in her hands and had her hold it out away from herself. As she had seen in many of the magazines, Sophie was instructed to place her right foot behind her left and angle her left foot out in front of her. The position was awkward and uncomfortable, but Sophie didn't utter one complaint. Once he had her head tipped perfectly, he shot the picture. For her close-up, she sat in a chair and looked off to the left. She imagined herself a goddess, waiting to be fed grapes.

Once the photographer had taken several shots, he gave Sophie his card. "I think you should consider becoming a model. I know several agents in Des Moines, whom I know would be very interested in these pictures. You should really consider traveling to Des Moines and meeting some of these men. I think you could model, and maybe even become an actress in Hollywood. I will write their names on the back of my card. If you meet with them, tell them I sent you."

Once again, Sophie beamed with excitement. Karoline didn't understand some of what the photographer said, but she could tell by his tone and demeanor he was lying. Was he trying to sell her more pictures?

Later that afternoon, when Sophie returned the clothes to Helen, she relayed every minute of her experience, especially the part when the photographer told her she could model. Helen, just as naïve as Sophie, fueled Sophie's modeling plans by dreaming with her. Sophie started plans for traveling to Des Moines to meet with these agents.

At the supper table the next evening, Sophie announced, "I am going to Des Moines to start a modeling career."

Unbelieving, Tinvald replied, "And when are you doing that?"

"Next week." With that declaration, she had her family's full attention.

Karoline, Tingvald, and Alex adamantly disagreed with her desire to travel to the capital city. Karoline said, "No, the city is no place for a young girl."

"There's nothing there but thieves. And capitalists. The way they work their employees, who are mostly immigrants, makes them the same as the thieves," Alex added with some authority.

Her family agreed: there would be no plans for Des Moines; there would be no discussion of Sophie going to Des Moines. She was not permitted to travel anywhere outside of their county, especially to such a wicked and large city.

As a way to placate her daughter, Karoline again offered a trip to Chicago. Sophie had been disappointed before when it never occurred; this time she already knew it would never happen, and she wasn't about to forget her plans in place of a fantasy trip. She was determined to get to Des Moines, certain her modeling career would begin as soon as she stepped off the train.

Sophie, furious at her backward and unsophisticated family, made her own plans. She was graduating from high school in the spring and could do as she pleased. In the time between, she needed to find a job and make enough money for her train fare. She assumed that as soon as she arrived in Des Moines, she would be taken care of by her agent.

Sophie spent the fall and winter working part time after school in the grocer's store. She cleaned the products and ran errands. She told her family she was saving her money for nurse's training, so they did not object to her getting a job off the farm.

Each week, Sophie counted every penny and put it toward her train ticket, which she had already priced. She was confident she would have the funds when the time came.

1907

Sophie

Seven months later, a week following her graduation in May, Sophie, bag in hand, crept quietly out of the house sometime around one in the morning. She picked a full moon to put the first step of her plan into place.

Crossing the road running in front of her house, she went down into the ditch and came out into a field, newly planted with corn. She hid her bag in a grove of trees, one she had to pass when she went into Soldier for work.

With her belongings recovered, she could board the train, requiring her to switch lines several times because there was no passenger train that ran directly from Soldier to Des Moines. Her family wouldn't discover her disappearance until she failed to return from work. By then, she would almost be in the city.

Her baggage stowed, Sophie retraced her steps, sneaking back into the house with no family members aware she had even left.

The next day, she wrote a letter to her mother, explaining her plans, so Karoline wouldn't worry. She hid the letter under her blankets, knowing when her mother was worried enough, she would search Sophie's bed. She said her usual goodbyes to her family and pretended to go to the grocer's for a normal day of work.

Once she arrived at the train station, she stood in line to purchase a ticket. She knew she could not afford first class, but she also knew she did not want immigrant class. The last thing she wanted was to catch some disease from an immigrant. She settled on coach and then sat down on a bench with her things to wait for the train.

As she expected, someone recognized her and came up to speak to her, curious about her trip. That person was Mrs. Henson, one of their church members. Once asked her destination, Sophie lied and told the woman she was heading to Chicago to visit her aunt. Sophie knew Mrs. Henson would eventually say something to her mother about running in to her. Her lie to Mrs. Henson would be the first bread crumb her family could follow.

Sophie was not new to train service. She and her mother had ridden the train from Soldier to Ute many times to visit friends and relatives. However, this train was much larger and full of passengers. Sophie hadn't thought about all of the strange people who would be sitting next to and across from her.

She boarded the train, looking around for an open seat. Passengers of various ages and sizes sat on the bench seats, which were on the outsides of the car with a wide center aisle. She would be required to sit next to and look across at another person. Women with young children filled many of the seats. Gentlemen is black suits sometimes sat together or sat across from each other, discussing the various issues of the times. Holding her belongings close to her chest, Sophie walked among them, looking desperately for an open spot.

She finally found one, next to a portly gentleman. He wore a traditional outfit: black pants, black vest, and a black coat. He wore a bowler hat and was reading a newspaper. His hair curled out from under his hat, and he wore his beard long. His wide bottom took up more than his allotted space, so she was required to sit closer to the outside aisle.

"Good morning, miss," he greeted her.

"Good morning, sir," she replied. Sophie hoped this would be the end of their conversation, and he would go back to his reading.

"Where are you traveling to?" he inquired.

"Des Moines," she responded and looked down at her feet, hoping her brevity would indicate she did not want conversation.

"And what is it that takes you to Des Moines? Will you be visiting family?"

Having not been taught to keep information to one's self with strangers, Sophie answered his question. "I'm going for a modeling career. I have two agents I plan to visit."

"Do you have an address? Do you know where you're going? Do you have an appointment? Do you have a place to stay?"

"I have an address but no appointment. I was planning to stop by their offices. I thought when I was given a job there would be a place provided for me."

"Oh, Miss…? I'm sorry, what is your surname?"

"Olson."

"Miss Olson. I'm afraid you've been misguided. When you go to those businesses, you may not be able to see the agent. You may need to make an appointment, and since they are quite busy, it may be several days to a week before you can get an interview. You'll need a place to stay until such time as you can interview with them."

Stunned, Sophie had not thought of any of these problems. She envisioned herself walking into the office, seeing the agent, and being hired. She did not realize it would be more difficult than that.

"I may be of some assistance to you by way of providing the name of a place to stay if you would like."

"Oh, yes please," she replied, her face alight with relief and gratitude.

"Good, then," he replied. "Let me be your guide. I, too, am heading to Des Moines. I can help you when it's time to switch trains. And I can find you a place to stay." His kind smile and offer of help put Sophie into his hands.

"There's a man by the name of Hyronimus Miller," he continued. "He and his wife run a respectable boarding house for young ladies at a reasonable price. When we get to Des Moines, would you like me to hail you a hansom cab and send you to their house?"

Because Sophie felt so fortunate this kind man had rescued her from a certain night of sleeping in the train station, she easily continued the conversation with him as they traveled east. She admitted to him she had run away, her family ignorant of her specific destination. She filled their time with information about her home and family and her desires to become a famous model. Her seatmate, such a kind man, listened patiently, asking her for details to fill in her life's history. By the time she gathered her belongings to exit the train, he knew every detail of her young life.

As he promised, her hero hailed her a cab, gave the driver directions to the boarding house, and told Sophie to use his name when she spoke to the boarding house owners.

Sophie could still hear her brother painting the city as a den of thieves, which made her silently laugh, because she had found nothing but kindness and charity.

1907

Sophie

Des Moines, the largest of Iowa's cities as well as its capital, showed some signs of being cosmopolitan, but it still held the state's conservative views. Churches abounded: Lutheran, Catholic, Presbyterian, Methodist, Baptist, Congregational, Quaker. And women's church societies sprung up from them.

Originally built from a fort on the Des Moines River, the city grew from its 1843 Army post, sprouting several newspapers, a library association, three colleges, and the Younker Brothers Department store—a large corner building with the latest fashions.

Des Moines, now a bustling city with brick paved streets, glinted like a jewel. The skyline was filled with monstrous buildings: the Observatory Building, Old Bankers Trust, the Fleming Building. Modern cars zoomed past Sophie's hansom cab. Ladies and gentlemen wearing the latest fashions went in and came out of glittering stores, carrying the most modern merchandise. She didn't notice any farm stores, and no feed wagons were pulled along these pristine roads. Sophie's eyes were wide with admiration as she traveled through the city.

Eventually, she came to the Courthouse District, aptly named for the Polk County Courthouse at the west end of Fourth Avenue. She saw a large white building and assumed it was the capitol building, standing proudly at the end of the street.

Like all large cities, though, it had its spoiled areas, often hidden from visiting businessmen and shoppers. South of the courthouse, the riverfront scarred the landscape, full of billboards, iron foundries, and row houses. The iron foundries, along with the industrial buildings and row houses, dumped their waste into the Des Moines River.

The cabbie traveled to East Second Street, stopping in front of a large, two-story Victorian house with a sagging front porch. At one time, the house was a grand affair with light green paint and purple trim. The paint was so faded one could no longer tell its true color, and the trim had turned to a dingy grey. The house desperately needed loving hands to bring it back to its former glory. In fact, the whole neighborhood, once beautiful, now looked poor and dirty and rundown. Small, ill-dressed children played in the streets well past suppertime. Women, or possibly just girls, loitered on the street, looking hungry and tired.

"Here you are, miss."

With some skepticism, Sophie asked, "Where am I exactly?"

"Exactly, this is east of downtown Des Moines, but we call it the Whitechapel District, like the one in London. Have you heard of that before?"

Not sure of her geography, Sophie said, "No, I don't think so. Is it famous?"

Incredulous, the cabbie questioned, "You ain't heard of Jack the

Ripper? The London serial killer?"

She had certainly heard of that man, but she failed to see how it connected to her destination unless he was now living in the United States. "I have, but I don't understand your meaning," she replied.

"This here's the red-light district, just like Whitechapel in London."

Completely out of her element and not wanting to sound like a farm rube, she decided to question him no further. She just wanted to get out of the cab and get settled in her room. She felt rumpled and smelly; second class had been crammed full of people with various bathing habits and picnic baskets full of odd and odiferous food.

Fortunately, the kind gentleman from the train had paid for her cab. The remainder of her funds would be required for her boarding, trips to the modeling agencies, as well as supper. Beyond those three things, there was no money for any sightseeing or even breakfast.

Stepping up to the front door, Sophie rapped lightly and waited. A large, hairy man answered the door and smiled at her.

"Good evening, miss. I'm Mr. Hyronimus Miller. Are you in need of a room or employment?"

"Yes, please. A room. And I also need to know where to buy some food. I haven't had any supper yet."

He ushered her inside the front door, taking her bag, and led her into a hallway. He helped her with her coat and hung it on the coat rack. In front of her were wide stairs leading up to the bedrooms. To her left was a large dining room for guests; to her right, a parlor. He led her into the parlor.

Sophie had never seen such opulence. She immediately noticed a button-tufted, red sofa with walnut legs and walnut scroll work above the fabric on the back. Matching red chairs rested in front of an expansive fireplace. Velvet wallpaper dressed the room. And a beautiful piano waited in the corner for someone to sit and play it.

Sophie had always wanted to learn the piano, but they didn't own one and didn't have the money for one.

The room was decorated with a large area rug, covering the oak floor; pictures of landscapes and fancy women hung on the walls; and trinkets perched decoratively on side tables.

"This is beautiful," she exclaimed, eyes as large as half dollars. "May I come in here to sit?"

"We often have guests in the evening, so you may come in any time you like other than the evenings. How many nights were you planning to stay with us?"

"Well, I'm not exactly certain," she said. "I need tonight and possibly tomorrow night. I'm going to see a man tomorrow about becoming a model."

"And how did you happen to choose our lodging house? You aren't from Des Moines, are you?"

"No, I was directed here by a kind gentleman on the train. By a Mr. Smith? He didn't give me his first name."

"Very good, very good," he said rather enthusiastically. We can certainly accommodate your needs. Have you had supper? We don't have a specific time; our guests can eat whenever they choose. Our cook keeps it hot in the oven. Breakfast and supper come with the room fee."

Sophie felt so fortunate to have met two men who were so kind and helpful. Hyronimus Miller sent her into the kitchen to retrieve her meal and then took her bag to her room.

The next morning, after a restful night and a filling breakfast, Sophie took a hansom cab to one of the addresses written on the Denison photographer's card.

The agent's tiny office, nestled among lawyers' offices and barber shops, didn't look very impressive. The interior was drab with only one desk and stacks of girls' pictures on top of it. A chair stood against a wall, which Sophie assumed was used to seat the models getting their picture made.

"What can I do for you this morning?" the agent asked when she walked in the door.

"I'm here about a modeling position. My photographer in Denison gave me your address and recommended I come and see you."

"He did, did he? That guy recommends every girl who takes a picture in his studio. He tells all of 'em they can be a model. You're a pretty girl; that I can see. But, see this stack of pictures? There are a hundred pretty girls and not many modeling jobs. I'll take your photo print and put it with the rest of these others. If I need you, I'll let you know. Right now, I don't need you, so you can go back to Denison or wherever you're from."

"I don't have my photo print." Sophie had left her prints at home, not daring to take such an expensive item with her.

"Then, I don't know what I can do. I won't even have a print to remind me of your image. I'm sorry, miss."

Sophie turned around and walked back through the door. She held back her tears, not wanting the people on the sidewalk to see her cry. She felt stupid. There was no point in going to the second agent's office without a print. She had no other option than to go back to the boarding house. She would gather her belongings and get a cab to the train depot, returning to her family to face whatever consequences they would dole out.

Her glum face told the story of disappointment when she walked into the boarding house parlor. She found it odd that none of the other young female boarders were out of bed yet. She had eaten breakfast alone, and now, an hour later, they still hadn't risen. More strange was the lack of Mrs. Miller, Hyronimus' wife. The husband told her his wife worked nights and slept during the day. She wondered what jobs hired women for a night shift.

"Back so soon?" Hyronimus asked, surprising her with his loud voice.

"Yes. It was terrible."

"Tell me your troubles. I'm a good listener."

Sophie again told about her life in Soldier, her running away, the agent's refusal of her, and her decision to return home. It felt good to pour out her troubles to someone who listened so attentively. Mr. Miller reminded her of the man on the train.

"You don't need to leave yet. I know a photographer who needs young women, such as yourself, to pose for him. Would you be interested in that?"

"Oh, yes," she said, enthusiasm showing in her eyes.

"I can send you to him this afternoon. You'll start today. You don't even have to pay for a cab because it's easily walked from here."

Just when Sophie thought all was lost and she would need to return home with her shame written on her back, another man saved her. Her mood, cloudlike, filled her with energy, making her skin glow.

As Sophie walked to the studio, she started to notice the dirty and run-down area she hadn't been able to see well when she arrived at dusk. Most of the buildings needed paint and repairs. Refuse dotted the sidewalks like blobs of clotted cream. The noticeable stench came from night waste being tossed into the streets.

Sophie found the studio easily; it was in between two saloons. The unkempt man sitting behind the desk looked up at her when she entered. He appeared fairly old with large mutton chops needing a trim, and his hair needed washing. He didn't address her first, so she stood and waited for him to address her.

Eventually, he said, "What do you want?"

"Mr. Miller sent me. He said you're looking for young ladies. You make pictures of them?"

His demeanor changed drastically. He was now very friendly. "Yes, of course. Are you interested in sitting for some pictures for me? We can start now! By the way, I'm Jack. And your name?"

"Sophie, and yes, I am ready to begin now."

When he stood up and walked, she noticed a prominent limp in his right leg. He hurried into his back room, and Sophie sat on the only chair available. After some time, he brought out a number of dresses and accoutrements. He laid them out for her and wanted to know which one she wanted to wear first.

The dresses were beautiful, but Sophie was shocked at the low necklines. They were also without sleeves.

Seeing her puzzled and somewhat distressed face, Jack explained, "These dresses are the latest fashions from Paris."

Not wanting to appear as if she didn't know the latest trends, Sophie picked out a dress and went into the back room to change. Once dressed, she was alarmed at her nakedness. The tops of her breasts plumped out of the dress, and her arms were bare all the way to her shoulders.

She walked out into the studio, looking worried and covering her breasts. "I'm not sure this is proper," she said.

"You look beautiful, just like those models in magazines!"

Sophie, although feeling like she was doing something very wrong, wanted to be amenable and sophisticated. She didn't want to let him know she was just a farm girl from a small town. Pushing through her feelings of embarrassment and shame, she said, "I'm ready whenever you want to start."

Jack put her in several poses, some of them rather unladylike in her opinion. He then asked her to lie down on the couch, which seemed to appear out of nowhere. She didn't notice it when she came into the studio. It was very similar to the one in the Millers' parlor, but it was rather frayed and worn.

The photographer posed Sophie on her left side, her hands clasped behind her head, which pushed out her breasts even more, and her right foot up on the arm of the couch. As he was taking the picture, he continued to tell her how beautiful and sophisticated she looked.

When she finished, he asked if she could come back the following day, and she said yes. However, he did not pay her. She supposed she would be paid at the end of the job.

When she told Hyronimus Miller she did not have money for the night's stay, he told her not to worry; he knew she was making money and would eventually pay her bill.

Sophie went back to the studio as promised the next afternoon. Jack had already chosen her dress. She would have no options this time. This outfit was also low cut and sleeveless, but it was also shorter. Karoline didn't allow Sophie's skirts to be more than an inch above her ankles; this dress would show her calves. He also directed her to omit her shoes and stockings. She again felt half-naked but said nothing and did as he asked. Again, there was no pay at the end of the session.

The next day she saw only undergarments laid out for her, a white cotton corset cover and silk drawers with stockings and garters. She couldn't possibly wear those in front of this man much less take photos in them for others to view. She was making a stand on this one.

"Jack, I cannot wear this. I will not be taking pictures in undergarments."

"I understand, Sophie. You are not the first model to be upset. These pictures are for French magazines. The French are much more modern, and the body is celebrated. Trust me, a woman in her undergarments appears even modest to them. And think about this: no one in America is going to see the photos, so you needn't worry about anyone you know looking at your pictures. It's just you and me."

While she still felt uncomfortable, she was willing to wear them to pose. The idea of her pictures in France, maybe in French magazines, excited her. Her family would never see them or know she had done such a risqué act.

She put on the garments and came out blushing. She covered what she could until Jack started to take the photos. At first, he had her standing; then, he put her back on the couch. At one point, she sat facing him with her legs spread wide. For the very last pictures, Jack arranged her outfit a little. He slipped down one of her straps and pulled the front material down more, showing most of her left breast.

"I know you're uncomfortable," he told her, "but the French models are often nude on top. This is nothing to them, and no one is going to see this picture."

She had been taught to do as she was told, especially by men who were older than she. She had also been taught not to complain. As uncomfortable as she was, she allowed him to take the photo, knowing what her family would think of such indecent behavior.

Once clothed, she could not look at Jack's face, embarrassed at his knowledge of her body. She felt protected in her clothing and was glad she would not need to stand mostly naked in front of him.

"I'll see you tomorrow, Sophie?" he asked.

"Mmm, I'm not sure, Jack. Maybe I should just take my payment now. I need to think about it. If I decide yes, I'll see you tomorrow at the same time. If it's a no, you won't see me again. Is that acceptable?"

"I understand. I gave your money to Hyronimus. He said you had debts at the boardinghouse that needed paid immediately. If there is money left over, I'm sure he'll pass that along to you. I hope to see you tomorrow, Sophie. You are very beautiful and an excellent model. I wouldn't be surprised if you become famous in France."

On her walk back to the boarding house, Sophie thought about his last sentence. She wanted to become famous more than anything. If she did become famous in France, perhaps she would be moving there? She couldn't imagine a farm girl from Soldier, Iowa, living in France as a famous model. Did such things really happen? Jack had taken the France pictures, so it wasn't necessary for her to continue, she reasoned. She would take her money and go home. She would give Jack her address, so he could contact her if she were needed in France. Her goal had been to become a model, and she was now a model. What else did she need? While she would have liked to stay in Des Moines, her family would be nearly hysterical. At this moment, she needed to go home. She would take the next morning train.

At the boarding house, there seemed to be no one around. Hyronimus, who usually greeted her, was gone. She went up to her room and packed her belongings. She then went and made herself some tea in the kitchen and sat in the parlor to wait. Eventually, a woman came down and saw her.

"Are you Mrs. Miller?" Sophie asked, hoping this woman would know when Mr. Miller would return.

"You could say that. We're all Mrs. Miller." Her tone was snarlish and unpleasant.

Sophie didn't understand. How many were there and what did she mean? "I'm sorry I don't quite understand. I've never met Mrs. Miller although I was told that she lived here and worked during the evenings."

"What kind of country bumpkin are you? There is no Mrs. Miller. The women in this house work in the bordellos. We work for Hyronimus. I assume you do as well." The woman was looking at her as if she were the most simple-minded soul who ever lived.

"No, I am a model," Sophie said with some hauteur.

"You don't say? What kind of model? Which studio is taking your pictures?"

"It's a few blocks from here, and Jack is his name."

"Oh, Jack. You mean the guy who takes nude photos."

"Certainly not! I am *not* nude. These pictures are for French magazines."

"Well, la dee dah. Aren't you the fancy one! I'm sorry to tell you, honey, but those pictures are being printed for any man wanting to stare at a naked woman. They aren't for French magazines. You're no better than the rest of us. You make your money on your back the same as us."

Sophie was outraged at this woman's audacity. She clearly didn't understand the circumstances. Sophie didn't know this woman's profession, but she had clearly mistaken Sophie's profession as something dirty.

When Hyronimus returned, Sophie asked him about her money. She wanted the remainder of it immediately.

"You don't have any remaining money," he informed her. "You had food and a bed to pay for."

"I thought the food was part of the board? And how much money did Jack give you?" Sophie did not know what she was being paid for her photo sessions. Society standards regarded women's discussing money as vulgar. Her mother often discussed money, but that was different. Her mother ran a farm and was an unconventional woman. Sophie saw herself as more refined and liked to follow societal etiquette.

Hyronimus' face changed from a smile to a sneer, and his eyes bored into her. Sophie could tell she had said something that made him angry.

His voice as sharp as a knife edge, Hyronimus said, "He didn't give me enough to cover what you owe. You have debts to pay, and you're not leaving until you do. You have two choices: either you can continue to model for Jack or you can go out and work with the other girls. Until your bill is paid, you won't be receiving any money. You also owe for tonight's lodging and food."

Sophie's felt the physical shock run through her body. She couldn't see a way out of this predicament. As long as she continued to stay, she would continue to owe money. She couldn't leave because she didn't have any money for train fare. She didn't even have enough to buy herself a meal.

She knew she had been trapped by this man, and she was afraid…afraid of what he could potentially do to her if she didn't do as he commanded. To appease him, she nodded her head yes and turned around to go back to her room.

Upon entering, she was surprised by another young woman occupying the bed across from hers. The woman seemed almost the same age or a little older. Her long blonde hair cascaded down her back. The young woman, dressed only in her drawers, had her back turned to the door.

"Oh, I'm so sorry. I didn't realize anyone else was in my room."

The young woman turned around, not embarrassed by her own nudity. Her heart-shaped face held two blue eyes the color of sapphires. "Hello, I'm Ruth. I'm sharing this room with you. What's your name?"

"Sophie." Sophie tried to look anywhere but at the woman. She had never been around anyone who was so casual about her body.

"I heard you was a model, one of those nudie kind."

"Oh, no. I'm a model for the French magazines."

"Sure. That's what they tell you for now. But you are going to be modeling naked soon enough."

"Absolutely not. I would never do something like that. I'm not planning to go back to the studio. Hyronimus said I could work with the rest of the girls. Is this some kind of factory work? Maybe sewing. I'm not very good at it, but I can learn pretty quickly."

"Sewing? That's a laugh. Do you actually have no idea what most of the girls in this house do? We're soiled doves. You know, sportin' women."

"I don't know what that is."

"Prostitutes. Ladies of the evening. Whores. Now do you understand? You're living in a house of ill repute. A bordello. We bring gentlemen back to our rooms. Well, not all of us. Some of us, like me, haven't worked up to that status yet, which is why I'm sharing your room. I work the streets with some of the others."

Sophie, stunned, sat statue-like. She began to put pieces of conversations together. She felt stupid and duped. While she hadn't wanted to be a fool, she realized she was.

"I'm not doing that."

"You don't have a choice. If you tell the big man no, he'll beat you. Last year, he broke a girl's nose when he thought she had stolen some money."

Sophie had never been beaten, whipped, or even lightly spanked. Their house had always had a no-hitting policy. When she and her sister fought, if either one of them laid a hand on the other, there were unpleasant house chores as punishment. She couldn't imagine Hyronimus hitting her in the face.

"I don't know what to do. I don't want to model anymore, and I'm not going out on the street. I want to go home, but I don't have any money. He has my earnings." Tears slipped down her cheeks. She was angry at herself for running away. She would pay anything to go back to boring Soldier. She would even clean the chicken coop if she could go home. For the first time in her young life, she appreciated her life. People she knew were kind and truthful. They watched out for each other.

"He means to keep you like the rest of us. Eventually, they will want you to go on the street. It pays more." Ruth had pity in her eyes. Sophie wondered about Ruth's story but thought prying was rude.

Sophie considered walking out the door the next morning without going to the studio or working on the street or paying her debt. She had nowhere to go, and she knew no one in Des Moines. She didn't even know her way around past the few blocks she had been traveling the past few days. She had allowed herself to be trapped like one of the rabbits her brothers ensnared. Perhaps Jack would help her.

Walking through the studio door, Sophie had no intention of posing for photos. She planned to beg Jack to help her, to give her a loan she would promise to pay back when she arrived home.

"I see you've returned. You're ready for another session?"

"No. I need your help, Jack. I want to go home, and I don't have any money. I promise to send it to you when I return. My family will pay the train ticket fee. Will you loan me the money?"

"Sophie, I can't."

"I promise you'll get it back," she implored.

"It's not about loaning you the money. Hyronimus has his boot on my neck, too. If I help you, then he'll punish me. You are the caged canary. Please, let's just get through the session. I don't want to tell him you won't cooperate. I know what he'll do to you."

"I can't take any more of the pictures like yesterday, Jack. I wasn't raised that way. I just can't do it!"

"How about I give you something that will make it easier? I promise, you won't even care. It will take away all of your embarrassment and inhibitions. You have to go through with this one way or another today. You can do this the hard way or the easy way. It's just a little shot."

Without waiting for a reply, Jack limped to his desk, opened a drawer, and took out a vial, syringe, and a spoon. Sophie watched him prepare the syringe.

"What is that?"

"It's something they gave me in the war for the pain when I got shot. I fought for one of the Illinois regiments; I'm from Galena. And you know what was the real kick in the head? I was shot sixteen months after Appomattox. The North and South weren't even fighting anymore, but it took over a year before all of the troops were notified. Getting shot for a war that wasn't even being fought ruined my life.

You think I wanted to make my living this way?" Jack asked. "Once Hyronimus Miller got his hands on me, my life was no longer my own. He runs most of the East End. You're one more little fly he caught in his web. And you are never going to get free. So, let's just get this started."

Sophie wished she were home again on the farm, but wishing didn't make the situation go away. Like Jack, she had no choice, but she also knew she couldn't do what he was asking. To make it through the session, she decided to consent to whatever Jack offered her. Sophie couldn't tolerate the sight of needles, so she turned her head while he injected the liquid into her arm. Immediately she felt an intense pleasure, and her body felt a warmth flood through her.

Jack led her over to the couch and removed her clothing. This time, she was completely naked. She laid down on the furniture and felt so drowsy. She knew Jack was posing her and taking pictures, but she didn't care. She wanted to sleep more than anything.

Eventually, she awakened enough to return to the boarding house. Walking back, Sophie felt so ashamed and stupid. How had she been naïve enough to get herself into this situation? Deep down, she knew how. She had been so anxious to leave the farm and show off her beauty to strangers she had allowed herself to believe anything she was told. She was disappointed in herself. She had been raised better.

Ruth was leaving for the evening, so they didn't have a chance to talk. Sophie stayed in her room until it was dark and then went to the kitchen for her supper.

Hyronimus interrupted her dinner, and his honey-smooth demeanor was now rough and terse.

"Jack tells me he has plenty of pictures of you now. I no longer need a model."

"Will you at least give me enough money to get a train ticket, so

I can go home?"

"Home? You're not going anywhere. You have a debt with me, and you're going out with the girls tomorrow."

Back in her room, Sophie thought about her family, specifically her father. She recalled many lectures in which he expounded upon the importance of one's character, especially a woman's, who must remain pure until her marriage. Her desire for fame led her to the very path she had been warned against. She could lie to herself about no one seeing the inappropriate pictures she had taken—but losing her virginity and being used by multiple men could not be hidden. She knew she would not survive this.

Without a plan other than sneaking out of the house and running, Sophie didn't care what alley she would sleep in or what garbage she would eat; she would not sell her body. Sophie waited until late into the evening, and when she couldn't hear anyone in the hallway, she crept quietly down the stairs, intending to sneak out the front door. Hyronimus stood near the front door like a sentry. He seemed to be able to anticipate her moves. Instead of leaving, she went into the kitchen to fix herself a cup of tea and brought it up to her room.

The next afternoon, Ruth, her roommate, laid out some clothing for her first night out. The sleeveless corset cover—a thin, see-through white cotton—would show her corset; a red skirt, well above her boots; and a black shawl to keep her warm would be her uniform for the night. Ruth then took out a rouge pot and liberally applied the makeup to her cheeks, making them an unnatural rosy color. She also spread some across Sophie's lips.

Sophie looked in the mirror and did not recognize herself. Her natural beauty now appeared garish. She imagined herself standing in front of her father and the expression on his face. She had never seen him hit any of them, but this may have prompted a quick slap.

"Are you ready?" Ruth asked.

"No, I can't do this. I wish I had the medicine in the syringe Jack gave me. At least I don't remember some of what I did. I could get through this better if I didn't care what happened to me."

"I can help you with that. Hyronimus gives us a pill that has the same effect. A couple of the girls go to the Chinese place and smoke a little before they go out. There are all kinds of drugs out there that can make this easier. If you prefer the needle, there's a girl here who can help you out."

Sophie didn't like the needle, so she opted for the pill Ruth held out to her. Ruth popped one in her mouth as well. The pill didn't work as fast, but she soon began to relax.

Once the sky darkened, the girls left the house—some in pairs, others alone. Ruth linked Sophie's arm in hers and proceeded to the door with a terse threat from Hyronimus about making sure Sophie was "broken in" properly.

Sophie walked out the front door, not knowing how her life would look from now on. She knew she could never go home again. She would never be the same Sophie.

1907

Alex

Alex lost his childhood the day he lost his foot. He could no longer play Keep Away with the rest of the children. He couldn't follow his brother around the farm. He sat on a chair and watched life rather than participated in it.

Once his mother discovered his talent for sums, she had him working with the Svensen brothers. They were like family, and they treated him like a son or younger brother. They taught him about their business. He sat on a stool and wrote up tickets of sale for them. He could see sums in his head like they were written on a chalkboard in front of him. Once he was older, he learned about the commodities markets and found his true talent. Stock prices, futures markets, commissions—these were vocabulary words he used as easily as those he was taught in school. He could predict when a bull market would turn. Instead of being a respected farmer, he was respected by the farmers, especially his father.

His father Kristoffer treated him like a man when Alex could understand and predict the stock market better than the adults. His father changed from seeing a ruined life for him as a farmer to a prosperous life as a commodity trader.

Alex took on other adult responsibilities as well. Alex was only seventeen when his father died, but he took on the task of planning his father's funeral, contacting their church minister, choosing the plot, putting a notice in the local newspaper. His mother often depended on him as much as she did Tingvald.

At the time of his father's death, he was engaged to Elizabeth Hanson. He broke the engagement, feeling a sense of responsibility for his family. Since he couldn't help with the farm, he took care of his mother's business matters. A year later, when she seemed able to take care of them herself, he moved into town, first living in a boarding house.

Money ruled Alex's life. He worked with it every day, six days a week. He thought about it at night. He counted his money and thought about how to make more of it. His father had always clambered for money. Kristoffer often told his sons the story of how he had saved to buy his first ten acres of land, how he had worked like a donkey to buy more land, and how he went and worked for someone else when the land wouldn't yield. His father always told him that for those who started their lives with money, they didn't know the value of it. But those who started poor never forgot its value even when they eventually had enough of it to live comfortably.

With his crutches, Alex's travel was not as easy as it was for others. Since he could not ride a horse, he drove a buggy; however, getting in and out of it proved challenging. As soon as he had saved enough for a car, he purchased a Model A, a simple open-air model he drove only in good weather. The roads to his mother's house were difficult to navigate, their deep dirt ruts often miring his tires in mud. The town's roads were somewhat better. He was one of the first Iowans to own a vehicle.

Even without a foot, his stock price as a bachelor was already high and going up. His handsome face with its fine dark hair, high cheekbones, and bright blue eyes attracted most of the females. Alex had an easy laugh and flirted with any female, no matter her age, marital status, or body type. Every woman from young singles to old widows blushed around Alex. He could get them in the palm of his hand better than a preacher in a church.

Even the men liked Alex. He could tell a yarn as well as Mark Twain yet give business advice and put on a sober poker face in a flash. The farmers bought their feed and seed as well as sold their grain to Svensen and Olson because Alex made them all feel like they were doing business with their brother.

Alex became a leader in the community as well as leading his family. His mother had worried needlessly about his future the day he lost his foot.

1907

Alex

Alex spent each day watching the ticker, the price of corn and beans rising and falling. His gift of figuring sums and understanding the markets put him in charge of that half of the business. Elfred sold feed and grain to the farmers, which was appropriate since he had the gift of gab. Alex preferred to stay in his office working with numbers. He was self-conscious of his prosthetic foot, a block of wood shaped to fit into a shoe. And, if it were bothering him, he could remove it, and no one was the wiser.

On the day of Sophie left, just as Alex was closing up the store, Tingvald's boy Milton came rushing into his office. "Uncle Alex, Grandmother needs you now! Sophie has run away!"

Without asking questions, Alex put on his jacket and went to his car. Run away? To where? He couldn't believe it was the emergency implied by his nephew. She was probably in Denison with some boy.

She would be in serious trouble when she came back late, but he was sure she would be back. Even though he felt like his mother was claiming fire on the prairie for just a campfire, he went anyway. His mother had taken the position of head of the family after his father died. All obeyed her commands.

When he pulled up to the house, his mother ran out the door and didn't even allow him out of the car. "Alex, Sophie has run away! She's gone to Des Moines to become a model." As she was speaking, she was holding a piece of paper in her hands. "She left a note. You need to go to Des Moines right now and get her!"

"Mama, just calm down. Let me get out of the car, and we can talk about this in the house. Where's Tingvald?"

"He should be in shortly. I sent Glenn to fetch him in the field. He's out planting."

Once Tingvald, Alex, and Karoline were seated, they began to discuss a plan. Karoline knew why she had gone to Des Moines and had a place to start the search. She told the men about the photographer giving Sophie addresses of Des Moines agencies. They would need to go to Denison first and retrieve that information and then drive on to Des Moines. Unfortunately, they could not start until the next day. The studio in Denison would be closed for the evening. That gave Sophie a day's start on them.

Because it was planting season, Alex volunteered to go alone and let Tingvald continue in the fields. He left early the next morning, bringing him to Denison by nine. To his dismay, the studio didn't open until eleven, which would put him in Des Moines by the evening. Another day she would have to get herself into trouble.

Alex completed some business at the bank while he waited for the photographer. At ten-thirty, sitting in his car, Alex saw the photographer coming down the street. Exiting his car, Alex moved over to stand in front of the door. "Are you the photographer?" Alex asked once the man approached him.

"I am! Are you here to have your picture made? A handsome man like you should have his likeness."

"No. I'm here to get the names of the agents you gave my sister several months ago. She ran off to Des Moines to go meet them. Do you know what kind of trouble you started? Are you getting some kind of kickback from those agents?"

"Certainly not! I have an eye for talent, and I pass along my expertise. That's all!"

Alex waited on the sidewalk while the businessman went into his studio and wrote the names on a piece of paper. Although the man protested, Alex didn't see the benefit of giving Des Moines agents business unless this photographer were getting something for his time as well.

The trip to Des Moines took Alex six hours, bringing him into the city by late afternoon. Alex found lodging between Walnut Street and Court Avenue at the Hotel Kirkwood, the best in the city. Its imposing size and ornate architecture towered over the other hotels on "Hotel Row." He ate a nice dinner in their upscale restaurant and thought about the whereabouts of his sister.

He had never been close to his twin sisters or his younger brother. Seventeen years sat between him and Floyd. He was more like a father to him than a brother. The girls were a different matter. Because he had been working at the Svensen Feed and Seed since he was old enough to add, he had spent his weekends and summers in town. He had little to do with the females in the house with the exception of his mother.

With a good night's sleep on an expensive mattress and a hearty breakfast in his stomach, Alex sought the first agent on the photographer's list. The photographer had given him four names, not remembering if he had given all four to Sophie. Therefore, he would start with the first one listed and visit all four throughout the day.

The first business wasn't even in Des Moines, but in an adjacent town, West Des Moines. He drove to Valley Junction and found the building. When he asked the owner if he had seen Sophie, he showed him her picture as well.

"No, don't believe she's come in here. Have you tried the other agents in the area?"

"Not yet. But I'm planning to do so. Thank you for your time."

Alex continued to the second address, which brought him back to Des Moines. The agent had not seen Sophie and was very sure about his answer. The third agency was closed for the day, requiring Alex to return if the fourth one did not yield the information.

When he walked into the fourth agency, the man was very busy and didn't want to take the time to look at Sophie's photo, pointing to the large stack of girls' pictures on his desk.

"I doubt I'll remember," he said, not even looking up from his work. "Young women come in here every day, looking to become a model. Most of them are off the farm, wanting something different than pigs and cows."

"This girl was from the farm," Alex said, holding Sophie's picture farther out. Exasperated with the agent's inattention, he put it right under his nose. "Have you seen her in the past day?"

Finally, without any other way to ignore Alex, the man looked at Sophie's picture. "Yes, I have seen her. Pretty girl. She came in here two days ago. She didn't even have a picture to leave me. She was pretty upset."

"Do you know where she went? Where she was staying? Did she leave you any information?"

"Sorry. I really can't help you. She just walked out."

Alex walked out the door and started down the sidewalk when the agent yelled for him. "Hey mister, wait a minute."

"Did you remember something?"

"No, but I just thought of another place you could look. There are only four of us reputable agents in the area. However, there are photographers who will take pictures of young women and promise them all kinds of things—like Paris magazines."

"Do you have addresses of these places?"

"You don't need an address. They are all in the same area. If you go east, right around the capitol building, you'll be in the right area. Some of them don't have a name on their door. I would suggest that you go into every business that's open, except for the saloons. You'll know those when you see them."

"Thank you for your help."

"I hope you find her, and I hope she's not in that area. There are some very powerful and ruthless men who run some of those places. Don't bother calling the police. They don't go into that area. They have an agreement with those bosses."

The next morning, Alex went to the East End and started searching. Looking at the run-down houses, refuse-strewn streets, and children clearly avoiding school upset him. People without means having to live among the gambling, drinking, and prostitution made him cringe. He had been to Chicago several times to meet with grain buyers, but he had always stayed in the nicer areas. He hadn't wanted to go to the seedier side of the city. Because Des Moines wasn't nearly the city Chicago was, he hadn't expected to see this type of area. Poor people living among the ilk of the hidden world, girls selling their bodies to live, men gambling away what little they had—it was all very different from life in rural Iowa.

In each establishment, there was always someone willing to point him to the photography studios, assuming he was looking for those kinds of pictures. Several times, he was accosted on the street by someone selling something: newspapers, fruit, girls. He also inquired about the boarding houses and bordellos, knowing she had to have a bed at night. Again, he always received plenty of information, the informant supposing he was looking for some company.

After a morning of fruitless searching, he walked through the door of a plain building, shabby like the ones around it. A skinny man with mutton chops and a pronounced limp was photographing a young lady in a very low-cut dress.

"Excuse me," the man said rather tersely, "I'm in the middle of a modeling session. You can come back later and buy photos if you like. I should be done in about an hour."

Alex went back out the door and continued to search, making a note to himself to return to the shop. The next business, a small grocer, gave him information about a house that offered beds to young women. It was only a couple of blocks away, so Alex decided to investigate while he waited for the photographer.

He could see the house had once been a beauty. Her light green frock with purple trim would have made her the belle of the block. Neglect had turned her once proud façade into a sad, old woman in a faded house dress.

Alex knocked on the door, and it was opened by a large man with plenty of dark curly hair, which was not only on his head but on his arms. A tuft of it peeked out of his V-cut collar.

"Hello, I'm looking for my sister. Her name is Sophie. Is she staying here?"

"I don't know no Sophie. Sorry." The hairy giant shut the door in Alex's face.

Alex first felt angry at the resident's rude nature, but he eventually felt perplexed. He had been treated well by every other person who assumed he was looking to spend his money. This man seemed angry at his presence. If he did know Sophie and she was doing something immoral, would he want to tell her brother?

He still had time before he could go back to the photographer. He got back in his car and found a small restaurant. He needed to sit down because his ankle had been rubbed nearly raw and his armpits were sore from crutch walking. He drove his car from place to place, but he still had to walk into the businesses.

While Alex sat drinking coffee and eating a stale doughnut, he thought about this sister of his. She was like a fish on dry land when it came to living on the farm. She was a smart girl but hadn't applied herself in school. Sophie was interested in fashion, beauty, and boys. Marrying a local boy didn't suit her. She thought she was destined for bigger things in life, the exact reason why she ran away. He supposed treating her dreams like they were unicorns had been hurtful to her, making her feel like her family didn't understand her. Trying to make her into the typical farm wife squeezed her into a box that was too small. They should have sent her to visit her namesake in Chicago. Perhaps that would have soothed her city soul and opened opportunities for her.

Alex drove back to the studio. This time, the photographer was alone. Alex determined he had gotten more information from people when they thought he wanted to spend money with them. He wouldn't mention how he knew Sophie. He would let the photographer lead the conversation.

"Are you wanting some pictures?" the man asked. "Do you want a particular type of girl? Or do you just want to look? I have a new girl, who is stunningly beautiful. I think you'll like her. Let me go in back and get my photos."

The photos were fanned out in front of Alex. Young girls, completely nude in various sexual positions, filled each photo. Alex looked briefly at each photo until he came to one. He quickly turned his head away from it. He had found her.

"Tell me about this girl," Alex said, pointing to Sophie's photo without looking at it again.

"She's a beauty. I have several poses of her if you'd like more than one photo. Some with clothes and some without. You have good taste."

"That's my sister," Alex said through closed teeth. "Where is she?"

The photographer backed away from him. "I don't want trouble, mister. I just do what I'm told."

"Tell me where to find her."

Hoping to stall the stranger until he could think of a way out, Jack said, "How did you lose your foot? This bad leg of mine, it comes from the war."

"Farm accident. Cows trampled me." Alex saw a way in with this man. "I was a little boy. Been on crutches ever since. Didn't give me much choice in life. What about you? How can you stand making a living this way?"

His guilt breaking through his fear, Jack said, "Believe me, this doesn't make me feel good. These girls are innocents, like your sister. I got problems and no way out of it."

"Can you tell me where Sophie is?"

"She's in a big Victorian house about two blocks from here. Big faded green house, but you won't get in unless they think you're a customer."

Alex realized he had already been literally close to finding her. And he had already ruined it. He would have to wait until she came out of the house before he could get her.

Trying to blend into the night, Alex stepped behind a hedge across from the house and waited. With each girl or pair of girls, his hopes rose and then fell. So far, his sister was not among them. This was both good and bad. He wanted to find her, but if she were with these women, then he knew how she was making her living. And, what would he tell his mother?

Finally, he saw her exit the door with another young lady. Sophie was scantily clad. Alex came out from behind a hedge and followed her from across the street. No one noticed him even though his crutches made a sound every time he put them on the ground. When she was several blocks away from the house, she and her associate stopped and stood underneath a gas-powered street light. The associate lit a cigarette and offered it to Sophie, who waved it away.

The cigarette smoked, the two women continued walking until they entered one of the many saloons. Alex had lost his chance to pull her in from the street. Now, he would need to devise a plan to snatch her from a public area.

Alex entered the saloon. The interior, lit by oil lamps, wavered in dim lighting with darkened corners. A piano sat in one of the corners, a player banging out upbeat tunes. A large bar stood across the side of the room with bottles of various colored liquids standing like pretty girls in a dancing line. Small tables with seated customers dotted the room. Pints of beer and glasses of amber liquid sat in front of each man. Women dressed much like Sophie sat on laps, danced with men, or circled about the establishment. The place reeked of stale beer and cigarettes.

Alex looked from girl to girl and finally saw his sister standing next to a seated man who was fondling her bottom. She seemed not to care where he put his hands. Alex wondered how long she had been visiting this saloon and allowing men to put their hands on her. Sophie had been gone from home for five days. He would need to get her attention and indicate she was not to acknowledge him.

He found a table in a darkened corner and watched for his opportunity. Several men were then passing her from lap to lap. Eventually, she was facing him. From his dark corner, he could see her lit by one of the lamps. Her face, expressionless, seemed far away from this seedy saloon. She could not see him in the corner.

When he turned away, distracted by a disturbance, she had

vacated a knee and was being led out the door. Quickly, Alex put his crutches under his arms and followed, trying not to attract attention, which was not usually the case.

He saw the couple walk down the street, turn a corner, and disappear. Alex followed as quickly as he could, but by the time he got to the corner, he found himself looking down a darkened alley. Into the blackness, Alex could just make out two forms standing close together. He wished he could sneak into the alley, but he had lost the ability to travel quietly the day he lost his foot.

While he was considering what to do, he heard the woman fighting against the man. Without taking more time to form a plan, Alex yelled out. "You there! Police! Don't move!"

The man, without lifting his pants up, started to run. The woman froze against the brick building. "Stop, I said!" The man continued to run.

Sophie was terrified by what the police would do to her. She turned to run but didn't have her bearings in the dark.

Alex started down the alley, his crutches making a distinct noise. "Sophie!" he yelled. "Stop! It's me, Alex!"

Sophie thought, *Alex who?* Her mind was so fogged she couldn't think of anyone at Hyronimus' house named Alex. She turned around and peered at the dark figure. As he came closer, she recognized the familiar sound of his crutches. Eventually, she understood the man coming toward her was her brother.

"Alex? Why are you here?" her voice telling of her disbelief.

"I came to find you. Did he hurt you? Did he do anything to you?" Once Alex reached her, he wrapped his arms around her. Sophie stood wooden-like, still not able to comprehend her brother's presence. Once it all came together in her mind, she wrapped her arms around Alex and began to cry.

"I want to go home."

"We can do that. Do you want to go get your bags? Who is that man in the house?"

"We can't go back there. He's the boss, and everyone is afraid of him. I would rather wear hand-me-down clothes from Ingrid than go back and retrieve mine."

"My car is close by. We can leave from here." Alex was flooded with relief. He thought about the consequence if he had come a few minutes later.

Once he had her safely installed in his car, he looked over at his sister, who had closed her eyes and was beginning to fall into a stupor. Alex would avoid questions until he delivered her to their mother.

1908

Betsi

Betsi had felt no sorrow when her father died. He had ruined her life, so she cut him out like a milkweed the day she was forced to marry Lars Berg.

At sixteen, she had gotten pregnant by a boy with the wrong last name and the wrong religion. Her father found a woman with the solution to that kind of problem. After her abortion, she had no desire to enjoy life. Her sadness sat in her chest like an anchor, holding her inside of herself no matter who tried to bring her back to life. The younger siblings did their best to make her laugh with their jokes and silly dances. Ingrid, her older sister, had tried to counsel her with no success. She knew she was a block, pulling down the family to a sadness only she and her parents understood. Her siblings knew something had gone wrong, but they did not know about the life that had been ripped out of her. She was not allowed to speak of it ever again.

Her parents—especially her father—had pretended as if nothing had happened. And worse, her father could no longer look her in the eye. His shame of her was too heavy a burden for her to bear.

Although her mother had made it seem as if it were a joint decision to force her to become Lars's bride, she knew it had been her father's doing. Betsi had heard him complain about her lack of "perking up" and being a part of the family. Six months after her procedure, he had convinced her mother that assigning her another life would allow her something else to think about other than the death of her baby. Together, they had presented her an ultimatum: marry Lars and become a wife or go work on someone's farm and become a farmhand. She was no longer welcome to live on their farm.

Marrying Lars did nothing more than give her work from sunup to sundown, taking care of him and his five children. She felt like a work horse: cleaning, cooking, doing the family's laundry, and taking care of the garden. She never had a moment for herself. Before the sun rose, Betsi was in the barn, milking their three cows, which she then repeated at the end of the day. She didn't particularly enjoy rising at 4:30 a.m. to complete the milking; she did enjoy the quiet of just her and the animals. Their warm bodies against her and their rhythmic chewing were soothing. Once she entered the house, chaos began and didn't end until she was back in her animal sanctuary. Once the milking was completed, she fed the children and put them to bed. Like her mother, she was completely exhausted at the end of the day and fell asleep immediately. She then woke, still exhausted, to begin the same day over.

The children ranged from three years old to fourteen years old. The older children resented her for taking their mother's place, and the youngest couldn't remember his mother and wanted Betsi as a replacement. A wall of ice built up between her and them. They treated her like she was their housekeeper, and she reciprocated as if she were. Ben, the three-year- old, clung to her, wanting her attention and love. Betsi, however, felt as if he were a rock chained to her; and she couldn't warm her heart to some other woman's child. She could only look at him and think about how her own child would have been, how he would have looked. She was sure it was a boy.

Lars was a kind man. He didn't beat or berate her—but he did not love her, nor did she love him. Theirs was a marriage of need: he needed someone to take care of his house and raise his children, and she needed somewhere to live. It seemed to her he took more than he gave. On their wedding night, she completed her wifely duty much like she completed the laundry. She felt relieved she was done but knew she would have to do it again. Betsi and Lars fell into a compatible roommate agreement. He made sure he put food on the table, and she made sure it was cooked. Once a month, he sought her in the night for conjugal relations, and she always complied, thankful she had the rest of the month in the knowledge he would not reach for her again. She assumed he found his natural relief with some other woman, perhaps a prostitute in another town, and she didn't care.

Their lives had not always been this way. During their first six months of marriage, Betsi wished to be happy. She got up each morning with a smile on her face. She fed his children and wished them a good day as they walked out the door, headed for school. Betsi did her very best to take care of his house and little Ben, but she couldn't find her own happiness. She prayed to become pregnant, so she might have her own child to love, and in turn, something to share with Lars. Her first pregnancy brought excitement into the house. She imagined her child's life as she prepared for his arrival. Within a month or so, she felt him slipping from her body with blood running down her legs. She felt as if the abortion had happened all over again, but this time it wasn't her parents' doing.

Betsi got pregnant several more times and lost her baby with each pregnancy. Her body seemed to reject her child as if punishing her for the one she had ripped away. She begged God to forgive her for her mistakes and allow her to make amends in raising at least one baby. She reasoned she needed to grow and nurture a life for the one life that had been taken. God either did not hear her or He did not see fit to grant her this chance to atone for her sins.

Her last miscarriage not only left her bereft of a baby but her own will to make herself happy. Betsi felt like she was climbing into a well. Each day brought her a little farther into the darkness. By the third year of being a wife and surrogate mother, Betsi was at the bottom of the well. She could no longer see light. The darkness enveloped her so much she could only feel her own pain. No one outside of the well came into her thoughts. Every day, she rose out of her bed even though she didn't feel like she could, and she went through her chores without caring about any other person but herself and her misery. At nineteen years old, she was weary of life and wanted nothing more than to end it. But she would never do that to herself, to her parents— even though they didn't deserve any consideration—or to Lars and his children.

Betsi Olson Berg accepted her lot in life, her fate as a punishment from God. She would continue to wear this harness and pull this plow of sorrow.

1907

Betsi

A throbbing ache on the left side of Betsi's mouth woke her from her dream. She had dreamt she was at her father's funeral, and instead of throwing flowers onto his casket, she was throwing rocks. Betsi dreamt some version of this dream several times a month. The dream always unsettled her, and she felt it was her father's way of punishing her for not attending his service. Lars had taken the children to both the visitation and funeral because it was the "proper" thing to do for one's in-laws; however, Betsi told him she owed her father nothing but bitterness and hatred and refused to go with him.

The throbbing in her mouth was a back molar and had been troublesome for several weeks. She had put off visiting the dentist because she knew the remedy for an aching tooth was extraction. She assumed strapping the patient into the chair was common practice, especially for women and children who were thought to be weak in bearing pain. Losing control of her own body and being held down to have a procedure done to her, especially having something ripped out of her body, made Betsi's skin turn cold and her body sweat. Knowing she would eventually be forced to have the tooth pulled made her no more ready to actually have it done. Instead, she had been nursing it along, avoiding chewing on her left side. Tonight, the tooth made its presence known in a demanding way. The throbbing synchronized with her heartbeat. Each beat brought a throb... throb...throb. She put her right hand on her heart and tried to focus on her heartbeat instead of her tooth. She could think of nothing else, nor could she avoid doing something about it.

In her pain, she suddenly remembered Lars kept medicinal whiskey in a cabinet. Betsi had seen her own mother rub it on her siblings' gums when they were teething, and it seemed to help. She could not remember if her mother had used it on her. She had never tasted alcohol, but at this point, she would do anything to alleviate the throbbing. Lars had used the whiskey for himself a few times, but he did not like the taste of it and certainly did not condone men who became controlled by it.

Betsi quietly traversed the hallway in her bare feet and went into the kitchen, finding the jar in the back of a cabinet. In western Iowa, many whiskies were home distilled and sold by a man who knew a man. The alcoholic beverage was delivered in a Mason jar. Serious whiskey drinkers bought it in bigger containers. Betsi opened the lid of the jar and was almost knocked onto her backside. The alcohol fumes had rushed from the jar and entered her nose, burning her nose hairs as they went through her sinus system. She took a tentative sip and held the liquid in her mouth. The taste did not agree with her palate, so she swallowed quickly. While the liquid slid down her throat, burning like a hot coal, the kick that came back up made her shudder and pucker her entire face. *How can anyone drink this stuff for pleasure?* she wondered. The need to reduce her pain was greater than her dislike of the whiskey. This time, instead of a small sip, she stole a big drink, thinking the burning, shuddering, and puckering would be the same no matter the amount she consumed. After she swallowed the next gulp, the liquid sat like a hot bun in the pit of her stomach and spread warmth throughout her body. Drinking the whiskey was horrible, but its effect was rather pleasing.

She put the jar back into the cabinet, went back to their bedroom, and slipped under the covers again. Lars was a heavy sleeper, so he had no knowledge of her night excursion for pain relief. Instead of tossing and turning, Betsi fell instantly asleep and had the best nightmare-free slumber in many years. When she woke in the morning, her tooth still hurt, but she wasn't exhausted.

While Betsi completed her house chores, her mouth continued to throb, more so the more she moved around. For the next two days, the pain gained momentum. She also noticed a swelling in her cheek. As afraid as she was to go to the dentist, she now had no choice and asked Lars to take her that afternoon. Their farm was closer to Dunlap than Soldier, sending her to Dr. McGuire.

Aloysius McGuire had a small office just up from the railroad depot. Its clean but drabby interior held only two rooms: the waiting room and the examination room. The waiting room hosted five straight-back chairs for his clients. The walls were bare, and other than sweating, nervous patients waiting their turn, there was nothing else to look at to keep one's mind from impending pain.

Dr. McGuire was a stocky man with stout forearms, black hair, and dark brown eyes. His low, soft voice was generally soothing to his patients.

Aloysius was a recent graduate of Iowa's dental school in Iowa City. He believed mechanics were as much a part of the field of dentistry as science. He had been trained to think of teeth like a machine with parts, ones that could be replaced. He had been very eager to start his own practice and apply his knowledge of mechanics.

Dr. McGuire was proud of his new dental tools—especially his chair—which allowed his patients to be tipped back. He also boasted of a newly purchased X-ray machine and a dental drill, which was electric instead of foot pumped. His dental tools, which were laid out in a leather case, stood shining and ready for use.

Betsi entered his office and sat down in his tiny waiting room. A small portable fan whirred, pushing around the humid air. No other patients were ahead of her, giving her no time to weasel her way out of the examination. She could hear low voices from inside his dental room and the occasional "ehhh" from a patient.

A large man came from the dental room, his mouth filled with bloody gauze. Betsi was called in, and she stood, eyes large, looking around at all of the dental equipment. She spied a number of tools that looked like pliers.

When Betsi sat in his chair, the dentist tipped her back and put a white cloth around her neck. As she looked up at his ceiling, she noticed a dead fly, hanging from a spider's web.

The doctor peered into her mouth, his breath smelling of coffee. He took his right index finger and poked at her inflicted tooth. She tasted the nicotine from a recently smoked cigarette.

McGuire's face showed a look of concern while his voice remained calm. "Well, I see you've got yourself a pretty bad tooth here. It's probably hurting you quite a bit because it has become fairly infected. We'll need to take it out."

Betsi's eyes widened. She had predicted the extraction but actually hearing it made her heart beat faster. "How much is this going to hurt?" she asked.

"I'm not going to shine this up like an apple; it may hurt a bit. If it weren't so infected, we may have been able to get you numb enough. I can't promise you won't feel some of it. You'll definitely feel me tugging on your tooth."

"Are you going to strap me down?"

With some indignation, he said, "Madam, I'm a dentist, not a sadist. Should we go ahead and get this done now?"

While Betsi wanted to say no, it wasn't practical. "Let's get this over, so I can go home and get on with my housework."

"You'll probably want to rest a few days. I'm going to give you a shot of Novocain and wait to see if we can get that numbed." He filled his syringe and came toward Betsi with the sharp end pointed up. The syringe was metal with a rather fat needle at the end. At the sight of it, Betsi felt light-headed.

After a few minutes, he tested the Novocain by poking her gums with a needle. "Can you feel that, Mrs. Berg?" Betsi shook her head 'no.'

Dr. McGuire directed Lars to hold her head, so she wouldn't move around while he worked. He then brought out a shiny pair of forceps, clamped the jaws around her left, back molar, and started rocking the instrument side to side.

Betsi felt a sharp pain and cried out. McGuire stopped his work. "Did that hurt? I was worried the infection would block some of the Novocain. I'm sorry, Mrs. Berg, but I have you as numbed up as I can. There is nothing to do but continue."

He placed the forceps back on her tooth and gave a good tug to the right. The rotted tooth crushed within the forceps like glass, leaving the lower half still lodged in Betsi's jaw. Betsi cried out in pain as he yanked on her tooth.

"Mrs. Berg, I apologize, but I'm going to have to dig out the rest of it." He took a scalpel and made an incision on the outside of her gum, so he could fold back the skin and see the bone. He then took the bone chisel and began to chisel the bone around the tooth. Betsi could feel him pounding on her tooth and writhed with pain as tears flowed down her cheeks. Her mouth filled with blood, and she could feel it trickling down her throat. He worked until he got most of the tooth out.

"We're almost done, Mrs. Berg. I just need to remove the root." She could see him coming at her with a screwdriver-like instrument.

"Mr. Berg, I'm going to be putting a lot of downward and sideways pressure on her mouth, so I need you to firmly hold her head."

As barbaric as the last step looked, there was no pain. The root and tooth removed, Dr. McGuire sewed up the skin on the gum.

Once finished, he packed her vacated gum with gauze and gave her a shot of morphine to dull her pain. With a mouth full of bloody material, Betsi allowed Lars to guide her from the office and out to their buggy. She vowed never to revisit the dentist.

1907

Betsi

Later that day, the morphine shot wore off, and Betsi's mouth was enveloped by pain. She tried to go about her floor scrubbing, but the throbbing only worsened. Taking the doctor's advice, Betsi laid down in bed with a cold cloth on her face. Nothing seemed to make the pain go away. Her brain searched through the house, trying to find relief. Ice may have dulled some of the throbbing, but they had run out of ice weeks ago, and it wouldn't be until the pond froze over that they would have it again. Thinking about the ice wouldn't help her now. Eventually, her brain came to the cabinet that held the whiskey. Betsi didn't relish the flavor or the way it made her body shudder once it was down, but any relief she could find would be worth whatever she had to go through. Lars would not approve of her drinking alcohol, so she waited until she was sure he was off the farm before she went to the cabinet.

This time, Betsi knew to take a large gulp the first time. It went down like hot metal and warmed her belly. Just for safe measure, she took a second and third drink. Very little time passed before she could feel nothing. Her entire face was numb, especially her nose, which she found very funny and giggled to herself.

Little Ben had been napping while she nipped from the jar. The other children were thankfully in school. She needed only to eliminate the smell from her mouth before Lars came for supper or the children came home from school. She had just the remedy: anise candy. She had made a batch of it several days ago. The flavor was delightful, and the scent was strong enough to cover her alcohol-perfumed breath.

Betsi intended to complete her daily chores, but her tipsiness prevented her from achieving anything. She started with baking bread, but she couldn't keep track of the measurements. Had she put in three cups of flour already? Or did she need to add one more? Because she didn't want to ruin her recipe, she left the dry ingredients in her mixing bowl to complete another time. Betsi moved from her baking to some mending. Her mending pile had become just that, a large pile. Betsi took up her needle, cut a length of black thread, and tried to thread the needle—except her hands wouldn't stay still enough to accomplish it. Usually an expert at putting the thread through the eye of the needle, Betsi missed the hole with each try. Finally, she gave in and sat on a kitchen chair to watch Ben, playing on the floor.

The older children's arrival from school began her nightly duties. She started Anna, the oldest girl, on fixing supper while she went out and milked the cows. Once in the barn, Betsi felt relief in not having to carefully pronounce her words or make sure she didn't stumble. The cows only cared if she fed them and milked them correctly. Upon sitting on her milk stool, she immediately lost her balance and fell backward. She also noticed her hands were clumsy as she placed the milk pail beneath the cow's udders and began to strip the teats. She had never been drunk before, but she assumed that was the reason for her clumsiness.

Several days passed before she thought about the whiskey again. Her tooth no longer hurt, so she had no reason to take another drink. It was for medicinal purposes only, and she had no pain. However, she had enjoyed that warm and slightly foggy feeling from the last time. She had not even thought about her situation in life, which was a first since the day she had been married off to Lars. The darkness that usually enveloped her soul had been lifted for a few hours. She almost felt like a girl again with no worries or troubles.

The more she thought about the whiskey, the more she wanted to imbibe it again. She washed the morning's dishes and told herself she wasn't going to drink any. She hung the laundry on the line, her fortitude beginning to wane. She told herself she would only take a small sip, just enough to warm her insides again. By the time she stood in front of the cabinet, Betsi figured if she were in for a penny, she might as well be in for a pound. As usual, she only had little Ben with her.

Lars had gone to the Dunlap auction to check out the price of hogs. He was thinking about selling some of theirs. He would be gone most of the day.

Betsi removed the jar and opened it, releasing the strong alcohol fumes; she took three large gulps. She did not hold the liquid in her mouth but let it slide down her throat. She was a little pleased she was getting more knowledgeable of how one should drink. Briefly, Betsi thought about what her father would think of her now. Just to show him she no longer sought his approval, she took one last swig. "That one was for you, *Fadir*."

The Mason jar was nearly half-empty. Betsi considered filling it with tea to cover her secret forays; however, that would dilute the rest of the whiskey. If she or the family were to get another illness, they would have nothing strong enough to remedy them. Since she could not replace the whiskey, she told herself she would leave the rest of it alone. If Lars asked, she would truthfully tell him she had taken it for her tooth, omitting the current event.

Betsi honored her commitment to leave the whiskey alone for two weeks, but a particularly hard morning brought her back to the cabinet, seeking refuge from her misery. Three swigs, her usual amount, soothed her bristled insides. The numbing of her face made her giggle, and every tense muscle relaxed. Betsi decided one more gulp for good measure would last her through the rest of the day. The fourth mouthful had more impact than she had anticipated. A feeling of warm sleepiness blanketed her body, and she decided to lie down for a few minutes.

Hearing a crash, Betsi jumped up, her head groggy from the whiskey. She heard Ben screaming from the back rooms. When she got to the back bedroom, her bedroom, she saw him on the floor in the midst of broken glass. His right hand was bleeding, a broken shard lodged in his tiny palm. He had pulled down a glass candlestick holder she and Lars had received as a wedding gift. She swiftly picked him up, sat him on her lap, and pulled out the glass piece.

After she cleaned up the glass, she realized how long she had been sleeping. During that time, Ben had had free reign of the house. He could have pulled the hot kettle onto himself or some other equally dangerous move. She felt guilty for having been so remiss in her duties. "No more liquor," she said aloud.

Betsi meant to keep her promise. Each morning, she arose with dedication to watching Ben and doing her household chores. Once Lars and the children left the house, she was alone with her thoughts. Her chores had become so ingrained she no longer needed to pay attention to her hands. Her mind was free to think about her life, both past and present. As she went about the house, the cabinet loomed large in her peripheral vision. She wanted so badly to escape.

After three days, she gave in. She promised herself no more than two swallows. She just wanted to feel a little lighter. There seemed to be a tipping point when she had consumed too much whiskey, and she could no longer control herself. Betsi reasoned two drinks would keep her coherent enough to continue in her daily work. She went to the cabinet and brought out the jar. Two swallows would put it under half full. If Lars pulled out that jar, there would be no explaining to him how she had needed it for her tooth. Clearly, she had been drinking it for pleasure. She would think about that tomorrow. Right now, she wanted the drink.

Once the jar was nearly empty, Betsi had to find a solution. She didn't know the name of the man who could sell her the illegal whiskey, and she couldn't very well go into a saloon and ask them to fill her jar. Her brothers, Tingvald and Alex, wouldn't buy it for her. Even if they would, she hadn't spoken to them for years. She could ask Elfred Svensen; he would know who sold it in a Mason jar. But if she asked him, he would surely tell her mother, who would insert herself into Betsi's life again. At the very least, her mother would tell Lars. Betsi held the jar out away from her and opened her hand, allowing the jar to crash to the floor, the remaining liquid spreading out over the wooden planks.

When Lars walked through the door, he said, "Whew, I smell alcohol! Is that whiskey?"

"Yes, I was cleaning out that cabinet, and the jar slipped through my fingers. The jar broke, splashing whiskey all over my kitchen. I cleaned up the mess, but it still smells awful. It's going to take a few days to get rid of the stench. And, we don't have any more whiskey for sickness. Do you think we should get more?"

A few days later, a new Mason jar of home-brewed whiskey sat on the cabinet shelf, but Betsi didn't dare drink any of it. She had already covered her indiscretion once, but she knew she couldn't do it again. As a result, she went back into her well of depression.

Betsi went through the winter months barely able to rise from her bed each morning. When the children asked her questions or needed her help, she gave them only enough to make them go away. Lars could no longer put forth the effort to try conversing with her. The entire family, except Ben, left her alone. And this fact made her feel more isolated. Feeling sorry for herself, Betsi inwardly chastised Lars for not even caring enough to try to break through her solitude.

1907

Betsi

Once a week, Betsi travelled to Soldier to sell her eggs. She had a chicken house full of laying hens, and the money raised from selling the eggs was hers to do with as she pleased. Often when she was in town, she stopped by to purchase supplies at the mercantile. While she grew and canned all their fruits and vegetables, she still needed to buy staples like flour, sugar, and material goods to make clothing for the family.

Several months into her depression, Betsi left Anna in charge of the children, including Ben, on a Saturday morning. She carefully positioned each egg in the straw, layer upon layer, nesting her eggs as carefully as the hens had laid them. She hitched up the team to the wagon, placed her egg container right behind her seat in the back to avoid too much jostling, and headed north toward town. As she passed along the path she used to travel to school, Betsi identified the very spot where she and Jimmy Sullivan had had marital relations, which produced her child. While only three years ago, Betsi felt like a completely different person. Then, she had giggled and smiled. Now, her face wore a permanent sour look with a turned down mouth. Then, she had worried about her studies and upcoming dances. Now, she worried about rain for the crops and an illness that might come for the children. Then, her chores at home were washing dishes, sweeping the rooms, and helping in the garden, which seemed like so much work. Now, at nineteen, those chores would only take up an hour of her full day of work. At sixteen she hadn't even realized how easy her life actually was. While she could admit she had ruined her life by getting pregnant, her father had made sure her life remained permanently ruined by making her marry Lars. Jimmy Sullivan had married Mary Hanrahan, another classmate. They now had a whole litter of Irish children. Sometimes she saw Mary in the mercantile, her many children trailing behind her, and Betsi felt cheated.

Soldier was not a large town, but it had a main street running north and south. On that street were the mercantile, a post office, a blacksmith shop, a drug store, and a butcher shop. Betsi's family brought one cow and one hog each fall to the butcher's to be processed into different cuts. Across the street from the post office was the *Soldier Tribune*, the town's only newspaper. Closer to the railroad tracks were a tile factory and the Green Bay Lumber Company. On the west edge of town stood another blacksmith shop, owned by Chris Johnson and Joseph Turpin.

Arriving on the outskirts of Soldier, Betsi noticed posters advertising a medicine show. She had heard of these travelling medicine men but had never seen one. Coming upon the center of town, she saw a man with dark, unruly hair and dark, scraggly mutton chops in front of a faded black, beat-up wagon, which was enclosed on all sides with an entrance up front. She could see it was a little house. The side of his wagon, in bright yellow lettering, advertised his business: **Doc Randall's Ole Medicine Show**. Under that in white lettering on a blue painted banner was written **Pills*Tonic*Music**. Standing on a soapbox, the hawker wore a dirty, ragged checkered green suit with a top hat. The suit did not fit him well: his rotund buttocks were straining the seams of his pants, and his jacket could not be closed over his voluminous belly. He was holding up two clear glass bottles with corks.

"Ladies and gentlemen, do you have aches? Are your teeth loose? Do you have bowel troubles? Doc Randall's elixir fixes all your problems. Ladies, do you feel low? Do you get nervous headaches? A little of this cure-all will get you feelin' better in no time. For just fifteen cents, all your troubles will be gone. Who wants to buy a bottle? Two bottles? You can trust me, Doc Randall. I've been using this elixir for years, and I am healthy as a horse."

Betsi stood in the back and watched Doc Randall peddle his wares; she also watched the crowd for their reactions. Some of the men took their wives out of the crowd and walked away. Some women gathered together to discuss the possibility of being better by this one tincture. Some townspeople had already gone up to the wagon to purchase a bottle. Betsi was definitely interested. She had refused to visit Doctor Olsen again, knowing he had been the one to steer her father to that horrible woman. Since then, she had seen no one for all of her aches and pains. If she had this elixir, she could doctor herself. She reasoned it might help with her dark feelings.

After twenty minutes of watching, Betsi went up to the vender. "Sir, would your medicine help with low feelings?" she queried.

"Madam, I guarantee you'll feel better the first time you use it. Just take two to three teaspoonfuls once a day. How many would you like?" The doctor's face showed his pleasure with another sale.

"I think I want just one."

"You realize I won't be through again for a while. When you run out, you'll be sick again. May I suggest that you buy at least three of them to keep you feelin' good until I'm around again?"

"That's forty-five cents. I can't spend that kind of money. I have supplies to buy."

Betsi had her egg money from her last sale, which was twenty-five cents, and she would be getting another fifteen from the owner of the mercantile.

Not wanting to lose his sale, Doc Randall said, "I want to make sure you'll have what you need. I can sell you three for thirty-five cents. I'm not making much profit from that, but I care about your health more than I care about my profits." He turned toward a man in the crowd and threw a wink.

Betsi felt obligated to take the three since he had been so thoughtful of her health. "I'll take the three. Thank you. But I'll need to pay you after I sell my eggs. Can you hold three bottles for me until I return?"

"Of course. Take your time."

Once Betsi arrived home with her goods, she took one of her medicine bottles and poured out two teaspoons' worth of amber tonic into a cup. She could smell the alcohol, but there were other unknown odors, too. She read the bottle to see if the ingredients were listed. They were not. In large capital letters she read, "RELIEVES INSTANTANEOUSLY," and under those words were listed the various ailments: headache, gout, nervousness, toothache, bellyache. She counted twenty-three different illnesses it promised to cure.

Betsi drank the potion and held it in her mouth. It was a pleasing cherry flavor and went down much more smoothly than the whiskey. While she appreciated the smoothness and flavor of the tonic, she wondered if it would work. She reasoned anything that tasted good or was mild in its effects would have no results. Since she had bought three bottles, she would continue to use the cure-all whether it worked or not.

Within half an hour, she could tell the medicine was working. She felt light and carefree as opposed to the silliness she felt with the Mason jar brew. She had energy she hadn't felt since she was a young girl. Betsi smiled and laughed with the children. She told them to forget their house chores for the day; they were all going fishing. Instead of baking bread, Betsi spent the day at the pond with her stepchildren. When Lars came in for supper, he found a happy house full of laughter. His wife hadn't cooked supper, but he didn't care if he ate cold leftovers if it meant his house would be a joyful one.

"Betsi, my dear, you are in such a good mood. What happened today to give you such a change in demeanor? Did you make up with your family?"

"Certainly not," she said. "I found a cure for my condition." She took the bottle out of the cabinet and showed him the potion. "I bought this today, and it really works! I'm feeling wonderful!" She gave him a big smile and a hug.

Lars smiled broadly. "I'm so happy for you, my dear."

By seven that evening, the medicine was wearing off, and she felt her old, dark feelings again. When Lars turned to her in their bed, she rebuffed him by turning over.

The next morning, Betsi rose out of their bed, went straight to the cabinet, and poured out three teaspoons of Doc Randall's medicine. Within a short time, she felt lifted. She had energy and felt happy and carefree. She couldn't believe she had suffered so long when something so miraculous existed. Betsi zipped through her chores. While she was milking her cows, she sang old Norwegian songs she had learned from her parents. She took Ben with her as she went about her day, chattering to him. The children came home from school and found their stepmother baking cookies for them.

After a month or so, Betsi felt confident enough to modify the amount she was taking each day. She took her regular portion in the morning as usual, and in the afternoon, she took another two spoonfuls. The extra quantity gave her the needed pick-me-up in the late afternoon and pulled her through the worst time of day. Now, when Lars turned toward her in bed, she reciprocated.

The mood in the house brightened like they had opened all their windows and doors. Betsi's fresh breeze swept through the family. The children wanted to spend time with her, and Ben became less clingy. Lars walked through the door with a smile on his face, finally happy he had the wife who had been promised to him.

1907

Betsi

Betsi opened her eyes at quarter past four in the morning. The room was still dark. She felt sluggish, and her body ached. As she sat up and swung her legs out, putting them down on the cold, hard floor, she felt shaky. Betsi needed her medicine quickly.

She pulled the bottle out of the cabinet and took a large drink. She no longer needed to measure out the amount; she knew how much she would need to get her going in the mornings. She would take another drink in the afternoon to stave off her lethargy and craving for more tonic. Recently, she had begun taking it before she went to bed. This allowed her a full night's sleep. Before that, she had felt the need to get up in the middle of the night to take another drink, calling these her 'night lifts.'

As the months passed, no matter how much tincture she imbibed, her depression returned, and she was irritable with the children and

Lars. Betsi liked to nap after her midday pick-me-up, and the children's noise when they came home from school woke her. She often yelled at them and made them go outside right away to complete their chores. There were no more after-school cookies, no more fishing, no more laughing. Their relationship had devolved into wary animals. She was the irritated lion, and they were the frightened gazelles.

During her naps, Betsi was allowing Ben to roam freely. When she awoke, sometimes she found him outside or in the barn. Once, he had gone away from the farm, and she found him in the neighbor's pasture. She knew children had gotten lost in the fields of corn and died, and she knew she should take better care of him. She admitted to herself that her negligence of this young child could result in his death; however, if she didn't nap, she couldn't think straight.

Once she finished the morning milking and got the children off to school, she sat down to drink her coffee, which was now the only nourishment she took for breakfast. Her role in getting the children ready for school was mainly barking at them to move more quickly. Theodore, 15, and Anna, now 13, took responsibility for helping the other two get ready. Anna made their lunches the night before and put breakfast on the table in the mornings. Theodore helped them wash their faces and put on their clothes. Betsi spent extra time in the barn after she finished milking, so she wouldn't have to feel guilty for consigning her duties to the older children. She returned to the house just in time to hustle them out the door.

She looked out the kitchen window and saw Ingrid, her sister, driving up in her buggy. She was alone, which was odd. Usually when she visited—which wasn't very often—she brought her youngest with her, who was near Ben's age. The children would play together, leaving the sisters to converse. Betsi enjoyed their conversation as long as Ingrid stayed away from nagging her about seeing the family, especially Karoline, their mother. Every time Ingrid went toward that subject, Betsi warned her she should turn in another direction or get back in her buggy.

As Betsi went out to greet her sister, she gave a warm, hearty "hello" in order to keep Ingrid from asking about her mental health.

"And good morning to you as well," Ingrid replied. "I was on my way to Moorhead to visit our sister Gunda and thought I would drop by to see you as well. I can make it a two-sister day."

Betsi's suspicions rose, and she could feel a fire rising in her chest. Her house was not on the way to Moorhead.

"Would you like some coffee? I just poured myself a cup."

The sisters sat at the kitchen table and started with very innocuous topics. Ingrid gave the updates on her children. Samuel had been down with a bad cold, but she was sure that it would pass. He hadn't given anything to Mary, her daughter, which was good. Her husband Stefan was out in the fields a lot since it was planting season. Betsi sat and listened, contributing nothing. She hoped her lack of response would send Ingrid away more quickly.

"Lars stopped by Mama's house, Betsi."

Betsi's face transitioned from innocuous to angry.

"He's really worried about you. We all are. He said that for a while you were doing really well…some new medicine you bought? But now you are worse than before. He said you don't bathe very often or comb your hair. You are napping often and leaving young Ben on his own. What is wrong with you?"

"Ingrid!" she yelled. "This is none of your business! And it certainly isn't the family's business! You can go home and tell our mother that my life—and more importantly, my body—are none of her concern."

Betsi got up from the table, opened the front door, and stood there until Ingrid left.

Betsi was furious with Lars, but she was also frightened. She hadn't been careful in hiding her condition, and now Lars had her family involved. Yelling at Ingrid had at least gotten her what she wanted—to be alone—but it would also make the family more suspicious.

As soon as Lars stepped through the door for supper, Betsi pounced. "What have you been saying about me to my mother? You have no right to tell her anything without my permission!"

"Betsi, I'm worried about you. I just went and asked for some help. Your family loves you and wants only your happiness."

"Huh," she grunted. "Their behavior when I was sixteen told me otherwise. I don't want their help or their concern. And I want you to stop talking about me to other people."

She realized too late she had brought up the abortion to him and hoped he would think she was referring to marrying her off so young.

"I am taking you to Dr. Olsen. We are going tomorrow."

"I'm not going to that man or any doctor, and you know it. You can't make me see a doctor."

"Betsi, I have been patient. I have tried to understand your feelings and give you a wide path, but I have had enough. You will go to the doctor even if I have to put you in the wagon myself and tie you in it. I would rather not do that to you, but this is the end of this mess. I will have a decent wife and a good mother for my children. I will do whatever it takes to make it happen—and we are going tomorrow."

Lars turned around, walked out the door, and went to the barn. This was the most she had heard out of that man's mouth since he married her. He had always given in to her tantrums and moods. She believed he would physically force her into the wagon. She decided her best move was to go to the doctor and convince him there was nothing wrong with her.

The only good thing about going to Soldier was getting a chance to buy more medicine. She was on her last bottle and saw the posters last week for the medicine show. Lars had no knowledge of how many times she had bought from the hawker. She used her egg money and some of the grocery money to purchase what she needed. She had been hiding the full bottles in the hayloft, and the empty ones were buried in her garden. As far as Lars knew, she was still on the original three bottles. Betsi would need to put forth a good show of her own tomorrow, and for that she would need a good dose of her medicine.

1907

Betsi

Betsi forced herself out of bed at her usual milking time. Her body ached as always. She went into the kitchen and took out her medicine, pulling out the stopper. She took two long drinks, double what she habitually required.

After her milking and sending the children to school, she and Lars got into the wagon to go to Soldier; it was her day to visit the doctor. They—or rather Lars—would drop Ben with Betsi's mother.

She took the opportunity to bring some eggs along to sell. She could use the money for her medicine purchase.

Arriving in Soldier, Betsi spied the small crowd in front of Doc Randall's medicine wagon. "I need to get another supply of my medicine, Lars. Can we sell my eggs and then get the medicine before we go to the doctor's office?"

"No, you can wait on those things. I want to be certain we get in to see the doctor. After that, I'll wait while you run your other errands."

When Betsi and Lars entered Dr. Olsen's office, she took a long look around to see if she saw the same things she saw in the dentist's office. There were only chairs, so she and Lars sat down to wait their turn.

Betsi had never been to the doctor's office. Dr. Olsen had been to their house when she was a child. He came when Alex had his foot amputated. He doctored her father's broken bones when he was dragged by the horse. He had come while her mother and brother Ole had smallpox even though she never saw him that time. Her parents, like other Soldier residents, only visited the doctor when there was trouble.

Shortly after they sat down, Betsi and Lars were called into the examination room. A table sat in the center of the room. It was made of oak, the bed part made up of three pieces of wood, which were hinged, so a patient could lie flat or sit up. The bed was attached to a large wooden box with six drawers on the left side and two doors on the right, which stored the doctor's instruments and supplies. A bookcase stood along the side wall, filled with anatomy and medicine books. Another half cabinet stood along the opposite wall with various glass jars, beakers, and a mortar and pestle. A small stool was parked beside the table.

Dr. Olsen asked Betsi to get up on the table. The backboard was positioned so she sat up with her legs resting against the bottom board and her heels in the shelves that jutted out from the leg boards. It reminded her very much of the dentist's chair, and she started to sweat from nervousness.

The doctor listened to her heart and took her blood pressure. He looked into her eyes, her ears, and her mouth. Picking up her left wrist, he counted her pulse. So far, he had done nothing invasive.

"Betsi, your heart rate is too high. Have you noticed your heart beating really fast?

"I don't think so."

"How do you feel in the mornings? Do you have a stomachache? Or a headache?"

"I feel groggy like everyone does, but other than that I feel fine."

"Are you still tired throughout the day?"

"We are all tired, aren't we? I work hard, and I get worn down. Fatigue is normal, isn't it? Other than that, I feel fit as a fiddle."

"Doc," Lars jumped in, "she's been taking medicine, and it seemed to help for a while, but now she's worse than she was."

Betsi scowled at Lars and tried to give him a stern eye, so he would quit talking about her.

"What medicine are you taking?"

"It's just a tonic from one of those medicine shows. Doc Randall's. I think it's been really good for me."

"Betsi, those tonics can be very harmful. They are mostly alcohol, and some contain cocaine or morphine. The one you are taking contains both. It would make you feel energetic and then sleepy. Does that happen to you?"

Lars interrupted again. "Yes, that's exactly how she's been. She's also kind of cranky and doesn't want to do anything around the house."

"You need to stop taking that tonic. There's nothing in there that is actually medicinal. Those ingredients are very addictive."

"We'll throw out what she has left, doctor. I can promise you that," Lars said.

Without thinking, Betsi blurted, "No! I need that medicine. It gets me through the day."

"How much are you taking? How much each day?" Dr. Olsen asked.

"Not that much. I take it in the morning when I get up. I start to feel horrible in the afternoon, so I drink a little more. And, it really helps me sleep at night, so I just take a tiny bit."

"Mrs. Berg, I think you have a dependence problem. I'd like you to step outside while I talk to your husband."

Betsi complied and stepped into the waiting room because the doctor had asked nicely, but she detested being talked about. She knew the men would be making decisions for her.

"Lars, your wife is addicted to that tonic. It's not medicine. Morphine could kill her. She needs to stop taking it today. Pour out any she has. Do you have any alcohol in the house?"

"Just a jar of whiskey."

"Pour that out as well. This isn't going to be easy for her. She will go through withdrawal: sweating, nausea, muscle aches or cramps, loose bowels. She will be horribly irritable. You may want to keep the children away from her. Perhaps they could stay with your mother-in-law?"

"How long is this going to last?" Lars asked, both concerned and surprised.

"The symptoms of withdrawal will be two to three days. Her desire for it will last…maybe the rest of her life. You should make sure alcohol is never in your house. She will probably drink anything she thinks will give her that same feeling. Or as close to it as she can. Good luck to you and let me know if you need me to come out to the house and look in on her."

Lars escorted Betsi out of the office and helped her up into the wagon. He could see some of the townspeople looking at the wares in the medicine wagon.

"I need to sell my eggs," she reminded him.

"I'll take care of that. We don't need to do that today—they'll last another day. I think it's best if we just go home."

The two of them did not speak as they rode along. Betsi was thinking about what little tonic remained and how she was going to get by when it was gone. There was the jar of whiskey. It didn't have the exact same effect, but it was better than nothing. She would need to figure out how to replace it, and she didn't care how that happened. She would go to the distiller herself if necessary.

Lars pulled the wagon up to the door of the house and jumped out. Usually, he helped his wife down from the seat and then put the horses away. Instead of performing any of these husbandly actions, he went straight into the house. Before Betsi could gather her things and climb down from the wagon, Lars came back out into the yard with her Doc Randall's tonic bottle and the whiskey jar. He pulled out the stopper from the bottle with his teeth and poured the liquid onto the ground. He threw down the empty bottle, and it sat like a dead friend among the weeds. Then, he unscrewed the lid from the Mason jar, pouring a full jar of whiskey onto the ground.

"What are you doing!?" she screamed. "I need that tonic! And, you're just wasting good money pouring out that whiskey!"

"The doctor told me you have a habit we need to break. No more tonic and no more alcohol. From now on, you can drink coffee or water or milk."

Betsi jumped down from the wagon and ran to the empty tonic bottle, picking it up and holding the bottle upside down above her mouth, licking up any small drips. Betsi then took her index finger and wiped out any residue from around the rim of the opening. Having done everything except break open the bottle and lick from the glass pieces, Betsi looked up at Lars from her crouched position among the weeds. "I hate you!" she screamed.

When the children came home from school, Lars sent them in the wagon to join Ben at their grandmother Karoline's house. Theodore and Anna helped the other two, Charles and Alta, pack clothing for a few days.

"Give Grandmother Olsen this note," Lars instructed. "It will explain why you are staying with her. You are not to read the note, understand?"

The children packed quickly, sensing something big was about to be unleashed, something they did not want to see or hear. They did not see Betsi before they left: she had barricaded herself in her bedroom.

Around suppertime, Betsi began to feel unwell. She told Lars since he was responsible for her feeling unwell, he could cook his own meal. He made scrambled eggs on the cookstove, throwing too much wood in and burning his eggs. He tapped lightly on her door and entered with her scorched meal, which she threw on the floor.

Lars left the bedroom, leaving the eggs splattered across the wooden floor, and went into the sitting room. He wanted to read *The Denison Review*, which was over a week old. The small towns—Charter Oak, Dow City, Ute—often sent their news to the larger papers. The Denison paper would include columns with news from some of these towns. He focused on the paper as his wife was tipping over furniture and throwing items against the wall in their bedroom. He saw J.B. Romans Co. now carried twine and remembered he needed some before winter. Ball-Brodersen Company was opening a new mercantile in town. He might take Betsi there to shop when she felt better.

No matter how hard Lars tried, he could not concentrate on the paper when he could hear her ripping apart their bedroom. His marriage to Betsi had not been easy. She came into his home at sixteen and had little knowledge of household keeping or child raising. Five children overwhelmed her, and she seemed to come with a large chip on her shoulder. Lars was not naïve enough to believe she wanted the marriage or would even love him, but he had fallen in love with her the moment he saw her. She seemed like a wounded bird to him. Her beautiful long hair fell in curls down her back. She had dark eyes, an alabaster complexion, and two dimples. He rarely saw her smile, though.

Lars had given her a wide berth, allowing her to lead in their marital relations. When she became pregnant the first time, she became a different woman, all smiles and blushes. Losing that child put her back into herself until her next pregnancy. When she lost the second one, she became solitary and quiet. He suspected she no longer told him when she became pregnant, not wanting to raise her hopes of a child because inevitably it died.

Over the four years of their marriage, her face had taken on a sour look, and the sheen in her hair had dulled. He knew she was unhappy, but he didn't know how to make things better. He gave in to her requests and whims, hoping to make her love him by spoiling her. So often, he wanted to take her in his arms, sit her on his lap, and comfort away her troubles—but any attempt to get close to her only led to her pulling away from him. When she first started taking the medicine, he thought his troubles were resolved, and they could start putting together a real family life. The children wanted a mother, someone who would love them. Now, Lars Berg had no mother for his children and no wife for himself; he had a wounded, broken woman.

After an hour of tornadic activity behind the bedroom door, Lars could hear nothing. He assumed she had worn herself out. Quietly at first and then growing louder, Betsi began moaning and crying, which ripped his heart apart. Lars was unsure if he should go into the bedroom to check on her. He decided he should in the event she was hurt. When he opened the door a crack, his mother's vase crashed up against the door.

"I hate you!" she screamed. "I never wanted to marry you, but my father made me!"

"I'm sorry, Betsi. I know I wasn't your first choice."

"Not my first choice? No, Jimmy Sullivan was my first choice!

My father duped you. Not only didn't you get a fresh girl," she spit out at him, focusing on the word *fresh*, "but you got damaged goods."

Betsi flung the door open and stood before him. Her eyes were watery, and her hair was in knots. Face shining with sweat, she continued. "I was pregnant, you stupid ox. My father had some woman come and rip my baby out of me. That's why I can't keep a child in my womb. Together, the two of you ruined my life!" She sunk to the floor and curled up in a fetal position, crying.

Stunned, Lars stood looking down at her. However, after a few seconds, he scooped her up and held her against his large chest, cradling her in his arms. He could no more leave his suffering wife than a suffering animal, no matter how hard her words were to him. He decided to leave her confession alone for now and give himself time to think about it. Lars's job right now was to get her through her illness and consider the future once she was recovered.

"Let's get you back to bed."

"I'm going to be sick," she said right before she vomited on both of them.

"I'll get you a pail and clean you up."

Lars changed out of his work clothes and put on his town clothes, the only other set of clothes he had other than his church outfit. He pulled Betsi's dress over her head, wiped her clean, and put her into her nightdress. He pulled up a chair next to their bed and encouraged her to continue drinking water as she heaved up the contents of her stomach.

By morning, Betsi woke, feeling less nauseous as well as tired and ashamed. Lars was sitting on one of their kitchen chairs, head down with his chin resting on his chest. He had stayed with her through the night, and they both had fallen asleep sometime before sunrise. Betsi could hear the milk cows mooing loudly in the barn, their milk bags heavy and uncomfortable. She would have risen and milked them, but she was still unsteady and feeling some of the effects of the addiction.

"Lars, Lars," she said, shaking his knee to awaken him, "the cows need milking."

"Sure, I'll do it," he replied without opening his eyes.

Betsi remembered her horrible behavior and was astonished Lars had chosen to stay with her through the night. He was gentle and ministered to her illness better than her own mother. He hadn't left the house, which is what she was hoping he would do. She wanted to be left alone in her misery. She had been thinking about the bottles buried in the garden, wondering if there were any drops left in them. She didn't know why he stayed, but she knew she would have to find a new place to live once she was on her feet again.

She was certain her outburst of the truth and her anger toward him would finally break the already cracked marriage. He would not want her now that he knew the truth. Betsi was unsure of her own feelings. She was frightened of being thrown out of the house. She was also confused by his tenderness toward her. She had never seen anything like it from her own father toward her mother. She was certain if it were her father who had learned this awful truth, he would have thrown her out into the night.

His chores completed, Lars came back into the house and proceeded to cook them some food. He didn't have an extensive repertoire of dishes, so he put lard on bread and added a glass of milk, bringing it to Betsi.

"How are you feeling today?"

"Better than last night, but not completely there yet. If I could, I would like to stay in bed for the day. I know there is a pile of dishes and laundry, and I was hoping to get out to the…"

"Betsi, don't worry about those things. I've asked your sisters to come over today to take care of your house duties. Your mother is watching the children. There is nothing for you to worry about other than to get well."

"You told my family?"

"Not exactly. I told them you had gotten very ill and needed some help around the house. They were happy to help you. You have a good family, you know?"

Again, people were coming to her aid when she had treated them so badly. She didn't deserve such love—not from her family and certainly not from Lars. She thought about how she had wrapped herself in pity and anger, pushing away anyone who tried to help her. Even though she did her best to stay unloved, her husband and family remained by her side.

Lars stayed with Betsi until her sisters arrived, and then he went outside to complete his own work. Betsi watched her siblings hustle around the house—sweeping, washing, baking—anything they could do to show their concern for her.

Afternoon came, and it was odd not to have the children rushing through the door, home from school. The house was quiet—too quiet she realized. Betsi thought about what it would be like to have the quiet all of the time—no one to need her, no one to love her, no one for her to love. She realized she didn't want that for herself. She wanted to love and be loved. For that to happen, she needed to make the first move.

Betsi got up from her bed, changed into a clean housedress, and began to cook supper. She wanted to make something special to show Lars her appreciation. She made traditional meatballs, ground beef with nutmeg, ginger, and pepper. She retrieved some carrots and acorn squash from their cellar and baked them.

When Lars walked through the door, he smelled his mother's cooking. She had always made traditional Norwegian dishes. Now, many of their people were adding other types of dishes to their diet, some from Ireland and Germany and England.

"Betsi, you have made my stomach leap! Supper smells delicious!"

"I wanted a way to thank you for taking care of me last night… especially after what I said to you."

"We're going to sit down and talk about that when you're feeling up to it."

"We can talk after supper."

Betsi tried to focus on their pleasant conversation about the children and the crops instead of steeling herself for the inevitable. Lars seemed to be in a good mood, which Betsi didn't understand. When they finished, they both resided in their usual chairs.

"Tell me what happened before I married you," he said to his wife.

Ashamed, Betsi took a deep breath and looked down at the floor. It was difficult to meet his eyes, but she knew she owed him the story. She looked up and locked her eyes to his, telling her account, leaving nothing out. She even admitted to choosing Lars over being made to become some family's farmhand.

"I wish I had known this information before we married," he said.

"I'm sorry my father kept that information from you. He wanted me to marry in order to get me out of the house. He took advantage of your situation and staked you to me. I'm sorry my family was so deceptive."

"I need to be honest with you here. I've been unsure of what I want to do. My first instinct was to pack your valise and send you back to your family—but I vowed until death do we part. And I take that vow seriously."

Betsi found herself relieved to hear those words. She had feared being sent back.

"I need a mother for my children. I can't raise them alone, and they need a woman's hand. But I won't allow you to continue treating them the way you have. None of this is their doing. They need better.

If you would just open your heart to them, I know you could love them. I saw that in you when you were taking the tonic. Why could you do it then and not before?"

Betsi shamefully admitted the truth, "I have been so bitter about the loss of my own child I didn't allow myself to fall in love with your children."

"*Our* children," Lars said. "It seems to me you've focused so much on what your life wasn't that you aren't willing to see what it could be. I've tried to give you space. I've allowed you to do what you wanted because I thought it would show you I loved you, but I can see it did no good. You don't love me, and you never will."

Betsi had no response. She sat on her chair, looking at her feet. She knew he was right. She had treated his children badly because she didn't see them as hers. And she didn't think she loved him. However, she was glad he didn't send her back to her family, not because she wanted a roof over her head. Her fear that he would send her home showed her she wanted to stay.

"Lars, I don't know what to say. I'm sorry. I want to try again. I want to try to get closer to your children. If I can love them, maybe I can stop pining over my own child. I know I'll never have a child come from my body, but I can at least be thankful for the ones I do have. As for loving you, I am going to try harder. Again, instead of focusing on what I lost, I want to focus on what I have. You have been so good to me. My own father never treated me with this much kindness and concern."

"I can't tell you how to feel about your father, but I can tell you this. When he came and spoke to me about marrying you, he made me promise to take care of you. He said his father-in-law made him promise the same thing, and he didn't feel he had fulfilled it. He wanted me to do a better job than he had done. He must have loved you enough to be concerned about your future and your marriage. I mean to keep that promise, which is why I would like to see if we can mend this marriage. What do you think?"

"I would like to try. Before I see the children again, I would like a few more days, so I am completely well. And…I will go to my mother's to retrieve them. I think I have some mending to do there as well." Betsi smiled at Lars and saw him for the first time as the man who loved her.

1908

Alex

Alex, like some grand-champion bull, was passed around Soldier from one home to another. Every mother with an eligible daughter sought his company for supper. They didn't care if he was Lutheran, Catholic, Baptist, or a heathen; they wanted their daughter to become his bride. His handsome face and bank account made him a prize.

Because he was a gentleman who never turned down an invitation as well as liking baked goods, Alex always accepted their offer and showed up with a bunch of wildflowers. He delighted the families with stories—some true and some not—making the dinner pass with laughter. At the end of the evening, he excused himself with a very busy schedule for the next day, kissing the young lady's hand and complimenting her mother on the meal. He never ate at the same house twice, wanting each family to understand he was not interested in their daughter.

The more elusive Alex was, the more desirable he became. His only sanctuary, the Seed and Feed store, sold almost exclusively to male customers. The farmers were only interested in discussing the weather and the price of corn, beans, wheat, and cattle. They did not invite him to dinner or talk about their daughters' fine attributes. Alex felt his best while doing his job.

At twenty years old, Alex was now the leading buyer of cattle in the Soldier Valley—as far north as Mapleton, and as far east as Blencoe. He bought cattle all the way down to Woodbine, often competing with the Dunlap Auction House. His business took him away from home often. Alex occasionally made trips to Sioux City, Omaha, or Chicago to do business. He was especially well known at the Union Stock Yards in Chicago, which he frequented more often than the stockyards in other cities. He always traveled by train, preferring to sit alone and read one of the many newspapers he subscribed to.

On a trip to Sioux City, the train overflowed with travelers, requiring everyone to double up in their seats. Alex always traveled first class, so the crowding annoyed him greatly until a ravishingly beautiful woman sat next to him.

Her raven locks were piled high on her head with tendrils of curled hair adorning her neck and face. She had bright violet eyes and creamy ivory skin, so flawless that it looked like a baby's. She wore an expensive lavender tiered dress with lace cuffs and collar. Her matching hat sat atop her gathered hair and was cocked at just the right angle to make her look rather jaunty. Her ears and wrist were adorned with diamonds. When she sat down next to Alex, she smiled at him, showing off two dimples. She looked to be around twenty-five.

Alex removed his hat and introduced himself. "Hello, ma'am. My name is Alex Olson. Are you headed all the way to Sioux City?"

"It's very nice to meet you. Yes, I'm staying on until then. My name is Cora Briggs."

Since she had joined the train in Smithland, a town north of Soldier and south of Sioux City, Alex assumed she lived there. "So, you are from Smithland? Why are you traveling to Sioux City?

"I'm not from Smithland. I actually live in Sioux City. I was visiting my aunt. And you? Where are you from?"

"Soldier. I buy cattle around the valley and sell them at the stockyards in Sioux City."

"How interesting. And are your cattle on the train with you today?" she teased, knowing they were on the passenger train, not the stock train.

"No, ma'am," Alex replied, chuckling at her humor. He wanted to keep the conversation going, but he had run out of topics. Normally, Alex was full of polite and witty banter, but he was so taken by her beauty he felt shy around her.

"Tell me more about your business," she said, relieving Alex of the burden of a new conversation topic.

Alex felt most comfortable when discussing what he knew. He could talk for hours about cattle prices and free-range versus feedlot cows. While he droned on about the stockyards and their unfair prices, Cora seemed rapt with his every word.

"I never knew there was so much involved in cattle selling," she said. "My husband and father are in banking, and it's as dry as dirt."

With the mention of a husband, Alex felt his heart sink. He had planned to ask her to dinner, showing off his big wad of cash at a pricey restaurant.

"Are you eating dinner with anyone?" she asked.

Alex was shocked by her question. *How could she read him so well?* he wondered.

"I usually eat alone, and it would be such a welcome change to have conversation while I eat. I know a lovely restaurant with a good wine menu," she said.

Alex's face looked stunned. He had never been approached by a woman, and this one was obviously very forward. He certainly had never spent time with a married woman. He could imagine his mother's disapproval.

"My apologies for being so forward," Cora said. "I normally don't ask men to dinner, but it has been so intriguing to hear about your business. I am also very interested in the valley that you spoke of. I've never been any farther south than Smithland. I was born and raised in Sioux City, so I'm not very knowledgeable of the country. I would love to hear more about country life. If I'm being too bold in asking you to dinner, feel free to turn me down. It won't hurt my feelings."

Alex was so taken aback by this woman that he wasn't sure how he felt. He was so physically drawn to her he couldn't look at anyone else, but he was also wary of her. He was not an especially risky person—except in business—but he was far away from home and knew he would not be seen by anyone who could report back.

"I would love to accompany you to dinner."

"Good. I presume you're staying at the Martin? My driver and I will pick you up at your hotel. Six o'clock."

"How did you know I was staying at the Martin?"

"It's the nicest hotel!" She smiled broadly at her cleverness, showing off a lovely set of dimples.

Cora excited Alex. Usually, he was the one chasing and then playing hard to get. This woman knew what she wanted and wasn't afraid to ask for it. *Was it her wealth or her status as a married woman that made her so bold*, he wondered?

Before they finished their trip, Alex wanted to tell her about his foot rather than surprise her when he got up. His crutches had been tucked away on the exterior side of the seat and were down on the floor, away from everyone's view.

"I don't want to surprise you; I've got a prosthetic foot. You can't see it with my trousers covering it." He held up his leg as he talked even though she wouldn't be able to see anything.

As a genteel lady, Cora showed no surprise. Her face remained as placid as water in a pond. "And how did you lose your foot if it's not too impolite to ask?"

"Ironically, I was trampled by cattle when I was a little boy. And now I work with cattle all day long. That irony just occurred to me. Do you think I'm compensating for something?"

"Maybe buying them and sending them to the slaughterhouse is your way of collecting an old debt." She giggled after she spoke, her laughter soft and musical.

Dinner with Cora thrilled Alex, who had never had such interesting conversation with a woman. The women in his family were all business, only thinking of gardening, farming, and raising children. The women he had courted were so vapid their conversations were merely trivial nonsense. Cora was not only beautiful but intelligent and sophisticated. Their topics ranged from politics to art and books. He could not keep up with her since his education had stopped after high school, and he was not one to learn about anything that didn't pertain to his business. However, this woman made him want to expand his world.

His only misstep was the wine. Alex had never tasted wine and certainly didn't know the etiquette of drinking it. When the waiter gave him the removed cork, Alex sniffed it, tasted it with the tip of his tongue, and handed it back. His glass only partially filled by the waiter, Alex—not realizing he was supposed to taste the wine for its quality—asked for a full glass and then directed the waiter to fill Cora's glass as well. Cora stopped the waiter from pouring more than enough to cover the bottom of the glass, picked up her glass to smell the wine and then taste it, and told the waiter that it was acceptable and to pour her an appropriate amount. Alex felt like a country hick and promised himself he would work on his knowledge of culture.

At the end of dinner, Alex chastely kissed Cora's hand, thanked her for the meal, and exited her carriage. A relationship with a married woman encompassed a firm line, and dinner had been enough of crossing it. He would do no more than that.

Once returned to Soldier, Alex visited the tiny library in town. He found two books Cora had recommended; he then visited Denison's Carnegie Library, checking out the remaining novels Cora had mentioned as well as any art books they had. He read them feverishly both at home and at work. He covered Henry James first and then moved on to Edith Wharton. Reading those novels brought him into a world he never knew existed. He soaked up the American aristocracy, their affairs and desires to leave their own class. His favorite novel was *Ethan Frome*. Alex especially liked this novel because the main character was a farmer.

He preferred her recommended artwork over books. *Le Violon d'Ingres* was a favorite of his as well as other Man Ray works. He also loved Rodin's sculptures but found the artist's personal life rather immoral.

Alex's mind had never been so stimulated. He never imagined he would enjoy anything outside of making money. His only regret was the lack of friends and family with whom he could discuss this learning. He could just imagine bringing up one of Wharton's books with the farmers in the back of the feedstore. He kept his learning to himself and never read outside of his office.

When Cora had dropped Alex at his hotel after their dinner, she gave him her address and told him to send her a note the next time he was in Sioux City, and they would go out for dinner again. For weeks, he thought about her open invitation, vacillating between whether he should see her again or go about his business with a clean conscience.

Four months after his first encounter, he returned to Sioux City on business. While on the train, Alex thought about all the new knowledge he had learned just for her, and he wanted to show her he too could be intellectually interesting. He mollified his conscience by telling himself they were doing nothing wrong: they were merely having a meal together with intriguing conversation.

Cora looked even more lovely than she had the previous dinner. She wore a dark green, short-sleeved gown with a low, square neckline. The style was Edwardian classic with an empire waist, accentuated with a ribbon below her bustline. Her neck was decorated with several strands of pearls, and matching pearl bracelets circled her wrist. Alex feasted on her rather than his dinner.

Cora complimented Alex on his new knowledge and praised his thoughts on some of the novels he read. Alex beamed with accomplishment and silently vowed to continue his self-education, so he could bring something new the next time he saw her.

The couple talked late into the evening, encouraged to leave by the staff's cleaning the dining room. "I've had another lovely evening, Cora," he said.

"Perhaps we can continue our conversation in your hotel room?" she suggested.

Alex blanched. He was sexually attracted to her body and intellectually attracted to her brain, but he wasn't sure if he was ready to be an adulterer. The Soldier Lutheran Church minister made it very clear this sin was soul-damning. He could not claim ignorance. A picture of his parents flashed in his mind. His church community and all of Soldier's residents were at the table with him. They shook their invisible heads from side to side. His answer to her invitation was obvious to him. "Yes, I would like that very much." Alex pushed away their chastising faces and escorted Cora from the restaurant.

The Martin Hotel, a Chicago-style structure, was one of the swankest hotels in the city, boasting of a large boiler room, which could heat the eight stories of rooms to a cozy warm even on the coldest of winter evenings.

The rooms were as posh as the exterior, with heavy draperies and plush furniture. Alex's view of Sioux City included the Missouri River. He wasn't sure which building his sister Gunda had attended for her teacher training, but he liked to imagine her in one of those fine brick structures overlooking the river.

Comfortable on the furniture, Cora and Alex continued their conversation. Alex called for room service, asking for some champagne and fruit. Neither one of them ate the fruit, but they both enjoyed the alcohol. The bottle empty, Cora and Alex felt a little drunk. Both confessed they rarely partook in spirits.

Warmed by the enormous boiler and the champagne, Alex removed his jacket and necktie, opening his shirt a few buttons to relieve his body. Cora removed her gloves. Both of them had taken off enough clothing to get more comfortable.

"Don't you need to go home?" Alex asked.

"Not really. My husband often sleeps at the men's club, especially when he's been gambling. I don't mind. I find it offensive when he comes into our bed smelling of whiskey and cigars."

"Sorry to be intrusive, but it doesn't sound like you have a very good marriage. You seem to spend a lot of time by yourself."

"I married him because he was in business with my father. They co-own the bank. Harold is quite a bit older than I. We've never been close. He needed someone to hang on his arm at society functions. I needed to marry someone in my own class. We got what we both needed. We don't have any children, and I'm thankful for that. I would hate to raise them in such a cold atmosphere with parents who only tolerate each other. It's your typical upper-class marriage of convenience."

Alex felt sorry for Cora. His parents had been in a tumultuous marriage, and he knew how unhappy his mother had been. He was surprised someone with so many financial means could have such a poor life. Many of his parents' problems had stemmed from a lack of money.

Alex reached over to stroke Cora's face, not intending to do more than show his sympathy for her. She took his hand from her face and kissed his palm. Moving close to him, Cora stared into his eyes, saying nothing. Neither one of them moved nor spoke. Alex no longer felt the pangs of guilt. He put his lips to hers and began their affair.

1908

Gunda

Gunda's career as a teacher was mostly smooth plowing, but she did encounter some rocks in her field. She began her school year in September with mostly smaller children. The older boys were still in the fields with their fathers and would be attending school when the harvest was completed in October.

The younger students loved Gunda, and she loved them in return. They were like baby birds; she, the mother bird, chewed up their knowledge and delivered it directly into their little beaks. They swallowed it gratefully and opened up again for more. A stern look from her was all that was needed when they began to misbehave. Occasionally, one of her pupils needed the corner for a brief period. Her dream classroom was not even as good as the real thing.

She started their mornings with reading, having the younger students recite poetry while the older students read prose from their

McGuffy Reader. Then, she flipped each group around and started the process again.

After reading, the students were given a short recess. In warm weather, they played outside with Gunda supervising. During the winter months, they played outside as much as possible unless the weather was bad, and then she provided art activities in the classroom.

Once returned from recess, the children were taught arithmetic, the older students helping the younger ones. Before lunch, the students practiced penmanship with the smaller children working on their letters and names and the older students writing out longer passages.

Following lunch and another recess, she read aloud various short stories; their favorites were written by Washington Irving. Then, it was on to grammar, followed by history, and ending the day with geography. Day after day, week after week, Gunda's teaching life was predictable and pleasant.

Once harvests were finished, the older boys joined her classroom. With all students finally in attendance, Gunda taught around twenty students. The older boys more often necessitated a firmer hand; a stern look did not often work with them.

Gunda tried a variety of methods: corner standing, detaining them after school, making them stand with their arms straight out like they were on the cross. She even tried the switch on one of them, but she was so much smaller than her student, bringing about a laugh as she laid the instrument across his bottom as hard as she could. These boys were the new rocks in her smoothly plowed field. But, for the most part, she was eventually able to get them under hand and run an efficient classroom.

The worst rocks were a pair of brothers, Lyle and Leon Pitts, fifteen and sixteen years old. The boys were referred to as Irish twins, children only ten months apart in age. They should have gone on to high school, but they didn't attend school regularly enough to graduate from country school.

They liked to sit next to each other, but Gunda had them on opposite sides of the small room, which only made them yell at one another when she was trying to teach. If she turned her back to the classroom for even a second, the boys were up to some mischief: throwing spitballs, pulling pigtails, arm slugging a younger boy. Gunda had started the practice of writing on the board while facing the students.

On the playground, they cursed and taught dirty words to the younger boys. One time, she overheard Lyle asking a little girl if she knew what sex was. Parents complained to her of their behavior, but no matter what she tried, nothing seemed to deter them.

One afternoon at recess, she saw them behind a tree, beating up one of the smaller boys. Instantly, she was enraged. Her job was not only to teach the children but to protect them as well. She had had enough of their cruelties and, before she could even think what she was doing, she yelled, "Lyle! Leon! Go home! Now! I don't want to see your faces for three days. Until you two can learn how to behave yourselves, you have no right to come to school."

The boys looked at her incredulously. She had never yelled at them before. And she had never lost control of her temper. As they stood staring at her, she extended her arm and pointed toward their home. "I mean it. Go home and stay there for three days."

Suspending students from school was a serious action, one that required notification of the county superintendent and the school board chief. She sent a note home with the chief's son and walked to the superintendent's home after school. She dreaded seeing him after what he had said about her size when she first met him.

She stood on Mr. Higgs's front porch and looked him squarely in the eyes. "I've suspended Lyle and Leon Pitts for three days. They were beating up a smaller boy."

"I see. I was worried you would have trouble with those two. They have tormented every teacher we've hired. Per protocol, you'll need to make a home visit before they can return to school. I would recommend sooner rather than later. Let me know if I need to intercede." With that, he closed the door.

The following day—a blissful one without the Pitts brothers—she walked to their farm. The Pitts homestead was buried among the steep hills away from other farms. The entire farm, including the house and outbuildings, looked like it had given up and was starting the process of dying. The house was once white, but now it was devoid of much of its paint, the grey weather-beaten boards showing through. Weeds overtook the perimeters of each building. A few wildflowers struggled through their weed counterparts. The outhouse, also devoid of any paint, was missing several boards, no longer providing the privacy one wanted. The barn, if one could call it that, had lost the fight to past windstorms and half of its roof now dropped into the building. Gunda walked up the sagging steps of the house and knocked on the door.

A small, stringy woman opened it, her grey hair tightly wrapped into a bun, pulling her skin along with it. When she opened her mouth to speak, Gunda saw she was missing quite a few teeth.

"Hello, I'm Miss Olson. I am Lyle and Leon's teacher," Gunda said as brightly as she could.

Without opening the door any wider than her weed-like body, the woman said, "I know who you are. You're the one who sent my boys home for fighting. They were just protecting themselves. I don't think they should have been punished for doing what they had to."

"No, they were beating on a smaller boy." The boys came into her line of sight. She noticed both had a black eye.

"Well, that's your story. And I don't appreciate you comin' to my house. You come around here again, and my husband's shotgun will show you the way home."

Startled, Gunda said goodbye and turned around, walking back down the stairs.

As Gunda walked home, she thought about how little she knew about her students. If she were in the Soldier school, she would know their parents, but she didn't know anyone from Moorhead and the surrounding hills except for the families who housed her. Her experience at the Pitts home taught her another side of home life, one definitely not like hers.

Her parents had provided a decent house with plenty of provisions. Even in the years of drought, they always had food on the table. Her parents didn't always get along, but they had been solid role models of how to live one's life. Her father would never have pulled a gun on anyone, especially a woman. He had never hit his children. When he punished them, he always made sure there was learning in what they were assigned. As tense as their home could be at times, Gunda felt fortunate she had been given good parents.

As she continued her walk home, she started to feel sorry for Lyle and Leon. They lived in a squalid house. They were both very thin, and Gunda now suspected they weren't being properly fed. Who knew what went on behind that front door? She assumed their black eyes had come from their father, punishment for being kicked out of school. Had she known they would be physically abused, she would have thought of some other form of punishment.

She decided she would pay them more attention and punish them less. Hadn't she been told in her training that children who were naughty were often seeking attention? Perhaps if she gave them praise, they would want to get more of it and behave better. She vowed to be more patient and try some different methods because negative punishments were clearly not working.

When the Pitts brothers returned, each had a swollen eye with deep purple coloring surrounding it. Gunda looked at them, and her heart sank, knowing she was the cause of it. The boys were sullen in class, refusing to answer questions or participate with the other children at recess. Gunda did what she could to communicate to them she was not holding their past actions against them. She smiled at them and placed a hand on a shoulder as she walked by. If someone needed to run an errand, she asked one of the boys to do it for her. The day was quiet, but this time, she didn't enjoy it.

After school ended, Gunda had a list of duties to perform. She needed to complete her weekly floor scrubbing. She also had a stack of theme papers to grade and didn't want to take them with her. By the time she left school at 5:30, the sun was already slipping under. Walking along the trail, she sensed someone was following her. She stopped to listen but heard nothing. At one point, she was sure she heard the crack of a branch. She looked quickly behind her and caught Leon ducking behind a tree. She realized the brothers were following her. Should she worry? Certainly, they wouldn't hurt a grown woman.

She continued to walk and then felt something hit her back. When she turned around, she saw a rock lying on the ground. Just as she looked up, she saw another one come from the tree line, which hit her on the side of her face, opening a gash. With blood trickling down her face, Gunda started to run. With her hands full of schoolwork, she ran awkwardly. Frequently, her petticoats tangled in between her legs, especially since she was required to wear two of them, and she had to stop to put them right again. The boys continued to lob rocks and sticks at her as she ran. Once she reached the farm where she was currently boarding, the projectiles ceased.

As she traveled back to school the next morning, she tried to formulate some kind of plan. If she sent them home, they would be beated again. Maybe she should put them both in a corner for the day?

Then, she would be back to giving them negative attention. She decided she would pretend nothing had happened, give them the same treatment she had the day before, and see if showing them she didn't dislike them would change their behavior.

She also wondered if she should stop at the superintendent's house after school and report what had happened to her. When she had gone to him before, he hadn't chastised her for her decision to suspend the brothers, but he had not offered her any advice either. In fact, he seemed rather annoyed she was on his front step. Gunda decided she would give the situation another day to see if more positive reinforcement would change their behavior.

Nothing changed. They remained uncommunicative in class, while she continued to show she cared about them. Instead of staying late, Gunda left her classroom by 4:00 p.m. She thought it was less likely they would accost her in the daylight. She hoped the dark's anonymity had made them brave.

As she walked along the path again, she heard them behind her. This time, they were not hiding in the trees. Instead of rocks, today they threw jeers at her. "Woo-hoo, Miss Olson, what happened to your face?" She continued to walk, not looking back at them, hoping they would go away. "Miss Olson, we know where you live. Do you want us to escort you home every day? We'd be happy to walk with you." They started laughing hysterically. Getting no response from her, the brothers quit their taunting but continued to follow her, once again stopping at the farm's entrance.

The next day after school, a day like the previous two, Gunda went to the superintendent's house. She would ask for his help.

"Miss Olson, more trouble?"

"The same trouble. It's the Pitts brothers."

"What did they do now? I take it suspension didn't work."

"They are following me home. The first time, they threw rocks and sticks at me. This gash is from one of the rocks they threw. Last night, they followed me and were taunting me. Each time, they followed me all the way to the farm."

"They've done that before," he said. "That's why the last teacher left. Anytime you discipline them, they want retribution."

"Can we talk to their parents?"

"Little good that will do. Their parents are drunk most of the day. They beat those boys and drink up what little money they have instead of buying food for them. They hate the school system and don't respect the teachers or me. We've been at this crossroads before. We can certainly expel them if that is what you wish."

"Then there are two problems: they will blame me and continue to trouble me, and they won't get the education they need."

"You are correct. We've had the sheriff on them before, but it didn't do much good. You could file charges for their rock throwing. Did you see them throw the rocks?"

"No. I saw one of them duck behind a tree right before the rock throwing started, but I can't verify they were the ones throwing even though we both know they did."

"What would you like me to do?" Mr. Higgs was asking sincerely and seemed as troubled by her situation as she was.

"Nothing, I guess."

"I would like you to have an escort after school. I can line up some men who can take you home or walk with you. At least we can make sure you're safe."

The escorts deterred the boys from following her home again. Their behavior in class returned to their pre-suspension normalcy. They antagonized, interrupted, fought, and cursed again. Gunda used every trick she could think up to deter them from interrupting the other children's learning. She continued to try to use positive reinforcement rather than punishment, and sometimes she thought it made things a little better.

When planting season arrived, she gave a sigh of relief. The big boys would be back in the fields and out of her classroom. Leon would not be returning. Students older than sixteen would not be allowed back into the country school. If they weren't bright enough to attend high school, then their formal education was completed. Gunda wished the best for him and prayed that Lyle, who would be returning next fall, would be more manageable without his counterpart.

1910

Sophie

Sophie didn't leave the farm for months after her misadventure. She was never so happy to feel the farm's land under her feet. Her brother's fields, once considered miles of nothingness, were now appreciated for their value in providing food. Her mother's strawberry patch, a drudge of picking and weeding, was now beautiful; and Sophie volunteered to tend it, sitting among the fragrant earth and sweet strawberries. She no longer desired brick paved streets or glamorous businesses. Sophie had learned to appreciate Soldier with its small businesses and honest citizens who cared for one another.

Sophie had been rather traumatized for a time, wishing to stay close to her family. She feared Hyronimus would find her and punish her for running away. She often suffered through nightmares of his return. Sophie agonized over how stupid she had been, foolishly thinking she knew better than her mother and brothers. She recognized her lack of worldliness and did not trust herself out in it again.

When she turned twenty-one, Sophie became worried she had become an old maid. Gunda was unmarried as well, which made Sophie feel less of an oddity. But, Gunda had a career, and Sophie lived at home with her mother. Sophie felt it was time to move on with her life, but she didn't know what life she wanted.

When she complained to her mother about her lack of a "life," as she called it, Karoline offered several suggestions. Sophie was not driven to a career, like her twin. Karoline thought Sophie might want to marry, which meant she needed to meet a nice man. Sophie would never meet someone hiding out on the farm. None of their church picnics or dances had produced a mate; therefore, she thought Sophie needed to cover more ground. Karoline suggested Sophie get a job in town. Several businesses had positions, but they hired only men: the post office, the Feed and Seed, the saloon, or any other store with men as their primary customer. However, Ericksen's Groceries and Hardware, which would hire women, had a position for a cashier. Sophie was a capable woman who could make change.

Dressed in her one good outfit—a black skirt and jacket—Sophie walked the six miles to town to apply for the position.

Upon entering the store, Sophie's eyes swept across the general layout. The front half of the store was dedicated to general merchandise: hardware, lamps, lanterns, brooms, pails, washtubs…and the list went longer than her memory. The hardware had tiny wooden boxes for each nail, screw, bolt, and washer. The pails were stacked according to size and sat next to the washtubs, which were presumably just a large pail, she thought. Each item in the store was next to an item that paired with it. For example, the brooms were next to the dustpans, which were beside the waste baskets. Sophie appreciated the organizational genius who had come up with this system.

The back half of the store contained the grocery items. Baking items—flour, sugar, spices, raisins, nuts—congregated together while cans and jars, like soldiers, stood side by side in another section, neatly arranged on the shelves. The grocery store did not have the splendid organization of the general merchandise, but every item was clean and had a spot of its own.

After Sophie had gotten a general sense of the goods for sale and how the store was organized, she sought out its owner. Walter Ericksen stood behind the counter in the front half of the store. Sophie noticed the grocery section of the store had a counter as well, but there was no one attending to it.

Walter finished with his customer and turned to Sophie. "Miss Olson, how can I help you? Are you looking for something in particular?"

"Yes, I'm looking for a job. My mother told me that you may have one available?"

"*Ja*, your mother? How is she doing?" Walter Ericksen still carried a thick Norwegian accent like the rest of that generation. He had emigrated around the same time as her parents. As a businessman, though, he had learned to speak English.

"She's well. Always busy with the farm, though." Sophie realized she needed to complete the prerequisite family information section of the interview before she could discuss the job.

"And your brothers? Are they also well? I see Alex a good bit since he's here in town, but I rarely see your older brother. And Gunda? I hear she's teaching over in Moorhead. How does she like that?"

Sophie was relieved her family was no bigger than it was. She may never get to the actual job. "Yes, they are all doing well. We don't see Gunda except one Sunday a month. She's not allowed to travel more than that unless, of course, it's an emergency." To speed this along, she added additional information. "And the grandchildren are all well, too. Ingrid's children are growing quickly. Betsi and Lars

were at the monthly Sunday dinner at Mama's house, and they seem
to be doing well. They're busy, of course." Had she covered everyone? "And your family? How are your wife and children?"

"*Ja, ja*. They're all good. My little one lost a tooth yesterday. He
thinks he's getting something for it. I'll put an apple next to his head
and see how he reacts." He chuckled, and his face lit up as he talked
about his family.

They continued their conversation, moving to several of the community members. Once the obligatory chat was concluded, Walter
told her about the job. She would be located at the back of the store,
in the balcony. He pointed to the cable system they had recently
rigged from the two counters. They put the customer's ticket of sale
and money into the basket; then, they sent the basket via the cables
to the person in the balcony. That person would make change and
send it back to the counter. Along with making change, the employee
would also need to do some light bookkeeping. Did she know anything about bookkeeping?

Sophie was impressed by the system in the store. She could envision herself in what she called the bird's nest, making change, but
she didn't know anything about bookkeeping. However, Alex probably did, and she could seek his help.

"Yes, I know a little about bookkeeping," she lied. "I am also
very good at arithmetic."

"Well, knowing your family, I'm sure you're a moral person, and
you'll work hard. So, you're hired. You start tomorrow at nine in the
morning. You finish at seven or as soon as the day's bookkeeping is
completed. Is that satisfactory to you? Oh, and we pay fifteen cents
per hour."

Sophie agreed even though the wage was lower than she
expected. She knew her brother paid the men in his store twenty-two
cents an hour, and she knew why she was receiving a lower pay even

though she didn't think it was fair. If Mr. Ericksen had hired a man for this position, who would be doing exactly the same work, he would be given the higher wage.

The first day of work, Sophie arrived fifteen minutes early for her job. She settled into her bird's nest and waited for customers' tickets. It didn't take long before the store was full of women wanting to get their shopping done in the early morning. Another employee, Jack Gorden, manned the grocery counter. Sophie discovered Jack was the one responsible for organizing the grocery half of the store.

Soon, tickets were coming from both counters. Sophie had to re-add the ticket to be sure there were no mistakes and then make change for the customer, sending the change in the correct basket. She had assumed only one basket came at a time; however, this was untrue because they put new baskets on the line as soon as they had one customer ticket completed. They didn't want to waste time waiting for her to complete her basket, allowing customers to stand in line, so they created a new ticket for the next customer, allowing the previous one to stand by the side and wait for the change.

Sophie worked as fast as possible. At first, she could sit down and do the work. But each time she needed to reattach the basket, she was required to stand up. All the standing and sitting became too much, so she stood the rest of the day. Once the last customer left the store and the sign was turned to "Closed," Sophie needed to start adding the tickets. Mr. Ericksen then directed her to put the amounts into the ledger. She also had to count the number of each item sold, look it up in the book that kept the wholesale price of goods, and add up how much they spent in merchandise. Once she finished her task, she could walk home.

Upon reaching her house, Sophie could feel the day's work in her body. Her feet ached, and her back had a stabbing pain in the center. Her brain felt fuzzy and tired.

"How was your first day?" her mother asked.

"*Uff da*. I'm tired, but I think I did alright. I've never done so much adding in one day. My brain is exhausted. But I made a little over a dollar today." Sophie realized she felt good about making her own money.

"Good. Did you meet any nice men?"

"I'm up in that nest all day. There's no one but me. Of course, there's Mr. Ericksen and his assistant Jack Gorden, but I don't have access to any of the customers, just their money."

"What's this Mr. Gorden like? Is he married?"

"Mama! Enough! I don't know anything about him. He looks older than me. I didn't see a ring on his finger, but that doesn't always mean anything. Are you satisfied?"

"I'm sorry I take an interest in my daughter's life. I won't pester you anymore." Karoline knew her daughter had taken an interest in Jack Gorden; otherwise, she wouldn't have known whether he wore a wedding ring or not. She was pleased Sophie felt proud of making money by using her brain.

Sophie worked for the mercantile from October through December without having any kind of conversation with her coworkers. She ate her lunch in the nest and then left after both men had finished. She had been given the responsibility of locking up the store. Sometimes Alex would stop by at the end of the day and offer to take her home in his car.

On a January evening, with a clear, star-filled sky and a bone-breaking cold, Sophie stepped outside, bundled in winter gear until she was barely visible. Sitting in his own automobile, Jack Gorden seemed to be waiting for someone. He waved her over. "I thought I would offer you a ride. It's too cold to be walking those six miles home. Get in."

Sophie didn't immediately take his offer. She was shy of being alone with a man, but when she considered her walk home, she swatted away her hesitancy. Sophie hopped into his vehicle. Even though she was inside, she kept the scarf wrapped securely around her neck and face. "Why did you think to offer me a ride? Weren't you already home with your family?"

"Family? Why do you think I have a family? I am a bachelor," he said, quite surprised.

"Oh! I don't know why I thought that. I apologize."

"I thought about you walking home in the dark and cold, and I started to worry about you. I hope you don't mind that I took it upon myself to look after you."

Sophie surprised herself by feeling pleased. Their conversation during the drive consisted of shop talk. How much prices had risen. How impatient some of the customers could be. Sophie found him to be rather pleasant and even funny at times. Once they reached the farm, Jack asked, "Do you mind if I give you a ride when the weather is too cold? I really hate to think about something bad happening to you. I would feel terrible if we found you, a frozen icicle, in a snowbank." He turned and grinned at her, and she responded with a smile of her own.

Through the rest of January, Jack drove her home each evening. She noticed his duties, which he used to complete well ahead of her own, now took him longer. He and she finished at approximately the same time. Their drives were filled with pleasant conversation: he asked about her family, and she did likewise.

Jack was originally from Ute but couldn't find a job, so he had moved to Soldier when Mr. Ericksen advertised his position. He was currently boarding at Minnie Eldridge's house. She cooked for him and washed his laundry.

Jack was an only child, and his parents still lived in Ute. His father was a butcher, but the business was failing, which was why

Jack sought out a new job. He now sent money to help his parents with their bills. Jack did not want to remain a clerk. He wanted his own butcher shop, but his father's would probably not remain open much longer and there was no money to start one of his own; however, he stressed to Sophie he was saving his money for the future.

Sophie did not share any of her Des Moines experiences. She told him after high school she stayed home and helped her mother raise her baby brother and take care of the farm. She wished she could erase that week from her past, but since she couldn't, she could at least keep it away from Jack.

By the end of February, Sophie was in love. Jack was a caring, industrious, funny man; and she wanted to marry him. To further along the process, her mother invited him to one of their Sunday dinners. Sophie worried the family would be too much for him, especially since he was an only child.

Their large table, its many extensions pulled out, was noisy and chaotic. Her mother, siblings, in-laws, grandchildren—when they were totaled up, they numbered twenty-three, and that counted Elfred Svensen, who was always invited to family functions. Children yelled, babies cried, adults argued over politics, and the clanking of pots and pans sounded the arrival of a delicious dinner. Sophie could just imagine a dinner at Jack's house, the four of them sitting at a small table with murmurs of quiet conversation.

To Sophie's delight, Jack jumped right in with her family. He played games with the young children, offered to hold babies while their mothers helped in the kitchen, and argued politics with her brothers and Elfred. At one point, Sophie's mother looked over at her and winked, giving Sophie her approval. The afternoon with the Olson family had gone well, and Jack seemed to enjoy himself immensely.

Jack even stayed after supper, inviting her for a moonlight walk. The full moon gave enough light to walk by. Millions of stars shone brightly in the black sky. Leafless trees, outlined in black, looked like actors on a darkened stage, the moon their spotlight. The wintry evening air was crisp and tingled their lungs as they drew a breath. Their boots made squeaking noises on the snow with each step. Both faces were cherry with cold. Jack reached over and grabbed her mittened hand. They walked for several minutes before either one spoke.

"Did you enjoy your time with my family?" Sophie asked.

"I had a wonderful time. I love all of the noise and chaos. My family dinners are so dull and quiet. I hate being an only child. I wish I had brothers and sisters like yours."

"Good. I was worried we would be too much for you."

"Do you think your mother likes me?"

"She does. I can tell by the way she kept offering you food like you were some starved bachelor in need of fattening."

Jack stopped walking and faced Sophie. He took both of her hands in his. "Maybe I am. Maybe I wouldn't mind spending Sundays with your family. How would you feel if I asked you to marry me?"

Sophie's face broke into a broad smile, and she squeezed his hands. "I would feel like I finally found the right man."

He kissed her for the first time and held her tightly against him. Sophie felt loved and protected.

"I'll take you to meet my parents" he said. "Do I need to ask your mother or your oldest brother for permission?"

"You don't need to ask anyone, but if you want to do this properly, I suppose you should ask my mother. And, she'll say yes. When should we marry?"

"How long do you need to prepare? A May wedding would be nice. That gives you almost three months."

The couple married in May. Sophie, like her sister Ingrid, wore her mother's wedding dress. She was a stunning bride and blushed with happiness. They did not take a honeymoon since they wanted to continue to save for a butcher shop of their own. Instead, they accepted Alex's offer of his rented house while he was in Sioux City for the weekend.

Afterward, they settled into Jack's small boarding room, saving up for their dream.

1910

Ingrid

Ingrid missed her father. She was his first-born, his little girl. He was her protector. Ingrid's relationship with her father was different from that of the other children. She felt close to him, even at times closer to him than she was to her mother.

During the visitation and burial, Ingrid stood beside her mother, offering comfort and understanding. She had witnessed many times the way her father had treated her mother. Ingrid sympathized with Karoline. Listening to how well he had treated other women, with such kindness and benevolence, was difficult for her mother to hear since those were not the words the family would have used to describe him, especially Karoline. Yet when Ingrid squeezed her mother's hand in understanding and solidarity at his gravesite, she felt like a traitor.

When Ingrid was a little girl, her father often picked her up and threw her high into the air. The more she giggled in delight, the more he responded, throwing her even higher. Ingrid was never afraid, knowing her father's strong arms would always catch her. In the evenings, she sat on his lap, snuggled into his soft, warm shirt while he read to her from the *Posten*, a Norwegian newspaper published in Decorah, or told her Norwegian fairy tales. Her father's lap was the safest place in the world.

When she was too old for his lap, she liked to sit on the floor near his feet and lean against his strong legs. Sometimes he would read interesting stories from the *Soldier Sentinel* to the family. She loved his deep, resonant voice and hearty laugh when the story was especially amusing.

Ingrid knew there was very little her father wouldn't do for her. Once, he even bought her a pony at the auction barn. She had begged him for months for a pony of her own. When he came home with it, she beamed with love for him. She named the pony Poky because he was so small compared to the other horses. Unfortunately, the pony, a brown Shetland, was meaner than cuss. Any family member who dared to sit atop the horse was instantly rubbed off on a fence or a tree. Sometimes, he would reach around and bite the rider's leg. Once, he had the audacity to bite her father on his behind. Poky's last mean trick was his final act. The Shetland had torn through Karoline's garden, ripping her tender plants out of the ground. Poky went back to the auction barn and was sold to another unsuspecting family. Ingrid was glad he was gone.

Her father's greatest gift to her was a parcel of land for a house and an opportunity for her husband Stefan to become part owner of the farm. She knew it was his way of making sure his daughter remained close to the family. When they built the house, he was always there, pitching in more than any other man. Ingrid could look around their home and feel her father's love wrapped around her, keeping her safe and warm.

When she brought their first child, her father's first grandchild, into the world, she named him Samuel Kristoffer Andersen. Her father's chest puffed with pride when he was told the child's name. He held that tiny baby in his arms and looked at Ingrid with pride. Every time Kristoffer came to their house, he immediately wanted to pick up his grandson. Samuel's first word was Papa. He followed his grandfather around like a puppy. He wanted to farm with his papa, riding in the wagon. She felt like she had given him the greatest gift ever made.

Ingrid named her second child, a girl, Mary Kristina. The baby was the tiny version of Ingrid. Seeing her father's large hands holding this small girl warmed Ingrid each time. Kristoffer visited his grand-children regularly, bringing small gifts. Sometimes they were baby bunnies or kittens. Other times, a wooden toy he had carved.

Kristoffer may not have always been the most loving father to all of his children, but Ingrid could see what a loving grandfather he had become. There was nothing he wouldn't do for her children. And for that, she loved him even more.

It saddened her that the children would not remember him. At three and two, they would not be able to hold onto all of the wonder-ful memories he had created with them.

Her mother, however, never seemed to be able to let go of her anger toward Kristoffer. Ingrid could perhaps understand her mother's feelings when it was between the time her father left for the north and his death. He had told her mother he wished she were dead. However, after he died of appendicitis, there was no reason for Karoline to hold a grudge. Ingrid thought her mother should focus on the good times they had had. She should appreciate how hard Kristoffer had worked for the family's benefit.

As with any marriage, nobody knows beyond what they see.

Ingrid knew that well. When she and Stefan were having problems, she did not announce it to the world or her family. The couple kept their problems and disagreements to themselves. Ingrid felt she had enough inside knowledge of her parents' marriage to know they had disagreements, but nothing worse than any other couple.

Her mother's behavior suggested she was a happy woman. Karoline hadn't worn black more than a month; Ingrid thought she should wear it until she married again. Karoline also didn't seem to want to marry again, not because she had lost her soul mate, but because she enjoyed being a widow without a husband.

Karoline's never putting flowers on Kristoffer's grave angered Ingrid. When Ingrid made her monthly trip to the cemetery, she noticed a few times there were flowers on Ole's grave, the brother the family had lost. She felt her mother could at least continue her wifely duties even though her husband was dead.

Ingrid never spoke her feelings to her mother. When she visited Karoline, she spoke only of the children and household matters. As the peacemaker in the family, Ingrid would not intentionally bring up disagreeable subjects. The only time she had ventured on an unpleasant topic was with Betsi, and that was only because she was concerned about her.

Ingrid, now twenty-one, happy in her marriage and happy in motherhood, had everything she wanted.

1910

Ingrid

Ingrid admired the beauty of the Loess Hills from atop her ladder. A rare frost in early October brought out all of fall's colors. Some of the trees along the ridges had turned gold, red, and brown. Others were still green. Ingrid could look down on the valley and see the patchwork of land. Some of it was yellow from the harvested corn. Pastures were still green underneath with weeds that had gone brown. The sumac in the ditches made a fiery orange and red. Layers of hills stretched out as far as she could see. The morning nip in the air had warmed, and the sun shone on her skin.

Ingrid and her two children were painting their hog shed on this glorious Saturday afternoon. They had been at the task for two weeks and were nearing the end of it. As Ingrid looked out from her vantage point, she noticed two men on bicycles nearing their house, carefully navigating the ruts, holes, and embedded rocks in the dirt road. She couldn't see how those skinny tires could withstand the bumpy terrain. *Country roads are no place for bicycles*, she thought. Large bundles were strapped to their machines, and Ingrid wondered how they could stay upright with such additional weight.

Ingrid had no interest in bicycling even though it had been the rage for both men and women for many years. She had seen the cycling clothing advertised in the fashion sections. Women wore blouses with tightly belted waists. They either wore split skirts or voluminous bloomers to keep their lower clothing from getting caught in the chain. In Ingrid's mind, those were still trousers, and women had no business wearing men's clothing. Ingrid did not view cycling as an appropriate women's activity. Women, flopping about atop a cycle, roamed the countryside unescorted by their men. *This was no proper way for women to behave*, she thought.

The two men, wearing identical riding outfits, pulled up to the hog shed so they could talk to her. They both wore knickers with long socks, a riding jacket over their shirts, and a Gotham newsboy cap.

"Good afternoon, ma'am," said the elder of the riders. "Can you tell me exactly where we are located?"

"You are near Soldier, Iowa." Ingrid responded without coming down from her ladder.

"How far are we from the Nebraska border?"

"I'm not sure," she said. "But, I know it's not a day's ride. May I ask your destination?"

The younger man responded, "We're destined for San Francisco. We started in New York City."

Ingrid had never been to New York City or known anyone from there. Her parents had landed in the city when they emigrated from Norway. And her mother went back through New York when she had returned to Norway with toddler Ingrid and not-yet-born Tingvald.

Ingrid climbed down from her ladder. She felt uncomfortable

having these men look up at her while she was in her dress. "Oh my. How long have you been on those bikes?"

"We've been traveling for over two months. We can cover eighty miles a day if the roads are good. We haven't been able to get as far lately because of the poor road conditions. Would you be willing to allow us some water?"

Ingrid showed them into her kitchen, bringing her children along for propriety, and gave each of them a glass of water and some cake. She was eager to hear about their journey.

"Why on earth are you riding bicycles across this country?" Ingrid asked.

"We are bicycle salesmen. We own a bicycle shop in New York City. We are promoting the leisure of cycling. Do you own a bicycle?"

"Certainly not! I don't think it's appropriate for a lady."

"Have you heard of Susan B. Anthony? The famous suffragette? She was a staunch proponent of the bicycle. She said she thought it had done more to emancipate women than anything else. Or how about Annie Kopchosky, the Boston woman who rode around the world? Or Maria Ward, who wrote 'Bicycling for Women'?"

"I've only heard of the first one. But, I still don't think it's for me. I think a woman's place is in her home, not out gallivanting around the country with her skirts flying about on a bicycle."

"Ma'am, are you not a proponent of the women's Suffrage movement?"

"I believe a woman's place is with her husband and her children. I don't want to vote. I wouldn't know who to choose. I trust my husband to decide. I have enough to worry about with all of my house duties and child rearing. I don't need to take on any extras. Voting and holding office is men's work. I don't want any part of it."

Surprised, the two men made their quick exit and continued on their way west.

***

Karoline dropped by to visit Ingrid and the children the next afternoon. The women usually chose one weekend each summer and fall to do their canning. Betsi would come with her troupe, and the three women would can until they practically fell down from exhaustion while the older children watched the younger ones. They would put up tomatoes, corn, beans, peas, beets, carrots, peaches, and pears. Anything that could not be stored in the root cellar went into jars. This canning session, the women were putting up pears and peaches.

Canning done for the day, Karoline and Ingrid sat on comfortable chairs outside, their faces to the sun. For a while, they didn't speak, contented to look at the fall foliage and watch the children play. They listened to the male cardinals high in the tree tops whistling their mating calls.

"Don't you think it's interesting the male species is the one concerned about looks while the females are not as showy? While human females are the showy ones and the males less so?" Ingrid mused.

"I think it's unfortunate. Look at what we do to ourselves. I hear some women are powdering their faces and rouging their cheeks and lips. And don't get me started on these corsets. They are the most uncomfortable thing man has invented. Notice I said the word *man*. I think it was a way to keep us from running away. We can't go very far before we're out of breath." Karoline chuckled, pleased with her cleverness.

Ingrid was sorry she had brought up the topic. As usual, her mother had gone into her man-hating mode. She decided to change the subject.

"The children and I were out painting the hog shed yesterday when two men on bicycles came by and asked for some water."

"That's not unusual. You've seen people out cycling before."

"They rode from New York City and are traveling to San Francisco. They are bicycle shop owners and are promoting riding. They even asked me if I owned such a machine. Of course, I told them how ridiculous it was, and they responded by telling me about these women who had ridden bikes. One bicycle lover was Susan B. Anthony. Can you believe that?"

"Huh. Never would have thought a woman that old would have been interested in bicycles."

"She said she thought it was the best thing to happen to women. Freedom for them, apparently. They actually asked me about the Suffrage Movement. They seemed to be all for it. I definitely told them my opinions."

"And, what are those?"

"That I think a woman's place is in the home and obeying her husband. There's no need for women to vote. I don't have the brain for that kind of nonsense anyway."

Karoline cringed at her daughter's words. She recognized them so well. Ingrid was definitely her father's daughter. She had wanted to please him so badly she was willing to mimic his words and his thoughts. She remembered Ingrid's wedding when she spoke her vows to Stefan, promising to obey him. Karoline had hoped her daughter wouldn't have to suffer the same kind of marriage she had had. As long as Ingrid lived her father's beliefs, there would only be peace in the Andersen house. Stefan made the decisions while Ingrid obeyed him.

"You have a brain as good as any man's. You can do anything you set your mind to," Karoline scolded her.

Ignoring her mother's comment, Ingrid added, "Those Suffrage women aren't in their right minds. Do you remember two years ago in Boone when they had that parade down their main street? The paper said there were nearly 150 women. What kind of woman marches in the middle of the street, carrying signs demanding the right to vote? I can't imagine what their husbands must have thought. I'll bet some of them don't even have husbands," Ingrid finished with some contempt in her tone.

As she finished her sentence, Ingrid realized what she had said. Her mother no longer had a husband and didn't seem to want one. She had hoped Karoline would marry Elfred Svensen, but she had turned him down, which was an embarrassment. The poor man had to put up with the gossip of a woman turning him away. He was a perfectly good man, and Ingrid didn't understand why her mother wouldn't marry him.

This fall, Ingrid saw her mother wearing her father's old pants and shirt when she was out in the field helping pick corn. This was not the first or only time her mother had chosen to dress in her deceased husband's clothing.

Ingrid was aware her mother was often the topic of conversations in some of the women's circles. A woman of forty-five had no reason not to marry. She still had good years remaining even if they were no longer child-bearing. With no husband, Karoline had the running of the farm along with Ingrid's brother Tingvald. It was absolutely shameful to see her mother take over men's jobs.

Throughout the conversation, Ingrid noticed her mother's reticence. And when her mother changed the topic of conversation back to canning, Ingrid knew she had deeply offended Karoline.

That evening, both women thought about the conversation. Karoline couldn't believe she had raised a daughter who was so unlike herself. And, while Ingrid felt terrible she had let her feelings about her mother not marrying show, she was not sorry she had spoken her beliefs about a woman's place. She just wished her mother felt the same way. It seemed the longer Karoline went without a husband, the more she became like those Suffragettes.

1911

Tingvald

When his father died, Tingvald got what he wanted—his portion of the farm. However, he got more than that; he now had the entire farm. The rope of responsibility had wrapped around him, and he now felt like he was pulling a tugboat.

Before his death, his father Kristoffer had purchased ten additional acres, bringing the farm to fifty. He had also added thirty head of beef cows. Tingvald had his brother-in-law Stefan, Ingrid's husband, to help him farm. Yet the decisions he made and the consequences that followed were ultimately his.

Kristoffer's arrangement with Stefan allowed him to work for his portion of the farm. Alex, Tingvald's brother, could not farm because of his missing foot; but he would still take his share of the proceeds if it were ever sold. There were other mouths to feed from the land and cattle: his mother; his twin sisters, Gunda and Sophie; and his youngest brother Gulbran Floyd. Tingvald was now responsible for every soul in the family.

The debts on the farm would need to be paid, without exception. There was sympathy for his father's death, but there was no leniency on loan repayments. He needed to make the mortgage each month, or they would start to lose their income, the cattle going first. After that, the farm would be sold acre by acre. He would be responsible for the loss of his father's dream.

Tingvald's own family also looked to him for care. When his mother suggested he move into the main house, he could not refuse, having given his savings to pay the missing loan payments, which he did not divulge to Ella Evensen, his fiancé. Tingvald now had neither time nor money to build a house for them. Living in his mother's house allowed him to watch over her, the only benefit to the family's moving in. For Ella, however, this did not fulfill the promise he had made her when he asked for her father's permission to marry. He built her a dream house, but that was all it was—a dream.

The weight of these responsibilities seemed to bury him a little more as the years passed. Now twenty-eight, he felt as if he were half-way into the ground. If the weather cooperated, and the prices of commodities remained high, and the health of all of the beings in his care was good, then he could get ahead and pay back the money they owed. Except all three rarely happened together. If the weather cooperated, the crop was in abundance, which drove the prices down. If there were poor yield, then the prices were high but not much crop to sell. He realized very quickly being a farmer was an occupation of worry.

Worrying put wrinkles on his face and grey in his hair. If he had enjoyed being a farmer, it would have been worth the sacrifice. However, he discovered within a few years of taking over his father's farm he did not like farming. It was body-breaking work and mental strain. He envied Alex, his brother. Alex sat inside, out of the pummeling sun, and used his brain instead of his body. He was an important man in town, part owner of the Feed and Seed store.

No matter how hard or long Tingvald worked, they never seemed to get ahead. They could meet the mortgage payments and take care of the family's needs, but that was all. There were no frills. His children wore patched, hand-me-down clothes, and his wife made her own dresses from the cheapest material. He did not have the money to buy the newest farming implements, nor could he borrow the money for them since they were already at their debt limit. He made do with what they had, as did everyone in his family.

When Tingvald had the reins around his neck and his hands on the plow, he envisioned himself in his own business. Perhaps he would own a little grocery store in Soldier. No wind, no rain, no cold or sun pounding his head. Tingvald would be inside, away from the elements. He could envision himself in clean trousers and a white shirt with an apron around his waist to keep the dust from dirtying his clothes and sleeve protectors to keep his white shirt pristine. Instead of the horses for company, he would greet customers and ask about their families. Perhaps he would be one of the leading merchants in town, and residents would seek his advice or listen to his gossip.

Instead, he came home each evening with a dirty, sunburned face; boots caked with mud or manure; and the smell of sweat and animal on his skin.

Tingvald knew his merchant dream was impossible. He remembered the fight he had had with his father before Kristoffer left to work up north. Tingvald had wanted his piece of the farm so badly he had badgered his father until his father yelled at him, calling him an "ungrateful mutt." Those were the last words he had heard from his father's mouth before Kristoffer died. Tingvald felt he owed his father; he needed to make peace with his father. The only way he could do that was to keep Kristoffer Olsen's dream alive, no matter the cost to himself.

1911

Tingvald

Three years after Kristoffer died, Tingvald married Ella and four months later looked into his son's face. They named him Chester Howard Olson but called him Howard. He was a fair baby with Ella's coloring: blonde hair and blue eyes. Like all new fathers, Tingvald was enamored with his child. Ella often brought him into their bed, so she could rest while she nursed him. After so many months of being transferred from his cozy drawer next to their bed, Howard wanted to sleep with them permanently. Tingvald complained gruffly it wasn't proper for a baby to sleep with its parents, but he secretly loved feeling his son next to him while he slept.

Karoline doted on her first grandson, remembering her mother coddling Tingvald when they were in Norway. She spent time with him while Ella completed her household chores. Karoline had kept the garden chores and loved taking her grandson out in the dirt, although Ella was irritated when Howard came in filthy with mud around his mouth, which she assumed meant he had eaten some of it. She often complained to Tingvald that Karoline was spoiling Howard. When Tingvald asked his mother to follow Ella's parenting rules, Karoline always answered his requests with "it's a grandparent's prerogative" to spoil them. She fed Howard cookies as soon as he was old enough to eat them. When she fed him her applesauce, Ella couldn't get him to eat his mashed green beans. Ella loved and respected her mother-in-law, but there was always unspoken friction in the house when Tingvald came in from farming.

Howard grew into a big baby with rolls of fat around his knees, elbows, and neck. He was never more jovial than when he was eating. He reached for the spoon and squealed with delight when it came close to his mouth. Ella was a small woman, not even reaching 5'2", with a tiny waist. Holding Howard made her look like a child.

Their second son, Glenn Merlyn, was born in 1910 when Howard was a year and a half, looking very much like Tingvald with auburn hair although his head was a crown of curls. Even though Ella and Karoline did not always agree on child rearing, Ella appreciated having Karoline in the house to help with the babies. When Sophie and Gunda were younger, they had pitched in with the child minding as well. The boys were spoiled by Karoline and the twins, but they were disciplined by Ella.

Before his second birthday, Howard contracted scarlet fever, giving it to baby Glenn as well. Howard's temperature climbed to 102 degrees, and his throat was blood red. Glenn's symptoms were much milder, averaging 99 degrees and some rash in his armpits and groin. As much as Ella and Karoline cared for the children, giving them cold baths and keeping cold cloths on their heads to help with the fevers, Howard succumbed to the illness. Glenn, thankfully, came through it.

Tingvald and Ella took time and grieved for the first few months. After that, like his father Kristoffer, Tingvald thought the best course of action was to work hard and not dwell on the death. He went back to his daily regimen. Karoline took special care of Ella, knowing what it felt like to lose a child. Ella never seemed to be her same jovial self even through her next pregnancy. This new baby, Milton, was born a year after Glenn in 1911; and the midwife proclaimed him a healthy baby.

Within a few days after Milton's birth, Karoline noticed Ella wasn't herself. The baby, like the others, slept next to Ella and Tingvald's bed in a drawer padded with blankets. When the baby cried from hunger, Ella put the pillows and blankets over her head to drown out the sound. Hearing the crying child, Karoline went into the room.

"Ella, your child is hungry. I know you can hear him."

Without removing the blankets, Ellsa wailed,"I can't! I'll kill him, too. You feed him."

"I don't have any milk. There is no one else to nurse him. You must do this."

Ella's response was to cry and bury herself farther under the covers. The only way to get food down Milton's throat was to allow him to suck on the end of a rag, which was dipped in cow's milk.

Karoline did her best to get nutrition into Milton, but the milk was too hard on his stomach, making him cry all day. He cried from hunger, and he cried from pain. Karoline tried several times to convince Ella to pick up her son and tend him, but Ella refused.

Ella also preferred to sleep the day through, ignoring her children and her house duties.

Ella didn't wish to be a bad mother, but her mind circled around the death of her first son. She took full responsibility for what had happened to him. Perhaps if she had kept a better house or fed him more? To keep her mind from repeating her faults, Ella started to count the cracks in the walls and ceiling. She took inventory of every item in her room and tried to memorize them. Eventually, though, she started to repeat over and over the things she had done wrong as a mother. She convinced herself if she were to die, the children would have a better chance at survival, being raised by their grandmother.

Karoline, concerned about her daughter-in-law, spoke to Tingvald. "Something is not right with Ella, Tingvald."

"She's still sad about Howard. She'll come around. She just needs to spend more time with Milton."

"I think you're wrong. This is more than sadness. She doesn't ask for the baby or about the baby. She only wants to sleep. Glenn whines for his mother all day, and I can't get her to take an interest in him either. I've heard about women going crazy after they've had a baby."

"She's not crazy, Mother. She just needs time."

Tingvald was never terse with her, but Karoline could tell she had hit a nerve with this topic. "I think you're wrong, but she's your wife. I'll respect your decision."

Ella didn't get any better. She stopped bathing, her beautiful hair matted and oily. Her body smelled like dried milk from her leaking breasts. Ella preferred to stay in her nightdress, sleeping day after day. After another week, Tingvald couldn't deny something more than sadness was wrong with her. With his mother's pushing, he finally requested a house call from the doctor.

Dr. Olsen had been their loyal family physician, making emergency house calls whenever he was summoned. He had retired recently, and a new Danish doctor, Hans Christensen, took over his practice.

The doctor, dressed in sharp black pants, white shirt, and a black jacket, went into the bedroom and came out again after a few minutes.

"Mr. Olson, your wife has a nervous disorder. You see, women are quite fragile, and the death of your son has been too much for her. I recommend a treatment called the rest-cure. I'm sure you're not familiar with it. A prominent Philadelphia neurologist by the name of Weir Mitchell found the best treatment for women's nervousness. I think we should follow his protocol.

You should start by giving her a very specific diet. She is to have only fats, like fatty meats and cream instead of milk, and lots of butter. She should have no fruits or vegetables. Mrs. Olson should be forced to rest in complete isolation as much as she possibly can. She is not to be disturbed by anyone, not even the children. This will give her time to allow her mind to settle. I am also going to leave tranquilizers for her. They will calm her mind and allow her to sleep more. She should take one right away in the morning and another in the afternoon."

"When will she get better?" Tingvald asked.

"This cannot be rushed. I don't think we can expect her to be cured for many months. We just need to give her time… and rest, as I said."

Karoline spoke up, "I don't mean to be impertinent, Doctor, but she's already spent a lot of time resting, and it seems to have done her no good. I think she has gotten worse. Don't you think it would be better if she were out in the fresh air and stimulated by conversation? She could help me with the flowerbeds; she loves flowers."

"Absolutely not! A woman's mind is not like a man's. It is easily broken and not easily fixed. She needs that rest to help her fix it. Something like this shows us why it is important for women to occupy themselves with children and housework. These are things that are natural for a woman's mind. These are things she can understand. Men want women to obey us, not because we are being cruel, but because they are better being guided by us. We can make sure their minds are not polluted by politics or money or men's matters. I'm sure I know what I'm talking about, Mrs. Olsen."

At the mention of the word *obey*, Karoline's hackles rose. And his description of a woman's mind infuriated her. However, she knew it was best to remain quiet. Nothing she said would change his mind, and she found she was more successful when she let a man think she agreed with him. She would talk to her son when the doctor left.

As soon as the doctor drove away, Karoline said, "Tingvald, that man is wrong."

"Mama, he's a doctor. I will make the decisions for my wife, and I say we are going to do as he says."

Karoline did not agree or disagree. She wanted to give Tingvald the respect he deserved as a man. However, she had made up her mind she would do what she thought was best for Ella. Tingvald was outside on the farm most of the day. If she took over nursing Ella, she could control what happened to her.

In the morning, Karoline took a pill and a glass of water to Ella, making sure Tingvald saw her with the medication. Instead of giving Ella the pill, Karoline put it into her apron pocket.

Once Tingvald was out of sight of the house, Karoline went into Ella's room, pulled the covers from her body, and made her sit up.

"We're going to put your housedress on you and get you outside. And, I'm not taking 'no' for an answer."

"Mother Karoline, the doctor said I was to rest."

"He wouldn't know what a woman needs any more than he would a porcupine. You're getting up and out of this house."

Once she got Ella dressed and up, she took her to the flower garden in the front of the house and had her sit on a blanket. She then went back into the house and got Glenn and Milton as well as some bread, fruits, and lemonade.

"Feed your son, Ella. He needs you."

Ella complied, not wanting her mother-in-law to think she was a bad mother. The women sat and watched the boys play in the dirt with a stick while Karoline talked to Ella about the bulbs she intended to plant in the fall. It didn't matter if Ella joined the conversation as long as she was being engaged.

Karoline assumed Ella would report Karoline's intentional disregard for the doctor's orders to Tingvald once he returned from farming. But she didn't.

Karoline continued the regimen of getting Ella out of bed each morning and making her become involved in the doings of the day. Sometimes they made bread together; other times they washed and hung laundry. It didn't matter what they did as long as Ella was being involved in daily life with her sons at her feet. Karoline also prepared special dishes for her daughter-in-law, ones with protein and nutrients. She knew fresh-grown fruits and vegetables were healthier than cream and butter.

Eventually, Ella showed signs of coming out of her depression. She spent more time with her children and took an interest in Karoline's daily doings. If it were a nice day, the women went for walks with the children in their arms. They became much closer through discussions of religion and women's roles in the family. Within a few months, she was more herself, completing her daily chores and looking after her children with less prompting from Karoline.

Doctor Christensen came occasionally to check up on her. Once Karoline saw the buggy pull into the front yard, she quickly put Ella back to bed and shut the door. He stayed only a few seconds with Ella each time he came and announced she was improving. When Ella was finally well, the doctor took full credit, spreading word around the area of how he had brought a woman out of her nervousness and into the health of life again.

1913

Alex

Alex continued his affair with Cora for several years. In the beginning, he altered his schedule so he could stay overnight in Sioux City at least twice a month. He and Cora always went to a restaurant and then back to his hotel room. She never stayed the night with him.

After the first year, they saw each other less until eventually he only stayed in Sioux City a few times a year. Occasionally, he met her for lunch when he was visiting for the day. Their relationship dwindled because she was married, and he wouldn't allow himself to become permanently attached to a woman he could never have.

At twenty-five years old, Alex felt his life had gone stagnant. He was no further along in his family life, and his business life had become rather repetitive. He went to the same auctions, met the same farmers, and sold to the same stockyards. For the first time in his life,

Alex was bored.

Therefore, he decided to change his business life. To do that, he would need to talk to his partner, Elfred Svensen. Alex had great respect for Elfred. If it hadn't been for Elfred and his brother Olof, Alex might have been sitting in a chair at his mother's house, thinking about the lives other people lived. Instead, they had mentored him and taught him the business, making him a respected figure in western Iowa agriculture.

Alex wanted to expand their livestock trading and drop the Seed and Feed store. The store didn't bring in nearly as much money and tethered Elfred to the counter full time. If Elfred joined Alex, they could buy and sell at a greater volume, bringing in more income for both of them.

Alex waited until Saturday afternoon, a day when they closed at noon. He invited Elfred into his office and offered him a glass of whiskey. Neither man was a big drinker, but when they had a good day or needed to discuss business matters, they always did it with whiskey. "Elfred," Alex began, "I'd like to talk about the future of this business. I think our business practices need to change. We could make more money if we sold off the Feed and Seed and spent more time with livestock. What do you think?"

"Sold off the Feed and Seed? Why?"

"You spend your days in the store. In the winter, we don't do that much business. We're busier during planting season, obviously. But, if we broke down how much we make hourly with sales at the store versus sales of livestock, I'm bringing in much more money than you are."

"Are you saying you're more valuable than me?" Elfred's face looked indignant.

"No. That's not what I'm saying at all. I'm just saying I bring in more money with what I'm doing than you do with what you're doing."

"So, this is a competition about who brings in the most?" Elfred's voice rose, indicating his anger.

Frustrated with his poor communication skills, Alex said, "Of course it isn't a competition. But I think you could be bringing in more money if you started to work with me."

"Now I'm to be your student? I'm the one who taught you this business. I don't like the way you're talking to me, Alex. You seem to forget how you started in this business. If it hadn't been for Olof and…"

"Elfred, stop. I know all of this. And I've told you many times how grateful I am you both took me into the business and taught me everything I know. I'm not trying to disrespect you. This is all coming out wrong. I'm just saying I want the business to make more money, and I think the Feed and Seed could be sold, so your skills could be put to better use."

"We're done here. I don't appreciate the way you're talking to me, and I certainly don't appreciate the way you've decided to take over the business and make decisions." Elfred put his still-full whiskey glass on the desk and walked out of Alex's office.

Frustrated, Alex sat at his desk, wondering how he had gone so wrong. After replaying the conversation, he realized he shouldn't have been so blunt in his opening statement. He should have led Elfred to the realization that the Seed and Feed didn't bring in nearly enough money for the time spent in the store. Alex should have worked his way into what he wanted or—better yet—he should have allowed Elfred to come to the plan for himself. Elfred was a proud Norwegian man and, like all Norwegians, he was stubborn and didn't like to be told what to do. The best course of action at this point was to leave Elfred alone for a few days and wait for him to come back on his own.

Several days, a week, two weeks—Elfred said nothing about

their conversation; in fact, he was distant and formal with Alex. Alex watched Elfred joke around with the customers and then turn to him and speak in a business tone, one Elfred had never used with Alex before. Their relationship had suffered a setback, and Alex was unsure of how to repair it. His mother knew his partner better than he did. She would know how to mend this situation.

Alex surprised his mother with an afternoon visit: he was usually so busy with work he barely had time to make the Sunday dinners. He found her shelling peas on the front porch—she never seemed to stop working. Alex had never seen his mother without her hands moving: soothing children, making food, milking cows, shelling corn. When he pulled his car up to the house, she looked up, and her face showed surprise. She waited for him to exit the car and sit down in the chair next to hers. "And to what do I owe the honor of seeing my son in the middle of the week?" she asked.

"I have a problem, and I need your advice."

"I'm happy to help you. What is it?"

"I've made Elfred angry, and he won't forgive me so that we can talk about it."

"What did you do?"

"I told him we should sell the Feed and Seed and he should work with me, so we could make more money."

"I see why he's angry. You *told* him; you didn't *ask* him. There's your first mistake. You have no right to speak to an elder that way. And, the second thing you did wrong was suggest to sell the Feed and Seed. That business was started by him and his brother, as you well know. It's all he has left of Olof. You are in the wrong, and you need to drop this and apologize."

"Mama, you don't understand business. If we sold the store and Elfred went into livestock trading with me, we could make a lot more money. Why wouldn't he want to do that?"

"Now, you're being impertinent with me." Her voice raised, and her face started to flush. "You know, Alex, money isn't everything in this world. Most people are happy to live with enough. Enough to put a roof over their heads. Enough to feed their families. Enough to keep them safe. Not everyone needs to drive a car and live in a big house. We raised you better than that."

"*Fadir* never had enough, and he always worked hard for more. He left us to go work on other people's farms just to feed his family. He worked day and night until he worked himself to death. I want something else. I don't want to worry about feeding my family or losing my home. I want to live with some pleasure in my life. What's wrong with wanting a little luxury and a little extra in your pocket? This is America. You and *Fadir* came here to make better lives for yourselves. And, that's what I want—a better life. Elfred is holding me back because of sentiment and stubbornness."

"I don't have any advice for you then. You're becoming someone I don't understand. Your *fadir* and I never stressed money other than what we needed to survive. And he never would have gone against one of his best friends in order to get more. He had his faults, but treating his friends disrespectfully was not one of them. He would be ashamed of you right now."

Alex stood mute, the sting of his mother's last sentence leaving him without words. He wondered why these old people couldn't understand him. Without saying goodbye, Alex turned around and walked back to his car. As he drove away, he neither waved nor looked back. He couldn't believe his own mother had taken Elfred's side against her son. Frustration and anger built inside of him as he drove back to Soldier.

Alex sat at his kitchen table, a cold cup of coffee in front of him, thinking about his predicament. He knew he was right in business decisions. If it weren't for him and his professional savvy, Elfred's tiny store wouldn't have grown to the degree it had. He would still be selling feed and seed to local farmers as well a buying a few animals to send to Sioux City. Alex could see there was no way of changing Elfred's mind, which meant he would have a decision to make. Either he would give up the business and find another way to make money or he would have to settle for his current life. Settling was not his strongest characteristic. Alex decided he would sell off his portion of the business and go out on his own. This would mean he would be in competition with Elfred in livestock purchasing.

Once Alex had formulated his plan, he asked Elfred to meet with him in his office after close on Saturday. Once again, they had glasses of whiskey in front of them. Alex's stomach vibrated with nerves. Instead of laying his request on the table like last time, he would give more background, building the groundwork first.

"Elfred, thank you for meeting with me again. First, I want to apologize for the way I spoke to you. I regret being rude and abrupt with you, and I hated the way we've been with each other since then. Our friendship is very important to me, and I do not want to lose that. You've been an important member of our family since I can remember. You gave me this job and trained me. I wouldn't be where I am today without you."

"Thank you, Alex. I appreciate the apology. I would like to start our last conversation over again. Please continue."

"I've been thinking about what kind of life I want to live. I appreciate everything Soldier has given me, but I would like more. I want to travel overseas. I want a grand house with nice things. I want a refined wife. In order to have these things, I need to make more money than I do now."

"I see. I didn't know this about you. And how do you propose to get all of this money?"

"As I told you last time, I think we could restructure the business.

Since the store doesn't bring in the bulk of our profits, I think we should let it go and spend our time with the livestock trade. I think we could easily bring in five times the profits we do now."

Elfred didn't say anything and proceeded to take out his pocket knife in order to clean his fingernails. Knowing Elfred's habits, Alex sat patiently and waited for a response. Cleaning his nails was always a sign Elfred was doing some serious thinking.

"Alex, I don't want to sell the store. My brother and I started it after we quit farming with your father. Did I ever tell you that Olof designed the layout? Every item on every shelf was decided by him. And I haven't changed one thing since his death. When I look around this building, I see him everywhere. I can't give that up."

"I'm sorry we've come to an impasse, Elfred. I was hoping we could work this out. I don't see any other way than to dissolve the partnership. You can buy me out for a fair price, and I will start my own business. Perhaps another man would want to become your partner? It's a good business. It's stable and provides security."

"*Ja*, maybe. I don't know. That's for another day. Right now, we're talking about dissolving the partnership. I suppose you're going to want more than what you put in."

Alex felt like the conversation was going better than he had hoped. He didn't expect Elfred to give up the store. He hoped for some kind of arrangement, which could be discussed in a calm and businesslike manner. So far, Elfred had remained calm.

"Well, Alex. Let me think about this. How about we both go through the books and come up with what we think is a fair price. Give me a week or so. Fair enough?"

"Thank you, Elfred. Yes, that's more than fair."

Always true to his word, Elfred took exactly one week in order to determine Alex's buyout price. Alex, too, spent the week determining what profits he brought to the business and what was fairly his. With whiskey in front of them again, the men decided to write down their figures and exchange them.

"I'm pleased that we are very close in our numbers," Alex said. "What do you think about splitting the difference down the middle?"

"I think that's fair."

"Good, now that we're done with our business matters, let's drink to our continued friendship." Alex lifted his whiskey glass and held it out to Elfred.

"There's one more thing before we conclude," Elfred said while picking up another piece of paper. "I want you to read this and sign it." He passed the paper to Alex.

Alex couldn't believe what he was reading. Elfred wanted him to give up all the livestock territory. He would have to seek out new customers and build new relationships. "Elfred, I don't think this is fair. I built those territories and fostered relationships with those clients. Those are my clients. Most of them don't even know you. I'm willing to give up the territory adjacent to Soldier Valley, but I'm not giving up the rest of it."

"Well then, we don't have a deal. Those territories belong to this business. The amount I'm spending to buy you out includes the proceeds from those territories; therefore, I'm buying your portion of those. You want all the money and the way to continue to earn it. You are leaving me with only the store. I don't think that's fair."

The two men sat staring at each other. Instead of two friends on the same side of the battlefield, they were now enemies on opposite sides. Leaving his full whiskey glass, Elfred left Alex's office without another word.

Alex needed advice, and this time he was not going to his mother. In fact, he wasn't going to ask anyone in his family. He needed to talk to another business person. Sophie's boss, Walter Ericksen, had also gone through a business split. Ericksen owned the hardware half, and Jakob Tow had owned the grocery portion. Jakob moved away, and the store was then solely owned by Ericksen.

After his impasse with Elfred, Alex left and went directly to Ericksen's store. Walter assumed he had come to see Sophie, who was in the bird's nest. "She's got some tickets to complete, Alex, but she'll be finished in a few minutes if you can wait."

"I came to talk to you, Walter. Do you have some time?"

"*Ja*, sure. Do you want to talk here at the counter or go back to my office?"

"Office, please."

As Alex walked through the store, he watched his sister, who was giving him a quizzical look. His brother-in-law Jack was busy with customers but glanced at him, too, wondering what could bring him into the store.

"Alex, have a seat. Can I get you anything to drink?"

"No, thank you. I've come to talk to you about when you bought out Jakob Tow."

"How's your family? Your mother? I haven't seen her for quite a while."

In his single-mindedness, Alex forgot that Walter liked to start with the socials first. Once that was completed, they got down to the reason for Alex's visit.

"Can you tell me how you and Jakob settled the buyout?"

"Sure. We determined the value of the business by evaluating its stock and building, its future earnings, and the debts we still carried. We came to a total value, and I paid him half."

"Did he have any special conditions? Like, what you could sell or what buyers you could use?"

"No, there was no need. He moved to Minnesota, so it was pretty clean. I don't like to be nosy, but what is this all about?"

Alex explained the situation as well as the negotiations with the amendment. He asked Walter if he thought Elfred was being fair.

"Alex, I've known Elfred since we all settled in Soldier. I've never known him to take advantage of anyone. Those territories were done under that business name. In my mind, they belong to the business. They are future earnings. I have to side with Elfred on this dispute, and not because he's my friend. I think you should let this go… if for no other reason than to retain the relationship. He's a member of your family and has been since your folks moved here. Your family will not side with you on this if it means alienating Elfred. Have you talked to your mother?"

"I have. She's siding with Elfred."

Alex had wanted to find someone who would agree with him. He wanted to be told he was in the right. His best chance was Walter, and not even he would side with Alex.

Alex knew he was on the wrong side of this argument, but his desire for money wouldn't allow him to admit his wrongs. Thinking about how to get around the agreement, Alex came to an idea. If his customers stopped selling their livestock to Elfred, then Alex was not taking customers. They were leaving on their own account, and they would be going to someone other than Elfred. It wasn't his doing if they came to him on their own. Whether they sold to someone else or to Alex, Elfred wasn't getting their business. Alex went back to the store the next day and signed the agreement. Their business dissolved amicably, and the two men finally drank to their friendship.

1913

Floyd

Floyd Olson, the youngest of Karoline's children, was the prince of the family. When he was seven, she gave him his own pony. He named it Lucky, and when he forgot to feed and water his horse, someone in the family always took care of it for him. Unlike his older brother Tingvald, he spent more time in the river with his school friends than he did helping out on the farm. He knew his mother felt bad that he had grown up without a father, and Floyd took advantage of that knowledge.

At eight years old, Floyd considered the farm his kingdom; and he, its king. He turned the chicken coop into his playhouse, and when he broke the eggs throwing them at the cattle, his mother only calmly explained why the eggs were important. If the other children had perpetrated such a crime, they would have received some horrible farm chore for weeks to help them remember the importance of those eggs.

Floyd nearly burned down the hog shed when he was ten. He and a neighbor boy had tried smoking cigars the boy had stolen from his father. One of them dropped a still-lit match into a pile of dried timbers. After seeing fire, both boys ran and hid in the barn. The family was fortunate Sophie had gone to the hog shed to see if the sows had birthed their piglets and, seeing the fire, ran to get help. The family doused the flames, and there was minimal damage to the shed. The brothers and sisters thought Floyd would surely be whipped for such a serious offense, but Karoline only made him help her outside for the next few weeks, something the other children had had to do as part of being in a farm family.

The community often discussed Karoline's last child, the one they called "the devil child." They blamed his behavior on a single mother not being able to raise a child properly. They whispered among themselves that she should have married one of those fine gentlemen—if not for herself, for the sake of her children.

One reason for Floyd's nickname came from his bright red hair, usually too long and definitely unruly. He knew manners but reveled in the shocked faces when he didn't use them. When he learned to make fart noises under his armpit, he often made them during a church service, especially when the minister asked for a quiet moment.

Floyd was also dishonest. When his mother brought him with her into any of the stores, he sometimes was caught pilfering small items. His mother always made him apologize and promise never to steal again. His apology was never heart-felt and was usually followed by a smirk. The community didn't want to hate Floyd, but he was very difficult to like.

To Floyd, the farm only meant work, which he hated. His brother Tingvald tried to take him to the fields so he could learn the trade, but Floyd resisted, finding excuses to stave off his brother. Sometimes his stomach hurt. Sometimes he had a lame foot and limped around for several days. Tingvald grew frustrated his mother never seemed to make Floyd do anything. When Tingvald was six, his father had taken him to the fields to work and to learn. Floyd would one day help run the farm, and he would need to start learning the business at an early age.

Floyd didn't want to learn the business; he wanted excitement. Plowing dirt and planting seeds bored him to sleep. He would rather do anything other than come home dirty every day, having walked behind a horse, back and forth across dirt. Floyd wanted to be a race-car driver or a motorcycle stuntman. He wanted to travel. He wanted to be famous. He couldn't decide on his occupation, but he knew he would never farm.

1915

Floyd

Iowa's conservative nature had started at its inception in 1847, the legislature restricting alcohol through licensing. In 1882, it went a step further and passed a total prohibition law, which was later struck down by the Iowa Supreme Court but then reinstated the following year with the power of prohibition in the hands of each county. Its women, Annie Wittenmyer and Ida B. Wise, fought tirelessly to keep the state's residents from imbibing the evil drink. Its famous son, Billy Sunday of Nevada, railed against the ills of alcohol from his pulpit.

Now, rumors of prohibition again drifted through Iowa. The state legislature, a conservative group of men, had been discussing making alcohol illegal state-wide. Each year, the topic came up but didn't make it through funnel week. This year, however, those gentlemen guaranteed their constituents they would make sure it not only made it through funnel week but would be passed in both houses. Many of them ran on the prohibition platform. They didn't dare go back on their word, or their seat in state government would be filled by another man's backside the next time they came up for election. Governor George Clarke guaranteed he would sign it. Prohibition, their panacea for the ills of society, was the most important issue of the 1915 Iowa legislative session.

Floyd overheard his brothers talk about its definite passage and saw his chance of visiting a saloon slipping away. He saw the saloon as the icon of manhood. Men standing up to a bar, drinking and discussing the day's business, was the modern-day Camelot. He had been waiting for his sixteenth birthday, four years away, hoping he would look old enough for the bartender to consider him "close enough." If the law passed, Floyd would never put his belly up to the bar; there would be no chance for any man to drink.

Floyd always followed the policy of doing and then asking for forgiveness, often forgetting the forgiveness part. He just wanted to see the inside of the saloon and perhaps get a drink of beer. Even if the bartender wouldn't serve him, surely some man would pity him and give him a few sips. He waited until his mother needed to go to town for some shopping. Uncharacteristically, he volunteered to go with her.

Once in town, Floyd lied to his mother, telling her he wanted to do some looking on his own. The holidays were coming closer, and he had some shopping to do. As soon as she entered the butcher's shop, he headed toward the Soldier Saloon.

Stepping inside, Floyd's eyes drank in his surroundings. The interior was dim, hiding the Christian drinkers in the corner. On his left, running along a good portion of the wall, stood a solid bar and a matching back bar, each made of oak. For the grown men, the serving bar hit the bottom of their ribs, allowing them to rest their elbows;

but for Floyd, if he stood at the bar, he would just be able to put his chin on the wood. A brass foot rail ran along the bottom of the bar, shined each week by the owner. Floyd looked at an ornate mirror decorating the back bar, reflecting the multi-colored bottles of liquor lining the shelves.

Signs, photos, and relics covered the walls. The owner, an avid hunter, proudly displayed his kills: heads of bear, deer, and elk. An old horse collar from his farming days hung directly in the center of the back bar. A very unusual sign—"All gamblers and fancy women must sign up with the captain before the boat leaves for New Orleans"—hung off to the side of the bar. Floyd didn't understand it, but he thought there must be something entertaining about its content.

Floyd stood inside the entrance of the bar, just looking at all there was to see, his eyes adjusting to the dim light. No one paid attention to him. The patrons, lined up at the bar like birds on a fence, were discussing life with one another; others, sitting at tables, were drinking alone and minding their own business. The bartender didn't see Floyd for a few minutes, but he eventually looked toward the door. "Hey, kid, you can't be in here. Where's your father? If he's in here, you'll still need to leave."

The patrons, hearing the bartender, looked over at Floyd. One of them said, "That's the Olson kid; he doesn't have a father. Just leave him alone, Clint. He's not hurting nobody. I'll buy him a Coca Cola."

"Art, mind your own drinking. He's not to be in here. If the boss sees him drinking anything in here, I'll lose my job."

Floyd stood still, waiting to see which side would win.

"Hey, you," another patron yelled over to him, "what'cha doin' in here? You know this ain't for kids."

With nothing to lose, Floyd decided to apply his charm. "I want the same as you all. A man just wants a drink once in a while."

The bar crowd broke out into laughter. Even the bartender showed a smirk with Floyd's clever comeback.

"How about one of you gents let me have a little beer before none of us can gather around here to drink together again?" Floyd asked.

His reference to the impending prohibition law set off the men. Angry words and curses for the legislators erupted from several of them. What would become of their saloon? Wasn't a man old enough to make his decision about what went into his body? Why did those legislators have the right to tell him how to live his life?

Floyd stood, listening to their arguments. Even without a drink, he felt like he was one of them.

Art, his first advocate, finally remembered the kid standing there, waiting to see if he would be served. "Clint, let me buy him his first—and maybe last—beer. The kid should know the taste of a fine ale among male friends." Pulling up a stool, he said, "Come here, kid, and take a stool. What's your name?"

"Thank you. The name's Floyd," he said, struggling to get settled onto the stool.

"You are Karoline Olsen's kid, right? You kind of look like her."

"Yah. I'm her youngest," he replied with a grin.

Clint finally relented, seeing he was against a wave of supporters. He poured a glass of amber beer and set it in front of Floyd, the beer foam running down the side of the glass. "Drink up, kid."

Floyd lifted the glass toward his fellow drinkers as a salute and then took a long drink. He could never have imagined what it tasted like, but he found it smooth and a bit bitter. He took another drink, wiping the suds from his lips.

As the other men settled back into their conversations, Floyd started to check out the other drinkers. Some sat by themselves at a table; others sat with companions.

Suddenly, the door opened, letting in bright light. A boy of about fourteen or fifteen walked through the bar and headed to the back. When he opened a door on the back wall, Floyd could see men sitting around a table with cards in their hands. No one else in the establishment paid attention to the boy or looked at the back room. Floyd wondered about the boy, who had something to do with the men playing cards in that room.

Before Floyd could go back to the conversation around him, the door opened again, but this time a woman's voice came from the bright light. "Floyd, get off that stool and come out here immediately before I whoop you!" his mother yelled.

The men hooted at him and told him to mind his mama. His face blushed pink, embarrassed to be treated as a child in front of his new male colleagues. He knew his mother was putting on a tough show; she would never lay a hand on him.

"See ya, gents," he said, waving goodbye to them. He could hear them belly laughing as he walked out the door.

His mother, angrier than he had seen for some time, grabbed him by the elbow, her fingers digging into his skin, muscle, and bone. She pulled him down the street while townspeople gave approving nods. "Why in the world did you go to the saloon? That's no place for a twelve-year-old boy."

"Had to know what it was like to be a man before alcohol became illegal. Don't get your bloomers in a knot!"

Her face turned red with rage and indignation. For the first time in her life, she laid a hand on one of her children. She slapped him along the back of his head.

Floyd was surprised, but not in pain. *She'll settle down in time,* he thought.

1915

Alex

Alex had agreed to stay out of Elfred's territory for cattle buying, which he technically did. He did not approach Elfred's customers. He did not visit their farms. He simply waited until either Elfred or his new associate showed up to buy their cattle, and his customers called him to ask why there was someone new. Alex explained the business split and suggested they send their business elsewhere—meaning, him.

Alex set up his new office a block over from the Feed and Seed. He bought comfortable lounge chairs covered in soft leather, copies of Matisse and Picasso paintings, and a large mahogany desk that took up much of the room. He even installed a modern telephone. He hired a young man to do exactly what he used to do when he was in high school, adding ticket sales and running errands.

Quietly, slowly, one after another, Alex took back most of his customers. He kept his word and didn't step foot on Elfred's domain. Instead, he used his telephone. With most people now using the device and the stock yards definitely doing business via phone, Alex no longer needed to leave his office. He sat behind his desk and made money.

Once a month, Alex traveled farther outside of his usual territory and met new farmers. He had gotten as far as Waukee to the east. He enjoyed traveling east because Waukee was close to Des Moines, which meant he could revisit the Hotel Kirkwood. While in the city, Alex ate at the best restaurants, visited the upscale saloons, and spent time in the upper-class brothels.

With his former clients and his new clients, Alex made more money in one month than he had in one year when he partnered with Elfred. He purchased new clothes and an expensive car. He certainly was the showiest and most dapper man in the county. He had not yet bought a house of his own, thinking a wife would want to pick out something with him.

His money piled up in his bank account. Along with trading livestock, Alex also traded other stocks. He stayed mostly with agriculture commodities since that's where his expertise lay, but he also put some money into railroad and oil stocks. Whatever he touched turned gold and made him more money.

A year after the business split, Elfred came to Alex's new office and confronted him about stealing his customers.

"Alex, you broke our agreement. You've been taking from my territory!" Elfred Svensen was rarely angry, but today his face matched the inside of watermelon. "I can't believe you lied to me!"

"Elfred, I've never stepped foot into your territory. If my old clients want to follow me, it's not my fault." As he said the words, Alex could hear how feeble his rationale sounded.

"I never thought you could be so underhanded. I didn't know I was partner to a *liar* and a *thief!*" Elfred was standing and pointing his finger right into Alex's face. With those words, *liar* and *thief*, Elfred struck Alex's chest with that finger. "I want you to give those clients back to me."

"Elfred, I'm not giving those clients back because they don't want to sell to you. I told you that when I suggested you go out with me. They don't know you or your new man."

"Your father would knock you to next Sunday if he were alive. He was as honest as the day is long." Elfred then turned around and walked out the door, slamming it behind him. The glass rattled and nearly broke.

Alex felt bad about the argument. He knew he was in the wrong, but he tempered his guilt by telling himself business wasn't personal. He still felt the same affection for Elfred as their family friend, but as a competitor, he felt nothing for him—or so he told himself.

With his expanded business, Alex had less time for his family. He missed most of the Sunday dinners and rarely saw his siblings. He purposely avoided his mother. He didn't want to hear her thoughts on the way he was spending money or the way he had treated their friend Elfred. Because he didn't go to the house, he didn't have the opportunity to visit Tingvald or his children. If he were driving by one of Tingvald's fields, he would stop his car, honk his horn, and wait for his brother to come to the car. They talked mostly of corn and cattle prices, but Alex always enjoyed seeing his older brother.

Several months after the fight with Elfred, his mother walked into his office. She stood in front of his desk, her hands on her hips. That stance was never a good sign. She stood silent, waiting for him to offer her a chair.

Alex rarely stood when someone came into his office: his prosthetic foot was unusable, and he needed his crutches to stand. This time, however, he made the effort to stand out of respect for his mother. Alex offered her one of his comfortable chairs and asked innocently, "Mama, to what do I owe the pleasure of your visit?" He knew exactly why she had come.

Declining to sit, Karoline said, "First, I wanted to make sure you were still alive. I haven't seen you for several months. I thought perhaps you had perished. And, second, I have no idea who you have become. You have treated our dearest friend—no, you have treated our family member—like some stranger. I have lost all respect for you, Alex. I want you to make amends with Elfred."

Because his mother had declined to sit, Alex was forced to continue standing even though he was uncomfortable. "Mama, you need to stay out of my business. This is between me and Elfred. This is not a family matter. And, I cannot give Elfred what he wants. Those clients don't know him and don't want to do business with him."

"And, why is that? Because you encouraged them to leave his business and sell to you?" Karoline stood staring into Alex's eyes, and then she quickly turned around and left the office, the door standing open.

Alex was irritated with his mother's intrusion. She didn't understand business matters and had no call to barge in on him and try to make him do as she said. A twenty-seven-year-old man didn't need to be chastised by his mother and told what he should do. He thought she should stick to what she knew best: raising flowers and children. And he was no longer a child.

Alex believed this feud with Elfred would eventually blow over. Elfred would come to his senses and make peace with him. Alex would continue to keep his clients from the old days but add no new ones from that territory even if they sought him out. He would focus on his new territories and build his empire. His decision to turn away new clients from Elfred's area made him feel like he was doing his best by Elfred.

With his new business doing well, there was only one thing missing from his life—a family. Alex decided it was time to seriously court an available woman and make her his wife. He wanted one who came from a wealthy family and had class and culture. He essentially wanted another Cora but one who was not already married. He wouldn't find that type of woman in Soldier. He needed to go to a larger city. He thought about Chicago since he was there frequently on business; however, he wasn't sure a woman from Chicago would be happy in this tiny town with few to no cultural events. He didn't want to go back to Sioux City: the social circle was very small with Cora knowing every available woman. This meant going to either Omaha or Des Moines. Omaha was a large agricultural city, which gave him a chance to get business done while also attending social events. Des Moines, though not as agricultural, was an Iowa city, which meant the woman would be used to what Iowa offered and didn't offer.

Several weeks after Alex had made his decision to actively pursue a wife, he planned a trip to Des Moines. He sought out his favorite place to lodge, the Hotel Kirkwood. In order to meet cultured women, he attended cultural events. Near the hotel stood the Princess Theater, a three-story white-washed brick structure. It had a green roof and a matching green awning. Passersby couldn't miss the structure with its large **Princess** sign affixed perpendicular to the building. On the awning, a sign attached to it advertised a new play, "The Man from Mexico," starring Margaret Lawrence and Conrad Nagel. Alex asked the concierge to purchase the second-most expensive ticket, which put him on the parquet, the main floor. He could have gotten box seats, but then he would be secluded from the other theater goers.

Alex dressed in his best suit, black with a crisp white shirt, and walked the block to the play. Upon entering the doors, he was brought into a lobby, which displayed artwork on its walls. As he stood viewing different pieces, several young women with their families came to view the art alongside of him.

One particular young woman caught his eye. She was tall with blonde hair and high cheek bones. Her emerald green dress brought out the green in her eyes. She looked to be about eighteen years old. Alex sidled alongside her father and introduced himself. Oscar Nilsson and Alex struck up a conversation about stocks and bonds, and Alex made sure to insert his line of business, trying to make an impression. At one point, he caught the young woman's eye and nodded at her.

Once escorted to his seat by the attendee, Alex watched the first half of the play. While he enjoyed the acting and plotline, he continued to think about the young woman. She was a good age and came from Nordic roots, Swedish not Norwegian, which his mother would still appreciate. Her father was a stock broker and seemed to make a good living, which was deduced by the family's attire and their box seats.

During the intermission, Alex purchased a glass of wine and continued to enjoy the artwork, hoping he would see the Nilsson family in the lobby again. As he scanned the crowd, he saw Mr. Nilsson with his daughter looking at a local piece of art. He went over to them and stood next to the daughter. "I'm sorry, miss. I haven't introduced myself. My name is Alex Olson. And, may I know your name?"

"Anna Nilsson," she replied, looking straight into his face with her large green eyes, then glancing at the crutches beneath his arms.

Alex saw her looking and decided to explain his situation so, if she were to reject him because of it, she would reject him immediately, and he could move on to another woman. "I see that you've noticed my crutches, of course. When I was a child, I was trampled and had to have my foot removed. I'm quite used to it now."

Anna blushed bright pink because she had been rude enough to be staring. "I'm so sorry for my poor manners. Please forgive me." She quickly shifted the topic and asked, "How are you enjoying the play?"

"There is nothing to forgive, and I like the play quite a bit. And, you?"

"Well enough. But, it's not Shakespeare. I love Shakespeare plays the best. Have you ever seen one?"

Once again, Alex found himself without enough culture. As much as he had read and studied, there was still so much more he needed to learn. "No, I'm sorry to say that I haven't. I would like to see one since you give such high praise."

"There is one next month. 'A Midsummer Night's Dream.' It's here. My family is planning to attend. Perhaps we'll see you then?"

Her invitation indicated to Alex she would not reject him because of his disability—at least not yet. "Perhaps you will."

At that point, Anna's father finished his conversation with another man and turned to escort her back to their seats. Alex saw no point in staying for the remainder of the play since he had accomplished his goal. He would go back to his hotel room and enjoy some whiskey and a cigar. His troubles with Elfred and his mother had not even entered his mind in his single pursuit of a wife.

1916

Ingrid

Ingrid and the other Olson women marked special occasions by going to Denison. Today was Karoline's fifty-second birthday, and Ingrid was accompanied by Karoline, Betsi, and Sophie.

Each woman was smartly dressed for this special day out. Each daughter wore the latest fashion, a dress with layered fabric; long, gauzy sleeves; and a high neckline. Their skirt lengths were fashionable, hitting just above their boots. They were all thankful not to have petticoats underneath, which not only bulked their figures but also made them hot. To compliment her dress, each woman had worn her prettiest hat, some with feathers and wide brims and some without sculpting to fit closer to her head.

Karoline didn't keep up with the younger women in their fashions, believing it wasn't appropriate for a woman her age to try to look young again. She wore her usual black skirt and matching black jacket. Her skirt length hit the ground, covering up her footwear. However, she had always loved hats and was wearing a new one with a wide brim that shadowed her face when she looked down. It had a smart red feather in the brim, which made Karoline feel rather lively on her birthday.

Karoline's skin was wrinkled and tanned from the sun. Her hair was mostly grey, but she still wore it up in a bun or braided and wrapped around her head. She had gained weight, but a woman who had birthed and nursed many children did not often keep her figure. Karoline's mind was sharp, and her body was as limber as it was in her 30s.

The women started early that morning. They had borrowed Alex's new automobile. He had purchased a dark green Cadillac Town Car with a black top, which fashionably matched its black wheels and running boards. Betsi had learned to drive it even though she and Lars had yet to purchase a car for themselves.

As she walked down the wooden sidewalk, Karoline thought about the two weeks it had taken her to traverse the state in a wagon with Kristoffer's body. If she had had an auto, she would have made it home before his body became unrecognizable with decay.

She also remembered stopping in Denison on her return to rest before her final push home. She had eaten at Koch's Café on Broadway; however, it was no longer there. Someone had purchased it and turned it into a pharmacy. Surprisingly, many of the stores had changed since her visit twelve years ago. There were two banks, instead of one. Many more mercantile stores could be found on Broadway and Main.

Denison had exploded in those twelve years, becoming one of the main hubs of western Iowa. Their school system, now two buildings with a fairly new high school on the east side of town, had added a Manual Training Department in 1908 and a Commercial Department this new school year. Denison students were fortunate in being able to be trained for any number of business jobs: shorthand, typewriting, bookkeeping. Karoline felt sad her children had not had all these opportunities.

The ladies began their shopping day by patronizing The Boys, a store with various merchandise, including ready-made clothing items. They were having a sale on coats. The October chill indicated the need for winter coats for themselves and their children. Children's coats sold for $1.98, and women's coats—which were usually $10.00— were on sale for $4.98. With those prices, they could afford to buy new ones for the older children and hand down their coats to the younger children. Betsi also needed new waist shirts, which were also $1.98. She had saved her egg money all summer for these fall sales.

As much as they hated wearing corsets, the women agreed they were necessary. The Ballo Brodersen Company, just down Broadway from The Boys, had a sale on them, $2.00 each, down from $2.50. Sophie thought it a shame something so expensive was not put on the outside for public admiration.

As they walked farther down Broadway, the women discussed the pleasure of being able to buy ready-made clothing. Karoline reminisced on how many nights she had sat up late, sewing clothes for the family. Now, it was less expensive to buy them on sale than to buy the material for them and spend the time making them.

On their way to eat lunch, they passed the same portrait studio where Sophie had had her picture made, but the ownership had changed hands. The girls convinced Karoline to have her portrait made after lunch. Even though Karoline thought it was very egotistical to have one's likeness on photographic paper, she agreed in order to please the girls.

Their arms loaded with purchases, they unanimously voted to eat lunch at The Kitchen Cupboard, a small café on south Main. They did not often eat out since they had food at home, and there was no reason to pay someone to cook something for them. However, since it was a celebration day, they were treating their mother to something special.

Upon entering the café, the women found a table for six in the center of the room. The interior of the café delighted them. The large windows facing Main let in bright light. Hung upon the walls were black and white sketches of the town and surrounding countryside. Red and white checked cloths covered the small tables. A fresh flower sat atop each table, theirs a wild rose, the state flower. The smell of freshly baked bread wafted through the café. The tables were completely filled with business people and other shoppers.

Handwritten menus sat in each spot on the table, indicating the day's set meals: one for breakfast, one for lunch, and one for dinner. The lunch menu was creamed dried beef, baked stuffed potatoes, and shredded pineapple. The women looked the menu over even though there was no choice in what they would order.

The waitress, a rather large woman with ruddy cheeks, her grey hair pulled tight into a bun, and dirty apron around her waist, came to their table to take their drink orders.

Karoline, whose spoken English was poor, didn't read it any better. She didn't understand there was only one choice for lunch. She looked at the three meals on the sheet and thought she needed to order one of those. In her confusion, she turned to Ingrid for help.

"Do I order one of these?" she asked in Norwegian, pointing to the three selections on the menu.

"*Nei, Mor. De serverer biff I dag,*" Ingrid explained.

The waitress, who had come to the table with a smile on her face, suddenly looked at the group with a hard stare. As Ingrid looked around the restaurant, she noticed all conversations had stopped. Diners were no longer eating but staring at them.

"We don't serve Germans here. You'll need to leave," the waitress rudely commanded in a loud voice.

Ingrid, confused, explained, "We aren't German. We're Norwegian. My mother's English is limited. She came from the old country."

"She needs to learn to talk English. And I don't care what you are. You'll need to leave."

With her usual quick temper, Betsi replied in a rather loud voice, "She said we're Norwegian. That's not German, and we'll stay to eat here," stressing the word *here*.

"Like I said, I'm not serving you. You can sit here and die of hunger if you like. But no one in this establishment is going to help you. I suggest you leave and find somewhere else to eat."

With those last words, the waitress turned around and went into the kitchen.

Confused and embarrassed, the women looked around the café. The patrons glared at them with hostile looks. They were waiting to see if the women would leave.

"What do we do now?" Sofie asked. "Should we just leave?"

Betsi, still angry at the exchange, replied, "They have to serve us. We've done nothing wrong."

Karoline replied, "I don't want to make a scene. Please, no more arguing."

Having no other choice, the women got up from the table. As they walked through the café, the patrons followed them with their eyes until they reached the door. They heard one man call them "Krauts" as they were walking by. Once they exited the door, they started walking toward their automobile.

"We'll eat in Soldier," Ingrid said. "At least we know we'll be served by our own people who know Norway is not Germany. You realize that woman didn't even know the difference between the two countries and didn't want to admit she had made a mistake."

"Did you see the way the other people looked at us? Like they hated us!" Sophie said.

"What about going to the studio for Mama's picture?" Ingrid reminded the group.

"Please, I would like to go home," Karoline requested. "I want to get back amongst my people where I am comfortable speaking my native language. We'll have it made another time."

***

When Stefan returned from his day's work, Ingrid relayed the incident at the café.

"Ingrid," he said, "you haven't been paying attention to what has been going on around you. Have you heard of the county Council of Defense?"

"No. What is that?"

"Each county has a group who encourage citizens to be patriotic. At least that's what they are supposed to do. But being patriotic has turned into spying on your neighbor. If you see German activity, you are to report it to this Council of Defense."

"We don't have many Germans in Soldier. There wouldn't be anything to report."

"They aren't just reporting German activity. Anyone who speaks a language that sounds German is also being reported. Just like that woman in the café today. She probably reported the incident to the Crawford County Council of Defense. She thought you were speaking German. I doubt she believed you when you told her it was Norwegian. People are making mistakes like that all the time. When I was at the Feed and Seed, the men were talking about incidents like yours happening across Iowa."

"Like what?" Ingrid couldn't imagine anyone being unkind to another person, especially an immigrant.

"A pastor was jailed for speaking Swedish at a funeral. The parents of the soldier didn't speak English, so he spoke their home language. It wasn't German, Ingrid. Just like today. I think you were lucky nothing happened to you. I don't want you speaking Norwegian any more. Your mother needs to stay in town and shop where people know her."

"What kind of world do we now live in where people treat each other this way?"

Like many Midwestern states, Iowa had been settled by poor immigrants looking for land to carve out a farm. They settled in areas where their own had already established themselves. Even though they all called themselves Iowans, they were more of a patch-quilt, each square sitting alongside the next but very different in content. These pockets of secluded countrymen viewed those not like themselves as "others." It took generations for them to marry together, speak English together, and see themselves as no longer German or Norwegian or Irish, but as American. Until such time, prejudice could show itself in times of stress.

Stefan continued, "I heard they actually jailed an elderly woman for speaking German. I'm sure they know she's not a spy. Like your mother, she just doesn't speak English very well. All of those first-generation immigrants hardly speak English."

"You know it is important to my mother we teach the children Norwegian. If we don't speak it, they'll forget what they already know. Can't we just speak it at her house and at home?"

"I don't think that's wise. We need to stress to the children they only speak English. It's too hard for them to sort out when they can speak Norwegian and when they can't. Unfortunately, your mother will understand a little less of what her grandchildren are saying. But we must think of the next generation. This isn't going to be easy for anyone. And if you think that's the worst, then I'm sorry to tell you more is coming. We haven't even gotten into the war yet."

"Do you think we'll eventually join the conflict?"

"I don't know. I've been thinking about what will happen to me if we do," Stefan admitted.

1918

Ingrid

Ingrid never believed a war on the other side of the world would come to them. Their farm in western Iowa seemed so isolated and far away from the conflict. Even though the papers had been full of news from Europe, President Wilson's reluctance to enter the war had given her a sense of security.

When the Selective Service Act was passed by Congress, Ingrid still wasn't terribly worried about Stefan being drafted into the army. He was thirty-eight as well as a farmer. They were only drafting men up to twenty-one. The army would probably never take anyone as old as Stefan, and farmers were essential workers and had deferment. He also had a family to provide for. All these conditions would surely insulate him from war.

Ingrid's family had thankfully also escaped the draft. Tingvald, like Stefan, was too old and also farmed. Alex had a missing foot.

And Floyd was only fourteen. No one in her family needed to worry about dying in the war.

Some of her neighbors, like Kristina Jorgensen, her mother's friend, had children who were also too old for the draft. Kristina's son Halstein was twenty-nine and had five children.

Other young men, though, were conscripted. There were six Olsons, unrelated to Ingrid's family, who would join, as well as all three Dickenson brothers. Her brother's friend, John Hedum, would also be required to show up for his registration date. Even though Soldier was a small community, it was being asked to do its part in this war.

Ingrid and Stefan went about their daily lives, farming and raising children. They, like many others, suffered shortages. Because there were many servicemen to feed overseas, Americans were asked to conserve food. The Food Administration encouraged meatless Mondays and eating potatoes instead of wheat.

Because the Olsons were farmers and had a large garden and animals, they could provide their own meat, milk, eggs, and vegetables. However, they wanted to be good Americans and do their part. The worst rationing they had to endure was sugar and flour. Instead of baking the usual sweets each Saturday, Ingrid and her daughter Mary came up with different ways to make desserts. Women shared recipes to help each other get through the war years. They made molasses gingerbread and applesauce cake. The government even put out a recipe called Trench Cake. It had currants, cocoa, nutmeg, ginger, and brown sugar instead of white. Women baked it and sent it to their soldiers in the trenches.

Canning fruits took a little more ingenuity. Fruits and berries took an abundance of sugar in the canning process. *The Extension Farm News* recommended a pint of sugar with a gallon of water in which to pack the fruit and berries. The *Extension* also recommended sugar replacements like corn syrup and sorghum. The fruit wouldn't be as sweet, but it would do.

Ingrid didn't mind the sacrifices she needed to make as long as she wasn't sacrificing a family member.

Just when Ingrid felt secure in her western Iowa nest, the government announced the draft in September 1918, for men up to forty-five years old. Stefan and Tingvald were required to go to the draft office located in the county seat; for Monona County, that was Onawa. Neither the men nor their wives were overly worried. Both being farmers, this was only a formality. The men would register, and then they would receive their deferment.

In sisterly solidarity, Ingrid went to her mother's house to sit with Ella, Tingvald's wife. They kept themselves busy by working on a quilt. While they quilted, the women talked about the war, those who had been drafted, and their own men who would be safe. Even though all three spoke with confidence, Ingrid couldn't help but feel a knot in her stomach. Until Stefan came home with his deferment papers, she would never feel completely safe.

By mid-afternoon, the men returned. When they walked in the door, their faces, serious and worried, told Ingrid the morning hadn't gone well.

"What happened?" Karoline asked before they could even take off their hats.

"I didn't get deferment," Stefan answered. "I'll need to report for a physical and then prepare to be shipped out for training camp."

Ingrid's stomach turned to water. Her chest tightened. "What happened? Do they know you are a farmer? What about Tingvald?"

Tingvald answered for Stefan. "They used farm tax records. When we paid off the loan on the farm, we changed the ownership to me and Mother. We never formally sat down as a family and worked out how much of the land was Stefan's. We've just been allowing him to take a portion of the profits and losses each year. Since his name is not on the land, they said he is technically a farm worker. They need him for the war more than they need him as a farm worker. I got a deferment."

Ingrid cried out, "You can't work the farm without his help! Did you tell them that? Did you explain the situation?"

"I did. Ingrid, we tried to get them to listen to us, but they're desperate for men right now."

"Would it help if I went with you?" Karoline offered.

"No, Mama. It would make it worse. Your limited English is only going to make them suspicious. I'm sorry, but I don't think there is anything to do at this point, except pray," Tingvald concluded.

"This isn't right. What can we do?" Ingrid had not given up on Stefan getting a deferment.

"Ingrid, there is nothing to do. I was not the only one in this situation. As we sat and waited our turn, we could hear other men arguing with those in charge. There is no leniency," Stefan explained.

Feeling defeated, Ingrid asked, "When do you have to leave?"

"I report for my physical in two days. If I pass that, then they'll tell me when I ship out for training."

Ingrid, only hours before, had felt sure her husband would never be sent to war. And now, it was happening to her and her children. Worry marched in and camped in her stomach.

"Where will you go for training?" asked Karoline, hoping it would be close to home.

"Camp Gordon in Georgia. We'll be transported by train."

"Why are they sending you so far away?" asked Ingrid. "Why wouldn't you train in Iowa? The papers say men are training in Des Moines at Camp Dodge. This doesn't make any sense." Frustrated, Ingrid could feel herself losing again. First, he had to go to war, and now he would be far away from them.

"I don't know. I am just telling you what they told me." Even though Stefan was trying to sound brave, Ingrid could hear the worry in his voice.

The family stood with eyes down, thinking about what this might mean for Stefan and Ingrid. Every day, they had looked at the lists of men in the *Soldier Sentinel*, men who had died in combat. Some of them were still boys, having just turned eighteen. Their whole lives—marriage, children, grandchildren—had been ahead of them, but now they were buried somewhere far away from home.

Stefan wanted to be patriotic and support his country, but he had a family who needed him more.

1918

Ingrid

Stefan shipped out for Camp Gordon on July 25 with his entire family at the railway depot. Karoline held him, her arms wrapped tightly around her son-in-law, reluctant to let him go. She put a basket of food in his hands for the train ride. When she reached around him for one last hug, she said, "*Jeg elsker deg.*" Karoline had never told Stefan she loved him, but she had such a foreboding feeling about his leaving she needed to tell him her true feelings.

Each brother shook his hand and patted him on the back. Each said "good luck" and told him they were sure he would be coming home soon.

The nieces and nephews also hugged him, some not truly under-standing his destination.

Stefan's mother, brother, and father stood among the Olson clan. His mother cried when she let go of his hand. His father gave him a hug and shook his hand. And his brother gave him a manly handshake and wished him well. With such a small family, his absence would be deeply felt.

Ingrid, Samuel, and Mary were the last to say goodbye. Stefan hugged and kissed each one of his children. He made Samuel, now fifteen, the man of the house. He would be taking his father's place alongside Tingvald on the farm. "Do your work well," he said. "You are replacing me, and Tingvald is counting on you."

Mary, a year older than her brother, was told to help her mother without complaining or arguing. "She will need you much more," Stefan reminded his daughter.

Even though Ingrid and Stefan had talked long into the night and made promises to each other, they couldn't resist one last goodbye.

"Please be safe," Ingrid begged. "And write to me as soon as you get to Georgia."

"You know I will. I'll come home again. You'll see. We'll write letters to each other. I'll let you know when I ship out. Tell me everything about the children, the doings of the family, and the gossip from town. I want to feel like I'm home again. I love you."

With a last wave to the family, Stefan boarded the train with the rest of the soldiers from Soldier.

***

Alex, who always brought the mail from the post office, handed Ingrid her first letter from Stefan, sent a few weeks after he arrived in Georgia.

25 July 1918

My dearest wife Ingrid,

I safely made it to Georgia, and my first impression is that it is very hot and humid. I know we've seen some scorching summers in Iowa, but there is nothing as bad as this. No matter how much water I drink, I can't seem to get enough of it. Other than being thirsty, I am doing well.

We drill all day long. I can't go into detail because I am not supposed to include any military operations in case any Germans get ahold of my letter.

How are the children? Has Samuel been helping my brother? Is Mary helpful around the house? Tell them I miss them terribly and look forward to seeing them again.

This camp is very unusual because the men here are not all Iowans. There are men from all states. Our division is the 82nd, and we are called the "All-American" division because the men are from across America. The men from the Southern states are very friendly. I have mostly remained with those from our state.

We will be embarking from Boston in a few weeks. We will land in England (I can't tell you which town), and from there we will join the war.

I know you worry about me every day. I'll be fine. Continue to write me letters. I love hearing the town's gossip. Kiss the children for me.

Your Faithful Husband,

Stefan

Even though she was fearful of him going overseas, she could at least rest easier in the knowledge that, for now, he was safe and healthy. After she finished reading the letter, she shared it with her children and then walked to her mother's house to share it with the rest of the family.

Ingrid tried to imagine his days of marching and carrying a gun. She felt Stefan would do well in shooting practice. He and his father had hunted the hills often. Ingrid had plucked many pheasants in the fall and had eaten deer meat in the winter.

Ingrid received several short letters from him before he shipped overseas. There wasn't much change in his daily activity. He was mostly wanting news from home, which she provided.

Once he shipped out, she didn't receive anything from him. Her brain told her it would take a while for the troops to settle. The mail from the front line would be slow. But her stomach was a constant knot of worry. Waiting for each letter made her days drag by. Finally, the first letter from the front came to her; she read it over and over.

12 September 1918

Dearest Ingrid,

How are you and the children? I miss all of you so badly. I hope my family is doing well. I've written several times to them. My mother is constantly worried about me. I think she has the entire church praying for me specifically. If you get a chance, I would like you to visit her.

We arrived in LeHavre, France. It is so beautiful here: it's a shame the landscape is ruined with shelling. I look at all of this beauty and wonder if it will ever look the same again.

The French are very welcoming. They are so thankful to see us here because they know we are kicking the Germans out of their country. They offer us food when they can. I hate to take it because I know they have so little. I wish I spoke French, so I could learn a little about them.

I do miss your cooking. Now that we're on the front line, the food is terrible. We usually eat tinned meat and biscuits so hard I could use them to pound in a nail. Sometimes we are given bread and jam. I enjoy this the most, but the bread is usually stale by the time it makes it to the front. I find myself eating all the food anyway and pretending it is one of your mother's famous Sunday dinners.

The conditions aren't much better. When I sleep, I sleep in mud. My feet are constantly damp, and I'm dirty all the time. I've been told I'm lucky to be here in the summer. In the winter months, the soldiers have been extremely cold, some of them losing toes from frostbite. There are rats as big as cats running through the trenches. Many of the men also have lice. I'm pretty sure I do as well. I laugh at this because my mother was so diligent in making sure none of us came home from school with lice.

My biggest complaint is the boredom. I'm getting to know my comrades really well because we have so much time to talk. I've told them all about western Iowa living. I have described hunting in the Loess Hills as a boy. I describe your cooking all the time. Their mouths water as I give details of every smell and flavor, and then they finally yell at me to stop. When I return, I never want to see canned beef again. I want my first meal to be those delicious meatballs your mother taught all you girls to make. I think about them often. Mostly the boys and I play cards and gamble. Please don't tell Mother Karoline. I know how she feels about that. But, there isn't much else to do.

Give each of my children a kiss and hug from their father. Tell your family I think of them often.

All my love,
Stefan

At their Sunday dinner, the family looked on the map for Le Havre. It sat on the coast of France, adjacent to the English Channel. The family assumed he had been shipped to England first and then brought by boat to France. Stefan had told Ingrid nothing of his route, following protocol for keeping troop movements secret.

That was the last letter Ingrid received from Stefan for nearly three months. She checked the list of soldiers killed every time the paper was published. Other boys from Soldier were listed, but she breathed a sigh of relief when Stefan's name was absent. She visited Alex to see if he had heard any war news in town. Every day, every hour that passed without word from her husband increased the panic that now sat permanently in her chest.

Ingrid visited her mother-in-law, Mary Andersen, to see if she had heard anything from Stefan. Her last letter was dated a few days before the letter Ingrid had received.

"Do you think something bad has happened to him?" Ingrid asked.

"We would have heard if he were dead. You would get a notification as his next of kin. I think no news is good news. Maybe he has been moved or is on the move? Maybe he's in heavy fighting and can't write? There are so many reasons why he wouldn't be able to write. I don't think we should assume the worst. Let's pray for him and remain calm until we know something concrete."

Ingrid appreciated Mary's rational thinking. There were certainly many possible reasons for his lack of communication. She would continue to pray for his safe return and keep herself busy to avoid imagining the worst.

Just when Ingrid thought she could stand it no longer, a letter finally arrived. The post date was old, and the envelope was dirty, looking like it had been to war.

7 December 1918

Dearest Ingrid,

How are you? I'm sorry it's been several weeks since I've written. Our division was part of a major battle, the St. Mihiel Offensive. You may have read about it in the newspaper. Our supplies were left behind us, so we haven't had much and certainly no letters. I haven't been able to get a letter out to you. I'm not sure when I'll be able to get this one sent.

We captured the city of Metz (that's in northeastern France) and had the Germans on the run. They were already retreating, so they weren't ready to fight. I can't tell you how good it felt to see them running for their lives. It boosted our morale.

Our supply trucks became stuck on muddy roads, so our only supplies were in our packs. We always carry a can of tinned meat, hard biscuits, sugar, coffee, and salt. There was only enough for a two-day supply. When we ran out of food, our spirits sat in the roadside ditches. I was lucky to have stuffed extra biscuits in my pockets before we went into battle. They were hard, but at least it was something to eat. I had to eat secretly since the other men had nothing. I felt ashamed I didn't share. I'm tired of being dirty and cold. I'm tired of this war. I'm tired of being away from my family.

We live with mud and water up to our knees and have to stand while we eat. Because of the conditions, some of the men have trench feet. Their feet swell to several times their size, blister, and become numb. Once the swelling goes down, I can hear them screaming from pain. One man shot himself in the foot to end the pain. While he probably lost his foot, at least he gets to go home. The men use the trench for every purpose, including the bathroom. Sometimes I look down, and I see defecations in the water around me. If men are killed, their body stays in the mud and water for days until the fighting ends; then we remove their bloated bodies. The smell of rotting bodies and human waste fills my nostrils. I can even smell it while I sleep.

Last night I went on something called a trench raid. We go into "No Man's Land," which is the land between us and the enemy. At night, we go into that area to fix the barbed wire, dig new trenches, or watch for activity from the enemy. The men who raid look for enemy soldiers who are either wounded or hiding. I found a wounded soldier and ran my bayonet through him. I never want to kill another human being again.

I know I shouldn't tell you these things. I'm sure I am upsetting you, but I need to reach out to someone other than these men to release my frustration and pain. I can never forget what I've seen and done. I am frightened for the man I have become. Only you, Ingrid, can make me whole again when I return.

I've been doing a lot of thinking about our future. I think farming is too hard a life. When I come home, I want to make sure Samuel finishes high school and goes to an industrial school. He should do something that doesn't rely so much on the weather. For me, I don't have much choice. I don't have any other training, so manual labor is all I can do. But he can do better.

As always, how is the family? Have you visited my mother? I think of you all every day and wish more than anything I could come home. Pray for me. Look after yourselves.

Much Love,

Stefan

Ingrid worried about the content and tone of his letter. He seemed frightened and depressed. She wondered if his mention of the future for their son was due to being in more danger than he relayed. She assumed he was keeping much from her. Ingrid prayed for his safety every night as well as an end to the war. That was the only way he would be coming home.

Ingrid devoured the weekly paper, looking at the list of men killed in combat. When she saw John Hedum's name, she covered her mouth and let the tears slip down her cheeks. She ached for John's family, but she was also crying for herself. What if that name had been Stefan's? She felt guilty for being glad it wasn't Stefan's name because another family was suffering their loss.

Ingrid and Karoline visited John's parents, bringing a jar of peach preserves with them. The kitchen was already littered with other dishes. When death happens, there is truly nothing for people to do but bring food. They show their thoughtfulness, but it doesn't make the hurt any less.

John was the only remaining Hedum son. The only other son had died in childhood, like Ole, Ingrid's brother. The rest of the Hedum children were girls. The day John's father died, the Hedum family line would disappear. There would be no one to farm the land, which had been broken by his grandfather.

The next time Ingrid didn't hear from Stefan for a long period of time, she did not worry. Every woman with a man in the war complained about the slowness of the mail. Ingrid felt comfort not being the only wife who had not heard from her husband for some time.

Winter came and made completing chores much more difficult. The abundance of snow kept them inside for days, the snow too heavy to remove with a shovel. At times, it was so bad they couldn't even walk to Karoline's house.

Weeks trapped in the house, sitting only with her thoughts, Ingrid started to imagine the worst. She saw Stefan dead in a field or in a trench. So many other young men had died in this horrible war. She wanted to believe Stefan would escape their fate, but the longer she didn't hear from him, the more she felt something was very wrong.

Her brothers read about the battles in the newspaper and listened to the war news every night on the radio, which they tracked with ink dots on a large map. Looking at each of the small dots on the map, Ingrid wondered if Stefan had been part of that dot. Where was he now? Why hadn't she heard from him?

When the weather was mild enough, Ingrid went into Soldier to do her trading. She, like everyone else in town, shopped at Ericksen's. As Ingrid was standing in line with her goods, Mrs. Haugen, a rather nosy member of her church, came up behind her and not-very-quietly said, "Mrs. Andersen, how is your husband? Have you heard from him recently? I understand there was a recent battle with many casualties. I was wondering if your husband made it through that?"

As Ingrid turned around to face this woman, she could see many of the customers staring at her, sympathy written on their faces, the same kind of sympathy she had given other families who had lost their loved one. "I'm not sure. I haven't heard from Stefan."

"That's not good, is it? I sure hope he wasn't killed! You haven't received word then? From him or the war department?" Mrs. Haugen had lit the fire of fear. Ingrid had been taught strict manners, but this time she could not bring herself to be social. Instead, she abandoned her basket of goods, turned around, and exited the store.

Ingrid's buggy ride home was filled with silent tears. This poorly mannered woman had spoken aloud her fears and opened the dam holding back her worries. She had exerted so much energy staying busy and keeping her mind out of the war trenches. Ingrid allowed herself only positive thoughts and made plans for Stefan's return. Four sentences, not even spoken with malice, had breached her bulwark of emotions.

A month later, March arrived with unusual warmth. To enjoy the warm weather, Ingrid took her rugs outside to beat them, getting rid of the winter grime. While she was enjoying the sun and warm breeze, her brother's green Cadillac drove across the rutted yard, past her mother's house, and pulled up to her front door. She was pleased to see him after the long winter months. She waved to him and went inside to put on some coffee, leaving her rugs hanging across the laundry line. Before she could enter the house, Alex yelled to her.

As he stepped from the car, she saw a piece of paper in his hand. His face was sad and solemn.

"Alex, what do you have? Why are you here?" Ingrid was afraid of the simple piece of paper.

"Ingrid, this telegram came for you. I brought it as soon as I was notified at the office." Ingrid didn't want to take the paper from his hand. The last time the family had received a telegram, it had announced the death of their father.

Alex stood beside his car, hand outstretched, holding the announcement.

Her face as white as her drying sheets and with a reluctant hand, Ingrid took the paper. She stood for a while, not looking at the message. As long as she didn't read it, Stefan was still alive. Once she read it, there was no changing history. At the top of the paper, she saw the official Western Union logo.

***

12 March 1919

To: Mrs. Stefan Andersen - Soldier, Iowa

Deeply regret to inform you that Private Stefan Andersen died yesterday from illness in a Nazire, France hospital. Our deepest sympathies.

Alex caught her as she sank to the ground, the wails of an injured animal coming from inside her. He pulled Ingrid to a standing position and guided her to the parlor, seating her in her rocking chair.

Alex had already read the telegram and was prepared to stay with her until Karoline arrived. He had sent word to Elfred Svensen, asking him to notify their mother.

Karoline hurried to her daughter's house, filled with guilt because she was relieved her sons were safe and away from this terrible war. She loved Stefan, and she had to admit he had been a good husband to her daughter. But she had had enough of funerals. It seemed no more than a few years between each time she unpacked her grieving clothes. Of course, death was a part of one's life, but every time it ripped something away, leaving a hole which could never be filled.

When Karoline arrived at Ingrid's house, her daughter was silent, sitting in the chair, staring out the window, looking at the barren fields.

"Ingrid, what do you need? What can I do for you?"

"Mama, there is nothing to do. What am I supposed to do without him? I'm not strong like you. I need my husband." Ingrid's admission of her present situation brought more tears.

"Ingrid, you need to rest and grieve. I will get my things and come back. I'm staying with you for as long as you need me."

Karoline remained with Ingrid for several weeks. She often heard her daughter crying in the night. Ingrid tried to put on a calm face for the children, but her eyes were always puffy and red. Ingrid was mechanical about her daily work. Her hands were moving as they always had, but her mind was not in the house or in Iowa.

Ingrid wondered about Stefan's death. How exactly did he die? Was he in pain? Did he die from bullet wounds? Where was he shot? The telegram had given her no details. Her brain wrapped around these questions and could not move to the future until she knew the details of his death.

Harder still, she would never see Stefan again, not even his body. He was buried in France with other American soldiers. She could not go to the cemetery to mourn him as she could her father.
Several weeks after her telegram, Ingrid received a letter. She did not recognize the sender. The letter had come from overseas.

03 May 1919

Dear Mrs. Andersen,

You and your family have been very much in my thoughts as of late. I write this letter to tell you that you have my deepest sympathy for the loss of your husband. It was my privilege to nurse your husband through his illness, and it saddened me greatly when he succumbed to it.

Two of his comrades came in with him, and they talked constantly of his bravery and compassion for his fellow men in the trenches. Private Stefan Andersen will be missed greatly by his company.

I wish to explain to you his death, knowing you were only told he died of 'illness' with no other explanation. Your dear husband came in with pulmonary tuberculosis. He was first brought to Nantes, France, and was diagnosed with pneumonia. When he was unsuccessful in recovering, they sent him to this hospital in Nazire.

I'm sure you are wondering how he became infected with tuberculosis. He may have had it before he left for train ing camp, he may have been infected while at that camp, or he may have contracted it in the trenches. Close contact spreads the disease quickly.

I wanted to tell you he was a model patient and spoke of you and his family often. He described the place where you live so well I could feel myself there. I could tell he loved his place of birth very much.

I hope this letter finds you and your family well and gives you solace in your sad hours. I also pray knowing his cause of death gives you some comfort. He died peacefully in a clean bed with love and care around him. He has been laid to rest with his comrades in Aisne Marne American Cemetery.

You can be very proud of his service to his country With much sympathy from all here.

Yours very sincerely

Helen Weatherall
American Red Cross

Ingrid appreciated the letter and the nurse who had taken care of her husband. She could lay to rest some of her questions. Her visions of his dying in the mud, being trampled by men, no longer haunted her imagination. The nurse's description of the clean bed and care replaced that ugly image. Ingrid wished she had a picture of his burial site, but perhaps one day she or one of her children would be able to visit France for a final farewell.

Ingrid knew her life would never be as it had been. Like her mother, she could not envision herself marrying another, but for different reasons.

Iowa would also never be as it had been. Its sons had traveled beyond its safe borders and seen things both ugly and beautiful. They

witnessed men's bodies being mangled by bullets, shrapnel, and bay-
onets. They heard the screams of the wounded and dying. Their once-
peaceful farm lives had never seen the horrors that only war can
make, and they would never be able to return to their naiveté.

Some would never return home completely after they had seen
France and Belgium. Sowing seeds and raising animals could never
compare to strolling the Seine, standing under the Eiffel Tower, or
climbing the towers of Notre Dame. Iowa's farm boys were restless
after the war.

1918

Gunda

In mid-October, residents of Moorhead and farmers from the surrounding area packed themselves into the small schoolroom—some crammed into the student desks, others standing along the walls and even filling the cloak room. A few of the men wore their Sunday outfits while others were still in their work clothing, but all of them had removed their hats out of respect. Some of the men wore white cotton masks over their faces. Other faces were bare.

Gunda sat in the front, off to the side, wearing her own mask. The board chief and Superintendent Higgs stood at her teaching podium in front of the classroom, also masked. The remaining board members were seated up against the blackboard behind the podium, some without masks.

The Iowa Board of Health had notified the state's residents they would be under quarantine within a few days. All public entities

—schools, restaurants, theaters—would close. The Spanish Flu had spiked in other states and was starting to infect Iowans at a fast pace.

The school board needed an official vote to close the school as so many others had already done. They had intended to meet briefly with a quick vote to do what was required; however, news of the impending close had traveled throughout the community and brought out those who wanted to add their voices to the dissenting side. Others in favor of the state mandate had come to support the board's decision.

Gunda had never imagined something as important as children's health would be an issue that divided people. But she was wrong.

The school board chief opened the meeting by welcoming the public and then handing the meeting over to the superintendent, who started by reading the quarantine mandate, which included schools. He then asked for discussion by the four other board members.

Three of the four members echoed their favor for closing the school, naming various community members who had already caught the plague. They also agreed with the Iowa Board of Health and called it their duty to abide by state government. Their speeches received praise from some of the attendees by way of clapping after their statements.

The fourth member, Chalmers Hansen, decided to disagree. Chalmers owned the largest tract of farmland in the school district, which he felt gave him more voting power than the other members. Even in a sitting position, he was a head taller than the other men; and, as he spoke, he gesticulated his feelings with his large hands. At one point he said, "This is our school, and nobody tells us to close it! Who ever heard of closing down because of a little flu? A cough. That's why we're pulling our children out of their learning?"

The school house erupted into cheers. Gunda could hear approvals: "They can't tell us what to do," "This thing isn't even real," "To hell with the government!"

Superintendent Higgs stepped up to the podium once again. His face was red, and Gunda could see a vein protruding from his temple. Although he was a man used to getting his way, he kept his voice calm and did his best to stop the stampede.

"Gentlemen, please remember that Miss Olson is among us. First, I want to remind you we are a public school and answer to the state. Therefore, we are required to follow state mandates. We have no choice here. But, I also want to make you aware of some facts about this flu. While some call it the Three-Day-Fever, it is beyond that. People are dying. Our county hospitals are full."

To support her boss, Gunda shook her head in agreement, hoping her siding with the superintendent would sway some of the dissenting men.

"We know there is misinformation out there: drinking liquor or smoking or using Vicks VapoRub. These will not stop this disease. Nothing has. If you read today's *Sioux City Journal*, you know Babe Ruth now has it. If a strong athlete can contract it, then what makes you think a small child won't? What if your child dies because you think he needs to learn to add and subtract? How will you feel then?"

Gunda looked around the room, and most of the men were looking down in shame. By bringing the topic to their own children, the superintendent had made this personal for them.

"There isn't going to be a decision here tonight. We will close the school until the state tells us we can reopen. Even if one board member votes no, this will still pass. You all should go and stay in your homes as much as possible. Wear the mask to save your own lives."

One farmer stepped forward and asked, "When will the school reopen? I need my boys in the fields by mid-May. If we don't go back for weeks, that's going to push the end of the school year, and I'm going to have to choose whether I keep them in school or pull them for the fields."

"I appreciate your dilemma," the superintendent said, "but we don't know how long this is going to last. I think we should all take this one week at a time and not worry about seven months from now. We'll do our best to get the children back in school, but we won't risk their safety."

Gunda appreciated his sensible answers. She felt he had overall done an excellent job in keeping the crowd under control. She remembered when they had first met, and she had felt he was rather abrupt and rude. Now, however, she could see his talents in being a leader.

The vote was quickly taken with Chalmers Hansen voting 'no' to save his reputation and favor with the nonbelievers.

After the meeting, Gunda discussed next steps with the superintendent. Because they were unsure of how long the quarantine would last, it was not prudent to send work home with students other than a few practice worksheets.

Since she would no longer be teaching, there was the matter of her wages. She had a teaching contract for the end of the term, which meant she was still an employee of the school. Gunda couldn't imagine what she could possibly do after she had given the school house a good scrubbing. Superintendent Higgs had other ideas. "I read in the paper other school districts are having their teachers continue to teach, but not to the children. They are going house to house to give lessons on hygiene to help eliminate this plague. I would like you to do the same."

"What exactly do you want me to teach these families?"

"Proper hand washing and mask wearing. Teach them about the spread of germs, especially through droplets. Make them understand how dangerous this flu really is. Can you do that?"

As usual, Gunda said she could even though she was wary about going around to the different farms and houses. From what she saw at tonight's meeting, she wasn't sure she would be wholly welcomed.

And she also worried for her own safety.

Gunda started with the town families. When she knocked on the first door, the child's parents thought she had come to bring work. They invited her inside and gave her coffee and a hot scone. Her young pupil was brought down to the kitchen, so Gunda could teach him.

"I'm sorry. You misunderstand. I'm here to help educate you on proper hygiene."

"You think we're dirty, Miss Olson?" the child's father questioned, his face showing disbelief.

"No, of course not. I'm here to instruct everyone on the importance of hand washing."

"We're clean people! I don't appreciate you telling us otherwise," the student's mother spoke up. "I keep my house clean and my children bathed."

"I'm sure you do." Gunda could see she had gone about her visit in the wrong way. Insulting people certainly didn't make them want to learn from her.

Once she quickly went through the information, watching both parents scowl at her, Gunda said her goodbyes and proceeded to the next house.

Next door, she had more success. Gunda convinced the parents it was important they and their children wear masks whenever they left their house. She also debunked the mother's belief that slathering Vicks VapoRub on their faces, necks, and chests would protect them from the flu.

Gunda's goal for each day was five houses. Within several weeks, she had most of the houses in Moorhead visited. She would not be able to visit more than two country houses per day. Since she didn't drive, the superintendent arranged for a buggy and driver each day. Often, he took the position himself.

Gunda found the farm families a little more difficult to teach.

Many of the farmers had not spent much time in school. They dropped out early to start farming, resulting in little understanding of scientific knowledge. She was told countless times that fresh air was the key to staying healthy. While Gunda didn't disagree that being outside was wholesome, she had a difficult time convincing them mask wearing was safe. They thought breathing in blocked air was unhealthy.

By the beginning of November, the contagion had spread throughout the state, the larger cities reporting overcrowded hospitals and dead bodies stacking up, the morgues unable to keep up with the demand. Western Iowa, with fewer large cities and more farmland, experienced less spread.

One of Gunda's last houses was the Pitts house. She had purposely put off visiting the family again, given the trouble she had had with the brothers and their parents. For this visit, she didn't need a driver since the farm was a walkable distance from where she was lodging.

Gunda climbed the same sloping steps, remembering her last conversation and the mother's threat of a gun. She knocked on the door and waited for a family member. As she waited, she looked around the farm, its sad buildings and fences looking even more dilapidated since her last visit. The barn had finally collapsed, and the outhouse was missing more boards. She had expected to see either Lyle or Leon outside since it was a bright, calm day. After waiting several minutes, she knocked again, this time as loudly as she could.

When no one answered the door, she became suspicious. No family member in the house or around the farm seemed impossible. They had no need to go to Soldier. They raised or hunted their own food. She had noticed a large garden area the last time she visited. The family was rarely seen in town. Taking a chance, she walked over to the window on the front of the house and peeked in.

She saw a sitting room, sparsely decorated with furniture, but there was no one in it. She could see past the sitting room into the kitchen. The table was full of dishes and empty canning jars, as if the family had been eating the contents of the jars and leaving them on the table. Nothing seemed unusual, but she also knew this family was not ordinary.

Gunda stood on the front steps, trying to decide her next move. She desperately wanted to write this down as 'no one home,' but she knew she would need to return. Every family needed to be checked off her list. She decided she would do more investigating before she left.

Gunda walked away from the house and went toward the remaining buildings that were still standing. She first went to the tool shed. The door was difficult to open because of an unkempt hinge. Once inside, she could smell the dust and oil. Tools were lying on the bench, looking like they hadn't been used in a long time. A grinding wheel was bolted to the tool bench awaiting someone's hands to crank the handle to make it go.

With no luck, she left and ventured toward the outhouse, hoping to find it empty. She could smell it well before she came near it. Obviously, the family needed to dig a new one. When she went to pull on the door, it caught. Someone had locked it from the inside. "Hello? It's Miss Olson, the teacher. I've come to check on your family." There was no reply. Her first thought was that a family member had locked the door as a joke. However, there was no way for someone to exit while locked inside. She decided to look inside where one of the slats was missing. In the gloom, Gunda could see Lyle Pitts lying on the floor. "Lyle, do you need help? It's Miss Olson. Lyle?" He didn't move. She couldn't see if he was breathing.

Gunda felt a chill go through her body. She was unsure what to do. She knew she had to alert the sheriff. But should she leave now or keep looking? She decided peeking into a few more windows was the proper thing to do. What if someone else needed her help?

She found a milk pail and carried it back to the house. Feeling like a 'Peeping Tom,' Gunda looked into the first window on the west side of the house. Inside, she saw a bed and a body in the bed. She wasn't sure if the body was alive or dead. Mustering her courage, Gunda went to the front door and opened it. Thankfully, no one locked their doors in the country. She went directly to the bedroom in which she saw the body. When she opened the bedroom door, a putrid odor accosted her nose. Leon was in his bed, partially covered by the sheet and blanket. His chest, up to his face, was red from pooling blood, and his body appeared quite bloated. She assumed he was dead.

Gunda quickly left his room and shut the door. She searched the house for the last bedroom. When she opened it, she smelled the same odor. Both of the boys' parents were in the bed, also dead. She backed out quickly, shut the door, and hustled through the house to the outside. Gunda snatched off her mask, bent over, and retched into the crabgrass growing up through the dead flowers.

Gunda began to run. She wanted to run all the way to Soldier, back to her own house; but she had a duty to do. Instead, she ran to the nearest farm, knocked on the door, and asked them to take her to the sheriff's office. On the way, Gunda couldn't get the smell of the dead bodies out of her nose. It had permeated her mask, which she was required to continue wearing. She also could not get the sight of the bloated, red faces out of her mind. She assumed they had died of the flu. *How long have they been dead*, she wondered? She started to think about the men at the school meeting who denied the severity of this disease. What would they think if they had seen what she had just witnessed? Of course, they had never considered their entire family being wiped out. It wasn't just a sniffle, or a cough, or the common flu. This was a serious disease that needed to be respected.

Tomorrow, having now finished her duties, Gunda would go home to her own family and stay until the school opened again. She prayed she would find her loved ones all healthy.

1919

Floyd

Floyd hated school. He dubbed himself 'the entertainment,' which—in his opinion—was sorely needed. Sitting in desks all day, doing work in their books was duller than walking behind a plow.

Miss Thorson, only five years older than fourteen-year-old Floyd, thought she could make him mind. Floyd, however, knew he had the upper hand. When he defied a command, her face turned red. The more he behaved like a mule, the higher her voice climbed. By the time he relented, she was a screeching, red-faced mess. The other students knew he controlled the class and snickered while watching the "The Floyd Show."

He generally put on his shows during reading time. The students were required to read aloud, going around the room like train cars. Each pupil read one paragraph. Floyd struggled with his reading skills, so he counted out the paragraphs and tried to prepare his before being made to read it. When his teacher didn't proceed methodically, it angered him because he always embarrassed himself struggling over the words. Most of the children two to three grades below him read better. Being corrected in front of the whole class caused him to shrink down in his seat and wish he were anywhere other than in his desk. To redeem his reputation, Floyd performed some funny antic, making the class laugh, forgetting his struggles with the paragraph.

Floyd battled with reading from the very beginning. His mother told him he was a late talker, which was the exact opposite of his siblings. She thought it was a sign he was a deep thinker. When Floyd started to learn his letters, he mixed up some of his consonants and later mixed up his syllables. Reading, his nemesis, often won the battle.

His teacher, as a way of taking back control after one of Floyd's shows, often chastised him for his slow reading. She would point out the youngest child and tell Floyd, in front of the whole class, the student could read so much better. She also punished him for his bad handwriting. When he finished work and handed it in, Miss Thorson made a spectacle of not being able to read his paragraphs. She read them aloud, struggling with each word. More than once, she had taken his paper around the room, using it as a display for sloppy work. Any chance she could take power from him, she did. When she did these things, she embarrassed Floyd, making him stare at his shoes.

Although history required reading, Floyd liked it. He was willing to crawl his way through sentences and paragraphs. He especially liked learning about the Vikings, as did the other children, because they were the warriors of Norway. He memorized the stories of their gods and sometimes acted them out with the other boys after school or during recess.

Floyd dominated math. Like his brother Alex, he had an affinity for numbers. He could see them in front of him even when he didn't write them out. While the other students struggled at the board, Floyd could figure the problem in his head before they had even started. Miss Thorson insisted he show his work, which irritated him because he had the correct answer without it.

Math time and recess made Floyd's shoulders relax. When he went out for recess, he and his friends burned off all their stored energy. They played tag, marbles, Hide and Go Seek, and Kick the Wickey. Floyd, the constant champion of Kick the Wickey, had advanced gross motor skills. He could kick the stick high into the air, and if he were the receiver, his hands seemed like magnets, always catching the stick before his peers. Floyd had natural athletic ability as well as natural leadership.

Most of the students in his class spoke English. Like Floyd, they had been born in America. Most of them also spoke a home language because, like his own mother, their parents either spoke English very poorly or didn't speak it at all. Some of the children attended their parents to the doctor or dentist to translate. Other children who were recent immigrants didn't speak any English when they walked through the schoolhouse door. A majority of them spoke Norwegian, but more outsiders were settling around Soldier; therefore, German, Danish, and Czech speech came from those young mouths.

The non-English speakers were put in the back of the classroom. Floyd, being an older student, was also in the back. He befriended these new students and did what he could to help them. If they spoke Norwegian, they had an advantage. Most of the students as well as their teacher spoke it fluently or pretty well depending on when their parents had emigrated. If they didn't speak Norwegian, no one— including the teacher—could help them. Floyd liked to learn a few words of different languages. He knew greetings mostly. The new students appreciated his easy friendship.

When school resumed after the Christmas holiday, Miss Thorson started the new year by explaining a new law that had gone into effect on January 1. Governor William Harding forbade anything but English in public settings. That meant nothing but English in their classroom, even amongst themselves, and nothing but English on the playground.

Students who always complied with rules sat silently, some looking toward the back of the room. Floyd was outraged. His mother and sisters had already experienced discrimination over his mother's Norwegian in a café, and he knew how hurt and embarrassed she had been.

"Miss Thorson, I think this is unjust!" Floyd declared.

"Floyd, our good governor is doing what's best for this country. We speak English in America, and anyone who comes here needs to learn it. I think everyone wants to be 100% American. Our state leaders know what's best for Iowa."

"Do you think our German classmate Franz isn't American because he hasn't learned English yet?" Floyd was not going to back down from this argument.

"We need to start our learning."

Floyd could tell she was irritated with him, and he saw his chance to make her look foolish. "No, I don't want to start our learning. This is so unfair! My mother doesn't speak much English. Is she not American? Is she a bad person?"

"Your mother is a very nice person. Please, Floyd, enough." Miss Thorson's face was starting to flush red.

"None of the people who settled this country spoke English except those from England. They considered themselves American and loved this country. Eventually they learned English or their children did." Floyd could see the other children agreeing with him and felt proud of his logic.

Miss Thorson, tired of wasting time arguing with a child and running out of her own logic, shut the argument down. "Our Governor said so. That's enough for me, and it should be enough for you. We are moving on, and I don't want to hear one more word from you."

Floyd, never one to back down from a challenge, thought about his next move. He wanted to best her more than he wanted to stand up for his classmates. He stood up.

"You're a terrible teacher, and you're stupid. Franz and his parents are just as American as you or me. Just because the Governor wants something doesn't make it right."

Her face turned a color Floyd had never seen, almost purple. She walked to the blackboard and took down the paddle. "Floyd, come up here and bend over."

Stunned, Floyd's feet bolted themselves to the floor. It was one thing for his mother to slap him alongside his head when he was a boy; it was quite another for a girl, who was hardly older than he, to spank him in front of the class.

"In a pig's eye!" he blurted. "If you lay that board on me, you're going to find it on your own back side!"

The room had been tomb-like; however, his last statement raised an audible gasp from the children. They imagined Floyd spanking Miss Thorson, and their eyes widened like twelve tiny owls.

Not knowing what to do, Miss Thorson pointed to the door. "Go home, Floyd! Don't come back until your mother is with you! You can come after school tomorrow."

In the cold and snow, Floyd stomped all the way home. He thought about his mother's reaction. Worse, he thought about Tingvald and Alex's reactions. This would be a family crisis.

Floyd finally arrived home, and when he walked through the front door, Karoline's face showed confusion. "Why are you home? It's only 10:00 a.m."

"I got sent home from school." Floyd told his mother the whole story, believing she would support his verbal tussle with his teacher.

"Tingvald is in the barn. Change your clothes, making sure you dress warmly. You're going out to help him today. We'll talk about this tonight."

Floyd felt confident his mother would take his side. He might receive a scolding for being disrespectful, but there would be no major punishment.

Karoline didn't disagree with Floyd's stance. She knew he was really sticking up for her. Floyd was certainly incorrigible, but he had a good heart. However, his disrespect for his teacher concerned her. Floyd often complained about her, and Karoline dismissed his complaints, thinking his dislike of school and challenges in learning manifested into a grudge against the person who taught him.

Karoline disliked being required to go meet the teacher with Floyd. She didn't enjoy going to speak with his teacher since her limited English made her feel inadequate as his parent. Usually, his teacher switched to Norwegian for her.

After supper, the family—those who lived in the house, plus Alex—sat down in the parlor to discuss Floyd's troubles. They agreed the new mandate was unfair. Floyd was only standing up for his fellow classmates and every other immigrant who couldn't speak English. For that, they didn't feel he had been in the wrong. They were ashamed of what he said to his teacher. His mouth had too often spewed vulgar language or impertinent statements. A punishment was appropriate. Taking over the milking would be his punishment. Floyd liked to sleep as long as he could in the mornings. Milking before the sun rose should give him pause the next time he opened his mouth to say something inappropriate.

After school released the next day, Floyd and Karoline took the sleigh to conference with Miss Thorson. Teachers stayed well beyond the school day—preparing lessons, cleaning the classroom, and bringing in coal. Miss Thorson was cleaning the board when they came into her classroom.

Floyd said, "Miss Thorson, I've brought my mother as you instructed."

"Very good. Please have a seat." Both mother and son sat in front-row desks. Miss Thorson sat behind her teacher desk. "I will need an apology from Floyd before we can continue any further."

Karoline looked at Floyd for a translation. She didn't know the word *apology*, so she missed the main part of the sentence. He translated her entire sentence into Norwegian.

"Mrs. Olsen, you'll need to speak English. As you know, we are in a public area, and you are required to speak only English."

Karoline reddened just like her son. She was embarrassed by her poor skills. She also knew Miss Thorson's family, and therefore she knew Miss Thorson's parents also spoke broken English.

"Please. I am sorry. Floyd, say sorry to her."

"I'm sorry I upset you." Floyd, trying to get out of an actual apology for his actions, hoped she would be satisfied with anything he would say that sounded remorseful.

"I don't accept your apology. Mrs. Olsen, your son is…bad. He is a bad student. He is a bad young man. Something must be done about him."

Her anger beginning to rise, Karoline responded to her in Norwegian just so she could say exactly what she wanted in the tone she wanted.

"My son tells me how you humiliate him in front of the other students. You make fun of him in class because he has troubles reading. You make an example of his handwriting even though it is not his fault. Yes, he's a bad boy in your classroom, but did you ever think about why this is so? If you treated him with respect and care, he would treat you the same. Being humiliated makes anyone fight back. Did you become a teacher because you loved children or because you wanted power? My son has a good heart. He was trying to protect those students who are like me and like your parents, by the way. He will not be apologizing for his argument with you. He was wrong when he called you names, but I can see now he was goaded into it."

"You have no right to speak to me that way. I am a teacher," she responded in Norwegian.

"Not a very good one. I will teach my son," Karoline retorted in English.

Floyd's mouth fell open when his mother withdrew him from school. He quickly envisioned lying in bed late into the morning. Hunting whenever the mood came upon him. Maybe even getting a job, so he could save up for his own automobile.

His ideas were pulled from under him when he came in from milking the cows; his mother had a place for school set up in the parlor. She had asked Gunda to loan her some books. She also had included the family Bible, which was written in Norwegian. Floyd found his new teacher much more demanding than his former one.

His mother tackled his reading for hours each day. She made him read aloud to her from their Bible, correcting him as he went along. She went through each subject every day. On Sundays, Gunda came for supper and filled in for their mother's shortcomings. When Gunda didn't come, Alex filled in. Alex had volunteered to work with him on arithmetic. Because of Floyd's aptitude, Alex taught him beyond his grade level. Eventually, Floyd worked with stock market scenarios to go beyond simple math functions. Alex discovered Floyd's excellent memory of numbers and complex reasoning. He was also swift when it came to calculating anything with money. Floyd enjoyed spending time with his favorite brother—and feeling like he was good at something.

With his family's diligence, Floyd continued to make progress.

Once he finished the eighth grade, his mother sent him to the high school where he would have different teachers.

1919

Alex

It didn't take long for Alex to decide Anna Nilsson was the woman for him. With her invitation, he made the trip back to Des Moines the following month and attended the Shakespeare play. Anna was attending again with her family, and this time, her father took more interest in Alex. By the end of the play, Anna's parents had invited him to their house for dinner the following evening. Alex knew her parents wanted to find out what kind of man was showing interest in their daughter.

The first time Alex visited Anna's house, he knew he had miscalculated how much money Oscar Nilsson made. The Nilsson home was a large colonial with a sprawling half-acre yard. The estate sat in the middle of other large houses in the wealthiest area of Des Moines.

Their dinner conversation centered around cultural topics: art, literature, and the theater. Occasionally, Alex had to admit his short-comings, especially with theater. However, his knowledge of art and literature could keep him respectfully in the conversation. Every time he looked over at Anna, her eyes shone with admiration for him.

After dinner, Oscar and Alex went into Oscar's office to discuss men's matters. Alex discovered immediately this was not a discussion; it was an interrogation by a father who wanted to be certain the man pursuing his daughter was worthy of her. Once Alex passed the test, proving to Oscar he had the means to take care of her and he came from a decent family, Oscar gave Alex his consent to court Anna. Within three months, Alex had asked Anna's father for permission to marry her. They planned a fall wedding.

Anna, her mother Hattie, and her sisters spent a fortune on their wedding attire. They traveled to New York City to have their clothes specially made instead of buying ready-made from Des Moines. Anna's wedding dress was designed by Ethel Frankau in Bergdorf Goodman's salon. Her dress was constructed of satin with a two- foot train and a veil that matched the length of the train. The cost of the dress was outrageous: $120.00. Her mother and each of Anna's sisters also had dresses designed for them. Hattie's designer, Jessie Franklin Turner, designed for Bonwit Teller's custom salon. Turner was the most sought-after designer at that time. Hattie's dress was also made from silk.

Anna and Alex's October wedding in 1917 was the social event of Des Moines. They had a small ceremony in Anna's family church but then hosted a large celebration in the Hotel Kirkwood's ballroom. Anna's parents invited everyone in their social circle, which amounted to a few hundred, and served a formal dinner. A full orchestra provided music for the dance. The ballroom was decorated with fresh flowers and candles.

Until the wedding, the Nilssons had never met Alex's family.

They knew only that their daughter was marrying a man with means, who came from a small town. Alex had told them his family farmed, knowing they assumed his family were big landowners. Alex had never lied to them, but he kept details of their life out of any conversation. The Nilssons were new money and only wanted their daughter's husband to keep her in the luxury she was used to.

Karoline and the other Olson family members attended the celebration and felt like sheep on ice. Their clothes were drab compared to the bride's family's attire. Even though they had worn their best and Alex had paid for some new things from Denison, their modest clothing stood out from the other guests. It was obvious they were farmers from the country.

Their manners also set them apart. When they sat down to the formal dinner, the number of forks beside their plates mystified them. They had only ever eaten with one fork. Since Karoline was a staunch supporter of temperance, they didn't drink alcohol—including the wine served with the meal, which the bride's family was especially proud of since they had gotten around Iowa's prohibition law—thus showing their influence with the right people. The first dish served was seafood, which Anna's family bought from the East Coast and had shipped in ice on a train. Karoline was the only member who had eaten seafood. In Norway, it was a staple, but in land-locked Iowa, seafood was rare. The rest of the Olson family didn't quite know what to do with the shrimp shells.

The wedding celebration complete, the couple traveled throughout the United States for their honeymoon. Because of the unrest in Europe, they had no choice but to stay in their own country even though Anna had always wanted to travel overseas like the European aristocracy did when they honeymooned. Anna also wanted to spend the year traveling, but Alex still had a business to maintain. Therefore, they settled on two months.

While they were gone, their house in Soldier was being built. The houses for sale didn't suit Anna, so they decided to build a new one. They chose the northwest side of town and picked out a lot looking down onto Soldier. They wanted a colonial style with two stories, much like Anna's childhood home. The house was made of red brick with black shutters. The front door was covered by a portico supported by four white columns. The most impressive exterior element was the circle driveway made of crushed red brick to match the house. The driveway wound around landscape sculptures and a fountain. Anna had asked for a tennis court, but Alex thought it was too much opulence for Soldier. He also thought it only added to the loan he had to take out from the bank to pay for a large portion of the house's expense.

The interior of the house was both new and old. Anna and her mother bought from antique dealers who had gone to England and purchased some of the furniture and architectural elements from aristocratic houses whose owners were unable to pay taxes on their large estates. The Olson house had two fireplaces from an English country manor. The salon furniture had been in a Duke's summer home. The rest of the furnishings came from various other places, but everything in the house told its visitors they were in the presence of wealth.

The builders finished the last details in early 1919. Anna Olson spent her days working to make her house a reflection of their position in life. She hired a professional decorator from Omaha to choose the paint, curtains, and the rest of the furniture to mix in with the antiques. She wanted her guests to feel like they could be in New York City among the newly wealthy. What she didn't realize until she had been in Soldier for a year was that she would have no visitors who would even know what the houses of the New York wealthy looked like.

Soldier women were wives of farmers, shopkeepers, grain merchants, and medical professionals. They did not know the finest families in New York or Omaha or Des Moines. They could not gossip with her over the lives of these other wealthy women. They hadn't seen the latest plays or read the newest books. They discussed their children—how to keep them healthy, how to get them through school, and how to choose a good mate for them—and their house duties, which included laundry secrets and delicious recipes. Their visits to the Olson mansion were uncomfortable for both them and their hostess.

By the middle of summer, after Anna had no more house projects to keep her occupied, she found Soldier to be unbearable. There were no cultural activities, unless one counted a barn dance as culture. There were no foundations or charitable boards for her to join. When she tried to raise money to put a sculpture in front of the community hall, she failed miserably. The town wanted to raise money to put a new roof on the building instead of buying the sculpture.

Two years into their marriage, in the middle of October, Alex came home to find packed traveling trunks. "Anna, are you planning a trip?" He couldn't believe she would go somewhere without him.

Anna had on her traveling clothes. She had been waiting for Alex's return to say goodbye. "I'm going to Des Moines. I'll stay with my parents. I can't stand another day in this town. I have nothing to do and no one in my social circle. I have no friends."

"Are you leaving me for good?" Alex didn't think their marriage had failed, so her desire to leave him was a surprise.

"Of course not!" she exclaimed. "I just need some time with my own people. It will only be a month. Why don't you come to Des Moines for a visit? You could stay a week or two. We could see some plays and visit some of our old friends."

"I can come for a visit, but I can't stay that long. You know I have the business to run. How else are we to pay for this grand house?" Alex could see his wife didn't understand how money was made. Her father had kept her ignorant of such things. *Perhaps a visit with her family would be good for her*, he thought. She would come back with all kinds of gossip and stories of shopping with her mother.

***

By the end of November, Anna still hadn't spoken of coming home. Alex had gone to Des Moines twice to visit her. He could see she was in her natural habitat. She now had occasions to wear her best plumage, and she strutted around the other women to show off her gowns and jewels. She took tea with them and chirped gossip about the other fashionable women. When Alex approached the subject of her returning to Soldier, she wrinkled her nose and pleaded for "just another month." Alex consented, hoping his generosity would make her feel obliged to return home.

The gossips in Soldier were cawing their speculations over whether she had left him for good. In their usual polite Midwestern way, they asked after her health, hoping to catch him in a moment of confession. Sometimes they asked if she would be able to chair a committee to raise funds for some ill resident. They would set the date of the fundraiser a month out, so Alex would have to admit she wouldn't be returning from Des Moines in time to help.

Nearing three months of Anna's absence, Karoline invited Alex out to the farm for supper. It was not their usual Sunday dinner, so he knew she wanted to talk to him—most likely about his estranged wife. Karoline, Alex, Tingvald, Ella, and their children sat around the large table and enjoyed a meal of ham, potatoes, carrots, and bread. It wasn't the fancy suppers Alex usually ate in his own house, made by his hired cook, but it felt good to be among his family and eating a meal from his childhood. He talked agriculture prospects with Tingvald and played with his nephews while his mother and

Ella washed the dishes.

Once the women were finished, Karoline asked Alex to take a walk with her. The winter snow was light that year, leaving the ground bare. There was no wind, which made walking rather pleasant.

Alex looked out over the land, the barren fields waiting for spring's planting. Life on the farm was so simple: plant the corn, hope for rain, and harvest in the fall. Each day's work replicated the day before and the day before that. Chores needed to be completed the same times every day whether it rained or shined, whether it was a Tuesday or a Sunday.

Alex appreciated the people of this area, who cared for one another. When his father was laid up with broken bones, the farmers had come to plant his fields. His parents had reciprocated many times over. Western Iowans used whatever talents they had to help those in need, whether it was farm work, cooking, or building. When Alex was in Des Moines, rescuing his sister, he had seen the exact opposite. They didn't give; they took.

The business with Elfred was still between them, creating a slight wedge, but Elfred was not his mother's intended conversation. Karoline was concerned about Alex's marriage. "Son, your wife has left you."

"Mama, she's coming home in two weeks. She'll be home for Christmas."

"Are you sure she's coming home? Are you having problems in your marriage?" Karoline had misgivings when Alex married Anna. She truly liked the young woman, but Anna was not right for Alex. Karoline knew all about marrying someone who came from a different background. While her husband Kristoffer was not as different from her as Anna was to Alex, he had been raised differently, which was the tear in their marriage fabric. Alex had been raised on bread and butter, and Anna had been raised on cake and ice cream. Karoline knew at the wedding Anna would never be happy in Soldier.

"I'm not having problems in my marriage. I love my wife. She just needs to go back to her people to have some company and entertainment. Soldier doesn't have enough for her right now. She's young; she'll get used to it eventually."

From her own experience, Karoline knew Anna would never get used to it. The more time she spent in Des Moines, the more she would come to resent returning to Soldier. However, Karoline's place was to support her son and his wife, not criticize them.

"I hope so, Alex. Anna is a lovely girl, and I only want happiness for both of you."

The next morning, while at his office, Alex received a letter from Anna. He wondered why she had sent him a message instead of calling him. When he read the paper, he understood why.

My darling, something exciting has happened. Gertrude Vanderbilt Whitney is coming to Des Moines to potentially sell one of her sculptures to the Jefferson Polk family. Maybe you remember them at our wedding? Mrs. Vanderbilt Whitney is arriving next month, and I would so like to meet her. Mother wants to host a luncheon for her. It seems silly to travel back to Soldier and then back to Des Moines. Therefore, I've decided to stay until after our guest leaves. The family would love for you to come here for Christmas. I trust you are busy with the business and won't even miss me.

Much love,
Anna

Alex immediately thought of his mother. What would he tell her now? How was he going to continue to behave as if his wife were coming home to him? Even if she did eventually come home, she would leave again. They would be that rich couple who lived apart from one another. He didn't have a marriage; he had a correspondence with a beautiful and cultured woman.

1919

Gunda

Gunda went back to her family's farm once she was released from her health duties. To her relief, her family was well. Her mother, Tingvald and his family, and Ingrid and her children had remained fairly secluded on their farm. Because they had plenty of provisions set aside, the family could stay away from others in town for at least six months. Sophie and Jack had more exposure: they had opened a small butcher shop in town and served the public. It too had been closed during the quarantine; however, the Governor had allowed businesses to open again after a few months. Her brother Alex and his wife Anna were also well. Anna had help she could send for provisions, and Alex completed business from his office. Gunda felt blessed her family had escaped this plague.

With little to keep her occupied after she came home, Gunda became interested in the Suffrage Movement, which was happening nationwide. She read all she could in the newspapers; however, only the *Sioux City Journal* seemed to write more than a story or two about national news. Gunda read about protests in other states where women, like Alice Paul, were arrested and jailed for their activities.

The question of whether Iowa would allow women the right to vote was on all Iowa women's minds. In 1916, the Iowa legislature had put the right to vote in front of Iowa voters, all of whom were men—and it failed. The 1919 legislative session would take up the question again. Gunda didn't want to sit back and watch what happened; she wanted to become part of it.

The statewide quarantine for schools lasted three months, until December 30. The children and Gunda returned to school after the Christmas holiday on January 2. While Gunda missed seeing her family every day, she missed her students more, but her return to school did not diminish her desire to become part of the movement.

The Iowa Woman Suffrage Association was hosting a rally in Sioux City in late February 1919. It was on a Saturday. Gunda could not get permission to attend a convention, especially one supporting something so radical, but she could get permission to go home to the farm. She would have to lie to the chief board member in order to leave Moorhead. The lie itself, if exposed, would get her released from her teaching duties.

Gunda didn't want to attend the rally alone, so she asked Betsi to attend with her. Her sister had become a modern woman and believed in women's rights. Betsi could also drive them, thereby eliminating the necessity of the train, which would expose Gunda to community members who would report her train travel. Lars, her brother-in-law, offered to drive over to Moorhead and pick her up after school on Friday to take her back to their farm. Technically, Gunda thought, she had not lied. She had come back and seen her family. She stayed with Lars and Betsi, not wanting to put the rest of her family, especially her mother, in the position of knowing she had lied and included them in that lie.

Betsi and Gunda left early Saturday morning. They had asked Alex to borrow Anna's red Ford Model T Touring car. Lars wasn't opposed to Betsi attending the rally, but he needed their truck for the farm work. The sisters invited Anna to attend, but she wasn't interested in such matters as Suffrage. However, she was willing to loan her vehicle to them. Even with the tan leather top covering them, the car was still cold in the February winter. Both women were bundled in winter coats, scarves, hats, and gloves. At one point, Gunda thought if they had taken the train, they would have been much warmer.

The rally was being held at the Academy of Music, a large brick building on the south side of Sioux City. It hosted a variety of theatrical performances as well as speeches. Susan B. Anthony had spoken there once before. Even though Anthony was now dead, her words were still carried through the movement. A woman dressed as Anthony would perform her most famous speech for the crowd.

Betsi and Gunda found a place to park their vehicle and joined the women streaming into the building. Most of the women wore black in protest, including their hats. Gunda had on one of her black teaching outfits and blended into the crowd.

The eight hundred seats were filled with mostly women but also a few men. Gunda looked out to the sea of black, realizing all these women had stepped away from their daily lives for a cause bigger than themselves. Many of them had made signs in support of the right to vote and were prepared to march outside with them after the last speech. The atmosphere buzzed with women's voices as they waited for the first speaker to take the stage. Gunda and Betsi were excited to be a part of this historic day.

The first speaker, Mary Jane Coggeshall, stepped onto the stage. She, too, wore all black, including the feather in her hat. She had a white sash across her body with **National Organization of Women** written on it. Mary Jane, who was originally from Indiana, was a graduate of Iowa State, which made her a popular Iowa suffragist. As she stood there, the buzz dropped to silence. Mary Jane lifted her voice and projected out to the audience.

"Poor, stupid Uncle Sam. He fails to see that the laws made for women a hundred and fifty years ago have not yielded to women's growth, and She is resisting the chains which confine Her, and therefore the home, her special realm, is the loser."

The crowd of polite, usually quiet women, jumped to their feet and erupted into a roar after her first line. Gunda felt the power of those united women running through her body. Goosebumps raised on her flesh, and her face flushed with excitement. The crowd went silent again as Mary Jane resumed.

"Iowa boasts of its absolute equality in matters of property. In the case of a certain excellent lady of Des Moines—a member of the Presbyterian church, her husband's acts becoming unbearable—they lived apart, he entering into a written contract with her to pay her a monthly stipend. This he soon failed to pay and the wife brought suit—but the Supreme Court of the state decided that a contract between man and wife 'was against public policy,' and today in Iowa it is not a crime for a man to defraud his wife."

Gunda was confused. Why was she talking about what a husband did to his wife? Betsi leaned over to her and whispered, "I can't believe that happened to this poor woman."

"Why is she talking about this?" Gunda whispered back.

"She's leading up to women voting against the laws that favor men over women, especially in marriage."

Now Gunda understood. The speaker was giving reason to the importance of voting. She wasn't just talking about its being important unto itself. These women were smart and good at constructing an argument.

Once finished, Mary Jane Coggeshall left the stage. She was followed by thunderous applause and waving signs. Gunda clapped until her hands hurt and hooted until her throat was sore. She had never had so much passion for something other than teaching.

Gunda felt a kinship with the next speaker, Carrie Chapman Catt, who was also an Iowa State alumna. Like Gunda, Chapman Catt was a teacher, but she had become a principal and eventually took the position as superintendent of Mason City Schools—the only woman to hold such a position. Gunda looked up to her and hoped to one day move up the education ranks as her heroine had done.

Carrie Chapman Catt gave a completely different speech, one that focused on the government's history.

"Woman suffrage is inevitable. Suffragists knew it before November 4, 1917; opponents afterward. Three distinct causes made it inevitable. First, the history of our country. Ours is a nation born of revolution, of rebellion against a system of government so securely entrenched in the customs and traditions of human society that in 1776 it seemed impregnable."

Gunda looked to Betsi for help. She didn't understand the reference to the November 4th date. A woman behind them leaned forward and said, "That was the last day of New York's Suffrage campaign. New York is the most populous state. It was a major victory." Gunda still didn't quite understand, but she latched onto the words, *rebellion* and *revolution*. She thought about how her country had come to be. Change only happened through rebellion. Women would not be taking up arms, but it would take a collective voice to get them what was rightfully theirs.

She thought about what her mother would say about her daughters attending this rally. She thought Karoline would be proud of them. However, her sister Ingrid would disapprove. Her husband Stefan had fought and died for their country's freedom. Ingrid would see this fight against her own countrymen as traitorous. Gunda even thought about her father. He would have hated this movement, and his wife or children supporting it would have been out of the question.

The final speaker was the one she looked forward to the most— "Susan B. Anthony"—who was a legend to all the women. The women once again jumped from their seats and shouted and cheered and clapped their hands. "Anthony" stood on the stage a full five minutes before she could finally get the crowd settled enough to speak. She talked to the women about their duty to help get the amendment passed. They needed to encourage their fathers, brothers, and husbands to vote for it. Gunda and Betsi looked at each other after this request; they both were thinking the same thing. Would their men vote for this amendment? The women thought Alex would vote yes, but Tingvald was questionable. He was rather old-fashioned in his thinking.

When the rally ended, Gunda felt powerful and alive. She vowed to herself she would do what she could to persuade the men she knew. She also thought about the young girls in her classroom. She needed to fight for them, to give them a chance for a better future. She would love to talk to them about this historical event, but the curriculum and the school board would never tolerate her talking about women's rights and the importance of standing up for themselves. She taught her girls to be pleasant and quiet. She taught them to obey men, especially their husbands. She wondered if any of them would go against her teaching and become a Carrie Chapman Catt or a Susan B. Anthony. She hoped so.

As she and Betsi exited the building, she ran into Peter Hoffman and his wife Maeve. The Hoffman children had been in Gunda's classroom several years ago. They looked as shocked to see her as she was to see them. "Miss Olson," Mr. Hoffman said, "I'm surprised to see you here." Gunda had no choice but to speak with them. Being impolite would only add to her list of current sins.

"Hello, Mr. and Mrs. Hoffman. It's so nice to run into you. Did you attend the rally?"

"Yes, we did. Mr. Hoffman has a client who wanted him to attend, and we couldn't say no. What did you think?"

Gunda wasn't sure whether she was supposed to like the rally or dislike it. The Hoffmans held her job in their hands. They were sure to report her activities to a board member. "I thought it was interesting. As a teacher, I couldn't resist attending an historical event. Someday, I can tell my students I watched history happen and retell some of the speeches these famous women gave. I think it will really add authenticity to my teaching, wouldn't you agree?"

Mrs. Hoffman's face became pinched. She looked like she had tasted something sour. She said, "I suppose it would. We must be going back. Do you have a way home?"

"Yes, I do. This is my sister, Betsi Berg. I came with her." The Hoffmans hurried away, and Gunda could tell they didn't approve of her attending the event.

Monday morning, when she entered her classroom, Superintendent Higgs was waiting for her. She felt her stomach sink to her shoes. "Miss Olson, did you attend the Suffrage rally on Saturday?"

"Yes, I did." There was no point in trying to get out of it. She would have to take whatever consequence came her way.

"You lied to the school board chief. And you attended an anarchist rally. You have disobeyed the rules of your teaching contract as well as led our young children astray with your behavior. Were you planning to start filling their minds with these rebellious ideas?"

"No, sir. I merely went to an historic event. This is America, after all. And I do have freedoms. Just because I am a schoolteacher does not mean I am not allowed my own opinions and freedom to go where

I please. I care deeply about children and would never teach them inappropriate things. But they should know what is going on in their own country. They should not be sheltered from its reality. They will have to live in it and whatever comes of it from these times." Gunda looked at Mr. Higgs with her head high and her eyes ablaze.

"I'm sure you already know you are fired. I will teach the children until we can find a suitable replacement. You may send a family member for your things. You can go back to your residence and pack up. I don't want to see you in Moorhead again." With those last words, he went and sat behind her desk.

Gunda walked out of the school house and back to the house where she was boarding. She felt a mix of emotion. She was proud for standing up for herself, but she was also embarrassed she had been fired. She packed her few things and called Alex's house, hoping to speak with Anna. Instead, Alex answered the phone.

"Alex, I need you to come and get me, please. I'll explain when I see you." Gunda worried about her brother's reaction. She had promised to teach until she paid off her debt to him for her schooling. She still owed him some money.

On the return to Soldier, Alex finally spoke. "So, you got into trouble for going to the rally, didn't you? Of course I knew you were going with Betsi to that event. Someone from Moorhead must have seen you, didn't they?"

Gunda appreciated not having to explain her situation to her brother. "I got fired," she admitted. "I don't know what I'm going to do now."

"I assume I'm taking you back to the farm?"

"I don't have another choice." And it was true. Gunda didn't have any place else to live. The farmhouse was already full with her mother and Tingvald's wife and four children.

"What are you going to do now without a teaching position? Will you look for another one?"

Gunda couldn't get another teaching position until the fall semester. She would need to travel well outside of Monona County and its bordering counties to find one. Superintendent Higgs would pass along her indiscretions to other superintendents. She wasn't even sure she wanted to continue teaching. She loved the children, but the restrictions of her occupation wore on her. Perhaps she could get a job in one of Soldier's businesses. "Maybe I could work for Mr. Ericksen and do the job Sophie vacated to work with Jack in the butcher shop?"

"You can stay with Anna and me if you get a job in town. Our house is plenty large, and I know Anna would enjoy your company."

Gunda didn't have a plan, but now she had a place to live. One of her problems was eliminated.

1920

Tingvald

Tingvald had despised the war. He was a peace-loving man and hated to see his fellow men kill one another. The death of Ingrid's husband Stefan shook Tingvald to the marrow of his bones. He thought often how he had narrowly evaded fighting. When Stefan had been conscripted and Tingvald himself had escaped, his sense of guilt grew on him like another layer of skin. It stayed with him and became part of who he was. Working daily with Stefan's son Samuel reminded Tingvald of the loss. At first, farming had been difficult without Stefan, but eventually Tingvald and Samuel had grown into a rhythm and were now farming together as if it had always been this way.

Although the war had killed many of his countrymen, it had boosted the farm economy. Land prices skyrocketed to $255 per acre. When his father had purchased the land in 1887, one acre cost $1.80.

The original thirty acres of land had swelled from $54 to $33,150. Before his death, his father had added another twenty acres, which were now free and clear.

During the war, the farmers produced corn to feed the troops and were paid well for it. In 1914, corn was worth $.60 per bushel. During 1919, the farmers were paid $1.30 per bushel.

Livestock, beans, wheat, and all other farm commodities boomed during the war. Farmers grew rich from the world's turmoil. When the war ended, the money they gained and hadn't been able to spend was sitting in their bank accounts, ready to be used.

In January, Alex visited Tingvald to speak with him about the future of the farm. Tingvald, at thirty-five, was in his prime and wanted a bigger life like his younger brother Alex. The two men sat at the kitchen table with cups of coffee and slices of cake between them. Karoline and Tingvald's wife Ella found chores to complete that kept them within earshot of the conversation. Women were not included in such financial matters, especially now that Karoline's children were grown men.

"Tingvald, I think we should purchase more land. The price of land continues to rise, and we should get in on the buying. Some of the farmers are going under because of their debt, which gives us plenty of options. I've heard our neighbor to the north cannot pay his loans. We could buy his farm and double the size of ours."

Tingvald hated the idea of taking advantage of another's misfortune. Prior to the war, farm prices had dropped. Farmers spent more to plant their crops than they did selling them. They owed the banks, who took their farms when they couldn't pay. In addition to the ethics of it, the idea of taking on debt made Tingvald shudder. They had survived the bank once, and he hated to invite it into their lives again.

Skeptically, Tingvald replied, "We would have to take on debt. We have no debt now. The war prices helped pay it all off. Shouldn't we just enjoy our financial freedom?"

"More land means more crops, which means more money," Alex replied. "We can make the payments and still have more money in our pockets. Trust me. I've been watching the markets. They've been steadily going up. This is a win. There is no chance we'll get into financial trouble. I know about these things. Do I ask you about farming practices? No! You know farming, and I know the markets. You need to listen to me."

Tingvald knew Alex was an expert in the markets. He was not. This could be their chance to become a big farming operation. They could hire more help. Perhaps he could manage the farm instead of going to the fields himself; however, he still could remember the worry the family had experienced when they nearly lost their farm in 1906. But Alex was right. If there were ever an opportunity to expand their operation, it was now.

"Alright. Let's buy the farm north of us." Tingvald silently prayed their decision would not be their ruin.

The auction was held on a cold February morning. Approximately fifty farmers had come to watch, some of them planning to bid. They were bundled against the frigid temperatures and stood in groups of three or four.

The owner had lost his farm because of multiple mortgages. Once he had gotten in too deep, he had taken out a second mortgage. Tingvald wondered what the farmer would do now without a way to make a living. He and his family would be allowed to live in their house, but what good would that do if the land around them wasn't theirs?

The auctioneer, a stout young man from Dunlap, stood up on a hayrack parked in front of the house. He was one of the best in his profession and had often stood on that hayrack, above the crowd, selling off men's dreams. The fellows with him would be spotters, calling out the men who bid on an item.

The animals were the first to be sold. The farmer had several mules and horses, each going for well below their value. They were followed by the farm implements, each one snatched up by another farmer looking to purchase at a low price. Tingvald thought about the irony of those items being sold first; without the animals and the implements, a farmer could not farm his land. Alex and Tingvald weren't interested in anything but the land.

Once the auctioneer finished the animals and equipment, the farmland was next. The Olson brothers moved closer to the auctioneer to ensure their bids were seen.

"Let's start the bidding at $200 per acre," he said. The price was well below the average for land.

Many hands went into the air. It was obvious to Tingvald they weren't going to get the land cheaply. The auctioneer then went into his bidding mode, an incomprehensible gibberish woven between the dollar amounts.

"Do I have $210? $220? $225?" The price continued to climb. Fewer hands were raised the higher he went. Once he got past $225, only four bidders remained.

"Do I hear $230?" Only two bidders raised their hands. "$235? $240?" Alex had raised his hand at $235. No one was willing to pay the $240. "$240? 240? 240? Sold! $235 to the gentlemen in front of me!"

The Olson brothers had just purchased a farm, adding another forty acres to their fifty. Their farm was now considered a 'large' operation.

Back at the house, Alex and Tingvald celebrated their purchase with a strong cup of coffee. Plans for extra men to help with the farming were discussed. They would need to hire at least four. Where to house them was the problem. Perhaps the farmer who sold the land would either leave his house, so they could rent it out, or he would take the men in for room and board. These were minor details once they had the men hired.

They also needed to decide what they were going to do with the land. Should they plant crops on all of it? Or should they put livestock on some and plant the rest?

Alex said, "I think we should plant some and put cattle on some. We need to look at the bushels per each acre. I definitely believe we should buy at least one hundred head of cattle. They too are going up in worth."

A little shocked, Tingvald questioned, "Do we need to start off with that many? We'll have to go back to the bank to ask for more. Maybe we should just plant the land with corn and see how that goes."

"Tingvald, I know what I'm doing. I buy and sell cattle all day long. Just like land, they've been rising in price. We'll buy yearlings, plant alfalfa on some of the land, and fatten them up for sale. We'll keep them for two years and then take them to market. I'm telling you; we'll make a fortune off those cows. Trust me. And the bank will be happy to lend us the cash. We can use the land for collateral."

Tingvald knew, of the two of them, he was the more conservative. Perhaps he had always been too conservative. His brother had done well for himself and understood the stock markets better than anyone. While his stomach felt a little sick with how much money they were borrowing, Tingvald allowed Alex to lead them in financial decisions.

He only hoped Alex had not led them into financial ruin.

1920

Gunda

Gunda knew she had gone down a road from which she could never return. She felt inspired and surer of herself after she had attended the rally. Her sense of empowerment awakened after the 19th Amendment had passed, giving women the vote. She'd always had opinions, but now she had a voice to express them. She hoped she would one day be voting for a woman President.

Gunda had spent months reading the papers thoroughly, looking for another teaching position. Though the longer she was out of the classroom, the less she desired to return. She had always understood women had certain rules that needed to be followed. However, she thought more about female teachers having even harsher rules than women outside the classroom. She felt oppressed by a male superintendent and an all-male school board. Gunda wasn't eager to go back to that situation.

Additionally, she had never intended to teach as long as she had. She had intended to get married before she was twenty-four, but her passion for her students had made time race by. Now, Gunda felt bitter about having taken care of other people's children while giving up the years she could have had her own. At thirty-one, Gunda was definitely an old maid. She was coming upon her barren years. No man would want her.

Most old maids were thrust upon one relative and then another. Gunda didn't want that, but she didn't have another choice. She could go back to Tingvald's house, but it was already crowded. She could live with her sister Ingrid; however, she didn't want to live on the farm. Alex had built a beautiful house in town. Anna was often away, which left Alex to run the house and his business. Perhaps she could be of service to Alex while finding a place of her own. To make sure she was not inviting herself into her sister-in-law's domain, she spoke to Anna first.

Anna had started a pattern of returning to Des Moines for two months and returning to Soldier for two weeks. She had been following this schedule for the last three years. In her absences, the help had made up their own rules and treated much of the house as their own. There were times when Alex returned in the evening to an empty house and no supper prepared for him. Dust was beginning to accumulate in the corners, and the wood floors needed waxing. Some of the silverware and dishes were being broken or misplaced, and everything needed a good polish.

Once Anna listened to Gunda's proposition of becoming their house manager, Anna felt relieved to have her in the house. Gunda could look after the help and Alex while she was away. Anna even offered to ask Alex for Gunda. He said 'yes' immediately.

Gunda occupied a bedroom on the opposite end of the house. She moved in while Anna was at home, so she could obtain house-management directions from her: cleaning schedules, menu options, the house budget, and payroll for the help. Gunda hadn't realized there was so much to running a household. Her mother and Ella did everything themselves.

Once Anna left for Des Moines, Gunda got an eyeful of why the house was in such disarray. The three cleaning ladies, who were supposed to come every day, often came twice a week but took payment as if they had come every day. Gunda confronted them about their dishonesty. Her ability to manage children came to her aid as she scolded them for their duplicity and threatened them with termination if they tried to cheat Mr. and Mrs. Olson again. Within two weeks, the house had returned to its spotless form.

Gunda next tackled the budget. She noticed the food bill, which came from the grocer each month, was far too high considering there was usually only one person eating two meals a day. Alex always ate lunch at one of Soldier's two cafes. Either the grocer was overcharging them or someone in the house was stealing.

Gunda spoke to the grocer first, asking to see the itemized charges for each month. There was far too much food ordered for one person. "Did you not wonder why this house was ordering so much food each month?" she asked him.

He replied, "How do I know how much food is eaten in a fancy house like that? Maybe they have many visitors. Besides, the more they order, the more money I make." He grinned at Gunda as if his clever remark was going to appease her. It didn't. She switched their account to Ericksen's Mercantile.

Determining that the grocer was only greedy, not dishonest, she turned her investigation to the person ordering the food.

Mrs. Thompson has been hired by Anna and was not from Soldier. Anna didn't trust any of the women in town to have the skills for large dinner parties (she really thought they couldn't cook well enough!), so she brought a woman from Omaha and paid her handsomely.

One afternoon, Gunda casually sat down on a chair in the kitchen while Mrs. Thompson was making supper. She could tell she made the cook nervous. After watching her for a few minutes, Gunda asked, "Mrs. Thompson, I'm curious why you order so much food every month when it has mostly been just my brother?" She noticed the sudden alarm in the woman's eyes.

"Mrs. Olson told me there would be many dinner parties, so I buy plenty of food. That way, I'm always prepared." The cook only looked into her pots and pans while she spoke, never looking at Gunda.

"Have there been dinner parties?" Gunda kept her voice smooth as if she were only curious about the workings of the owners and their house.

"Yes. At the beginning, Mrs. Olson had several of them."

"But there haven't been any in the three years since. Is that correct?"

"I'm always prepared, though." Mrs. Thompson had determined the purpose of the questioning and was now defiant in her responses.

"What do you do with the extra food when you don't use it?"

"I throw it away." Gunda watched to see if she glanced at the garbage can, which anyone would have done if they had actually used it.

"Let's just see, then. We'll go together and look at the garbage."

"I'm not a pig! I don't root through garbage! I'm a trained cook!" Mrs. Thompson's anger signaled her guilt. "I don't need to be treated this way! I quit!"

Gunda hadn't found out the truth…yet. But she had what she wanted. She was now rid of a dishonest employee, and she hadn't had to fire the woman.

The laundress, Miss Every, a young, kind woman with a slight frame, told Gunda everything. Mrs. Thompson had been selling the additional food, allowing her customers through the kitchen door.

To save herself from repetition, Gunda gathered the entire staff

—cleaning ladies, laundress, handyman, and gardener—to the dining room. "I am the mistress of this house when Mrs. Olson is away. Anyone not doing their duties will be fired. Anyone stealing in any way from this house will be turned over to the authorities. You will do your jobs to the best of your ability, or you will no longer have a job. Am I clear?" She stared defiantly into their eyes.

She heard low mumbles of assent from the staff. Gunda decided she would investigate no more and give them the opportunity to keep their jobs.

Gunda felt good about her work. She had found a new purpose. She would still be an old maid living with relatives, but these relatives needed her.

1921

Ingrid

Two years after Stefan's death, Ingrid received another communication from the American government. President Harding had committed himself to bringing home the bodies of the fallen soldiers, now buried across Europe. When she received the letter, she had to choose whether to leave Stefan in France with his comrades or whether to bring him home to his family. Wanting Stefan to remain close to her, to be able to visit him when she wanted, made her decision easy. She chose to have his body brought back to her.

Six months later, Stefan's body returned to her by train, and the family gathered at the station for him once again. Karoline and all of Ingrid's sisters, brothers, and their families as well as Mary, Stefan's mother, along with his brother Anders and sister Elizabeth stood at the train depot. Their faces were pensive as they waited for Ingrid's reaction.

Stefan's body was not the only one returned to Soldier. He was accompanied by many other soldiers, their families also standing on the depot platform. This large crowd stood mute, looking down the tracks, sad anticipation vibrating through their bodies. The train finally arrived, sending out a large whoosh of steam, as if fatigued from its weighty journey.

The caskets, draped in American flags, were carried one by one from the cargo by army personnel. Each family cried fresh tears as they found the casket labeled with their loved one's name.

Seeing Stefan's military casket covered by his country's flag, Ingrid felt her immeasurable loss again. The three years had allowed a thick scab to form over her heart but being so close again to her husband ripped it off. Silent tears slid down her face. His voice and laugh resounded again in her ears. Ingrid reached out and laid a hand on the flag, feeling all the way through the wood and onto her husband's body. She didn't want to think about what he now looked like, only how he had looked the last time she had seen him, standing on this same platform, saying goodbye to her for a final time.

Anders put his arm around Ingrid and encouraged her to cry into his shoulder. Instead, she stood tall and followed her husband's death trail to the funeral home where he would lie until his second burial in the Lutheran cemetery.

Ingrid had agreed to bury Stefan with the other veterans on the northeast end of the cemetery. The white marble grave markers were lined along the cemetery fence. A week after the return of Stefan's body, his family had requested only a graveside service, a young bugler playing "Taps" on his instrument while the Andersens and Olsons stood around his grave.

Ingrid's compromise in taking him away from his fellow soldiers in France and laying him beside his comrades of Soldier was not an easy decision since she would not lay alongside him some day. People generally assumed a young widow, such as Ingrid, would eventually marry again, and she would be buried with her second husband, the one she would be married to for a longer period of time. Ingrid, however, didn't see herself marrying again. Her time as a widow had made her feel closer to her mother and a little more understanding.

***

A month after his funeral, on one of the windiest days of May, Ingrid was hanging clothes on the line, looking out over the valley as she often did, thinking about her life, the children, her memories of Stefan. She put an extra pin on each piece of clothing to hold it in place while her hair blew out of its tight knot and let loose strands whip her face. Her skirt and blouse clung to her body as the gale pushed against her.

Because her house sat on the hill, she often saw visitors arriving well before they reached her. Today, she recognized the horse and buggy of Stefan's brother, Anders Andersen. Anders had stopped by several times to check on her and the children after his brother's death. She was touched by his concern and generosity as he usually brought something for the children even though they didn't need it. She noticed he was wearing his pastor uniform today, dressed completely in black.

Anders was Stefan's younger brother by just one year. He had escaped war because he had a weak heart. Ingrid did not know him well. They had spent more time with her family due to proximity than they did with Stefan's family in Moorhead. Anders became a pastor of the Lutheran church in Willmington, a tiny town ten miles northeast of Soldier. His flock, as he liked to call them, were fewer than fifty. The church, like the town, was dwindling in numbers. Anders expected to close the church in the next few years and was looking for a position in Ute, Charter Oak, Mapleton, or Moorhead.

He wanted to move closer to his family. He had yet to marry and start a family of his own, which was probably responsible since he couldn't afford to feed, clothe, and shelter them.

Ingrid didn't mind Anders stopping by while he was on his way to see his mother; however, something about him made Ingrid edgy. Anders looked like Stefan, which made Ingrid sad; but he unsettled her in a very unexplainable way. She couldn't say whether it was the topic of conversation or the lack of space he gave her when he stood and talked to her. When he stopped to see them, she always invited him inside, fed him a sweet, and gave him news of the children while making sure someone was always in the house with her. She tried to ignore her feelings, especially since he was a man of God, but she could feel her body relax when he was back in his buggy and driving down the hill.

Both of Ingrid's children had married and moved out of the house within the last year, so Anders had less reason to visit unless he wanted to catch up on the family's news. Since he conveniently came by before lunch, Ingrid would, out of politeness, have to feed him. She felt uncomfortable with him in the house for such a long period of time, but it had to be endured, especially since he was Stefan's brother. Because she had no ready-made lunch, the visit would take even longer.

Once invited inside, Anders sat at the kitchen table with his cup of coffee and relayed Moorhead news. After the obligatory cup, Ingrid started their lunch. As she stood at the stove, cooking a ham steak to go with last night's leftover fried potatoes, Anders left his chair and wandered around the kitchen and parlor, picking up objects, looking at them, and setting them down as he imparted religious philosophy to her. She offered him the newspaper to read while he waited, but he declined and continued to pace around like a tiger.

Each time he came into her kitchen, he put his head over her shoulder, so he could monitor the progress of her cooking. Each time she sensed his presence, Ingrid jumped. She could feel his hot breath on her neck while he was peering down. The hair stood up on her arms, and she wanted to tell him to wait outside or sit in the parlor. She was so uneasy with just the two of them in the house together.

As a woman, Ingrid deferred to men, especially those in prominent positions. She was also brought up with a catalog of protocols to be used with a variety of people. These ingredients only created a woman who would not react on her instincts, which at this point were telling her to ask him to leave. Instead, she smiled at his jokes, answered his questions, and allowed him to get too close to her while she was cooking. To politely inform him he was invading her space, she lied and said he was making the kitchen hotter with all his moving and she didn't want him peeking at the food she was preparing. He didn't act on any of her subtle messages.

As Anders stood in the kitchen, hands on his hips, he took up the only path leading out of it. "When are you planning to marry again, Ingrid?"

Turning around to face him, Ingrid replied, "I hadn't really thought about it much. I still miss your brother terribly. I can't even fathom sharing my life with someone else."

"I was thinking it is my duty to make sure you are well provided for. I don't make much as a minister…"

Ingrid held her breath, waiting for what she thought would be an offer of marriage.

"So I thought I might find a good man to provide for you."

Relieved, Ingrid replied, "I really do appreciate your concern for me. I'm sure Stefan would have appreciated it as well. I am doing well, and my children are now grown and on their own. My mother is nearby, and my family is very good about taking care of my needs. I still receive part of the farm proceeds, so I am financially set. You don't need to find someone for me."

In order to separate herself from the awkward conversation, Ingrid turned back around to face the stove, hiding her discomfort from her brother-in-law.

"Oh, I see," he replied in a dejected tone.

His tone told her he had actually meant himself as her new spouse. She could feel the tension behind her back and didn't turn around, hoping he would move from her path.

Instead of moving out of the kitchen, Anders stepped directly behind her. She could feel his breath on her neck. He took the few flyaway strands of her hair and tucked them back into her bun. Then, he put his lips to the back of her neck and kissed it.

Whipping around to face him, Ingrid tried to push him away from her, but he caught her along her side as she was turning. His arms wrapped around her, pinning her arms down, and he picked her up, laughing like a little boy playing a joke on a friend.

"Put me down!" she commanded him.

"You like this. Admit it. You *need* this. You haven't had any fun for over two years."

"Anders, no! Please put me down! Now!"

As Ingrid struggled to release herself from his hug, he was pushing her down onto the kitchen floor. Ingrid was terrified and was frantically thinking of a way to release herself. He then laid her on her back and sat on her stomach, his knees straddling her. He began to tickle her. His actions only served to bring his face closer to hers. Suddenly, his laughing and joking turned to something else. His face twisted into one of distress, and he laid his cheek onto hers.

A whining voice into her ear said, "Just let me take care of you. I'll be a good husband. I promise. It's just one brother for another, Ingrid."

As he was saying these words, he was now completely on top of her, holding her with his weight. He was easily a foot taller and a hundred pounds heavier. Ingrid started to panic, knowing what was coming next.

"I'm just so lonely, Ingrid. I need a wife."

Ingrid struggled to free herself all the while saying "no, don't" over and over.

Anders continued to repeat, "I'm sorry. I'm just so lonely" as he was releasing his belt and unbuttoning his trousers.

While he was lifting her skirt and tearing her undergarments, she attempted to roll him off her, but she didn't have the strength. Knowing he would not stop but intended to rape her, Ingrid began to scream as loudly as she could, recognizing there was probably no one near enough to the house to save her. With no one to help her and no way to free herself, Ingrid knew she was defeated.

As he forced himself inside of her, Ingrid squeezed her eyes shut and thought about Stefan. They had created their children through this same act, but it was done with love. If Stefan were alive, he would kill his brother with his bare hands.

Finished, Anders stood up, pulled up his trousers, and offered to help her from the floor.

When Ingrid pushed her dress down and curled into a ball, Anders said, "Ingrid, I plan to marry you. It's alright. We'll be husband and wife." His tone was desperate; he was trying to make his actions not only legal but moral. "You'll see, Ingrid. We'll be together." Not receiving any response from her, he walked out of the house, leaving the door open.

Ingrid laid on the floor and cried, wishing for Stefan or her father. She had never felt so vulnerable as a woman. She could only wonder why she had allowed him to do what he did. Why hadn't she asked him to leave? Why hadn't she listened to her inner fear? She knew why.

Her father had taught her to obey men. He trained his daughters to believe a man was better, smarter, more capable. He made her believe men were protectors of women. Now, she knew he was wrong. She could no longer feel safe among men.

Even a man who wore the uniform of God was still a man, one who could be flawed like anyone else.

Ingrid picked herself up from the floor, locked the door, changed her clothes, and scrubbed herself clean, repeating to herself "nothing happened." She spent the rest of her day scrubbing every corner of her house.

When the children came to visit the next day and found the door locked, they pounded until their mother opened it. She told them the latch was broken, and the door needed to be locked at all times to keep it from springing ajar.

Ingrid did her best to act as though nothing had happened; she served them food and asked about their lives, not really listening to their answers. However, Mary detected something wrong and asked about it. Ingrid feigned a headache and asked the children to leave early.

Once they were gone, she was regretful she had asked them to leave; she was alone in her house with no protection. Ingrid didn't know how she could live. She didn't want company, but she also didn't want to be alone. She felt out of place in her own world.

Ingrid felt unsafe in her home, and the farm now felt empty and forlorn. It had always been a part of her life, a comforting entity, which provided for her and her family. A sameness and a solidness that never changed.

Now, the fields around her were wide spaces that harbored danger. Yipping coyotes, once soothing sounds of the wild, called like men taunting her, waiting for her. The night winds wailed like crying women who were being harmed. Ingrid, too afraid to sleep at night, slept in spurts during the day with her bedroom door locked.

1921

Floyd

At sixteen, Floyd had grown into a handsome young man. His red hair, parted down the middle and smoothed down, set off his bright blue eyes and pale skin. His rakish smile with dimples sent the girls after him. He had Alex's charm and Karoline's stubbornness. He teased girls and often conned them into kissing him. A few of the girls, those with less stringent morals, had allowed him to go beyond kissing.

One afternoon, coming out of the hardware store, Floyd saw a young man exiting the back of the saloon. He was the same one Floyd saw the day he was in the bar. The youth had brown hair and, with his hands in his pockets, a sloping walk. He looked like he was taking a stroll in the park.

Full of curiosity, Floyd sidled alongside him and introduced himself. The fellow offered him a cigarette and struck up a conversation. With so few young males in town, friendship was a valued commodity.

Frank Hogan, nineteen years old, lived in Dunlap but often came to Soldier to run illegal poker games in the backrooms of certain legitimate establishments. When Floyd saw him several years earlier, Frank had been running errands for the man who ran the games.

"Do you play poker, Floyd?"

"No. I've never even seen it played."

"Want to watch a game and learn?"

"I'm not sure I can. Where and when?"

"This Friday night in the back of the hardware store."

"Really? I was just in that shop. They don't have gambling—do they?"

"Just come and see for yourself. Seven sharp. And keep your mouth shut. The players don't like nobody yappin' while they play. Come in the back door. Knock four times, so I know it's you. And don't say nothin' about it to nobody."

Floyd's body vibrated with excitement. His feet practically danced his way home.

On Friday night, he told his mother he was meeting some boys at the theater to see "The General" by Orson Wells. Floyd felt a little guilty, but his adventurous spirit talked him into being lenient with the truth. Karoline generously handed over the shiny dime for admission.

He would never admit to his mother he was involved with cards. She hated gambling as much as she hated liquor. His Uncle Elfred Svensen often told him stories about how he, his brother Olof, and Floyd's father would go to the barn and play cards. Karoline wouldn't allow cards in her house: they led to gambling. Elfred's telling of the stories breathed life into Floyd's imagination and made his father come alive for him.

Standing outside the shop door, Floyd felt his stomach dancing the Fox Trot. His hand, out of rhythm with his stomach, shook a little and sweated. He considered turning around and going to see the film, but this chance would never come again. He knocked four times.

Frank, cigarette hanging from the corner of his mouth, gave a nod toward the interior, indicating Floyd's admission. Floyd squinted through the haze and whiffed the bouquet of cigarette smoke, men's sweat, and hard liquor. Six men sat around a table, five players with cards in hand.

Frank monitored the game and poured liquor from a jug into their glasses, keeping the players lubricated. Floyd's eyes bulged: they were drinking moonshine. He was in the midst of a full-blown illegal party. Floyd found a stool near the edge of the poker table and sat eagle-like, soaking in the game.

The dealer shuffled the cards and laid down one card for each player, face down, repeated the process, and then dealt another one, face up. "Jacks are wild," he said.

Each player lifted the smallest corners of his face-down card and sat waiting for the other players.

The men threw money into the middle of the table, the man with a Jack beginning, throwing down a quarter. One player said, "I'm out." The remaining four received three more cards face up, and one more face down. Another player bowed out. The three fearless gamblers threw more money into the pot. Selecting five of their seven cards and throwing the other two, the remaining men squared off for a game of chicken. One of the men who had a thick mustache called the game, and the players were required to reveal their hands. "A pair of fives," a player looking through thick eyebrows said with smugness.

"Ha, I have a pair of tens," said a large man with a discernible hump.

"Three of a kind, ladies. And thank you very much," the last player with a missing pinkie announced. He laid out three 8's, sweeping the money from the table.

Some grumbling from the other players broke out, but Frank

topped off their whiskey to help them forget their loss.

The dealer gathered the cards, shuffled them, and dealt another hand to each man. *Eyebrows* scowled and cursed the dealer for a bad hand but stayed in. *Hump's* face stayed calm as he bored holes into the other players. The quitter from the last game quit early again, and Floyd wondered if he ever lost any money. *Mustache's* lips lifted slightly, and Floyd thought he saw a grin. *Pinkie* drummed his fingers on the table and complained about the slow pace of the game. *Eyebrows* began the bet with two quarters. Each man followed with no one folding. The dealer sent out four more cards. *Eyebrows*, not seeing what he wanted, folded. *Mustache* started the new bet with a crisp one-dollar bill. *Hump* followed suit. *Pinkie* cleared his throat and folded. The last player (Floyd was calling him *Chicken* because he had been gnawing on a chicken leg) grabbed his chest and pretended he was dying but tossed in four quarters.

The dealer, chewing on a cigar without lighting it, threw out another round. *Hump* folded but *Mustache* and *Chicken* were still alive. *Mustache* slapped another dollar on the table, and *Chicken* raised when he threw in a five. *Mustache* folded, giving *Chicken* the win. The dealer wiped up the cards without Floyd's being able to see *Chicken's* hole cards.

Several more hands were dealt, and one by one the men packed up and left the game. In the end, only three players remained. Another hand was dealt, but Floyd needed to return home. The movie had finished at nine, and it was now eleven. His mother would have his hide.

"Floyd, how about we meet for a drink tomorrow. I'll meet you in the back of the saloon at one," Frank said before Floyd left.

Not knowing how they would drink in the saloon, Floyd let his question dissipate and gave a quick nod before he rushed out the door.

On his way home, Floyd replayed the games he had watched. He had never been so interested in something before. He told himself he would eventually play one of those games.

The next day, Floyd skipped school and hung around Alex, who chastised him for playing hooky.

"It's only the fall play today," Floyd said, defending his truancy. "I'm not missing any learning."

Alex offered him some pocket money if he would help figure some commodities tickets. Floyd worked with his brother until one o'clock and then feigned hunger to skip out.

Frank lounged against the back door of the saloon, cigarette dangling from his mouth and a dark brown Fedora hat pulled low over his brow. Frank Hogan was the slickest guy Floyd had ever seen. Floyd planned to replace his Newsie with a Fedora as soon as he had some cash.

"Hey, pal!" Frank yelled out. "How's about a drink?" He opened the back door and, bowing low, made a sweeping motion with his arm, pretending Floyd was some dame and Frank, the gentleman. "I just picked up a deck of Luckies and thought we could smoke, throw back some hooch, and chin a bit."

Floyd, embarrassed by his own proper grammar, tried to imitate Frank and threw in some of his own slang.

"So, who's the Big Cheese? Who runs these games?"

"Sorry fella. I'm keeping that one under my lid. Can't name him. If you want a job, I'm sure he would take ya on."

Nervous, Floyd changed the subject to avoid the question. "What's your story, Frank? How did you get into these games?"

"My uncle. He used to run 'em, but he went to the big house. Now they're mine. I make pretty good dough. What about you? You got a skirt? A squeeze?"

Because Frank quickly changed the subject, Floyd sensed he was getting too personal with his questions, but he had to know about the liquor. "Where do you get the lightning?"

"My boss knows the guy who makes it. He's in Templeton. You ever heard of Templeton?"

Floyd shook his head, feeling like a farm bumpkin.

"Templeton's got all kinds of distillers. You don't dare go into the woods in case you run across a cook. I've been there, and I've seen 'em. Corn liquor, rye liquor…Hell, they make it outta anything you want."

Floyd went back to Frank's first question, wanting to get back on familiar territory. "No, I don't have a squeeze. I've smooched with a few, though. You?"

"You bet. She's a Sheba."

"Sheba?"

"You know, va va voom," he said, his hands making an hour-glass silhouette while he spoke.

"Frank, can I ask you a question about the game last night?"

"Sure. Do you want me to explain somethin'?"

"Do you remember in the second game when the guy with the big mustache gave in to the guy chewing a chicken bone? Why did he give in? With the cards I saw, the ones facing up, there was no way that Chicken Guy could have had anything higher than one pair. Mustache most likely had two pair or three of a kind."

"How do you know that? You don't even know the rules of the game."

"I don't know all of the combinations, but the simple ones I could figure out. I remember numbers really well, and I can figure probability in my head. I kept track of the discarded cards. I may be wrong about that hand, but I still think Mustache should have stuck it out."

"You some kind of genius?"

"I doubt it. But I think I could play this game pretty well. Do you think I could get in on a game?" Floyd could feel his heart beating faster as he pictured himself at the table with a cigarette in his mouth and a drink at his hand.

"How much money you got? The game you watched wasn't a high stakes game, but you still gotta have some dough. At least ten."

Floyd didn't have much dough. His pockets seemed to have a hole because as soon as he put the money in, it went right back out. He needed a job. He could work for Tingvald on the farm, but there had to be an easier way. He would ask Alex if he could work with him. Floyd was sure if he could make the first ten with labor, he could make the next ten with cards.

"Can I get into the next game at the hardware store?"

"That's a closed game. Those guys have been playin' since my uncle started the game. Besides, you don't want that game. Those old Norwegians are tight with their money. They play for pocket change. I can get you into a different game in Dunlap. They play Five Card Draw. If you want that game, then you gotta have at least twenty bucks. You let me know when you got the money. I can help you learn the game before then."

Floyd felt a rush of excitement run up his body. Playing cards with a bunch of men, drinking bootleg liquor, and winning money— life didn't get much better than that.

1921

Ingrid

Fatigue had taken over her body from the moment he slinked away. After her children left, she slept dead-like for three days, trying to hide from her reality. She ignored visitors at her door. Locked inside her bedroom, she pulled the covers over her head and curled into a tight ball, an animal wanting to protect itself. Her brain muddled Stefan making love to her and Anders raping her.

Ingrid's brain protected her and Stefan's memory, turning her rapist into something else, something much more sinister. Anders, who reminded her so much of Stefan, could not be her attacker. Instead, he became the Devil in disguise. The Devil, who was after her body, to spawn his seed and take her soul.

On the fourth day, while lying in bed, she heard Anders knocking on her front door, calling her name with his rapping. When he didn't get a response, he started looking into her windows. Tap, tap, tap.

"Ingrid, please. I want to talk to you. I want to marry you."

The tapping sounded like a bird, its beak wrapping on the glass. *A black bird*, she thought. *A crow. The man in black has returned*, she thought. *He has turned himself into a bird*, and *He's going to come down the chimney. He wants to put his seed into me again and make me his bride.*

Ingrid ran from her bedroom and threw logs into the fireplace, lighting the kindling as fast as she could. If she could get a fire going, the crow would stay away. He would turn himself back into a man, and a man couldn't get into the house with the windows and door locked.

Having made a roaring fire, Ingrid went back to her bedroom, but her locked door was no longer safe enough, so Ingrid crawled under her bed and into a corner, making a nest with blankets and pillows. She spent many of her days and nights holed up in her sanctuary. She listened for the return of the Devil as either a man or a bird. Every day, she could hear his rapping, tapping on her door and windows.

Ingrid needed to keep the fire always burning, so he would not turn himself into a bird again and fly down her chimney. She never knew when he would return—sometimes it was during the day, and sometimes it was at night—so she could not sleep longer than an hour before she needed to add another log.

By August, her breasts felt tender, creating suspicion he had achieved his mission. She knew she carried his child.

She thought about the joy she had felt when she found out she was pregnant with her first child. She glowed with love for that growing baby. Every month of pregnancy brought new wonders for her and Stefan. They celebrated the impending birth and became closer than they had ever been. They talked many nights about its future. Their second child was much the same. Even when she had two miscarriages, she felt love for those unborn babies the second she knew of their existence.

Day after day, Ingrid felt less certain it was a baby until she denied it altogether. With every cell in her body, Ingrid knew with certainty this was something evil growing within her because she experienced none of her previous feelings. Instead of joy, there was anger. Instead of love, there was only hate. Children were gifts from God, and she knew this was not from God.

It was from the Devil instead. She dreamt it was a weed and knew when she awoke it was true. She waited to see if this thing would die of its own accord and fall from her womb.

Ingrid loathed the weed growing inside of her. She imagined it sprouting from Anders' vile seed, eventually becoming a tall thistle like him. Right now, the roots were imbedding themselves into her womb. Its hairy fingers, tentacle-like, were reaching out for nourishment.

Could she kill this weed like she did those in her garden? If she drank a poison, it would travel through her body, into her womb, and kill it. The weed would wilt, shrivel, and die. Could she survive the poison? Did she even want to? Uncertainty settled into her soul and lived there.

Day by day, month by month, she envisioned the weed growing. Five months into her pregnancy, it was now a thick stalk and prickly, pointed leaves unfurling. Sometimes, she could feel the leaves as they opened.

***

Karoline walked to Ingrid's house once a week to drink coffee and keep her company. She knew of the loneliness that could set in with an empty house. While the children lived there, she had not worried about Ingrid as much, knowing the daily task of living and taking care of them would keep her mind occupied. When both children left in the same year, Karoline made an effort to stop by more often.

Ingrid understandably went into a depression after Stefan's death. She seemed much more settled once Stefan was buried in the cemetery, and she could go visit him. Since May, however, Ingrid seemed to be reverting back to her old habits: staying in bed longer each morning, allowing herself to become untidy, ignoring her cleaning duties. Ingrid also now kept the door locked, ascribing it to a faulty door catch, and only after Karoline knocked for a long time and called out to her did Ingrid open the door. Karoline intended to ask Tingvald to send one of his boys to fix the latch, but by the time she returned home, her head full of new thoughts, she forgot every time she visited.

Karoline hadn't seen Ingrid since September and decided she would walk to her house and check on her. The last visit had been so strange, Ingrid clearly trying to shorten their conversation. She was also oddly dressed, wearing more layers than appropriate for the weather. Each time Ingrid was maintaining a roaring fire even though the house was stuffy and hot from the summer weather. Karoline's mother-sense told her something was very wrong with her eldest daughter.

Ingrid's door was locked as usual, so Karoline pounded on her door and called out her name. She stood on the front step for ten minutes, waiting for her daughter. When Ingrid didn't appear, Karoline went around to the windows, looking in to see if she could get Ingrid's attention. When she didn't see Ingrid and knew her daughter had not left the farm, Karoline went back to her own house to retrieve a tool to open the door.

She brought Tingvald and a crowbar. Once the door burst open, they stepped into the dank house, smelling of unwashed dishes, soiled clothing, and spoiled food. They heard nothing. The house seemed to have been vacated. Each called out to Ingrid and eventually heard a slight movement. They followed the sound to her bedroom.

Dirty clothes were lying on the floor, and the bed was stripped of its blankets. The curtains were securely closed, creating a tomblike atmosphere with stale air. They stood, looking around the room, until they could hear heavy breathing. Karoline got down on her knees and peered under the bed. Two eyes stared back at her. Curled into a ball and covered with a blanket, Ingrid lay in the corner on the dusty floor. Karoline gestured to Tingvald to leave the room.

"Ingrid, please come out," Karoline said gently, recognizing this fragile animal. After Inger died, she herself had become this animal, hiding in her own bed in the dugout.

"Ingrid, I want to help you. I will take care of you. You don't need to be afraid of me. I'm your mother."

Karoline crawled under the bed, uncovering her daughter. "Please, my dear. Come with Mama."

Slowly, Karoline coaxed Ingrid from under the bed. As she held her daughter up against her, she felt the bulge.

Horror, pity, and sadness overcame Karoline. Her defenseless daughter had been overcome by a man, she was sure. But who? And when?

Holding her daughter out away from her, Karoline looked Ingrid in the eyes. "Ingrid, who has hurt you? Who has been with you?"

Terror showing in her eyes, Ingrid said, "The man in black! He's trying to take me with him!"

Karoline didn't understand. But she did know she needed to take her daughter to her own house, to get her away from this dirty place, which was certainly the scene of something horrible.

Back in her home, Karoline tucked her daughter into her own bed, bringing her warm milk and toast with honey. Someone had attacked her daughter, who was now out of her mind, and Karoline was determined to bring her back to health and find the perpetrator.

Several weeks of warm baths, warm food, and loving family

around her, Ingrid uncurled and came out of the bedroom. By the looks of her, Karoline suspected she was five months pregnant. She would keep Ingrid in her house and watch over her, coaxing back her sanity.

An evening in November, a month after their discovery, Stefan's brother Anders came looking for Ingrid. He stood on Karoline's doorstep, dressed in his black minister uniform. At the sound of his voice, Ingrid fled to Karoline's bedroom and scooted underneath the bed, her belly making her movements more difficult.

When Karoline went to tell Ingrid she had a visitor and found her once again under her bed, the mystery of Ingrid's rape burst like a bubble in Karoline's head. Karoline marched back into her parlor and, like a protective bear, attacked Anders, slapping him across the face. "You raped my daughter, didn't you?!"

"No, never! We made love. I'm going to marry her. I've been trying to see her to ask for her hand, but she won't let me into her house. Can you…"

Karoline interrupted his pathetic lie, "No, you attacked and raped her! And you are going to pay for this. You will be arrested and tried." She pushed him back out her door and slammed it, going into the bedroom to rescue Ingrid. Karoline squeezed herself under the bed with her daughter and laid her hand on Ingrid's face.

"Was it Anders who attacked you? Did Anders rape you?"

"The man in black! It was the Devil!" Terror swept across Ingrid's face, her eyes shining like a wild animal's.

Karoline could understand her daughter not being able to face the truth: her attacker was not only a family member but a man of God as well.

Karoline left Ingrid alone in the bedroom the next morning when she went out to the coop to gather the eggs. When she returned, Ingrid was lying on the floor in a pool of vomit. Karoline's bottle of plant killer was empty next to her. Karoline felt relieved she used no poison in her herbicide—just soap, vinegar, and salt. While she was thankful there was no harm done, Ingrid's action made Karoline face the truth: Ingrid was not getting better. She still believed a weed was inside her stomach and had tried to kill it, even if it meant she would kill herself. Ingrid needed to be watched more closely as her pregnancy progressed.

Karoline called a family meeting, requiring attendance. Once the siblings and grandchildren were gathered, with Ingrid safely asleep, Karoline gave them the details of Ingrid's situation, including the name of her attacker. Their first task was to set up a schedule of taking care of Ingrid, never leaving her from their sight. With such a large family, many eyes were available to keep her safe. Their discussion broke down when the topic of Anders' punishment came about.

"We should beat him to death!" Floyd interjected.

"That's not reasonable," Karoline countered.

"He's a minister, and she's not right in her mind, Mama. He's not going to be punished," Betsi protested as a way of agreeing with Floyd.

"I agree with Mama," Alex added. "This isn't the Wild West. We can't serve our own justice. But Betsi is also correct. And I have no intention of allowing him to go unpunished."

"Maybe there's a way to carry out both ideas," Tingvald said.

"How?" Gunda wanted to know.

"The men of this family will need to visit Anders. Maybe we can persuade him to turn himself in. If not by logic, then perhaps by force."

The group of men—Alex; Tingvald and his sons; Lars; Ingrid's son, Samuel; and Floyd—would go to the parsonage and, if necessary, drag Anders all the way to the sheriff's office to confess his crime.

When they showed up at the parsonage, a mob of angry men, Anders began denying the rape, insisting they made love. He cried and sniveled, asking them to believe him. He lied and told them he had asked her to marry him, and she said yes. None of them believed him and finally, Samuel lifted his baseball bat and whacked Anders across his back. "Tell the truth!" he screamed. "You raped my mother!"

The pain of the bat was enough for Anders, who admitted to his crime and agreed to tell the sheriff. He still maintained he was planning to marry Ingrid. The story of his arrest and prosecution splashed across the local newspapers all the way to Sioux City. The headline always read the same: "Minister rapes woman." The scandal shocked the residents of the Loess Hills who always thought of themselves as safe from everything but petty crimes. For the first time, they locked their doors. Church pews were empty for a time as people realized ministers could be capable of something evil.

With careful watching, Ingrid continued to grow her child. She still refused to recognize it as anything other than a thistle. She talked about it getting taller and adding leaves. She believed when it bloomed its purple, spiky flower, it would come out of her.

The morning of her delivery, a cold January morning, Karoline found her under the bed again. How she had managed to squeeze her large belly into that small space defied logic. Ingrid was panting like a wolf. When Karoline reached for her, Ingrid growled, warning off any interference.

To retrieve her from under the bed, Karoline directed Tingvald and his sons to lift the bed and move it. Once completed, they could lift Ingrid up and place her on the bed, preparing her to give birth.

As the baby came through her birth canal, Ingrid screamed about the barbs of the plant scraping her insides. She commanded her mother to get a knife, so they could chop it up once it left her body. Through her pangs of pain, Ingrid continued to scream, "Kill it! Kill it, Mama!"

After six hours of pain, screams, and rants, Ingrid delivered a boy. She became confused when he began to cry a human sound. She stopped her wild accusations and lay still, trying to make sense of what she was hearing. Hoping to make her daughter see sense, Karoline took the wrapped child and laid him on Ingrid's chest. "Look, Ingrid, you have another son. Isn't he beautiful?"

Ingrid turned her head to the side to avoid looking at the infant. Her eyes rolled up and her mouth twisted into a grimace. "This is the Devil's child. Kill it before it kills us," Ingrid said emotionlessly, pushing the baby from her chest.

Karoline quickly caught the baby and took him from the room. For the first time, she admitted Ingrid could not come back to herself.

1921

Betsi

The news of Ingrid's delivery prompted Betsi to take the truck and see her sister and the new baby. With every new baby, Betsi was both happy and jealous. She still yearned for a child.

Arriving at her mother's house, Betsi was alarmed at the current situation. Her sister had rejected her own child, declaring it evil, and her mother was now tasked with raising a grandchild.

Betsi took the small wrapped bundle in her arms. The boy had a shock of dark hair, which stood straight up. When he finally opened his eyes, she saw they were chocolate brown. She ran her finger down his face, feeling the velvety softness of his skin. His tiny fingers wrapped around hers, and he let out a perfect baby yawn. She put her nose down to his head and smelled his innocence, laying her lips on his soft hair and kissing his head. She felt such a strong love for her sister's baby, an intensity she had never felt for any other child.

Once she laid the baby in his bassinet, she and her mother had coffee at the kitchen table.

"How are we going to feed him?" Betsi asked her mother.

"I sent one of Tingvald's boys to the general store to get the supplies. I never fed a child formula, but we don't have another option. He needs to eat."

"Does he have a name?" Betsi asked while peering at the infant.

"I was hoping Ingrid would name him, but I'm less convinced with every hour. She refuses to touch him, calling him only the Devil's child. I was hoping once she saw him, she would want him."

"Is she ever going to come out of this?"

"I'm not sure. When Ella was in a bad way after her birth, I knew she would eventually become well. It just took time and care. But this is not the same. Ingrid has suffered so much trauma she has gone crazy," Karoline replied.

"What if she never gets better? Will she just live here? Who will take care of her? We could put aside our lives to take care of her when we thought it was temporary, but if this is permanent…"

"I've done nothing but think about this. I considered calling the doctor, but I don't trust him. If I had done what he wanted with Ella, she wouldn't have healed. I can't imagine what he would prescribe for this."

"What do other people do? Ingrid can't be the only struggling person," said Betsi.

"There is a hospital in Cherokee for the mentally insane. I don't know anything about it. I would like to give this a month or so to see if we make any progress with her."

"And the baby? Are you going to take care of him, too?"

"I can't. Taking care of her is all I can handle. And maybe your sister would come to herself again if anything having to do with the rape were gone. What do you think?"

"I would like to take him home with me. The children no longer need my care. I would love to cherish and love my sister's baby for her." Betsi's usually bright eyes had gone soft with love for this new creature.

"What if she doesn't get better? If he starts off with you and then we have to take him somewhere else, it won't be good for him."

"Lars and I will raise him if need be. Ingrid will be your responsibility, and he will be mine."

Betsi hadn't asked Lars to take on such a responsibility, but she knew he loved children, loved her, and would want her to fulfill her lifelong dream.

After she brought the baby home, she and Lars doted on it, calling him Bubba. Betsi, who had settled into her life as a step-mother, found she had maternal instincts so strong it was as if Bubba were the baby she had lost. She responded to his every whimper and noise. She cherished every moment she held him whether it was to feed him in the middle of the night or to cuddle him in the morning when he awoke. Betsi marveled at every finger and toe and told anyone listening every move he had made for the day.

Every minute of joy also brought fear. Would her sister finally become well and want him back? Would her mother change her mind and decide to raise him? As much as her brain told her to keep the mother thread severed, her heart wound that thread around herself and Bubba so tightly there was no room for air between them.

Betsi even thought of proper names for the baby. She loved the name James, but it was too close to the name of the boy who had gotten her pregnant. Charles was her second choice. They could call him Charlie, like Charlie Chaplain. She didn't even dare ask Lars his opinion, knowing he would warn her of becoming too attached to a baby who wasn't theirs.

At 34 years old, Betsi felt her life starting over again. She had a good husband, wonderful children, a safe home, and an opportunity for a baby of her own. She hadn't felt this blissful since she was sixteen years old.

1921

Floyd

Floyd spent six months getting the twenty dollars he needed to get into a poker game. He worked on the farm, doing anything Tingvald would pay him to do. He worked for Alex, sweeping floors, running errands, and figuring tickets. The family members were too concerned about Ingrid's state of mind to pay attention to Floyd's accumulation of money, so they asked no questions and happily paid for the help.

In the interim, Frank Hogan taught Floyd the various games of poker. Occasionally, Frank brought his friends along to fill out the number of players. Sometimes they played for money; other times they played for bragging rights. Frank taught Floyd strategies in betting, and at first, Floyd lost his pennies. As he grew more confident in his gamesmanship, he began to win more often until eventually he won more money than he lost. At that point, Frank decided Floyd was ready to play for serious money and found a game looking for another player.

Saturday nights in Charter Oak, a town north and east of Soldier, held a decent poker game. Players came to challenge each other in the back of the general store. When Floyd questioned why they went all the way to Charter Oak, he was informed the town did not have a lawman.

Once he had lied again to his mother for his late night, Floyd hopped into Frank's Flivver and held on tight. Frank, a maniac driver, pushed his old car to go speeds beyond safe, especially on the curves.

Floyd, still wearing his Newsie, sat down at the table, introduced himself, and settled in for his first game. As the host of the game, Frank poured glasses of whiskey for each man. Floyd took the drink but sipped slowly, wanting to keep his thinking clear.

"Five Card Draw, gentlemen. Here's the rules of the game: no more than a three-card exchange, two rounds of betting, and the minimum is half the pot with no limits." Each player, including the dealer, anted a quarter. The dealer dealt five down for each player.

Floyd picked up his hand: a pair of twos, five of diamonds, six of clubs, and a three of diamonds. His pair of twos probably wouldn't win him the pot.

The player to the left bet a quarter. The next guy folded, the following bet, and the last guy folded.

Floyd threw three of his cards out and picked up another three: he drew an eight, a nine, and a queen. Nothing to add to his pair of twos.

The next guy kicked out three cards along with the dealer. Floyd detected a slight flush in the other guy's face. He speculated the draw had given him something better.

The dealer called, Floyd called, and the guy bet a dollar. Floyd didn't think he had enough to beat this one unless the player was bluffing. Floyd decided to play conservatively and folded. The dealer folded. The winner laid his hand face down and picked up his two-dollar win.

Curious, Floyd reached over to the winning hand and started to turn over the cards when the winner slapped his own hand on top of Floyd's. "Nobody looks at the cards, kid. First rule you learn in poker."

Shocked, Floyd pulled his hand away. He had embarrassed himself.

With the first game finished, the men drank from their glasses, draining them, while a new man became dealer and shuffled the cards. Floyd brought the liquor to his lips but took only enough into his mouth to wet his tongue.

The new dealer sent out five cards for each man. The ante remained the same. Floyd held a pair of fives, not a bad beginning hand. The first player bet one dollar, and Floyd folded. If he risked by bluffing and lost, he wouldn't have enough money for another game. So he sat and studied the other players as they went up against each other.

Several more games into the night, Floyd had won one hand and folded on several more. Overall, he was down two dollars. For an inexperienced player, he didn't consider himself a loser.

The drinking continued, each fellow having imbibed several glasses. Floyd noticed their playing was more erratic: their bets were larger and they bluffed more often. At one point, Floyd was watching after a game finished, and a player set his sweating tumbler on a card. He slid his glass to the edge of the table; the card stuck to the bottom of the glass. The other players were giving the original dealer a hard time and telling jokes, so no one saw the card had not only stuck to the bottom of the glass but had then fluttered to the floor when the player slid the glass off the table.

Floyd glimpsed down at the card, making sure the player didn't notice; it was an ace. The man placed his foot on the card and brought it closer, his shoe remaining on the card. Floyd was witnessing a cheat.

Floyd was unsure of his next move. He didn't know these men, and they were much older. He was uncertain how they would respond to his accusation. He lied and said he was out of money, so he could sit out the remaining games and see what happened with the errant card. Making sure he sat in a position that would give him no view of the cheater, giving the player an opportunity to feel like he was in the clear, Floyd took a seat on the outskirts of the game. If the man bent down, Floyd would know he used the card.

The competitors played two more games with no one noticing the missing ace. On the third game, the man reached down, pretending to scratch his leg, and palmed the ace. He held the card until he asked for another one. Smoothly, without even looking down, the player switched out his new card for the ace. He won the pot with three of a kind, three aces.

Floyd felt somewhat mixed about the cheating. On one hand, he didn't want to play with someone who cheated, and he certainly didn't want to lose to one. On the other hand, the deftness with which the player set up the con and switched out the cards made Floyd admire this fellow. Floyd wondered how often the competitor played dirty. He supposed the guy was never caught, which gave him the courage to perpetrate the scam.

Although Floyd walked away from the game one dollar poorer, he gained valuable experience. He didn't plan to return to that particular game; he did plan to continue to play and see if he could eventually start making a profit.

Frank put Floyd's name out there as a substitute player, and either because of his young age or Frank's reputation, Floyd was invited to play every week and often more than once a week. He never allowed himself to lose more than three dollars, a sum he had set for himself after the first game, and always played conservatively once he was up by ten dollars.

1923

Floyd

Floyd wanted to win enough poker money to buy a car. With a car, he could take out young ladies and have a more private place for them to spend time together.

Floyd found a 1910 Model T for sale. The owner wanted $50.00, not bad compared to the $360.00 cost if he bought the car new. The standard black paint on the car had dulled with years in the sun. The right front fender, like a lame hand, had crumpled in from the car being run into a fence. The automobile was not the beauty he had hoped to buy. But it had wheels and an engine, which after it was hand cranked to life, brought the car's top speed to 45 miles per hour, outrunning a fast horse.

Once Floyd had saved enough winnings, he purchased his machine in March, on his eighteenth birthday, telling his mother he had earned it working for Alex, with Alex loaning him the rest of the money needed. Alex had agreed to keep Floyd's gambling secret although he warned Floyd about the dangers of ruining his reputation.

With his jalopy, Floyd felt more confident in courting some of the most beautiful girls around. Elsa Gustafsson, a pretty Swede from Kiron, was known to be the most stunning girl in five counties. Kiron, north of Denison, was quite a distance for Floyd, but with his auto he wasn't deterred. Thinking of her long, blonde hair and big blue eyes, Floyd would drive any distance necessary if he thought he had a chance of courting her.

Floyd's opportunity came with a barn dance outside of Kiron. He was certain she would be there as any social event was well attended. He was not disappointed. When he walked into the dim barn, lit by lanterns and decorated with checked cloths covering the hay bales used for seating, he saw her in a crowd of young ladies. She wore a blue dress with a matching blue bow. Her smile lit the space around her, and her laugh drew all the young men's eyes. Looking beyond her group, Floyd noticed groups of young men gathering courage to ask her for a dance. Floyd could see he would need to outcharm his competition.

Each reel brought a new partner for Elsa. She was following a decades-old system of dancing one dance with each gentleman who requested, keeping the list of them on a small card. Because Floyd had arrived late, he ended up being at the bottom of a long list. He was concerned the dance may not last long enough for his turn.

At the end of one dance and before the next, Floyd brought Elsa a glass of water, butting his way between her and her dance partner. As she took the glass, he put his hand on her lower back to guide her outside. Before she realized he had cut her off from the rest of the dancers, he had wrapped his jacket around her chilled shoulders and blanketed her with his charms. Elsa forgot about her other dance commitments.

Each time Floyd drove his bent-up Ford to squire Elsa about, she was very prescriptive in their social activities. She wanted to see the pictures in Denison, play games with friends in Kiron, and attend dances in Schleswig. Floyd didn't mind. He enjoyed showing her off to all the young men who were jealous Floyd had caught himself such a beauty.

Once, they double dated with Frank Hogan and his latest girl, eating steak in Dunlap. Frank, showing off for his date, used all his modern slang and flashed wads of cash, even paying for Floyd and Elsa's dinner. Elsa didn't care for Floyd's friend and preferred to spend time with the people she knew. Floyd wasn't offended. Frank grew on people gradually, like moss. Not everyone appreciated his showy ways and bawdy humor.

Elsa appreciated the finer things, and Floyd spent wads of cash to keep her happy. He bought her small gifts along with paying for dinners and picture shows. He was gambling twice a week to keep up with his expenses. He never realized once he had something nice, it would take work to keep it.

When he graduated from high school in May, his mother nagged him to settle into an occupation, pushing him to start farming with his brother. Floyd never wanted to work on a farm. He wanted to work with Alex, but there was no full-time position available. Besides, he wanted to spend time doing what he wanted, arguing he had been tied to a school desk for many years. Floyd preferred fishing with friends, playing poker, visiting some of the Speakeasies, and tooling around with his girl beside him. "This is the 20's," he told his mother. "This is the age for young people, so I want to do what they do. And it isn't walking behind a horse and plow."

After five months of courting, Floyd and Elsa's relationship evolved into something more physical. Floyd pushed to see how far she would let his hands wander, and Elsa signaled her consent with small giggles.

One summer evening, Floyd and Elsa were parked on a country road, colloquially known as the Seven Dips. The lovers were locked into a passionate kiss as Floyd's hands moved to Elsa's knees. His hands decided to explore unknown territories and wandered over Elsa's body until they slid under her skirt as far up as they could. No hand reached out to stop him. No verbal objection barred his way. Floyd conquered her completely. He didn't care about consequences.

Having ruled her body once, Floyd now had full access whenever he chose. No challenge remaining, Floyd began to lose interest in Elsa. Before, he didn't mind her petty demands. Now, she seemed a burden. She burned through all his money. She controlled his free time, so he no longer saw Frank or his other friends. She didn't approve of his gambling. Floyd felt tied by her apron strings. He had more freedom in his mother's house. After nine months of seeing her, Floyd decided he would let Elsa go—gently.

He practiced his speech in his room. He thought about how he would comfort her if she cried but not let her feminine tears dissuade him from his goal. Hours before their final date, Floyd felt the butterflies of his nerves, but he was determined to cut the strings that bound him.

Floyd and Elsa were parked on a country road, and Elsa turned to him and said, "Floyd, I'm pregnant." His stomach felt a lead weight drop into it. His wings of adventure were ripped from his back. The cord of responsibility wrapped itself around him and tied him to Elsa. "We need to get married," she said. Elsa expected him to marry her, and their parents would make sure it happened even if her father needed a shotgun to get him to the church.

Instead of years of fun and freedom, Floyd now needed to find a stable job and a place for his family. He realized his dreams for travel and adventure were now dead, replaced by long days of work and a lifetime of responsibility. The most adventure he could hope for was traveling from work to home with a wife and baby waiting for his pay envelope. His soul sank into a depression.

He felt obliged to tell his family the unhappy revelation. He worried they would be disappointed in him; they would be angry at his reckless behavior. He decided to announce his mistake at their next Sunday dinner, a tradition from his childhood.

"Everyone, I have some important news," Floyd started as the potatoes were being passed around the table. "Elsa is pregnant, and we are planning to marry."

Instead of anger or disappointment, his mother showed approval. "You'll settle down now. You can farm with Tingvald."

"*Ja*, I can put you to work right away. I always need men."

"I don't want to farm. I don't understand why you and Mama can't understand that." Floyd was not only irritated they had refused to allow him his own plans, but they also seemed happy this had happened to him. His mother seemed relieved.

"What is it you think you can do instead of farm?" Alex asked.

"Maybe I could work with you?"

"No, I don't need any more help. I'm sorry. It's time to grow up, Floyd. Many men do things they don't like because they have responsibilities. However, you are good with numbers. Perhaps I can ask around and see if something else would suit you. Until then, I think you should do farm work to start making money for your family."

The family agreed on the plan, and Floyd felt a little more hopeful something would come through.

***

Floyd and Elsa married in September, a few weeks after his announcement, her parents insisting on a quick, private wedding with only family attending. Her parents barely spoke to him, showing their disapproval. Elsa told him they blamed Floyd entirely for ruining her. They didn't like that he was Norwegian, drove a fast car, and drank liquor. They were stout Lutherans, who didn't drink, smoke, or gamble and had their own plans for Elsa's future, hoping to marry her to a Swedish dairy farmer in Sac City.

After the wedding, the couple moved into Ingrid's empty house, giving Floyd proximity to his job. Every morning at 4:30, he walked to the barn and milked the ten cows. After he ate breakfast with his family, he and Tingvald started the daily feeding of animals and then headed to the fields for harvesting.

When he returned to Elsa for his lunch, she was often still in bed, and no lunch was prepared for him. They argued often over her assumed responsibilities. Floyd had always seen his mother and sisters working as hard as the men in the family. They had even come to the fields to help pick corn. Elsa would not be picking corn, she didn't have much skill in cooking, and she detested working outdoors; therefore, gardening was out of the question. On top of that, she was a poor housekeeper, spending her days reading books instead of keeping the house clean.

Elsa delivered a little girl in March, two days after Floyd's nineteenth birthday. The baby looked very much like her mother with blonde hair and blue eyes. Floyd tried his best to be interested in spending time with his daughter, but every time he looked at her he only saw another responsibility. His mother-in-law moved in with them for two months to help with the baby. She often hinted at his lack of responsibility in finding them their own home. He spent more time outdoors, trying to avoid her.

Floyd was horribly unhappy. He had made a mistake in marrying Elsa. No, he had made a mistake in getting Elsa pregnant. In dating Elsa. He wished daily he could go back in time and undo his decisions. He longed for his freedom, his friends, his adventures.

A little over a year after he started to help Tingvald on the farm, Alex came to the house with a job offer.

"I have some contacts at the Denison Bank," he said. "They can offer you a job as a bank teller. It doesn't pay much at first, but there is opportunity to advance. Are you interested?"

"Interested?" Floyd responded excitedly. "I'm thrilled! When can I start?" Floyd pictured himself wearing white shirts and dark trousers. He would have clean fingernails. No more manure. No more mud up to his knees.

Floyd moved his family to Denison the following week. They rented the upstairs of a large house owned by an elderly widow. It had only one bedroom and a small sitting room. They cooked meals in the widow's kitchen. It was only temporary until he could make a weekly wage large enough to rent something bigger.

Elsa was happy to move off the farm and into a town. She would have more opportunity to shop and make friends.

For a time, their relationship improved.

1923

Ingrid

Six months after giving birth, Ingrid often spoke of the Devil's child. Since the infant was no longer present, she believed her mother had done as she requested and killed it. She felt safer with no evil in the house, but evil still existed outside. Ingrid refused to go beyond the door, preferring to sit in her bedroom. If a visitor stepped into their home, she screamed and hid under her bed until the intruder left.

One September afternoon, Gunda, bucket in hand, came from the fields to the house pump to retrieve some water. The family were picking corn, and Gunda had been elected to make the journey.

Deciding to check on Ingrid, Gunda entered their house and immediately smelled smoke. The acrid fumes slithered from under her mother's bedroom door.

Rushing across the parlor and down the short hallway, Gunda flung open the door. Inside, a pile of clothing was aflame, the conflagration growing with each second. Gunda quickly grabbed the blanket from the bed, threw it on the pile, and stomped on it until it died. The room filled with smoke as the pile smoldered.

Ingrid was missing. Gunda called for her sister with no response. It was unlikely she had left the house. Her sister seldom stepped from the room she shared with their mother.

Finding no one in the remaining rooms, Gunda went back into her mother's bedroom and looked under the bed. From the far corner, she could see two eyes peering out. Ingrid was hiding in the corner.

Frustrated by this common behavior, Gunda grabbed her sister's dress and began to pull. Ingrid slid across the floor until she was free of the bed.

"Why did you start a fire?" Gunda demanded of her sibling.

"They have the Devil's seed," Ingrid replied while staring at the burnt remains of her skirt and waist shirt.

Gunda now understood. It was the outfit Ingrid had worn when she was raped. Each family member owned four changes of clothing. They had not thought to throw out a good set of clothes after they had discovered Ingrid's violent attack.

Settled down to eat their supper, the family discussed Ingrid's predicament. Having a family member attend her at all times was impossible. A farm required outdoor work, and Ingrid refused to leave the house. They never imagined she would be unsafe inside.

Today's near catastrophe had proved their efforts were not working. Another alternative was needed, and they all knew what alternative was necessary.

Cherokee's Lunatic Asylum was well known to everyone in western Iowa. Children joked about needing to go there. Parents threatened their naughty children with its confinement. Men put their wives there to seize possession of inherited land. It seemed to be a malevolent presence, pervading everyone's conscience.

The asylum, which was located well outside city limits, was a compound of large brick buildings sitting on 600 acres of land. Its beauty was marred by the fence keeping lookers out and patients in. The facility could house 1,000 patients in 550 rooms and was one of four asylums in the state. It was dubbed a 'city within a city' with its own farm, bakery, newspaper, cannery, and broom-making workshop.

Residents within the facility had been brought there by their families and had various illnesses. Some of them were men brought by their parents. They had returned from WWI with shell shock. Some of the women were diagnosed by their local physicians with nervous exhaustion, especially after having given birth. There were men and women with manic/depressive psychoses, moral insanity, schizophrenia, addiction, hysteria of various forms, and neuroses.

Women who were not insane also resided at the facility. They were outspoken, willful, unfaithful, disagreeable, or promiscuous. Families or husbands solved their 'female problem' by shutting it away. The women went into the asylum, mixed with the other female inmates who were violent or insane, and never returned.

The residents were divided by their level of danger to themselves and others. The most dangerous inmates were housed in a separate building, surrounded by its own fence, and monitored by many more staff. Those patients who were not dangerous and could work in one of the many facilities were housed in several other buildings. The catatonics, although not dangerous to themselves or anyone else, took more care and, therefore, had their own floors. However, none of the patients received enough care due to the shortage of help.

Getting Ingrid to the facility was challenging. With her refusal to leave the house, the family sought help from their doctor. He gave them a heavy tranquilizer to put into her morning coffee. Once she was asleep, they could transfer her to Alex's car and drive her to Cherokee. That part of their plan worked well enough. It fell apart when Ingrid woke up.

Fully awake, Ingrid looked around her and realized she was in a car instead of her bed. She immediately began to scream and flail her arms, trying to get out of the vehicle. Her son Samuel and her brother Tingvald were in the backseat with her. They battled her surprising strength and finally were able to get their arms around her. Karoline, sitting in the front with Alex, worried she would hurt herself or one of them and regretted the trip.

Once they were on the asylum grounds and pulled up to the main office, two large gentlemen came out from the building to assist the patient. As soon as they put their hands on Ingrid, she started to scream and flail again, kicking her legs and trying to bite the men. A nurse came out with a straitjacket, and the three of them held Ingrid down and put her into the contraption. Ingrid looked like a deer caught in a wire fence. Her eyes were bulging and looking wildly about. The nurse took a syringe out of her apron pocket and gave Ingrid an injection. She quickly went limp.

Ingrid's son, brothers, and mother felt helpless as they watched her being put into the straitjacket. She had yelled out their names, seeking help. Karoline cringed as she watched her oldest child, feeling for the first time she was useless when her daughter cried out for her. The nurse directed the family to the main office to fill out forms for Ingrid and assured them Ingrid would be put safely into a bed.

Having filled out various papers, one of them making her a ward of the state, Karoline asked to see her daughter before they left. She wanted to assure herself Ingrid was comfortable and being attended to.

"You may see her in two weeks," the nurse informed the family. "It's best to get the patients settled and into a routine before we allow them visitors. I assure you we'll take excellent care of her. She'll see one of the doctors by tomorrow and start receiving the help she needs. Have a safe trip home."

Karoline didn't understand. She had a right to see her own daughter, didn't she? They couldn't keep Ingrid from her. Standing dumbly in the middle of the entryway and not knowing what else to do, the family left the facility and departed for home.

The Olsons returned in two weeks only to be told Ingrid could not see visitors. "She's having a difficult time adjusting," the nurse told them. "We have to keep her restrained in her bed; otherwise, she wants to crawl under the bed and stay there. The doctor has been trying some new methods. We hope they'll calm her down. Next time you want to visit, please phone ahead, so you don't make such a long trip for nothing."

"We want to see Ingrid," Alex said in his most commanding voice. "We have a right to see her. We're her family."

"I'm sorry," the nurse replied. "You aren't allowed to see her unless we say you can. You gave over your control of her when you signed the papers. I understand how much you would like to see her, but we don't think that's best for her right now. You can try again in another two weeks."

"I would like to talk to her doctor," Samuel said. "I'm her son."

"Certainly. We can make an appointment for the next time you visit." The nurse then herded them out of the lobby and through the doors.

On the way home, the family rehashed their visit. They all felt angry and frustrated. Karoline couldn't understand why she couldn't see her own daughter. "We have no rights, Mama. We gave them full control of her," Alex explained.

Three weeks after they took Ingrid to Cherokee, they called the facility to make an appointment with the doctor. The day of their visit, they called again to be sure they were able to see Ingrid. They were told she may be sleeping, but they would at least be able to look at her.

Once there, they were escorted first to see Ingrid's doctor. Not all of the family could squeeze into his office, so Tingvald sat outside and waited. Karoline wanted to be sure she could understand the doctor, so she asked Alex to translate his every word into Norwegian.

The doctor was quite young. He had obtained his degree from Minnesota and studied under a prominent psychiatrist. He assured the family he knew the most inventive methods used in modern psychiatry.

"How is she doing?" Samuel asked. "Is she getting any better?"

"She's struggling," the doctor replied. "She is still terrified of everyone, especially men. She refuses to go outside of her room on her own. We've been bringing her into our dayroom to visit with the other patients. We've had to strap her into her bed at night and strap her into her wheelchair during the day. If we don't, she runs, and we often find her under her bed."

"What has been done to help her?" Samuel, as her grown son, had taken over the questioning. Karoline and Alex listened, Alex translating.

"We've given her ice shock therapy and administered bromides. The therapies are not working, but the bromides put her into a very tranquil state."

Karoline wanted to know what ice shock therapy consisted of. She pictured Ingrid being strapped to a block of ice.

"Ice shocking is very simple," the doctor explained. "The patient is put into an ice bath for several hours. We hope the jolt to their system will shock the brain into normalcy. Sometimes when we take them out of the ice bath, we put them into very hot water. However, it has not worked for Ingrid. We just haven't found anything that has helped."

"May we see her now?" Alex asked.

"Certainly. I'll have you escorted by one of our attendants."

The family left the office and followed the male attendant down a long hall and through a locked door. Once the door was opened and they had stepped into the women's dorm, a powerful urine odor accosted them. Karoline took out her handkerchief and held it over her nose and mouth.

The family looked around them in horror. Patients were sitting in wheelchairs along the hallway. Some of them were restrained at their wrists and ankles. Others were slumped over in their chairs, pools of urine beneath them. Some of the women were in stages of undress. A completely naked woman sat on the floor with a baby doll in her arms. They could hear wails and cries coming from unknown places.

Once they reached the end of the hall, they came to a day room. More women sat around. The ones who were more in control of themselves played cards or danced to a record on the Victrola. Over in the corner, next to the window, they saw a thin woman with long hair hiding her face. She was strapped into the wheelchair, and her head hung down onto her chest.

The attendant said in a cheery tone, "Ingrid, your family is here." Karoline had not even recognized her own daughter. The family walked over to her chair. Karoline reached under Ingrid's chin and lifted her head. Ingrid's eyes were glazed, and she gave no response to the people she was supposed to know. There were distinct red patches on her temples as if something had been clamped to her head.

"Ingrid, it's Mama." Karoline looked directly into her daughter's dead eyes. When she released Ingrid's head, it flopped back down onto her chest. Karoline shook her daughter. "Ingrid, please. Look at me!" A long line of saliva dropped from Ingrid's mouth onto her lap.

Karoline looked back at her sons and grandson. Their expressions were a mix of shock and terror. Karoline said, "We can't leave her here. We need to take her home…today!"

Karoline turned around and marched back down the long hall, followed by the rest of the family, and waited for someone to unlock the door. Once through it, she marched right to the main office and demanded to see the administrator.

They sat for some time, waiting for him. Once in his office, Karoline said, "We are taking Ingrid home today!" She stared defiantly into his eyes, daring him to deny her.

"Please sit down, ma'am," he said pleasantly. He gestured to chairs, indicating the whole family sit. "Let's talk about this, please."

"I just saw my daughter. She is…stupid," Karoline said, searching for a word she knew to describe her daughter's condition. "We will take care of her at home."

While Karoline was speaking, the administrator was searching through his files, looking for Ingrid's. He did not respond to Karoline as he read the reports.

"I see we've tried several procedures on her, and nothing has seemed to help. However, there are other methods that we are planning to try. Right now, she's sedated…stupid because she has been given some drugs. They keep her calm and allow her mind to right itself."

Tingvald, who had been patient long enough, interrupted, "My mother said we're taking her home to recover, and that's what we're going to do." His brother and nephew nodded their heads in agreement.

"You can't. You signed over your rights to us. We will decide when she goes home, and she's not going home with you today. It is our duty to see to her well-being, and this is the best place for her right now."

Karoline stood up and leaned across the administrator's desk. "Something has happened to her. I saw red marks." She pointed to her temples. "What did you do?"

The administrator hesitated and shuffled through the papers in the file. He pretended he was reading in order to stall. "Well, hmm. I haven't spoken to her doctor yet. I believe it came from the cold baths. It's nothing to worry about."

"Cold water made those marks?" asked Samuel.

"As I said, I haven't talked to her doctor. I'm sorry, but I have no more time today. I'm sure I'll see you again." He walked to his door and gestured for them to leave.

Once outside the facility, the family stood there and stared at the front doors. They were all thinking the same thing: they had made a grave mistake in bringing their loved one to this horrible place.

Every two weeks, Karoline made the trip to see Ingrid. She was always driven by one of the men in the family, who also served as a translator when needed. Every visit they saw the same thing. Ingrid was strapped into a chair and left to herself. Sometimes she was in the hallway; other times she was in the dayroom. The asylum kept her in a drugged state, presumably so she would not go into a fit of fright.

Karoline felt deeply guilty for having Ingrid committed. Although her daughter at thirty-nine was no longer a child, Karoline still took responsibility for the well-being of her children. She had always done her best by them; this time her best wasn't enough.

1924

Tingvald

Although Tingvald earned his living as a farmer, in his heart he was a fiddler. Inner peace came to him as soon as he laid his chin on the red spruce wood, taking up the bow in his right hand and drawing it across the strings. His worries about the crops or the mortgage or the cattle melted away and were replaced by music. His mother's father, Gulbran, had given him the violin when he was a young boy. He couldn't remember this old man exactly, but he did remember someone playing the instrument while he danced. His mother had hired a man from their church to teach him to play it.

Jalmer Johannson wore a white beard that matched his long white hair. Before he played, Jalmer tied up his beard and tucked it under his chin and violin, so it wouldn't get tangled between the strings and the bow. He closed his ice blue eyes when he played a sad song, but during a dance tune, they were open and dancing with the music. Jalmer fascinated Tingvald. The young boy wanted to play as well as his teacher, so he practiced at home even without his mother's cajoling. When Tingvald was twelve, Jalmer invited him to play with their local band at one of the community dances. Even though Tingvald was toward the back of the stage, being above everyone dancing made him feel important.

Jalmer had died many years ago, and Tingvald took his place at the front of the stage, standing straight with his head cocked to the side, his chin nestled against the wood of his instrument. On this fall evening, he was playing at the Halversens' barn dance to celebrate the end of the harvest season.

The spacious barn was lit by gaslight, which gave it a surreal feel. The Halversens had pulled down some of their hay bales from the loft and made a ring around the outside of the barn to provide seating for their guests. Tables, many of them brought by community members, dotted the edges of the barn for the large meal preceding the dance.

Each invitee was asked to bring a dish. Women took pride in their cooking and brought only their best fare. The food was arranged by categories: meats, vegetables, and desserts. Butchering occurred in the fall, so beef and pork were in abundance: large, cured hams in their juices along with beef roasts sliced into thick slabs. Bounteous gardens provided roasted carrots, potatoes, and sweet potatoes with the occasional dish of canned green beans. Pickles, sweet and dill, accompanied the sides. Desserts, the main attraction, showcased the women's talents. Devil's food cake, Brown Bettys, and varieties of pie loaded an entire table. Orchards provided apple, cherry, and peach. Traditional Norwegian desserts of *krumkake, kringle*, and *lefse* could still be found, brought by the older generation. Many second-generation women had now moved more toward American cooking, which was a conglomeration of many ethnicities.

The tables cleared, the dancers moved into position. The band leader barked out the call for a traditional Norwegian dance. Men and women paired and walked side by side, making a large circle while the single austere pull of Tingvald's violin bow brought them together. The violin picked up pace and the pairs, still side by side but now with hands together, walked more rapidly around the circle, some of the women holding out the sides of their long skirts. The violin picked up again, and the pairs now faced each other, the men walking backward as they twirled their women, occasionally showing off by making a complicated foot maneuver: a kick to their hand behind their back, a swoop down on one leg and back up again, or a jump with heels together. The barn began to heat up with the bodies packed together.

Tingvald's violin, now warmed after the first song, anxiously awaited a night of hard work. The rest of the band joined in for the next song, and the dancers shifted into position to the call of the next dance. Some of the dances were Norwegian folk while others came from other lands, a conglomeration of songs representing the mix of people. Songs like "Sweet Betsy Pike" and "The Dying Californian" were newer, coming from recent American events. Even though it was mid-November and the barn was chilly, Tingvald felt moisture wetting his face and underarms.

Ella, gathered with a group of women, put food away and cleaned up refuse. Tingvald's three teenage sons—Glenn, Milton, and Milton—had already found young ladies and were on the dance floor. Glenn had his grandmother's coloring, auburn hair and blue eyes. Milton and Maynard looked like Ella with dark hair. All of his sons were handsome and danced most of the evening with different partners. Edna, his beauty with her long chestnut hair and high cheekbones, drew the attention of many young men, who wrangled with each other to garner the most dances. As Tingvald stood on the stage and watched his daughter, he now understood his grandfather Gulbran a little better. He too had stood with his fiddle and watched Kristoffer dance with his daughter. How protective he must have felt, Tingvald mused. None of those young men were good enough for Edna, and Gulbran must have felt the same way about his son-in-law, especially when his mother had returned to Norway with stories of neglect. If any man neglected or abused Edna, Tingvald, who never showed his temper, would take him to the shed.

At midnight, his instrument lovingly placed back in its case, Tingvald finally sank into his bed. He dreamt of dancing and music. At one point, his violin notes turned into cows' bellows. His dream shifted into the cows being in the barn with the dancers. With louder bellows, Tingvald came from his reverie and realized the cows were real, were his, and were outside of his window instead of in their pasture. "Damn it!" he cussed, using his strongest language. "The cows are out again!"

This was the third time this month, not to mention past incidents in the spring and summer. He thought he and the boys had found the hole in the barbed wire fence and fixed it. If they were in his yard, then they were certainly in the neighbors' yards and gardens. Fortunately, the cornfields, cleared from harvest, had no stalks to munch or trample.

Wearing long drawers and an undershirt, Tingvald jumped out of bed, yelling for the boys. "Glenn, Milton, Maynard! Get up! The cows are out again. Just grab your boots; there's no time for dressing."

Tingvald, lantern in hand, was out the front door before the boys had responded, boots pulled up with his drawers tucked inside.

Tingvald's sons shared the small bedroom. They, too, jumped from their beds; however, they took the time to put on their pants and shirts. To them, the cows were only a nuisance rather than hundreds of dollars. They headed out the door after their father.

Tingvald directed Glenn to head north; Milton, south; Maynard, east; while Tingvald took the west. Seventy-five head of cattle, which had been roaming the pastures all summer, would not be easy to herd back into their enclosure. He did not know how long they had been free; perhaps they had already escaped while he was at the barn dance and had been roving for several hours. Fortunately, cattle generally stay together in clumps, but there would be strays.

During his cattle searching, Tingvald's emotions came in the form of anger that he was the one hung with the responsibility of the farm. Chasing cattle in the middle of the night was no dream, no goal, and no life. He desperately wanted to sell the farm, split the money with the family, and take his portion and start again with his own dream.

Tingvald knew his father had seen himself farming alongside his many sons. They would be a close family—praying together, celebrating together, and working together. This was the way in Norway, and it was to be the way in America. His mother saw the farm as not only a way to provide but also a way to keep them as one unit. Offering Stefan and Ingrid a plot of land and a way to become part landowner was Kristoffer's way of making sure his daughter remained close. Lars and Betsi were only a few miles away. The other children settled close by, so the time traveling home did not impede their desire to join in every event. If there were no farm or house, having moved his mother to town with him and Ella, there would be no homestead, no place to return to. The children would scatter like petals on a flower and blow in the four directions. After all his mother had endured with her husband's death and the work she had put into the farm, he could not take away the only thing that really mattered to her—her children.

With as many cows back in their pen as possible, Tingvald directed the boys back to bed. He would send them out again tomorrow to round up the stragglers. Too worked up from running around,

Tingvald sat in his rocker and picked up an old edition of *The Soldier Sentinel*. Instead of reading the news, he focused on the store ads, noting the types of sundries they carried and for what price. If he had a store, what would it carry? Anders Halverson already ran the dry goods store, which catered mostly to women. If he had a store, he would want men folk as customers. He could envision himself, his foot on a crate, jawing with the farmers in the back of his store while his hired clerk took care of the sales. They would all call him T.A. instead of the odd name his mother had given him, which she insisted on using. It wouldn't be a feed store, of course. Elfred already had that covered. Perhaps he would sell farm goods, and only farm goods. He could carry the usual items, like twine and nails, but he could also specialize in certain items that had to be ordered from a catalog or gotten from the big towns, like Denison. Tingvald got excited thinking about his impossible dream.

However, Tingvald was a realist. He would never own a store. His place was on the farm. His sons would farm after him and their sons after them. His father Kristoffer had envisioned a legacy, and it was his responsibility to carry it through.

1928

Tingvald

Easter dinner at the Olson farm was a special event, one that Tingvald's children never missed. Ella spent days baking, cooking, and cleaning. The day always started with Easter service, followed by a spectacular feast. Each of the married couples brought a dish to share, and each unmarried person helped with the dishes at the end.

The family sat down at the long dining table. Ella, looking at her oldest son, said, "Glenn, I haven't seen you in church for a while. During Easter, you should be going to church."

Glenn said quietly, without looking at his mother, "I'm planning to join Alice's church."

All eating stopped. The family looked at Glenn and waited for the explosion.

Tingvald, his face beginning to flush, could feel a stubborn anger rise in him. He ripped the napkin from under his chin and threw it onto his full plate of food. He looked at Ella, got up from the table laden with Easter abundance, and strode out of the room, the sound of a door slamming somewhere within the house. Quietly, Ella followed him.

The remaining family members looked at one another and then at the couple. They didn't know if they should partake of the feast or leave it. Glenn took Alice's hand, and without saying a word to the family, led her out the door.

The remaining family filed out of the house, a fully cooked meal uneaten.

Glenn's new wife, Alice Gibbs, was both German and Catholic. Glenn, raised Lutheran like all Norwegian people, had married outside of his faith but had assured his parents he would continue to attend services in the family's church. On Sundays, Alice would go her way, and Glenn would go his.

Alice Gibbs had transferred to Soldier High School from Ute her junior year. Even with the new addition, the class had only twelve students.

The junior class enjoyed spending time together. High school athletics was both an inexpensive and entertaining way to partake in teenage fun. One winter evening, they loaded into three cars and traveled to a basketball game in Dow City, Alice needing to sit on Glenn's lap because of the cramped conditions in the car. Even though she was not what his parents would have chosen for him, Glenn was smitten.

Having completed their education, Alice went to Normal School to become a teacher, and Glenn went to work on a farm for Howard Ulvan, his mother's cousin. They married four years after their high school graduation.

Sitting in their bedroom, waiting for everyone to leave the house, Ella asked, "How could we have done such a poor job raising that boy?"

"It's not us, Ella. I knew it was a bad idea when he married Alice. Even though he swore he was going to remain in our church, I had a bad feeling. And I was right."

Glenn had never been a disobedient child. He took his responsibility as the oldest very seriously. He helped with the farming. He treated his grandmother respectfully and always had time for her when she needed something from him. He was helpful and pleasant to the women in the house. This news shocked them to their toes, because Glenn had never gotten into trouble, except for one time.

Like most Americans, Glenn was a passionate baseball fan. He and Tingvald had listened to games on the radio. Of course, like every baseball lover, Glenn admired Babe Ruth, who played for the New York Yankees. In the spring of Glenn's senior year, Ruth was playing an exhibition game in Sioux City. Glenn and the other eight boys in his class skipped school and drove to the game. Glenn knew both the school and his parents would punish him, but he felt it was worth whatever he was given. The school gave all the boys detention, requiring them to help the janitor clean the schoolhouse. His parents made him clean the winter manure from the barn, a most unpleasant job.

Easter evening, Tingvald sat in his favorite chair to consider the day's tragedy. His own parents and others of that generation came from a country that did not include outsiders. There was little chance for them to intermingle with anyone other than those who were Norwegian. When they emigrated, the likelihood of being exposed to an outsider was greater although they tended to live among their own people and married from within their community.

With Tingvald's own generation, more people had moved into their community, and not all of them were Norwegian. Since the number of men outpaced the women, it was not uncommon for a man to marry a woman of a different culture. He knew many men who married Danes or Swedes.

With his own children, they seemed to have weaker ties to their country of origin; therefore, marrying a German girl did not seem unthinkable to his son. His mother Karoline said nothing to her grandson, but she dearly wished he had found a nice Norwegian girl. Even one of his twin sisters had married someone outside of her culture.

But to marry outside of one's faith was unforgivable. Italians married Irish, which was a clash of cultures, but at least they were both Catholic. Danes and Norwegians were both Lutheran.

When these culturally mixed marriages did not work out, the trouble was always blamed on not marrying your own kind. When Glenn married Alice, Tingvald worried the difference in their religions would tear their marriage apart.

His head and his heart were on two separate spheres. His community would expect him to disown his son and daughter-in-law. His heart could not conceive of never seeing his son and his grandchildren if there were any. As he vacillated between head and heart, he rocked and smoked his pipe.

Waking to an empty and cold bed, Ella came into the chilly parlor to find Tingvald still rocking and smoking.

"Are you staying out here all night?" she asked. "I've been thinking about all of this since noon."

"I don't know. I'm torn, Ella. I don't know what to do about this catastrophe. I know what my father would have done."

"What would Kristoffer have done?"

"He would have disowned Glenn and Alice. He was a firm believer that you married your own kind. I remember when my sister Betsi got mixed up with an Irish boy. I don't really know all the details; it was kept pretty quiet. But I do know he was resolute that she was not to marry either an Irish or, worse yet, a Catholic. I can imagine what he would have said about Glenn and Alice's marriage. I am certain he wouldn't have attended. He would have cut them out of our family like a disease."

"Is that what you're planning to do? Will you disown our son because of his choices? Alice is a good girl. She's a teacher. She comes from a good family. They both come from a Christian religion. What is it that we want for our children? Because I want for them to be happy. She makes him happy.

"When he converts, we obviously won't attend, but what is the worst that can happen? Will the sky fall down? Will he die? As long as they live an upright life, I don't care if she's Norwegian or Irish or Catholic. If she makes him happy and is a good wife, I can ask for no more. I don't know what you will do, but I will not cut my son from my life. I have already lost one son—that couldn't be helped—so I won't intentionally lose another," Ella stated.

Tingvald decided nothing needed to be done in the middle of the night and going back to bed was his most prudent action at this point. He could feel the sense of Ella's reasoning. Children were invaluable. His family had already lost several of them due to illness. If his mother could have brought Ole or Inger back to life, would she have done it if she knew they were going to change their religious beliefs? He was sure she would have done so.

Although Tingvald tried to live the path his father had set for him, this was one detour he would take. He would not make the same mistakes, which had cost Kristoffer his daughter Betsi.

1929

Alex

On Thursday, October 24, Alex sat in his office. The weather was unseasonably cold. Raging winds screamed outside his window, and dark western clouds with potential snow were building and being blown into Soldier. *The Farmers' Almanac* predicted an early winter. Alex thought about the crops and whether his brother could finish harvesting them before the first snow.

Alex had spent the majority of the morning going over his book-keeper's ledgers. He used the same man for both his business and personal finances. His business was a hilly road: it had its ups and downs. The farming economy in Iowa had been good in the early 20s but had points of depression and then recession. Families who had borrowed too much were losing their farms. Farm auctions, like the one Tingvald and Alex had attended, were now a common occurrence.

His personal finances had done very well. He invested a great deal of his cash in the stock market. His stocks had risen like a hot air balloon and seemed to never intend on coming back to earth. He had been smart and divested his interests. In the beginning, he had invested only in agricultural stocks. Fortunately, since agriculture in the Midwest and South had struggled on and off, he had put his money into other investments like tin and tires. On that October day, he was nearing $300,000.00 in stock profits. It wasn't cash in the bank, but it could be whenever he decided to sell his shares. His actual cash was no better than when he worked with Elfred. He was better off than most but certainly not cash rich. He had a modest sum in savings.

As Alex worked, he could always hear his stock market ticker going in the background. Its ticking had become quiet music. When he was concentrating, he rarely heard it unless the stock market started rapid selling. Then, it began to sound like a woodpecker on a tree. Alex smiled, thinking how much he loved hearing the sound of money being made. He also had his Stewart Warner radio on, playing pleasant music. He was waiting for the afternoon news from Omaha. As his stock ticker was clicking rapidly, the radio announced a major catastrophe on Wall Street. With the words *Wall Street*, Alex focused his attention on the radio. He reached behind him and turned up the volume. The radio announcer said, "The Dow Jones has fallen by nearly twenty-one percent. Trading has stopped to allow the markets to calm down."

Twenty-one percent, Alex thought. He has just lost $60,000 in stock worth. It hurt, but he didn't want to panic. He still had profit and could wait it out. The stocks had taken large dips before, but they had always come back up in a day or two.

He went over to his stock ticker machine and looked at the hill of tape lying on his office floor. As he looked through the different companies, he had to recalculate his worth. Some of his companies had taken a bigger loss. As he averaged them, Alex figured he had lost more like twenty-three percent, bringing down his worth closer to $231,000. It was still a large sum of money, but it worried him greatly.

Alex left for lunch. Instead of eating at the café, he was going home. Anna was there, and when she came home, he spent as much time with her as he could.

Anna was always happy to be home, until she wasn't. While she was there, she and Alex ate meals together and enjoyed any social event in town. They also attended the Olson Sunday dinners.

Alex missed seeing his mother at the head of the table. She had finally succumbed to old age. It had been two years since her death. The family felt her loss greatly, and Sunday dinners didn't feel right without her at the head of the table.

When Alex walked through his front door, Anna always greeted him and said, "How was your day?" Every time, he responded with "very well," but today it would not be true. He would say the words anyway because he did not want to worry her.

Once settled down to a delicious lunch, the conversation revolved around Des Moines' society doings. Even though Anna was in Soldier, her mother still relayed the gossip to her over the telephone.

"Alex," she said, "I think we should do some remodeling on the house."

"Really? And what would you like to remodel?" Alex could see the bills mounting up over this busy project.

"First, I think we need to make the kitchen bigger. And, I would like to put in electric lights. Now that the town has electricity, we should put it into the house. I also think we should get some new furniture. Ours is already nine years old. It's horribly out of date. What do you think?" She looked at him, her eyes bright with the potential of a big project to keep her occupied.

"I think electricity is a grand idea. The town has had it since '24, and we wouldn't be the first to put it into the house. Others are ahead of us. I think the other things can wait, especially the kitchen." Alex thought if he gave in on something, she would be happy enough to wait on the rest. If he had said 'no' to everything, she would have asked until he gave into her.

Alex had promised Anna to take Friday off and spend the day together. He was taking her to Sioux City to watch a play at one of their favorite theaters. Instead of going to the play, Alex wanted to sit in his office monitoring the ticker. He wanted to reassure himself the markets would bounce back. He reminded himself whether he watched or didn't watch, the markets would do what they were going to do. There was nothing gained by disappointing his wife.

While he was out of the office, the Dow had risen by .06%. When Alex went in on Saturday, he saw the market climbing in the right direction. He reassured himself there was no reason to panic. He knew it would go back to its original worth. He and Anna spent a lovely weekend going to church and visiting the family.

Monday morning, October 28, Alex returned to work. Instead of working on anything, he put his chair in front of his ticker machine to watch the markets closely. The trading was heavy, investors trying to get out of their stocks. Alex thought about selling his, but those who panicked in this profession often found themselves wishing they had stayed steadfast. The economy had been so good for the past decade he could hardly believe the markets would go down anymore. The rise on Saturday made him hold his ground. Unfortunately, by early afternoon, he had lost another twelve percent, $36,000 more.

While he still had over $195,000 worth of stocks, he had half of that in outstanding debt. He had borrowed the money to build his house, to buy his business building, to purchase automobiles and other items for the house. Alex had allowed himself and Anna to live well beyond their means. His stomach felt sick thinking about how much money he had lost in the last few days. He decided to close the office for the rest of the day and go home. A nice lunch with Anna would perk him up.

Tuesday morning, October 29, Alex went into the office early. He wanted to be there when the markets opened. He turned on his radio to listen for any additional information. Alex had gone to the horse races only once in his life. Waiting for the markets was his race. He was nervous and anxious for the gates to open and let his horses run. He hoped they would show well and pull him from his circumstances. The trading was immediately heavy again. Panicked investors were dumping all their stocks. Some companies' stocks had no buyers. Alex had a few high-risk investments that went under immediately. He had also put his money into some of the well-known companies, like Ford Motor. While they also lost value, they were strong enough not to go completely under. His total Tuesday loss was fifteen percent, another $45,000. He had $150,000 remaining in stock value if he could get anyone to buy, which he couldn't. While he was rich in stocks, he was cash poor.

The Omaha radio news reported catastrophes on Wall Street. Men were jumping from their buildings. Men were killing themselves by hanging or gun. They had lost everything. They woke as millionaires and were paupers by late morning. Alex sat in his office chair with his head back, looking at the ceiling. He thought about his own circumstances as well as those of other men he had met. While he pondered, his telephone rang several times, but he did not feel like discussing the current events with anyone.

On his way home for lunch, he considered telling his wife about their circumstances. As it was with most wives, she had no knowledge of their finances. She only knew there seemed to be money for anything she wanted. His office secretary brought him bills from Des Moines, Omaha, and Sioux City. Anna bought new clothes for each season. She wouldn't wear anything beyond two years and liked to 'spruce up' her wardrobe each spring and fall. She wouldn't think of buying ready-made clothing. Her dresses were designed and hand-made. Alex was unsure of her reaction when he would be forced to tell her they needed to curtail their spending.

When he walked through his front door, he could tell something was very wrong. The hired help looked as if they were walking on glass as they tiptoed around the house. Their faces were stricken. Alex caught Miss Every, the laundress, by the arm and asked what was amiss. "Mrs. Olson's father," she whispered, "he's dead."

"Where is my wife?"

"She's upstairs. In bed."

Alex couldn't imagine how her father had died. Heart attack? Anna had said nothing about her father ailing in any way.

Alex took the stairs two by two, rushing to his wife's bedroom. She reached out for him, and he wrapped his protective arms around her. "Anna? What has happened?"

"My father," she wailed. "He's dead!"

"How did it happen? Did he have heart failure?"

"My mother wouldn't tell me. We need to go to Des Moines… right away!"

Unlike Anna, Alex knew why a cause of death was not men-tioned. It was shameful. Thinking about the men who were killing themselves in New York, Alex felt certain Oscar Nilsson had killed himself. Each time Alex visited the Nilssons, he and Oscar sat in the library and discussed stock trading. Alex knew Oscar had purchased risky stocks to get the bigger dividends. Alex speculated that Oscar must have taken his secure stocks and exchanged them for the uncer-tain ones. He had probably lost nearly everything.

The next morning, Alex and Anna took the train to Des Moines. The weather seemed very precarious, so it was best not to get the car stuck in a storm. The railway was safer and more reliable.

When they arrived in the late afternoon, they went immediately to the Nilsson home. Anna's mother was entombed in her darkened bedroom. Anna's uncle, Oscar's younger brother Nils, lived near Des Moines and had arrived the day before. Alex and Nils went into the library to talk.

"He shot himself right in this room," Nils informed Alex. "He sat down at his desk and put the gun into his mouth. Anna's mother found him lying behind the desk in a pool of blood." Nils shuddered from the thought of the deed.

Alex looked at the wall behind the desk, but there was no blood to be seen. The servants had cleaned the mess.

So much had happened between him and Oscar in that library. Alex remembered his first visit to the house and Oscar taking him into the library to determine whether he was suitable to marry Anna. Oscar had often drunk whiskey with Alex while giving him stock tips. Even though they came from different worlds—Alex, a farm; and Oscar, the city—Alex always felt Oscar had accepted him. It couldn't have been easy to allow his daughter to marry a disabled man. But Oscar had seen his potential and the love he had for Anna and took him into his family. Alex knew he owed this man a great deal, and he vowed he would somehow repay him.

The Olsons stayed in Des Moines for two weeks. Alex shut down the office, which had no business anyway. Gunda could take care of the house without them.

Anna's mother Hattie was not faring well without Oscar. Unlike his own mother Karoline, Hattie was frail and had no sense of how to get along in the world without her husband. She didn't know how to pay bills. She didn't know anything about their finances.

Oscar's funeral was as lavish as Anna and Alex's wedding. A few from their society circle attended. Six black horses and footmen

carried the walnut casket. Fields of flowers adorned his casket. A tall
obelisk marked the beginning of the Nilssons' graves. Oscar had a
large tombstone with an angel on top, all carved from marble. A
bountiful reception fed the funeral attendees.

During the two weeks, Alex spent time calculating their own
finances. He had already determined he would let his office building
go back to the bank. There was no business to conduct, so there was
no need for a building in which to conduct it. The bigger question was
the house. He could pay the mortgage on it for six months, but then
they would be depleted of all cash. With little revenue for an indeter-
minate amount of time, they needed to save as much cash as possible.

Eventually, he was forced to make the decision to let the house
go as well. Since no one in Soldier had the money to buy it, the bank
would reclaim the property. He dreaded telling Anna they would have
to move into Ingrid's house or Tingvald's house. There was also
Gunda to think of. She, too, would need to move. He wasn't sure
what to do with the furnishings. They couldn't take them into someone else's house. He didn't know of a space large enough to store
them. And when they did get a new house, it wouldn't be nearly as
big as their current one. They wouldn't need all of those wares.

Their three cars should be sold as well—if he could find buyers
for them. They were too fancy for anyone in Soldier. Perhaps someone in Omaha or Des Moines would be interested.

Alex found no silver linings. There was nothing but bad news to
tell his already-grieving wife. He didn't think she could handle more
of it. Instead, he kept quiet and continued making financial plans.

At the end of the two weeks, Alex broached the subject of returning home.

"I can't leave my mother!" Anna exclaimed. "She needs me! I'm
not sure when I'll be able to return. I need to get her back on her feet.
Uncle Nils will stay as well. He's starting to sort through the

finances. But I understand if you need to return to the office."

Alex decided to take the train the next morning. He would do what needed to be done and then return to Des Moines. Without a business to run, there was no need to stay in Soldier. He could stay in Des Moines for as long as the family needed him.

That evening, Nils requested to speak privately with him. Like many times before, Alex found himself in the library discussing finances.

"Alex, I met with the banker today. It's worse than I could have imagined. Oscar put every dollar he had into several of the stocks that are no more. He has no cash, no stocks, no bonds. Nothing. Fortunately, the house is paid for. However, there is no money to run it. They can't even afford to pay the help what they currently owe them. Hattie and Anna are ignorant of their financial situation."

"Why on earth did they have such an expensive funeral? Where did the money come from?"

"They haven't paid for the funeral yet. When merchants think you're wealthy, they are more than willing to extend credit. That is, until you can't pay the bills. I was hoping you could suffuse the family with some cash to get them turned around?"

For the first time, Alex spoke the words: "I'm broke."

"You have nothing?"

"Worse," Alex said, "I have less than nothing. My debt exceeds my cash. I can't help Anna's mother."

Alex explained his financial situation to Nils. When he told him they would soon have no house, Nils had an idea. "You should live in this house. It's certainly large enough for you both. There is more opportunity to find employment here in Des Moines. Hattie needs her family around her right now. She leans on Anna."

As Nils ticked off the reasons why they should move to Des Moines, Alex couldn't argue with any of them. They were all true.

His wife would be so thrilled to live in Des Moines again that she wouldn't mind losing her own house…he hoped.

When Alex explained their financial situation to his wife as well as the plan to move to Des Moines, he was relieved she took the news well. She lamented some of her furnishings she would lose, but the other benefits exceeded those losses. She would be a city girl once again and enjoy the restaurants and entertainment. She would be around her people.

Alex felt a pang…of what? Regret? Longing? Western Iowa ran through him like his blood. The steep hills covered in spring green, the palette of fall foliage, the sound of cows lowing, and the mating call of the cardinal—all of this would be replaced by city streets, automobiles, and throngs of people. He would wake up in the morning and look across flat land. Instead of the farm, there would be neighborhoods.

Alex knew his ties to Soldier and the farm would remain strong, but he would never live there again.

1932

Sophie

After five years of working at Ericksen's and saving money, Jack and Sophie finally achieved their goal and started a butcher shop. They took out a bank loan for the building and put their savings into the equipment for the shop. They located their new business on the north end of First Street in Soldier.

The shop was a small, wooden, white building with large front windows. A meat counter with a glass front met customers as they walked through the door. The counter was full of porkchops, hams, sausages, roasts, and steaks. The back of the shop, where Jack did the butchering, was very small. A large table and his implements filled the space. Only he could be back there when he had a hog or steer on the table.

Outside of the shop, in the back, three animal pens butted up against the building. Farmers would bring their animals into town and release them into a pen until Jack could get them butchered. A small wooden sign hung over the building: Gorden's Butcher Shop. The day they opened their own business was the happiest day of their lives. They held hands while they stood on the street, looking at their accomplishment.

The butcher shop was a thriving business. Sophie worked the counter, selling meat to the customers, and Jack processed the animals. They had many loyal customers who swore their meats tasted the freshest. On Saturdays, their patrons queued up in front of the counter and often went out the door and down the sidewalk. There was seldom a lull in business. At one time, there was even talk between the couple of opening a second shop in Ute, where his father's shop had gone under.

A small apartment sat above the butcher shop. A sitting room, two bedrooms, and a tiny kitchen comprised their living quarters. Sophie had filled their home with used furniture. The apartment was organized and clean. The couple had hoped to use the second bedroom when they had a child, but sadly that hadn't happened. Most evenings, they sat and listened to the radio programs coming from WEAU in Sioux City. They both enjoyed *Music Shop*, and Sophie was very fond of *The Book Club*. While they listened, Sophie repaired clothing while Jack completed bookwork for the business.

Jack and Sophie had dreams of buying their own house one day. They scrimped and saved every available penny and put it into the bank. Jack and Sophie worked closely together and enjoyed their growing relationship. They dreamed and planned their life while they lay in bed.

The volatile farming during the Twenties caused many banks to close. Banks in Iowa relied heavily on farmers' business. Soldier's bank, however, remained strong during that time until farm foreclosures doubled and then tripled at the end of the Twenties into the Thirties. The Soldier Bank could not survive. When word got out the bank was closing, customers rushed to withdraw their money. Unfortunately, Sophie and Jack's house savings were lost in the bank closure.

On top of losing their savings, their business declined. The butcher shop could buy animals cheaply, but there were few customers to purchase the processed meat. People did not have money for meat. They grew vegetables in their gardens and lived off the free food. No customers meant no money to pay the loan on the business.

Jack began to drink more than the occasional Saturday night beer. Sophie, like her mother, didn't like liquor and nagged him about his consumption. With the bad economy, Jack became bitter and didn't appreciate Sophie's condemnation while he was trying to relax after a discouraging day. He took his anger out on Sophie. If she made a small mistake, he yelled at her, often in front of other people. Jack's smile had turned to a permanent frown. Sophie's feelings were constantly hurt from the way Jack treated her, so she began to pull away from him. They no longer dreamed together. Sophie went to bed early, and Jack stayed up drinking.

By July of 1931, Jack and Sophie were facing the reality of their shop needing to close. They could no longer make their mortgage payments. Not only were they losing their business, but they were losing their home as well. The entire building would go back to the National Bank, the entity that had taken over Soldier Bank's loans. While the Soldier banker knew the couple and would have given them more time, the National Bank was a large Chicago institution that didn't know them—and didn't care about their business or where they lived. They wanted the loan repaid, or they would repossess the building. Sophie and Jack closed their shop and packed their possessions at the end of July.

Because of Ingrid's unfortunate circumstance, her house stood empty. Once she had gone to the Insane Asylum, the family finally had to resign themselves she would never come home again. Her children had married and moved out of the house. There was plenty of room for the now homeless couple and even some children should they ever be so lucky. In return for their free rent, Tingvald asked Jack to help on the farm.

Jack couldn't refuse, but farm work was distasteful to him. He had gone from his parents' butcher shop to working in Ericksen's Mercantile to his own store. Jack did not like working outside in the heat and snow. But there were no jobs to be had, and he and his wife needed a place to stay. Begrudgingly, he acquiesced.

At first, living in a larger house pleased them both. Ingrid's belongings were nicer than their used furniture. They had plenty of room. They could get a little more space between them, so they weren't constantly on each other's nerves. However, it did nothing to abate Jack's drinking.

By October, the newness had worn off, and Jack was angry every morning he had to rise early to help with the milking. With the shorter days, he was working more often in the dark and cold. His mood matched the outdoors. He came home tired and resentful. He complained about the way Tingvald treated him, believing he got the dirtiest chores instead of Ingrid's son Sam, who was still working for Tingvald. After being his own boss, Jack didn't like to be bossed around and thought Tingvald lorded over him. Sophie listened to his complaints and tried to suggest another way of seeing things. That only irked Jack, and he accused her of taking her family's side. They bickered nonstop from the time he came home until Sophie gave in and went to bed.

In November, after the nightly chores, Jack began to go from the farm to the Speakeasy instead of going home. He didn't want to listen to his wife standing up for her family over him.

The Loess Hills had enough land to make finding the bootleggers difficult—unless one knew where to look. Some of the locals visited a small barn three miles east of the Olson farm. From the outside, the building looked abandoned. The paint was faded, and the roof needed new shingles. But on the inside, there were a bar and tables with mismatched chairs on a dirt-packed floor. The interior smelled like an abandoned barn with old hay and animals. The bartender served only one thing: corn liquor. Their customers could never be certain the liquor was safe to drink, but with little else to choose from, they took their chances.

Jack heard about the barn from a former customer. He had been curious but had never had the impetus to look for it. With his lost luck and poor circumstances, he decided to see it for himself, so Jack walked the three miles to his destination. Once inside with a drink in front of him, he found comfort with other men who were in his same situation. They, too, had lost everything and were trying to drown their woes in illegal hooch.

A cold November evening, Jack was sitting at the bar when a fellow patron sat next to him. The man was tall and thick around the chest. He had ruddy cheeks and nose with a dark walrus mustache. They drank silently together until the man finally introduced himself.

"Name's Walter. What's yours?"

"Jack."

Jack and Walter started a conversation. Like everyone else, they talked about the hard times. Walter had been a traveling salesman, but he no longer had a job with that company. Now, he said, he sold something illegal. Jack wasn't aware of any other illicit item besides liquor… unless it was drugs. He didn't figure it was alcohol since they were already sitting in an unlawful bar, so it must be drugs. Jack wasn't interested and started to move away from Walter. Just as he was getting up, Walter said, "Jack, I got something special for you.

You like pretty girls?"

"Who doesn't?" Jack, thinking Walter was into prostitution, wasn't in the mood for some whore. He wasn't the kind of man who cheated on his wife.

"Take a look at these beauties." Walter laid five picture postcards down on the bar.

In the dim light, Jack could see the women were naked. He was slightly interested in looking, but he didn't want to appear to Walter as the kind of man who disrespected women. Jack thought of himself as higher class than the men who drank at the bar.

"Jack, just take a look at this one. She's the prettiest." Walter held the postcard in front of Jack's face. He glanced at the picture, looked again, and then looked at it closely. His first reaction was shock and disbelief. Jack snatched the picture out of Walter's hand and held it close to a candle on the bar. Blood began to creep up his body, turning his face scarlet red.

"She's a looker, ain't she?" Walter mistook Jack's actions for interest in a pretty, nude girl. "I'll sell it to you for a dollar."

"Where did you get this?!" Jack exploded.

"I bought it in a Des Moines shop," Walter said defensively. Walter now knew the picture had infuriated his prospective client.

Jack got down from the stool, picture still in hand. As he marched out of the bar, he could hear Walter yelling at him for stealing his merchandise.

Jack's shock and horror as he walked the three miles home fermented into rage. He continued to glance at the photo, which only built his revulsion.

Jack burst through the front door of the house, slamming it shut behind him. He gripped the picture in his left hand. Sophie was at the ironing board, smoothing out wrinkles in Jack's Sunday shirt. When she looked up, she saw a hand coming at her. Jack's hand. The crack of the slap across her face reverberated throughout the quiet house.

"You filthy whore!" Jack screamed at her, thrusting the picture into her face.

Sophie could only take a quick glance, knowing what it was before Jack punched her in the stomach. The wind knocked out of her, she fell down onto the floor, crying, "Jack, no...stop!" She tried to hide under the ironing board. Jack picked up the board and threw it across the room, exposing Sophie to his rage.

Sophie felt her husband's fists pummeling her body. He seemed to be hitting her anywhere he could find as she curled into a ball on the floor. Each punch landed with his full force—her side, her back, her head. Then there was a lull, and she could hear him breathing heavily over the top of her.

"You cheated me! You lied to me! You're dirty! You're nothing but a slut!" Before Sophie could respond, Jack grabbed her by her long, dark hair and dragged her into the middle of the room. Sophie screamed as she felt her hair ripping out of her scalp. "Jack! Stop! Please!"

Once he got her into the middle of the room, where he had more space to beat her, he began kicking her wherever he could land a blow with his boot. Sophie's body began to feel like tenderized meat. With each strike, he called her another name: "whore," "slut," "prostitute," "harlot."

Sophie could only stay curled into her protective ball, waiting for Jack to wear himself out. Eventually, she heard the front door slam and uncurled to find herself alone. She used a chair to pull herself up from the floor. Her ribs were a mass of pain. Clumps of her hair lay strewn across the floor. She went to the bedroom mirror and looked. Her nose and mouth were bleeding bright, red blood. Her left eye was beginning to swell from where he had punched her. Her whole body would soon be a mass of purple bruises.

Terrified he would return and beat her again, she limped the one-sixteenth of a mile to Tingvald's house. As she traveled, Sophie could only think of that vile picture—one she hadn't thought about in many years, one she could barely remember being taken. And it brought her back to that couch in that shabby studio. She remembered believing no one she knew would ever see the picture. Now, she wondered how many of them were out there and who had seen her naked. Twenty-four years had passed since that awful experience. So many years she felt safe in the world she had built. Today, her past found her.

Inside her brother's house, Sophie listened to Tingvald rage while Ella ministered her wounds. Her left eye was swelling shut. She had a swollen lip and a gash on her scalp, in which flowed bright, red blood. Ella thought she had two cracked ribs and a dislocated shoulder. Alex had installed a telephone in their house in case of an emergency involving their mother, so Ella used it to call for the doctor.

Ella put the coffee pot on the stove to warm it and gently moved Sophie into the kitchen to sit on a chair. With her damaged ribs, lying down and getting up again sent shoots of lightening pain through her body.

The three of them sitting at the table, Tingvald asked, "What would ever cause him to beat you this way? Was he drunk? Did you provoke him?"

Only her mother and Alex had known what happened to her in Des Moines. Her mother wanted very few details, just enough to determine how best to bring Sophie back to herself. Alex, however, had seen those pictures. That shared knowledge bound them together. The three of them decided there was no benefit in telling the rest of the family.

Sophie had hoped this day would never come, the day her shame slithered back into her life. She choked out the whole story—her pictures, the drugs, and her near-slip into prostitution. Tingvald and Ella's faces showed their incredulity with wide eyes and open mouths. But quickly their eyes sagged or filled with tears, expressing their final feelings of pain. They were also afraid others had seen, and possibly purchased, a photo of her. They felt helpless in being able to do nothing to stop her reputation from being destroyed. They would wait and see what came of the situation.

For the present, though, Sophie was worried Jack would return. To protect her, Tingvald and Ella insisted she stay with them. With two of their sons married, there was now more room in their house. Tingvald would wait for Jack's return to the farm. If he didn't show up for work the next day, they would assume he had probably left for good. If he did or didn't return, the decision of what would happen to Sophie's marriage was Jack's to decide. Sophie assumed he would divorce her.

Sophie didn't want a divorce. She wanted their lives to return to the way they were when business was good. She loved Jack. She had never been happier than when they were the couple who owned the butcher shop, but Jack couldn't unknow what she had done. Their marriage was changed forever, and he may never want her back.

A year later, Sophie received divorce papers. She cried with the knowledge he would never return to her. She desperately wanted him back. The stigma of divorce would stay with her like a permanent smell. Gossips would speculate as to the reason for their split, and rumors of her broken marriage would travel with the wind through Monona County. A moniker of "divorcee" would attach itself to her for the rest of her life.

1932

Tingvald

Farming boomed at the beginning of the Twenties. Land prices shot up; corn, hogs, and cattle prices rose; and the stock market became a permanent, uphill climb. After he and Alex had invested in more land and cattle, the prices dropped considerably. Their purchase price of $235 an acre dropped to $210 an acre and then in 1922, $174 an acre. Instead of panicking and selling land, Alex talked Tingvald into buying more at the lower price. They purchased two more farms, for a total of 250 acres.

Tingvald and Alex also bought another 200 head of cattle and 250 head of hogs. The Olsons had one of the largest farming operations in the county. When Tingvald went into town, farmers noticed him and whispered. Tingvald knew they were pointing him out as a major land owner. To farm this much land, he and Alex had also borrowed money for newer machinery. They bought their first tractor, plow, and planter. His sons and nephews helped farm if they wished to make some money; otherwise, Tingvald hired men in the planting and harvesting season just as his father had done.

When Tingvald read about the stock market crash in '29, it was far away from their farm. He could see no reason why Wall Street had anything to do with Soldier farmland. In 1927 hogs sold for $6.20 per hundred pounds. By 1931 they had dropped to $3.25. Gradually, Wall Street did affect farmers in Iowa. Corn prices had also dropped from 43 cents a bushel in 1931 to 23 cents in 1932.

Anger smoldered as prices continued to decline, more farmers lost their land, and families could not feed their children.

A farm rally in Des Moines added fuel to the growing fire. Farmers in their best attire lined up to march around the capitol. Farmers were banding together to try to bring farm prices back up. They wanted a guaranteed price for their products and a moratorium on further farm foreclosures. They did not get what they wanted.

Within months after that, milk farmers outside of Council Bluffs banded together and picketed along Highway 34. The peaceful picketing morphed into blocking the highway, so farmers could not bring their goods to market. A standoff ensued between the sheriff and the men blocking the highway. The sheriff brought in more law enforcement and escorted farmers who wanted to take their products through the line. News of the impasse spread, and one thousand men started toward Council Bluffs to give aide to the farmers who were in jail for picketing. The sheriff fought back with his own men holding submachine guns and riot guns outside the jail, who were told to shoot should any man try to storm it. Nothing came of the conflagration. No help for the farmers. No change in prices.

By July, the fire of discontent raged closer to home. Tingvald began hearing whispers of a farm strike in Monona County. He wasn't sure how he felt about that. Tingvald had always minded his own business and did what was best for his own family. He held the mantra that other people's problems were theirs to overcome, except in sickness or death.

Near the end of August, his neighbor to the north stopped by his fields to inform him of a meeting in John Anderson's barn. Tingvald suspected it was about a farm strike. He considered staying home, but he didn't want to miss the information.

When Tingvald finished supper, he told his wife he was going to a farm meeting. When Ella asked him what kind of farm meeting, he only replied with a vague "about farming." Ella could easily get worked up over conflict, and since he didn't know what he would do if there were a farm strike, there was no need to get her started on her worrying.

When Tingvald stepped into Anderson's barn, he was surprised to see nearly seventy-five farmers gathered, sitting on bales or standing along the sides. Once the meeting time came about, John Anderson stood on a chair, so the men could see and hear him plainly.

With a loud, authoritative voice, John boomed, "I've called you here tonight to talk about our problems. I don't know about the rest of you, but I can't pay my mortgage this year. I've only made enough money in the last two years to pay what I owe on taxes. That ain't putting food in my kids' bellies or buying my wife a new dress. Somethin' has to be done about this. We can't count on the government; we can only count on ourselves and, hopefully, each other."

The men in the barn gave audible assents and shook their heads. One voice came out from the crowd. "I hear ya, John. But what can we do? We don't control the price of corn or cattle or hogs. We git what we git. Our good President Hoover is doin' all he can for us. He's one of our own."

With the mention of Herbert Hoover, the crowd showed divided reactions. Some nodded in agreement while others called him the "do nothing" President, who didn't seem to care about his own people from Iowa.

Tingvald was torn on the topic of Hoover. His mother had taught him to respect the man in the office. But he had to admit he felt like the man in the office wasn't doing much for his ailing people.

Another from the crowd brought the topic back to the purpose of the meeting. "What are we supposed to do about this situation, John? You brought us here. Did you have an idea?"

"I can't see who said that, but I'm glad you asked. I do. I'm suggesting we go on strike."

The word *strike* brought silence. Men looked down at their feet, some shuffling uncomfortably. Most of the men were skeptical. If it hadn't worked for the milk farmers, then why would it work for them?

A few of the farmers spoke out, questioning how it would do them any good. They didn't work for a company they could walk away from. Their company was their own land.

"How are we supposed to strike?" a voice from the middle of the barn said.

"What's gotten us into this mess," John explained, "are the prices. We need to fix the prices. The only way to do that is lower productivity. We've always known prices drop when commodities are plentiful. Slaughter your hogs, and what you can't eat you should bury. Burn the corn in your fields."

What he was suggesting was sacrilege to these farmers. They watched and worried over their corn. Their cows were part of their families. They smiled at the piglets when they came out of the sows. To treat their products like this went against every cell in their bodies. The men gasped audibly, some turning red in the face and shaking their fists at their leader.

"I know how this feels to you." John tried to calm them down so they would listen long enough to hear him out. "I feel the same way about my cows as you do about your animals. Hell, I've got some of them named. I've spent time and fuel in my fields to grow my crops and at the end just set it on fire? I'm no different than you. But, unless we do something drastic, we're going to lose our farms. And then what will you do?"

"It didn't work for the milk farmers. Men died in that fight! Why would it work any better for us?" Tingvald couldn't see who made the comment, but what he said was true.

Many of the men in the group agreed with him. If it had worked for the milk farmers, they would have considered what John was suggesting.

Tingvald understood the logic in John's proposal, but his heart pushed away from the logic in his head. Wasn't getting something for his crops and animals better than nothing? He could at least pay the bank something, hoping they could not foreclose on everyone and would come up with an alternative plan. Besides, if they all didn't do it, then those who sacrificed did it for nothing. He didn't want to be the one who burned his crops and killed his animals while the rest didn't. He would be a fool.

***

By the end of November 1932, corn prices were at an all-time low of 23 cents a bushel. It cost more to put the corn in the ground than they were paid for it when it came out. They couldn't even afford the gas to bring it to market.

Tingvald had continued farming, hoping each year prices would rise. When they didn't, the family became more indebted to the bank. Not only couldn't they pay their farm mortgage, but they also could not pay their taxes. When things became dire, the bankers did not go to the farms to warn the farmers; they required the farmers to sit in their offices.

In December, the Olsons had a meeting with the bank. Tingvald brought Alex with him, and they sat on chairs outside the banker's office. They could see another farmer and his wife inside, and judging by the tone of the voices, it seemed rather grim. When the couple came out of the office, the man's face exploded with red, angry blotches; and his wife's face was pale with fear.

The banker, his youthful face looking serious, motioned the men toward chairs in front of his desk. He looked much younger than either of the Olson men. He wore a clean, dark suit and a white shirt. His nails were clean and his hands soft. Tingvald could tell he had never put them into dirt. "Gentlemen, please have a seat."

Alex and Tingvald sat uncomfortably on the chairs. Alex had worn one of his suits, but Tingvald wore his town clothes, which consisted of a less-patched pair of overalls.

"As you are both aware, your family owes $32,000 to the bank. For the last few years, you've only paid the interest. This year, you've paid nothing. Your family as well as you, Alex, have been excellent bank customers. We've held off as long as we could. But we now need payment."

"How much do you need?" Tingvald asked, dreading the answer. He was aware the bank had been calling in loans for the full amount.

"We need half. Because you are valued customers, we aren't asking for the full amount."

"You might as well," Alex replied, his teeth clenched and his voice low. "We can't even come up with half. Even if we sold everything, we would still owe."

"Is there nothing else you can offer?" the banker asked hopefully.

"Nothing. You'll have to take the farm," Tingvald replied, resigned there was nothing he could do. That sentence was the one Tingvald had feared, had fought against, since the day his father had died. He felt responsible for losing his father's dream.

"You fellas know if this were still a local bank, we would work with you. Ever since we were bought out by the Chicago firm, we have to follow their rules. I'm sorry to do this to your family. You're good people."

The banker set the auction date for the third of January.

When the men were out of earshot, Tingvald turned to Alex and said, "You said you knew what you were doing. You told me to trust you. We've lost the farm. I've lost my father's legacy." Tears welled up in his eyes, but he blinked them back, not wanting to cry in front of his brother.

"I'm sorry. I don't know what else to say. I can't take it back, and I can't fix it. If I could, I would. You know that. I've let down our entire family. We have no other choice but to move on. If we let this divide us, then we've truly lost everything."

Tingvald knew Alex was right. However, Alex hadn't been put in charge of maintaining the family's legacy. Their parents had left family, crossed an ocean, and worked like pack mules to buy the farm. Every bit of their dreams and sweat had gone into the soil. Their father had worn out his body working his land, so he could build something for his sons.

If only they hadn't gotten greedy. If they had maintained their father's original acres, they would not be losing the entire thing. Their vanity had done this.

Alex could go back to Des Moines. He had business skills he could employ in finding another profession. Tingvald did not. He had never known anything but farming. He would be forced to work another man's land to survive.

1933

Sons & Daughters

Each new year excited Tingvald. A new year meant new crops, green sprouts poking out of the good, black soil. A fresh start in the fields. The hope of healthy corn—pregnant with many ears, nourished by gentle rains—flooded his waking dreams. He envisioned a better yield, his grain wagons full to the brim with golden kernels. Anything was possible in a new year.

This new year was different. No new crops. No new beginning. Only the end—the end of their livelihood, the end of their family's home, and the end of their father's dream.

Tingvald rose at 5:30 a.m. and met Alex, who had come the night before from Des Moines for the occasion. They sat drinking coffee in the parlor and talked of the weather and their siblings.

The brothers walked out of the house at 6:00 to start the ending of their legacy. The frozen earth was snow-free, but the ruts from the farm machinery last fall made walking difficult. The sky, overcast with a solid sheet of clouds, had not seen sun for several days. A slight breeze made the already cold atmosphere bite into their faces as they walked together. As Tingvald looked up into the sky, he wondered whether it would sleet or snow. Bad weather would keep folks from attending the sale, but he didn't care. The money went to the bank, not the family.

The sale was to be conducted in front of their barn. The auctioneer, the same one who had sold them the extra land years ago, was already at work, setting up for the day. All of the men were bundled in heavy coats, caps, and gloves. Their work boots, now clean of mud from the fall, would keep their feet warm for a few hours. After, though, it would be miserable walking with frozen toes.

"What'll ya say, John? All ready to go for the event?" Alex asked the auctioneer.

"Easy peasy," John responded. "You fellas did a good job here."

Most of the family had pitched in the last few weeks. The contents from each of the out-buildings had to be emptied and organized. Harnesses, pitchforks, rope, chains, tools…and the list went on. Each had to be inspected to ensure they were in good order and then put into piles of like items.

Some of the items would be fought over by bidders. Other items, like their single tine plow—the one their mother used in the field when their father had broken his leg—would no longer be wanted. Newer machinery with better methods had taken its place. Some of those out-of-date pieces were covered in dust and cobwebs. Family members had found some of them in the hayloft or stored in a back corner. They still needed to be put up for sale, though.

Tingvald and Alex separated, and each man surveyed the piles one last time. Their memories of childhood and their parents were embedded into each item.

By 6:30, Lars brought Betsi and Ingrid's child Bubba, who was now ten years old. Betsi went into the house to help Ella, Sophie, and Gunda prepare the food for the day, starting with breakfast for the family, the auctioneer, and his men.

Sophie and Gunda were preparing a breakfast of eggs and bacon with bread. The meal wasn't fancy, but it would stay in everyone's stomach until lunch, which wouldn't be served until the end of the auction—hopefully by 1:30 in the afternoon.

Ella had started the sandwiches for the people coming to bid on their lives. The women were shocked when they found out they had to feed the people who were buying their things. "If you want them to stay until the end," the auctioneer said, "you've got to make sure they don't want to leave for lunch." He was right, of course, but it seemed to them this was insult after injury. The family would receive less than their farm was worth, and they had to give the buyers a full stomach to do it.

When Betsi entered the house, a wave of delicious scents hit her: the fat frying on the bacon, eggs sizzling in the bacon fat, toasted bread, salt and brine and smoke from the ham Ella was slicing for sandwiches. Once Betsi had tied on one of her mother's many aprons, she jumped in to help Ella. She buttered the bread and laid one slice of the smoked ham on top, repeating her actions over and over. The women also needed to brew gallons of coffee. On a cold day such as this one, chilly hands wrapped around the warm cup of brewed liquid kept the bidders' minds attentive to the auctioneer rather than their frigid hands.

All of the family who could make the auction were now at the farm. Ingrid was absent due to her condition. Before Karoline died, she had made the journey every two weeks to Sioux City and back to visit her daughter. Each time she came home despondent and didn't rouse for two days. During that time, she lamented constantly of letting her daughter down. The rest of the family did their best to visit Ingrid when they could, but their sister didn't recognize anyone.

Of course, no one in the family expected Floyd. His move to Denison with Elsa, his wife, had physically separated them. They visited fewer times after the baby was born, supposedly because it was too difficult to travel with her. And then months went by without word. Their mother was still alive the last time they had seen Floyd and his family. Then he disappeared. Never came home from work, leaving wife and child to fend for themselves. A few months after Floyd's mysterious disappearance, their mother had died, probably of heartache, they thought. No one had seen Elsa or their niece for the last six years; she had moved back to Kiron to live with her parents. Floyd's siblings didn't know if their brother was alive or dead.

The auction began sharply at 8:00 a.m. By 7:00, farmers and townspeople were beginning to arrive, navigating their vehicles over the deep, frozen ruts in the farm yard. They parked in the north field, the one directly behind the house.

Some of the men brought their women with them. All were bundled in warm gear appropriate for the outdoors. Most of the farmers wore their bib overalls, the good ones they reserved for running errands in town. Their winter caps had ear flaps, which were held down by the string tied under their chin. Most of the men, however, left their flaps up until they could stand the cold no longer.

Their women had less protection from the outdoors. While their top half was kept warm with layers of sweaters under their winter coat, their bottom half was bare below their dress hem. Their naked legs were exposed to the cold and wind, which would send them back to their vehicle or inside one of the buildings within a short amount of time.

All of the visitors were picking through the piles. They were holding up items, inspecting them for flaws. The once-neat piles were soon strewn, blending one type of item into the next. Murmurs of judgment could be heard as they looked at the goods. Some of them complained about the assortment, claiming that "there weren't nothin' there worth anything" or that they "ain't seen this thing used in a long while." Other potential buyers were looking at the large machinery, specifically the tractor. They sat on the seat with their hands wrapped around the steering wheel, or they crawled under it to inspect the engine. One man was checking out the cultivator, inspecting its condition as he crawled over and under it.

The women walked around with their hands tucked into their armpits for warmth. They looked into wooden crates and poked around the piles. They were not interested in any of the farm items. They were looking for household things. Some of them wandered up to Ingrid's house or Tingvald's house. They peered into the windows with their cupped hands against the panes, looking to see anything of interest. A particularly nosy women had gone around the back of Tingvald's house and was looking at Ella's crocks. Ella used them for pickling, but they were currently empty. As the intruder started to turn one on its side, looking for cracks in the pottery, Betsi opened the back door and yelled, "Hey! That isn't for sale! None of the housewares are for sale. Get out of our yard!" The startled woman soured her face and walked briskly back toward the barn, muttering under her breath about "some people."

Most of those who had come for the auction were strangers. They had traveled from adjacent counties: Harrison, Crawford, Woodbury, and Ida. To them, this sale was an opportunity. A few of the family's friends had not come to buy but to support the family. They saw this event as the tragedy it was.

Elfred Svensen drove up to the house in his ancient Ford truck. Elfred, now sixty-five, was still spry for his age. After their mother died, they hadn't seen as much of Elfred. Their loss was his loss as well. The children noticed that the twinkle in his eye when he talked about or to Karoline was now gone. When Elfred stepped to the front door, he went right in instead of knocking, which was always his way. It was a sign of his being a family member instead of a visitor.

"Hello, Olson women. I just come to see what's cooking in the house. Always something good, *ja*?" Elfred had never lost his Norwegian accent, and almost every sentence was punctuated by one or two *ja*'s.

The women smiled and giggled. Elfred was their favorite adopted uncle. Their real uncle, Valter Olsen, was never welcomed in the house but always seemed to show up just when they needed him the least.

"Elfred," Betsi said over her mound of sandwiches, "you'll eat breakfast with us. It's ready. We're just waiting for the men. Have a seat at the dining table."

Just as Betsi finished her sentence, the men came in to eat. They removed their boots at the door and hung their coats on the coatrack. Their faces were bright red with cold, and they were rubbing their hands together while blowing warm air between their cupped fingers.

The auction men sat at the kitchen table, and the Olson men sat at the dining room table, Alex choosing to sit as far away from Elfred as he could. Auction conversation started at both tables while the women laid down plates of eggs, toast, and bacon.

Not more than five minutes after the food had been laid, Valter Olsen came to the house. He walked through the front door and headed straight to a chair at the family's table. Valter, now seventy-nine, looked ninety-nine. His long, stringy hair had turned white, which matched his long, unkempt beard. His pungent odor from lack of bathing overpowered the delicious breakfast scents.

Valter had shown up a few times after Kristoffer died. The first was to marry his brother's widow, the second to beg for money, and the third to steal a hog. Each time he was rebuffed by Karoline or—in the matter of the hog—shot at. Once Karoline nearly took off his hide, Valter had stayed away from the farm. A few times they were missing some chickens, but they didn't know if it had been Valter or a fox. Karoline said she hoped it was a fox—at least the fox was decent.

As the family sat eating and discussing the day, Valter declared, "Well, if I had taken over the farm as was my rightful place, none of this mess would be happening today. That one there," and he pointed with his fork to Tingvald, "don't know how to run a place properly. You done run yourselves into the ground."

Betsi stood up, leaned over the table at him, and pointed her finger, "Hush, you old fox! You don't know what you're talking about. You aren't even a part of this family! I don't know why you came today other than to rub it in!" Having said her piece, she sat down and promptly picked up a piece of bacon and popped it into her mouth.

The rest of the table's inhabitants looked at her, shook their heads, and smiled. They could always rely on their fiery sister to speak what they were thinking and too polite to say.

By 7:45, the family had finished their breakfast. All of them wanted to watch the auction, so the women directed the grandchildren to clean the dishes.

John, the auctioneer, stood on the hayrack while the crowd stood down in front of it. His men brought items up to him for bid as well as watched the crowd, scanning for signs of bidding.

John started with the smaller items, knowing most of the serious buyers were there for the bigger machinery and would stay until the end.

First up, two horse harnesses. "Who will give me five dollars? Five dollars?" When no one bid, John went down in amount. "How 'bout three dollars? Three?" No one moved. The crowd knew it was a bank sale and weren't willing to give their hard-earned money to the entity ruining lives. "One dollar? One dollar?" Out of the crowd, a man raised his chin to indicate his interest. "Yep! One and a half? One and a half?" No more bids. "Sold! One dollar!"

Item by item, crate by crate—the process went on for three hours. John started with the number that ought to be given, and the bidders let him know by their reticence they weren't paying the price. Items went for well below their worth or didn't sell at all.

The family stood in back of the crowd. Each item had a memory: the horse collar that had been put on so many times when they hooked up the wagon, their father's saw he had used to cut down the trees to clear the land, the hammers he and the Svensen brothers had used to build the house, the ice tongs that lifted blocks of ice from their pond in winter.

The Olson women were upset when their sleighs were brought to the front for sale. Their father had made them as Christmas gifts when they were children. He cut oak trees down from their timber, making planks from the raw wood. He spent evenings in the barn, planing and sanding the wood, making it smooth for their small hands. The wooden runners were curved and rubbed with wax to make them go fast. Their parents had pulled them up the hill and run beside them as they went down, only to repeat the process. Often their father sat on the back of the sled and held his children against his chest, his big hearty laugh in their ears as they went from the top to the bottom. These were the childhood memories they kept, tossing the arguments and tension out like rubbish.

In a gesture of love for his wife and her sisters, Lars bid on the three sleds, claiming Bubba would enjoy them. Betsi looked over at her husband, a warm smile on her face.

One of the last items was the single-tine plow, its handles shiny from wear. The single tine, a lone soldier fighting against the rocks and dirt clods in the field, dug its way back and forth from one end of the field to the other. Their father's hopes and dreams had gone from his heart into his hands, gripping the wood as he grappled with the field's obstacles until the wood was smoothed down, soft as velvet. Miles of land had been plowed with that implement, their father walking behind the plow back and forth across his fields. Even their mother had put her hands on the wood as she struggled with her small child in tow, trying her best to complete the planting when Kristoffer had broken his leg.

The auctioneer started at $1.00 but could get no bids for the plow. The outdated implement was thrown on the junk pile and would be burned with the other unwanted items.

The drawn-out process of the sale was bittersweet for the family: fond memories resurfaced but then were sold away.

The sale moved into the bigger items: two wagons, two plows, a binder, rake, mower, disc harrow, cultivator, and pulverizer. All implements were in excellent shape. Tingvald knew the value of a dollar and made sure to take care of his things. With farming in such a slump, the farmers were unwilling to buy extra equipment. The wagons and plows, the heart and lungs of farming, sold for a good sum. The other pieces went for twenty dollars or less.

With no more farming equipment, Tingvald felt a sadness in his heart. As often as he had told himself he hated farming, with no more equipment, there was no possibility of going back. Even if they could magically rebuy the land, he would have nothing with which to farm it.

"Gentlemen, next up we have land. Two hundred and fifty acres of prime soil. The whole lot is to be sold. There will be no parceling it. And the houses on the land do not go with the land. Those will be sold separately."

The song of the auctioneer started the bid at $50 an acre. Alex and Tingvald had paid $235. The bidding was slow: no one from out of county wanted the land because it was too far away to farm. Their neighbors didn't want the land because they had enough troubles making their own mortgages. The auctioneer started again: "$45? Do I hear $45?" No bids. He continued to climb down… $40, $35, $30, $25. At $25 an acre, he finally got a man from northern Harrison county to purchase it. The farmer planned to keep his cattle on this extra farm. The soil would be reseeded and go back to grass. It would be as if it had never produced crops.

The Olson children felt an emptiness in their souls. Their lives had started on the land and grown as tall as the corn. Their hopes were planted in the soil and sprouted, each one harvesting a dream. Both of their parents had put their love and sweat into the dirt—all for the benefit of their children. Now, it was gone. Their roots were ripped from their home and would be planted elsewhere. Some would grow again; others would not.

The last items for bid were the houses. Ingrid's house came with nothing but the parcel around the house. Karoline's house came with the outbuildings: barn, hog shed, chicken coop. Both Karoline's and Ingrid's homes were free of debt. The family would take the money and purchase two houses in town: one for Gunda and Sophie; and one for Tingvald's family. If they didn't receive enough money, then Gunda and Sophie would live with Tingvald and Ella. The situation would not be ideal, but they would do what needed done.

Thankfully, the houses went for a fair price. The farmer who bought the land wanted both houses for his hired men, one of whom had a family. The sale of the houses would be enough to get them the two houses in town.

With the sale finished, the family went back into the house for their late-afternoon lunch. The dark clouds of the day seemed to follow them inside. The usually large, rambunctious family was quiet as they sat in the parlor, waiting for the meal. Each child reflected on personal thoughts and memories. For them, a funeral had happened that day. They had buried their parents all over again. In some way, each Olson member felt a small or a large part of the blame.

Elfred purposely sat next to Alex. The two men had not spoken for many years. Because he was the one at fault, Alex spoke first. "Elfred, I want to apologize for my behavior. I was so very wrong to treat you in the way I did. I let money rule my heart instead of family. Can you forgive me?"

Elfred looked at Alex and held out his hand. "I forgave you long ago. I didn't want to let this continue between us. We're family. And I know it would make your mother so happy to see us rekindle our relationship, God rest her soul."

The packing of the houses would start the following day. By the end of the week, their childhood home would be swept clean—void of their lives. They would take their memories with them and pass them down to their grandchildren and their great-grandchildren.

The land would pass from one family to another, each with their own dreams until no one would remember that it had once been called 'the Olson place.' Generations of new people would replace the old, and eventually the Olsons' individual names along with their family name would be wiped from the town's memory. It would be as if they had never existed. The only markers of their existence would be their graves in the Soldier cemetery.

1927

Karoline

Karoline sat on her favorite rocker just inside her open front door, enjoying the breeze and the warm sunshine of the September afternoon. She smelled acrid smoke from someone burning leaves somewhere, the smoke drifting across the hills. Her family's voices, echoing through the valley, floated to her door. Their chatter and bursts of laughter, music to Karoline, made her smile. Darting across the front of her house, a red squirrel gathered seeds and nuts for his winter stash, racing up a walnut tree. A woodpecker rapped furiously on a tree somewhere in the grove behind their house. Karoline loved fall more than any other season.

The exterior sounds juxtaposed against the silence behind her. Seldom did she have the opportunity to enjoy solitude in her own home. Usually, a cacophony of her children's voices; her grandchildren running about, crying and fighting; household work being done filled the house to its ceiling. Today, however, her family were in the fields picking the hard ears of ripened corn and throwing them into the wagon.

Karoline held a clear, glass bowl with the last of the season's strawberries in her lap. She had been keeping them in the root cellar and was sifting through the rotten ones and pulling out the good, cutting the stems from the berries. Later, she would slice the sweet, red orbs and sprinkle them with sugar, making a strawberry syrup that would dribble down her fresh angel food cake. Karoline baked a cake and served the strawberry mixture each time there was a birthday during strawberry season. For the winter birthdays, she covered the cake with whipped cream, flavored with cinnamon. It was always an angel food cake.

Karoline felt all of her sixty-two years in her back and knees. If she sat very long, a pain crawled up her spine, and her knees began to ache. Her back had supported the eight children she carried—in her womb, strapped to her front, and finally on her hip. Her knees had felt the hard earth and wooden floors as she knelt for hours gardening or cleaning. Even though it was giving out on her, she appreciated her body's faithfulness.

As Karoline watched the squirrel scamper around her yard, chattering and running up and down trees, her hands became silent, resting in the bowl on top of the strawberries. She often stopped her work to sort through her memories. Something today—a sound, a smell— brought her back to her husband's funeral.

Like those new picture shows, she played the day back. Her body had been so weary from traveling across Iowa, taking him home for burial. Her heart had vacillated between hurt for the loss of her spouse to anger for his final cruelty toward her. She had had to play the brave widow when she wanted to shut her door away from the mourners who had not known how awful Kristoffer could be.

The twenty-two years without him had given her ample time to let go of her bitterness. Yet, his final communication to her had cemented her anger. She supposed she would die with it embedded into her heart.

After their last fight, when he told her he wished she had died instead of their son, he sent her a letter once he had arrived in Cedar Falls. When she returned with his body and read the letter, it was his final words of their fight, ones she could not rebut. Even though she had tossed the correspondence into the black hole with his body, she could never erase his words. The physical ones were buried with him, but the memory stayed with her.

Kristoffer had apologized for his thoughtlessness; however, he wiped out his apology with his condemnation of how she conducted herself as a wife. His final punishment was a permanent separation. They would no longer behave as husband and wife.

The ember of resentment flared again with the kindling of memory. Twenty-two years and six feet of dirt could not snuff out the flame. Instead of allowing herself to become angry over a dead man, Karoline shifted her thoughts to her children.

Had she been a good mother? If she asked her children, she wasn't sure what they would say. Her oldest daughter Ingrid no longer knew her or herself. She sat in a chair, her mind in a dark cave, never to see the light again. Karoline grieved the loss of this oldest child as much as she did Ingrid's twin sister, Inger. They had been perfect, beautiful babies. Karoline often revisited their decision to put her in a hospital, but she could see there had been no other choice.

Tingvald, her stolid son, had raised a fine family and was a successful farmer. He had suffered his father's words as well as she, yet he fought daily to keep the farm alive. Karoline recognized his disappointment in farming. It had not brought him a life of leisure: hard work from sunup to sundown, his hands gnarled with swollen joints, his days chained to chores—never allowing him to go too far or for too long—weather or the price of corn keeping him from his sleep. The life of a farmer was all-consuming. Yet Tingvald shouldered his father's dream and prepared his own sons for the life. Even though she was aware of his unhappiness, one of her sons had to sacrifice to keep their only accomplishment. Someday, his sons would take over the farm and continue the Olson name. Karoline saw generations of Olson men working the land. It would be theirs for centuries.

And Alex. Karoline worried about Alex. When he was a little boy, she had blamed herself for his accident and fretted over how he would make his way in life. Karoline worried his life would be as stunted as his leg, but he had never used it as a reason to allow himself to fail. She had been so proud of his intelligence. A man as smart as he would rise, which is exactly what he did. Kristoffer had been so proud of his accomplishments at the Feed and Seed. But then, like his father, he focused too much on wealth. There was no satiating him when it came to money. Instead of his body, his soul had become stunted. Cheating Elfred had shamed her greatly. Alex had chosen money over friendship, loyalty, and love. Choosing Anna as his wife was also about money. Karoline knew her son was building his own dream, one of termite-eaten wood that would eventually crumble. She was certain Anna would one day leave him and go back to Des Moines. She felt certain if Alex did fail, it would be money's doing.

When Karoline thought about Betsi, a smile came to her face. She had been certain they had ruined her life with the abortion and forced marriage to Lars. Betsi had hated them and held her grudge to her father's grave, and Karoline feared she would hold it until the day she, too, would die. Karoline had worn that kind of depression and anger after she lost Inger. The deep well of depression had swallowed her as well in the days before she went back to Norway, and she was scared Betsi would take her own life. After her struggles,

Betsi finally had come back to herself and to them. Pride swelled inside of Karoline while she watched her daughter became a loving wife and mother. It saddened her Betsi could have no children of her own, but she was raising Ingrid's son to be a fine man someday. Karoline thought about how this fiery daughter of hers was closest to herself.

Gunda, her bright star, had earned the education Karoline herself had longed for. Never speaking of her own desire to go to school to become a nurse, Karoline felt her chest swell with pride when Gunda announced she wanted to become a teacher. Before Alex had offered the money, Karoline was already thinking of what she could sell to pay for Gunda's education. Gunda was a strong, capable woman who would find her way. Karoline felt certain she would eventually marry, having her own strong daughters whom she would raise to speak their minds and follow their own paths.

Sophie, her beauty. Had it not been for her unfortunate time, Karoline wasn't sure what would have happened to her. Her vanity and selfishness had almost ruined her. Once Karoline knew she was safe and well, a small part of her was grateful it had happened. Sophie had been a beautiful, wild horse who decided to run; and Karoline wasn't strong enough to reign her in. Only her own horrifying experience had broken her for good. After that, she had thought no more of leaving the family, and she had gained some humility. Sophie had finally settled down and found a good man, and she was now on the right path of marriage and family. She and Jack were making their own dreams with the butcher shop. She hoped they would soon have their own children.

Floyd, she knew, was her own failure. She had spoiled him. She had allowed him his way and given him anything he wanted. Karoline did not have the heart to discipline Floyd as she should have. If Kristoffer had raised his last son, Floyd would have known hard work and ethics. He would have tamed Floyd's wildness and broken his spirit.

Once Floyd married and moved to Denison, he separated himself from his family, angry over their desire to see him settle down. They squashed his dreams of adventure and lauded his marriage and daughter.

Floyd, in retaliation, had pulled away from them. The day her daughter-in-law called her, relaying his disappearance, Karoline wept for her last child. Had he run away and left his family? Was he out there somewhere? Would he ever come home? Karoline could not believe he had intentionally left his wife and child. While he did not always make the best decisions, he would never desert family. Something horrible must have happened to him; otherwise, he would have returned from work that day. She hoped someday he would walk through her front door and explain himself. Her mother-sense was mute; she could not feel whether Floyd were dead or not.

Karoline rested with her thoughts, going back beyond her children, over the ocean to Norway. She scrolled through her childhood days with Runa, giggling, telling secrets, dreaming of their futures. The melody of her father's violin as he practiced for the upcoming Christmas festival sounded in her ears. She could hear her mother in the kitchen making *krumkake* for the party, the smells of cardamon and cinnamon bathing her nose. The house was warm and comfortable, wrapping its safety around her like a warm, Norwegian sweater.

Karoline's head dropped into her chest. The bowl slid from her lap, landing on the floor, scattering strawberries and broken glass. She was home again.

Afterword

Once again, there is both truth and fiction to this story. The stories attached to the children are mostly fiction. And that which isn't, didn't happen to them but to other members of my mother's family. The description of Karoline's death is accurate. Her grandchildren found her sitting in her chair. She is buried in the Lutheran cemetery in Soldier, Iowa. Her gravestone only says "Mother Caroline" with the date. Christopher's stone is an obelisk with his and some of the children's names on each side.

The only Olson child I know is Tingvald's son Glenn, my grandfather. Glenn met Alice Gibbs in exactly the way I described. She was Catholic, which was a source of contention in this Lutheran family. The story of the Easter dinner happened as I wrote it, but the conversation between Ella and Tingvald at the end of the chapter was in my imagination. I do know Glenn was not disowned. When I was a child, I can remember going to my great-grandfather Tingvald's house and listening to him play his violin. So, it must have turned out well somehow.

My favorite Glenn story was when he skipped school with his male classmates and went to Sioux City to see Babe Ruth play. My grandfather was the most honorable man I have ever known. When he told me the story of skipping school, he always had a twinkle in his eye and a smile on his face. He didn't regret the truancy or the punishment that followed. He was a passionate baseball fan, often watching two games at the same time, and seeing the Great Bambino was one of his fondest memories.

The Iowa events are based on research. I was surprised by a few things: early prohibition for Iowa, the Whitechapel district in Des Moines, and the English-only law. Many of the historical events I put in the story are true. I read old issues of the *Denison Review* to get ideas for the book. The men riding their bikes across the United States, a woman being raped by a minister, the milk farmers going on strike— they all really happened. I am extremely lucky to have a copy of Soldier's Centennial book, which they refer to as "The Bible." I pored over those opening pages about the origin and oldest residents of Soldier so many times I almost know them by heart.

As with the first book, I've been trying to find information on name spellings. Norwegian last names are derived from the father's first name with the words *son* or *daughter* added on. Olson came from Ole's son. The emigrants arriving in the 1800s spelled their last names with *sen*, not *son*. The Norwegian word for son is *sønn*. However, it is pronounced *sen*. When emigrants boarded a ship, they wrote their own names on the passenger list. I believe they spelled it the way it sounded with English letters since the ø is not in the English alphabet. After the first generation (Karoline and Kristoffer), the second generation started to spell *son* the way it is spelled in the English language. You may have noticed Olsen being spelled two ways in the book. Karoline spelled it Olsen with an *en* as did the older generation. The younger generation switched it to *Olson*.

My grandpa Glenn was always very particular in the way his last name was spelled. He did not want to be mistaken for Danish.

Acknowledgements

I am grateful to Dr. Anthony Paustian and the people at Bookpress Publishing for helping me get this second book published.

I would also like to thank my friend, Kristin Jeschke, who helped me with this book. Kristin is an excellent teacher, friend, and writer. She gave her time freely (and I do mean free) to give me feedback on the book.

My husband, John Kotz, is also on my list to thank. As crazy as this dream has been, he has supported me all the way—taking me to events, carrying my boxes of books, encouraging me with every step.

My family has also been a support. My brother, Dr. Tim Hanigan, was as excited for me as he would have been for himself. He also helped in the writing of the dentist chapter. If you squirmed while you read it, I can only thank Tim. My sister Beth sold books for me when I was double booked. My other siblings encouraged my success and celebrated when I finally found a publisher. I appreciate the support they've given to their little sister.

My former student and pseudo-son, Josh Skipworth, spent some time researching for me.

My first editor, Malory Wood of Missing Ink LLC, gave me excellent feedback on this manuscript. Thank you, Malory, for making me aware that I'm terrible at putting in time signals. I learned a lot from you.

Finally, I need to acknowledge the internet. I can't imagine how much longer this book would have taken had I not been able to click on a site. I read research papers, websites, and back issues of newspapers to find out what Iowa was like during the time period of the book.